*This book is dedicated to Paul, my loving husband, critique partner, and scene enhancer, and my father, without him consistently placing fantasy books in my hands, my love for fantasy and sci-fi would never have grown.*

# Fantastical Realm Publishing
## Book List
## *Author Sarah M. Wasson*

### Chronicles of Atlantis

The Beginning of the End – Book 1
The Journey Continues – Book 2
The End of Atlantis – Book 3 - Forthcoming
Royal Line – The Search – a Chronicles of Atlantis Short Story

### A Prophecy Foretold Novel

Twins of Fate – Book 1
Wizard's Hat – Book 2
Infinite Medallion – Book 3 - forthcoming

### Short Stories

To Train a Falcon

# The Journey Continues

## Chronicles of Atlantis
### Book 2

Self-Published by
Sarah M. Wasson

FANTASTICAL REALM

PUBLISHING

Copyright © 2025 Sarah M. Wasson
Edition 3 — book size — 5.4"x8.5"
**ISBN: 979-8-9994821-1-2**

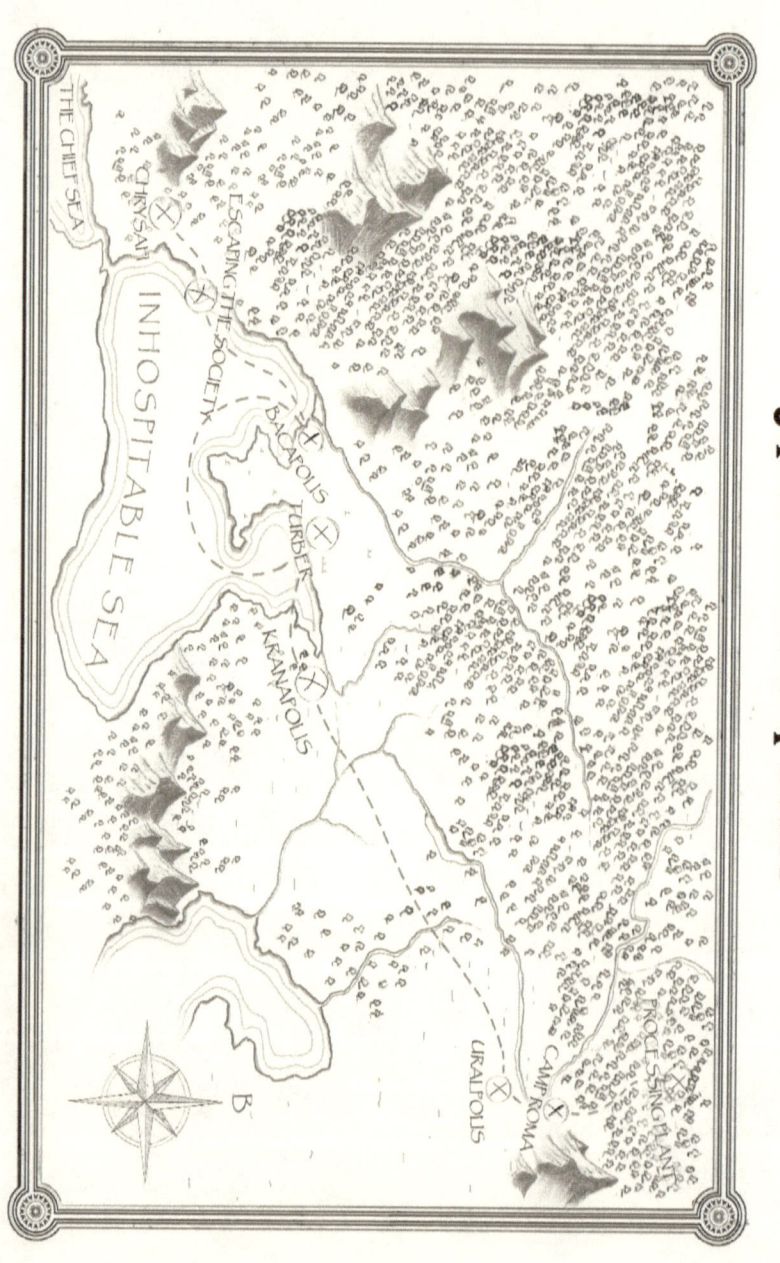

# Neiaphi's Path

## ∞ PROLOGUE ∞

"**WE** will complete the final test tomorrow, Sir," Crelian said, his gaze fixed on the swirling liquid in the holding tank below from his vantage point on the catwalk. Sen approached quietly, his movements careful and deliberate. When Crelian spoke, Sen froze, caught off guard.

"Good, good," Sen replied. He joined Crelian at the railing, peering down into the tank with a shared, contemplative silence.

"Any additional problems?" Sen asked.

"None, Sir. My crew is planning a celebration for tomorrow night after the final test. You and your men are welcome to join us if you wish."

Sen grunted thoughtfully. "I'll let my men know. Where is this to take place?"

"We thought the conference hall would be the best location."

"That will be fine." Sen's mind raced. The conference hall was situated far from the main gates. With everyone gathered in one place at the rear of the camp, they'd have no easy escape. It was the perfect setup.

Crelian glanced at Sen, his sinister grin faltering when he met Crelian's gaze. His expression quickly turned impassive. "Report to me after the test tomorrow, before your celebration."

"Yes, Sir."

Sen took one last look at the tank before turning to leave the catwalk.

"What did he want?" Georgios asked, emerging from the other side of the catwalk.

"Nothing unusual," Crelian replied. "Is everyone ready to leave?"

"Yes, Sir. The women and children are prepared to move at a moment's notice. When do we depart?"

"I told Sen we're holding a celebration tomorrow evening after the final test. He'll assume we'll all be at the conference hall at the camp's rear. I want all children older than five to be outside the walls with some of the servants disguised as part of a nature lesson," Crelian instructed.

"Have all the servants go to the conference hall early to set up the celebration to get them out of the way. All the women and children should be in their houses, ready to leave at a moment's notice. Make sure all the animals are packed and prepared for the move. I'm scheduled to meet with Sen right after the final test. Everyone should head toward the gates as soon as that meeting is over. If I don't make it out, keep moving—don't wait for me."

"What do you think Sen might try to do?" Georgios asked.

"I don't know, and I don't plan to find out," Crelian replied. "Let's just hope we manage to get away from here and reach Atlantis safely."

Georgios nodded in agreement. Crelian reassuringly gripped his shoulder and led him off the catwalk.

Cret sprinted up to his father, coming to an abrupt halt. "Father, did Japster tell you what happened at Camp Roma?" Cret panted, struggling to catch his breath.

"Slow down, Son. What are you talking about?"

"I overheard Hepluosis talking to a Local about an attack on Camp Roma from about half a month ago," Cret said between gasps. "He mentioned that the same people have been spotted heading this way."

"Japster didn't mention that," Crelian said, his expression darkening. "Thanks for the information." He headed off to bed early that night, the weight of the news heavy on his mind. Despite his worries about the following day, sleep came quickly.

Cret was jolted awake by the sound of screaming. He fumbled to light the candle by his pallet in the darkness and hurried to the window. The camp was engulfed in flames. Hooded figures moved through the chaos, using torches to set fire to anything flammable. Locals struggled to contain the fires, but their efforts were overwhelmed by the onslaught.

Suddenly, the front door of their house was thrown open with a deafening crack. Several hooded men stormed inside. Cret raced to the main room, where he found his father already there, ready to face the impending danger.

"What's the meaning of this?" Crelian demanded, his voice cutting through the chaos.

"Gather what you can and follow us. You're in danger," one of the intruders replied urgently.

"Son, help your mother and sister," Crelian instructed. "Camtis, get the animals ready. We're leaving tonight."

Amid the chaos of the burning camp and the hooded figures wreaking havoc, Crelian's men and their families slipped away unnoticed. They traveled through the night and into the next day, driven by the constant fear of being pursued. Though no one spoke of it, the anxiety in the group was palpable, keeping them moving swiftly. It wasn't until dusk that the hooded men finally allowed them to rest.

Crelian approached the man who seemed to be the leader of the hooded figures. "Who are you?" he demanded.

After a moment, the man turned to face him and pulled back his hood. The others followed suit, revealing their faces. Crelian, half expecting them to look markedly different, was taken aback to see they were similar to himself.

"We call ourselves the Loyals," the leader said. "We are dedicated to Atlantis and saved your life last night. I must admit, I'm impressed with how swiftly you managed to gather all your belongings and animals."

"We were planning to leave this evening," Crelian said. "Over the past several days, we packed everything in secret. What brought you to us yesterday?"

The leader responded, "We have spies at the Plant and at the place you called Camp Roma. We learned that you were scheduled to be executed tonight." Several people gasped in shock. "Even though you planned to leave, you wouldn't have made it out in time. We decided it was best to act swiftly before Deleon could ensure your complete eradication."

"Thank you for saving us," Crelian said. "I'm Crelian. And you are?"

"I'm Simos," the leader replied.

"Why would Deleon want us killed? We're no threat to him," Crelian asked, puzzled.

Simos explained, "Deleon's hostility stems from a long-standing issue. It's rooted in the story of Poseidie and the replacements sent by Romota." As Simos detailed the background, Crelian listened closely, his mind racing. He shook his head, reflecting on how most people were easily swayed by whoever promised them security. It seemed the Society would face little opposition on this planet.

"How much further until we reach Atlantis?" Cret interrupted, breaking Crelian's thoughts.

"Several months of hard travel," Simos answered. "We'll need to stop for the winter and continue in the Growing Months."

"Several months!" several voices exclaimed in disbelief.

Crelian glanced around as people huddled closer, their concern growing.

"What happened to Addident and Neiluios?" a woman's voice called out from within the crowd.

"Their guide, appointed by Deleon, is one of ours," Simos explained. "They're on their way to Atlantis and will likely arrive a month ahead of us. Our route is more direct, and we have access to technology that the Society hasn't destroyed yet. But for now, everyone must rest. We have a long journey ahead, and you'll need your strength."

From the back of the crowd, Japster and Hepluosis glared at their rescuers. "I'll ensure we never reach Atlantis," Japster said quietly. "And you'll assist me, my son."

Hepluosis grinned at his father. "Whatever you say, Father. I'll do as instructed."

# ∞ 1 ∞
# FLEEING

"**CRELIAN**, please, we must go back to Camp Roma," Meli pleaded, her voice breaking. "Our boys are still there in the special school for exceptional learners. They said they would join us in a month. We can't just leave them behind." Tears streamed down her face.

"I'm sorry, but we can't go back. I wish we could, but it's impossible. I'm not even sure what their fate is. Camp Roma was attacked some time ago."

"No! Why weren't we told?" she cried, collapsing to her knees.

"There didn't seem to be any point," Crelian replied flatly, his gaze averted. "There was nothing that could be done."

"Ma'am, please try to calm yourself," Simos interjected. "It was us who attacked the camp."

"Where are my boys? When will I get to see them?" Meli cried.

"I'm sorry, but you might never see them again," Simos replied sadly.

"What? Why not?" she demanded, her voice rising with anger.

"The Society deemed them hazardous because they refused to accept their teachings. By the time we arrived, they already had their minds erased and had been moved to a new location, presumably given to a new family. Do not worry—

we are still searching for them, and when we find them, we will have them returned to you."

Caiaphas wrapped his arms around Meli and gently led her, sobbing, back to their tent.

Cret returned to his family's tent while the adults discussed their journey to Atlantis. Inside, he found Camtis preparing the evening meal.

"Who do you work for?" Cret asked sternly.

"Excuse me, sir?"

"Who do you work for?" he repeated.

"You and your family, sir. Why do you ask?"

"You were appointed to us by Deleon, weren't you?"

"Yes and no, sir. Deleon assigned me to work for one of your families, but Net chose me specifically for your father."

"Neiluios's servant?"

Camtis paused his preparation and turned to face Cret, clearing his throat as he met Cret's gaze. "Yes, sir. In the short time, Net was with Neiluios, he began questioning what we were told about you. He knew I had an open mind and urged me to volunteer for the first placement, advising me to use my best judgment regarding those from Romota."

"And your conclusion?" Cret asked flatly.

"I no longer believe what I was told. You are good and decent people, not the evil monsters they made you out to be."

"And your current intentions?" Cret asked.

"To serve your family until I am no longer needed, sir. I take it our liberators have filled you in on a bit of history," Camtis said slowly.

"They have. But why didn't you tell us the truth when you realized we weren't the evil monsters you thought?" Cret asked.

"The timing wasn't right. I knew Sen would never allow your people to leave. I hoped they might integrate you into their group and everything would be fine. But after a few days, it was clear that would never happen. I began packing supplies secretly in case your father decided to flee. He's an intelligent man—I knew he'd see through Sen and his followers eventually. It seems our liberators from The Loyals just beat him to it."

"I'll inform my parents about our conversation. The decision will be theirs." Camtis nodded and returned to his work. Cret continued to watch him, wondering if he was truly being honest. Only time would tell.

Crelian, saddened by the news, shook his head. "Everyone, please try to get some sleep. We have a hard day of travel ahead." He glanced toward the back of the group, where Japster and Hepluosis stood, sinister grins on their faces. Japster locked eyes with him before quickly departing. *What were they up to?* Crelian wondered.

"Come, my husband, you need to follow your orders," Sephi said, taking him by the arm. He allowed her to guide him to their hastily assembled tent. Inside, Sareen was already asleep, curled up with a doll he had bought her. Outside, Cret sat by the fire with Camtis, lost in thought as he stared into the dancing flames.

Sephi continued toward the tent, urging her husband to lie down and rest. But Crelian stopped and leaned in. "I'll be in shortly." He smiled, giving her hand a reassuring squeeze. Sephi reluctantly let go of his arm and slipped inside the tent. Crelian sauntered over to the fire and sat beside his son. With a slight nod of his head, he signaled Camtis to retire. Camtis acknowledged the gesture and quietly departed.

Cret didn't seem to notice when his father joined him. They sat in silence for a few moments. "I'm sure she's fine. She's almost to Atlantis and probably giddy with joy," Crelian finally said.

"Oh, Father, you startled me," Cret said, jumping. "When did you get here?"

"A while ago. I'm sure she's fine."

"Who?"

"Neiaphi. Isn't that who you were thinking about?"

"Usually, but not at the moment," Cret replied, shaking his head.

"Do you want to talk?" Crelian asked after a moment.

"I was just thinking about Caiaphas's two boys. I never told you, but I found the criminal camp soon after we arrived and witnessed them there. I helped those boys escape, hid them in a cave, and brought them food. Guards found them a few days later and almost caught me delivering more supplies."

Crelian placed a hand on Cret's shoulder. "Why didn't you tell me? I could have gone to Addident and had them released."

"I didn't think Deleon would comply with Addident's request for their release. I didn't want to put anyone else in danger. I'm sorry, Father; I feel terrible. Not only that, but I tried to help them, but I probably made things worse."

"I would have done the same. Don't feel bad. If these Loyals aren't able to locate them, they have a chance at a new life without Romota's memory. I think they'll be just fine either way."

"Yeah, I'm sure you're right. Thanks." Cret hung his head and ran his fingers through his hair.

"Come, let's get some rest."

"I'll be right behind you. I want to make sure the fire is out first." Crelian patted him on the back and ducked into the tent.

Cret stared into the fire for a moment before turning his gaze to the stars. Amid all the commotion of the past few days, he hadn't thought much about Neiaphi. She never truly left his mind; she lingered in the background of his thoughts. He kicked dirt over the fire, watching as the last ember slowly faded. "I'll be with you soon; don't give up on me," he whispered into the darkness before retiring into the tent.

## ∞ 2 ∞
## RIVER

**THE** Loyals woke everyone early the next day. The air was thick with humidity, even though the sun had yet to crest the distant horizon. The hastily erected tents were taken down and packed as quickly as they had been set up. Everything was done in silence; the mood was somber. The Loyals urged them to hurry, pushing forward without stopping until midday when they finally came upon a large lake.

Simos led Crelian's group around the lake and into the looming forest. He halted them at a small hillside. "Crelian, I must speak to all of your servants alone," Simos said.

"What are you going to do?"

"There's a truth machine inside this cave." He pointed to a small opening, barely large enough for a man to enter without stooping. "I will find out which servants are loyal," he said flatly.

"Yes, that must be done." Crelian nodded.

Hepluosis overheard this and eyed his servant, Six, who stood beside him. Would they allow him to stay? He wondered.

Simos and his men escorted all the servants into the cave. Some balked and began to resist, but the resistance ceased when several men drew their swords.

A short time later, Simos returned and announced that a few servants were allowed to stay, but most would be dealt with. Crelian opened his mouth to ask what that meant but decided against it; at this point, it didn't matter.

After the Loyals finished with the servants, they informed the small remaining group that they needed to keep moving. They traveled through most of the night, using torches to guide their way. Pushing hard and resting little, they finally earned a reprieve two days later when the Loyals allowed their weary companions to sleep.

hey stopped near another lake, where the women and young children bathed while the men set up camp. Crelian and Cret helped Camtis pitch their tent in silence, each lost in thought about how everything had shifted once again. What lay ahead?

"How long do you think they'll let us rest?" Cret asked his father after they had finished setting up the tent and cooking fire.

"Simos said we'd leave again in the morning. After another two days, we can travel by river for a while," his father replied.

"That will be welcoming," Cret replied. "Do you trust these Loyals, Father?"

"I don't know yet. So far, they seem more truthful than Deleon and his followers, at least. I feel like Simos is hiding something from us, but…" He trailed off, shrugging. Camtis sat a short distance away, trying not to listen to their conversation but failing.

"Sirs?" Camtis finally asked.

"Yes, Camtis," Crelian replied.

"I know a lot about the people helping you. The Society and the Loyals are, so to speak, at war with each other."

"What do you mean, 'so to speak'?" Cret asked.

"There's minimal bloodshed between them, and no outright battles are occurring right now. However, a war is raging between them. What Simos said about Poseidon and the replacements is correct.

"The replacements set out to undo or destroy all that Poseidon and his sons had accomplished.

"The Society emerged as the people's savior from oppression. Whole towns flocked to them for protection from what they called inhumane treatment. Initially, they could walk into most villages, take over the governing bodies, and remove the officials and guards.

"They put their own people in charge or elevated trusted townsfolk. I feel fortunate to have grown up in my own town—I've heard stories of others that fell into poverty under The Society's rule, with corruption spreading through the ruling class," he said thoughtfully.

"At first, I didn't believe those stories. I dismissed them as Loyalist blasphemy. But now..." He shook his head. "Seeing how The Society was planning to handle a group they deemed a threat, I realize that your people's only crime was arriving at this planet, unknowingly holding the truth. I've started to question everything—everything I learned, heard, and saw. These past few months have truly tested me."

"We're all very grateful for your service, Camtis. We're glad you've opened your mind to another side of the story. Your help will be needed in the near future; I'm sure of it," Crelian said, placing a hand on Camtis's shoulder. Camtis nodded but said nothing.

True to Simos's word, two days later, they arrived at a river where two large flat-bottom boats awaited them. After loading their supplies, they pushed off. The boats were equipped with a unique propulsion system that allowed them to silently and rapidly slice through the water.

Crelian, Cret, and most of the other men gathered with Simos and the Loyals, eager to learn everything they could about the planet and Atlantis. In contrast, Japster and Hepluosis kept to themselves, further deepening Crelian's mistrust of Japster's motives. He couldn't help but chuckle at the unfolding dynamics.

"What do you find humorous, Father?" Cret asked.

"Oh, just reflecting on how my distrust for Japster has grown since leaving the plant," Crelian replied, shaking his head.

Cret laughed. "Now that you mention it, I feel the same way! It's quite the thought—distrusting him even more. As if he could get any more untrustworthy!"

"We have to keep an eye on him and Hepluosis," Crelian said.

"I already have been. They're definitely scheming—probably trying to figure out a way back to the Society to reclaim their status. Since we landed, Hepluosis keeps talking about how his 'qualities' will be recognized here, how he's destined to be a powerful leader. I used to dismiss those remarks, but now they worry me. I don't believe he has what it takes to lead, but I do think the Society will use him and Japster however they can. They'll do anything to stop us from reaching Atlantis."

"I agree, my son. We'll need to find a way to leave them behind."

Simos stood at the bow of the lead boat as it cut swiftly through the river, which twisted through the countryside, narrowing in places and widening into broad expanses that looked more like lakes. He marveled at their rapid pace downstream, watching trees blur past in streaks of green.

Suddenly, the boat slowed to match the current's speed. Simos made his way to the stern, where the captain was steering. "Is something wrong, Mida?" he asked.

"Not at all, sir. We're approaching the first settlement along the river. We don't want anyone to notice how quickly we're moving, so we slow to the current whenever we're near villages or other boats."

"Right you are. Thank you. Please proceed," Simos said, nodding before making his way back to the bow of the boat, where he spotted Crelian approaching.

"Good day, Crelian. Are the gods smiling on you and your family this morning?"

"Uh, yes, I suppose," he replied, visibly uncomfortable. "Do you know why we slowed?"

Simos smiled. "I just asked the captain the same thing. We don't want to draw attention to ourselves, so we'll slow down whenever we pass settlements."

Crelian nodded. "That makes sense." They continued their short walk to the boat's bow. "Do you know how many days we will be river-bound?"

"I don't," Simos replied. "Several, I'd imagine. This river is quite long—I've never traveled this far south on it." He paused, glancing at a group of villagers on the riverbank. "I've been wondering—do any of your men or boys know how to handle a sword or other weapons?"

"No, sir, not to my knowledge. We're officials and, more recently, engineers. Most of us probably haven't even picked up a rake, let alone a sword. Why do you ask?"

"It would be wise for all of you to learn. Here, all boys over ten—and therefore all men—know how to wield some kind of weapon, even farmers and peasants. They may not be highly skilled, but they can at least attempt to defend themselves and their families."

"I see. Do you have anyone who can teach us?" Crelian asked, turning to look at his people lounging on the deck in small groups.

"Two or three of us have enough skill to teach you the basics. When we make landfall around midday, we'll find suitable wood to craft practice swords and staffs. Later, we can purchase real weapons if the opportunity arises."

"It will be good to touch solid ground for a short time. I'll inform everyone." Simos nodded and turned his attention back to the water ahead.

## ∞ 3 ∞
# TARGET PRACTICE

"**NICE** shot, Alexa," Greish said proudly.

Alexa turned and beamed. "When did you learn to shoot like that?"

"In my village, all girls were encouraged to learn archery to protect our families if needed."

"Can you teach me?" Neiaphi asked.

"Sure, but I must warn you: it's not easy. It'll take a lot of practice and sore arms," Alexa replied with a serious expression.

Neiaphi met her gaze sternly, and then they both burst into laughter.

Andonis looked at Neiaphi with a puzzled expression. "What's the matter?" she asked.

"Back on the boat, I handed you a bow when we were being chased. Why did you take it if you didn't know how to use it?"

"Oh. Well, I figured I could at least hit someone with the bow if they boarded us. I didn't want to seem useless. If I were sent below with the other women and children, I would have gone crazy." She looked down at her hands in her lap.

"Well, I'd never have guessed you didn't know how to use it. You took it from me as if you expected me to hand it over."

"I was, in a way," she murmured, gazing into Andonis's eyes. When he opened his mouth to ask what she meant, she shook her head, and he, puzzled, held back from pressing further.

"If you want to learn, there's no better time than now." Andonis sprang to his feet and extended a hand to help Neiaphi up. She accepted it eagerly.

Alexa handed Neiaphi her bow and an arrow, and they moved ten paces closer to the target. "Alright, hold the bow in one hand and the arrow in the other. See that notch at the back of the arrow? Place the string there. Then pull back, aim, and shoot."

Neiaphi followed her instructions, but the arrow dropped at her feet. "That didn't go as planned," she said, disappointment clear in her voice.

"Not to worry; let me help you," Andonis offered. Neiaphi held the bow and arrow again, and Andonis stepped behind her, placing one hand over hers, his chest close against her back. "Turn your body toward the target," he guided, adjusting her stance. "Now, pull the string back until your hand is at your cheek." His hands guided hers as she drew the string back. "Take a deep, steady breath, hold it, aim—and release." " Neiaphi's arms trembled slightly. "You need to stop shaking," Andonis chuckled.

"Sorry," she whispered, her heart pounding as she struggled to focus. It was difficult with Andonis so close, his hands on hers and his breath warm against her neck. Sensing her tension, Andonis gently released her hands and stepped back, giving her space. Neiaphi took another steadying breath, relaxed her grip on the bow, and lifted the arrow into position again. She inhaled deeply, held it, and closed her eyes briefly to calm herself. Opening them, she felt a sudden surge of determination. Almost unconsciously, her fingers released the bowstring. The arrow soared through the air, landing with a solid thud in a distant tree.

"Nice shot, Neiaphi!" Alexa exclaimed, jumping up and down. Cypress, roused from his nap, barked at the commotion.

"Very nice," Greish praised.

"Yes, indeed! Where did you learn to shoot like that?" Andonis teased.

"I had a good teacher," Neiaphi replied, her smile wide.

Alexa handed her another arrow, and Neiaphi eagerly accepted it, repeating the steps she had just learned. After drawing back the bowstring, she opened her eyes and released the arrow, thrilled to hear it land with another thud against the tree.

"Natural," Andonis said, giving her a friendly pat on the back.

Neiaphi looked at all the smiling faces around her, and a tear slowly slid down her cheek.

"What's the matter? Did I pat you too hard?" Andonis asked, concern etched on his face.

Alexa stepped closer and wrapped Neiaphi in a warm hug. Neiaphi wiped away her tears. "No, you didn't hurt me. I was just thinking about how nice it feels to have friends again. Other than Cret, I haven't had any friends here on Earth."

Greish nodded in understanding, and Andonis placed a reassuring hand on her shoulder, giving it a gentle squeeze. "You have no idea what my family has been through. We had heartache long before we even made it to Camp Roma."

The ever-watchful Net stood nearby, keeping a vigilant eye on Neiaphi. When her first arrow struck the tree, he couldn't help but cheer. He scanned the area for Neiluios, but there was no sign of him. As her second arrow hit the mark, Net rose to his feet; he needed to find Neiluios.

A short distance from the camp, Neiluios was deep in conversation with Mace. Net glanced back over his shoulder at Neiaphi, who was still surrounded by her friends, then hurried on.

"Is something the matter, Net?" Neiluios asked when he saw Net approaching rapidly.

"No, Sir, but I think you should come see something."

"Excuse me, Mace."

"Of course." Mace bowed slightly.

As they returned to the spot where Net had been weaving a basket, Neiluios spotted Neiaphi among her friends. She held a bow confidently, stepping back five paces before taking aim. With a steady breath, she released the arrow, which flew through the air and struck a distant tree. Her friends erupted into loud cheers, and even Cypress joined in, barking excitedly.

"You have a natural marksman in your family, Sir," Net said.

"So it would seem," Neiluios replied, surprised. As they drew closer, he called out, "Nice shot, dear."

Neiaphi beamed with joy; it was the happiest he had seen her in a long time.

"Oh, Father, you saw that! Isn't it wonderful?" Neiaphi exclaimed.

"She's a natural, Sir," Greish added.

"I had a good teacher. Andonis gave me some pointers," Neiaphi said, glancing at him.

"Very few pointers. You're gifted, Neiaphi," Andonis replied proudly.

"Thank you, Andonis. Would you join us for this evening's meal? Altesse will be eager to hear about Neiaphi's latest accomplishment," Neiluios said with a warm smile, glancing between Neiaphi and Andonis.

"I would be honored, Sir." Andonis bowed formally.

Neiaphi eyed her father and Andonis, a flicker of uncertainty crossing her face. She wasn't sure she liked whatever was unfolding between them. Alexa, noticing her friend's uneasy expression, stepped in smoothly. "While you all bask in Neiaphi's success, we'll go for a walk," Alexa announced, quickly taking Neiaphi's arm and leading her away.

Once they were out of earshot, Alexa slowed their pace.

"Thanks," Neiaphi said, letting out a breath.

"Not at all. I know your parents said they'd give you plenty of time to choose, but that looked like a decision," Alexa replied with a knowing look.

"To you as well? That was just scary. I don't want to go home tonight."

"If I were in your place, I wouldn't want to either," Alexa murmured. They walked in silence for a while, until Neiaphi glanced back and spotted Net trailing behind. She sighed, signaling for Alexa to pause. Turning, she gave Net a small nod of acknowledgment before the girls settled under a shady tree.

"Maybe you should talk to your mother before Andonis arrives," Alexa suggested. "She might be able to steer the conversation if needed."

"Possibly," Neiaphi replied, chewing on her bottom lip as she fell into deep thought.

"Do you want to talk about it?"

Neiaphi jerked her head and bit her lip a bit too hard. "Oh, ow. Talk about what?" She rubbed her lip gently, trying to shake off the sting.

"Whatever it is you're so intensely thinking about."

"Sorry about that. When Andonis showed me how to shoot, he stood so close and held my hands. He's never been that close before." She shook her head. "I don't know how to understand my feelings."

"Excited, nervous, unsure, happy, and scared all at once," Alexa suggested.

"Yeah, something like that. Is that how you felt when you were with Greish?"

"At first, yes. But not anymore. I'm comfortable around him now. I just feel happy."

"Has he talked to your father yet?"

"No," she replied, a hint of sadness in her voice.

"Have you talked to him about it?"

"Oh, that wouldn't be proper," Alexa replied, shocked. "If he brought it up, I could ask questions, but he has to start the conversation."

"So many differences. We share a lot of the same traditions, but it's the little things that make it hard to know what's right," Neiaphi said, shaking her head. "Let's head to my tent. I want to talk to my mother."

"Do you want me there?" Alexa asked as they stood, smoothing out their dresses.

"I think it would help if you don't mind."

"Not at all," Alexa said, linking her arm with Neiaphi's and leading the way.

"Mother, are you inside?" Neiaphi called as she approached the tent.

Altesse emerged from under the low tent flap, shielding her eyes from the bright sunlight. "Hello, dear. Hello, Alexa. I just put the boys down for a nap." She motioned to a nearby patch of shade. "Come, sit with me for a while. I feel like I haven't seen much of you two these past few days."

"Sorry, Mother," Neiaphi said, but Altesse waved off her apology.

"Did you need something?"

Neiaphi cleared her throat. "Father invited Andonis to share the evening meal with us tonight."

"He did, did he? Do you know why?" Altesse asked.

"I showed Greish, Andonis, and Neiaphi my bow earlier, and Neiaphi wanted to learn how to shoot. Andonis helped her, and Neiluios saw her excellent shots," Alexa said. Altesse looked at her daughter with surprise.

"That's wonderful, dear."

"Thanks, Mother. Father found out that Andonis gave me a couple of pointers, and he wants him to tell you how much of a natural I am. Oh, and make it sound like you haven't heard the news before. They don't know I was planning to tell you," Neiaphi said with a sly smile.

"No problem," Altesse replied, placing a hand on her daughter's knee. "So, what are you two truly concerned about? It can't just be that."

"I'm worried that the conversation will shift to other topics—ones I'm not ready to discuss yet."

"I see. How can I help?"

"If you sense the conversation changing, could you redirect it?"

Altesse stared at her daughter for a moment. "If I can, I will."

"Thank you, Mother." Neiaphi hugged her tightly. "I'll be back in time for dinner."

"Goodbye, girls."

"Bye, ma'am," Alexa replied.

The girls whispered to each other, arms linked, as they walked toward Alexa's tent.

"There you are, Neiaphi! Net and I are going into Chrysafi in the morning. Would you and Alexa care to join us? I want you to pick out a new dress for your mother," Neiluios said.

"Yes, please!" Neiaphi beamed.

"I'll have to ask my father, Sir," Alexa replied.

"Your father is joining us. I'm sure he'll say yes," Neiluios teased.

"Do you know when we'll be traveling again?" Neiaphi asked.

"The day after tomorrow."

"I'll see you tomorrow then, Neiaphi. Good night." Alexa leaned in, whispering, "And good luck."

Neiaphi smiled. "Good night, Alexa. Cypress, come back here!" The dog had dashed off after an unseen object. "I'll be right back, Father."

"Don't be too long," Neiluios called after her.

"I'll help you retrieve Cypress, Miss," Net offered.

"Thanks. I don't know what's gotten into him. He doesn't normally run like that."

Cypress dashed to the forest's edge, standing with his hackles raised, a low growl resonating from his throat.

"What is it, boy?" Neiaphi asked, eyeing the dark trees. Cypress looked up at her and whined. "Come on, boy, it's time to eat. Come on."

"We need to return to the camp, Miss. I don't trust this forest. Something is watching us; I can feel it," Net said.

"I feel it, too. Cypress, come!" she commanded, her voice firm. This time, Cypress obeyed.

Neiaphi and Net hurried back to the relative safety of the camp. Spotting Greish sitting alone on a boulder, keeping watch, she said, "I need to ask Greish something. I'll catch up with you soon."

"Okay, miss." Net continued toward their tent with Cypress in tow.

"Hi, Greish. Do you have a moment?" Neiaphi inquired.

"Sure! What can I do for you?" he replied.

Neiaphi sat down beside him and patted the guard dog resting at Greish's feet.

"Have you thought any more about Alexa?" Neiaphi asked.

"All the time. Has she said anything to you?" Greish replied.

"I already told you she likes you and wouldn't mind if you spoke to her father. What else is there to think about?"

Greish shifted the focus of the conversation. "Have you made up your mind yet?"

"I'm not here to talk about me," Neiaphi said.

"Why not? It doesn't sound like you've made up your mind. I know two people who want to get to know you better."

"Who?" she asked, feigning ignorance.

"Like you don't know. Chartis has already spoken to your father, and I know Andonis likes you."

"I don't like Chartis that way, and I don't know Andonis that well."

"Get to know him, will you? You're all he talks about, and I'm getting tired of hearing it," Greish said with a smile.

"If you promise to talk to either Alexa or her father, I'll consider getting to know him better."

"Which one should I speak to first?" Greish asked.

"Well, Alexa told me that if you spoke to her father, she wouldn't say no. But she also mentioned that she'd talk to you if you brought it up. It's just not proper for her to start the conversation. She's getting sadder every day you two talk without discussing your future. I can tell she really likes you."

"What's our future going to be?" Greish asked. "How can I talk about it with so many unanswered questions? Where will I be stationed? Will I be able to support her? Will I make a good husband and father?"

"They're all good questions," Neiaphi replied. "I don't have solid answers for you. But I do know this: Alexa will make sure your home is well cared for, no matter where you're stationed. And I truly believe you'll make a great husband and father."

"Really? How can you be so sure?" Greish asked, a hint of doubt creeping into his voice. "I may not have been brainwashed by the Society like Hepluosis, but I was still taught some things about keeping 'your woman' in line. It sounds rough being a woman on this planet."

"Tell me about it," she said, letting out a dramatic sigh. "But listen, you've already acted like a father in many ways. I've seen how you are with Cypress and the other dogs, and how you look out for your fellow guards and friends. You'll make a wonderful husband."

Thanks, Neiaphi. I really appreciate that," Greish replied, offering her a small smile. "You'd better get back to your family. I have a lot to think about."

Neiaphi patted him on the shoulder reassuringly. "You'll figure it out." She turned and made her way back to the tent.

## ∞ 4 ∞
# ]]EEDED SKILLS

**SHORTLY** after midday, Crelian's small party found a suitable landing spot along the lake's edge. As the boats touched the shore, everyone eagerly disembarked, grateful to stretch their legs and feel solid ground beneath them.

"I wish to stay here for the evening. Who's with me?" Georgios asked. Several voices grunted in agreement.

"Alright, let's make it official," Crelian said, raising his hand. "A show of hands for camping here tonight." Every hand went up.

"Then it's settled. Let's set up the tents and get a few fires going." Crelian glanced at Simos, who nodded and began giving instructions to his men.

A few of Simos's men went hunting, while others searched for suitable sticks to craft swords and staffs.

That evening, the group practiced basic drills with the staffs. The men took turns first while the boys observed closely. Meanwhile, the younger children and women sat around the fires, chatting and sharing stories.

When it was the boys' turn, Cret found himself paired with Hepluosis, who glared at him with a smirk. "You'll be looking up at me from the flat of your back when I'm done with you," Hepluosis sneered.

"We'll see about that. You have to catch me first," Cret taunted, swiftly spinning out of the way of Hepluosis's first strike. With a quick movement, he swung his staff low, striking Hepluosis's ankle. Hepluosis yelped in surprise, then growled and lunged at him. Cret easily dodged to the side as the strike whooshed past him. Cret easily dodged out of the way. The match quickly drew Simos's attention, and he paused his instruction with the younger boys to watch. Hepluosis lunged, swung, and slashed, but each time his staff sliced through empty air as Cret nimbly evaded. Then, Cret's foot snagged a root, causing him to stumble. Seizing the opportunity, Hepluosis struck Cret's shoulder. Gritting his teeth, Cret spun away from the blow, regaining his balance.

Hepluosis charged forward, his staff crashing against Cret's with a sharp clack. He pressed in closer until their faces were just inches apart. "You will lose," he growled through gritted teeth.

"Honestly, I expected more from you," Cret taunted.

With a swift shove, Cret pushed Hepluosis back and darted past him, landing a flurry of strikes on his back and legs as he moved.

"That's enough, boys. Come here," Simos called out to the two winded combatants. Cret walked over proudly, though his eyes remained on Hepluosis, wary of any sudden moves. Just as he reached Simos, he caught sight of Hepluosis's staff swinging toward him from the corner of his eye.

Simos moved to intercept Hepluosis's strike, but Cret's staff was there first, meeting Hepluosis's blow with a resounding crack. Hepluosis growled, pressing his weight into his staff, trying to force Cret off balance.

Simos wedged his staff between the two boys. "I said stand down," he commanded sternly, his gaze fixed on Hepluosis. "What's your name?"

"Hepluosis," the boy snarled.

"And yours, young man?" Simos asked Cret.

"Cret, sir. Crelian is my father," Cret replied.

Simos nodded. "Have either of you sparred with staffs before?"

"No, sir," Cret answered. Hepluosis merely shook his head, refusing to break eye contact with Cret.

"You, my boy, are a natural," Simos said to Cret. "Tomorrow, I think I'll put a sword in your hand and see what you can do."

"I'm already skilled with the sword," Hepluosis replied proudly, puffing out his chest.

"So, you say. We'll see tomorrow. Where did you learn to use a sword?" Simos asked.

"I trained with the guards back in Camp Roma," Hepluosis replied.

Simos nodded. "Next time I say 'stand down,' I mean it. I won't always be there to save your skin." He shifted his attention back to the younger boys.

"Tomorrow, when we spar, we'll see who the better man is. You and me, with swords," Hepluosis declared, jabbing his staff at Cret. "These staffs are for women, not men." With that, he tossed his staff at Cret's feet and stormed off.

Crelian approached his son, picking up the discarded weapon. "Was that wise? You know you have issues with him. Why invite trouble?"

Cret shrugged. "I didn't mean to provoke him; I was just trying to avoid his attacks at first. But he was so sloppy in his form that it made it unavoidable." A grin spread across his face. "I saw a couple of Simos's men spinning and dodging earlier, and it looked easy, so I thought I'd give it a try. Hepluosis just couldn't keep up." He paused, then continued, "But I've never picked up a sword, so I'm sure he'll have the upper hand there. Thankfully, it'll be a wooden sword."

"Just watch your back. When we board the boats again, I'll put Japster and his family on the other boat. No sense in causing an issue if it's not necessary."

Cret nodded in agreement.

"Good morning, Cret."

"Good morning, Tycho. How are you today?" Cret asked, addressing the boy two years his junior.

"Oh, so sore. I had no idea learning to spar with a staff would be this painful. I watched the guards train; they made it look fun," Tycho replied with a pained wince.

"I'm not feeling too bad, but Hepluosis didn't land many hits on me," Cret said, grinning widely.

"Can you teach me some of those moves?" Tycho asked, his eyes bright with curiosity.

"Sure! They're going to show us swords today," Cret replied.

"I thought we were moving on," the younger boy said, frowning slightly.

"No, my father decided we needed another day of rest, and Simos agreed. So, we have all day to spar—swords this morning, and I think archery later."

"That doesn't sound like resting," Tycho replied with a hint of sorrow.

Cret slapped Tycho on the back. "Well, I think the resting is just for the women. Come on!" Together, they headed to the clearing used for sparring the day before. A couple of men were already practicing with staffs when they arrived. Simos smiled and waved them over.

"Are you two ready to learn the art of the sword?" Simos asked.

"The sword is an art?" Tycho replied, looking confused.

"Most certainly. Wielding a weapon, regardless of its kind, is an art form. Any crafted skill can be considered a form of art." Simos picked up a practice sword and demonstrated swinging, slashing, and pretending to block. He spun and ducked down gracefully.

"How you move with your opponent—attacking and defending—is like a dance. Anyone can take a sword and hack at a defenseless tree, but not everyone has the nerve to perform when their adversary fights back and is motivated."

"Very nicely put, Simos," Hepluosis said, joining them. With a flourish, he drew his sword and drove the tip into the soft, lush grass as if daring anyone to challenge him.

"That is a fine weapon you have, but you won't be using it yet," Simos said. "Today, we'll be practicing with practice swords."

"I haven't used a practice sword in months. I've outgrown that level of skill."

"That may be, young sir, but the others aren't at your skill level yet. No one will be injured today. Please sheath your weapon." Hepluosis frowned but complied.

"You'll spar with me first, Hepluosis, as I demonstrate some fundamental techniques to the others."

A massive grin spread across Hepluosis's face as he grabbed a practice sword. Simos and Hepluosis squared off, each eyeing the other intently. Simos waited, allowing Hepluosis to make the first move. Hepluosis lunged, but Simos easily blocked the strike. As they traded blows, Simos narrated to the observing boys, pointing out specific techniques used by both himself and Hepluosis.

"Good job, Hepluosis. Now, the rest of you, grab a sword and pair up," he instructed, stepping back. "Hepluosis, take a break."

Crelian stood a short distance away, observing the boys as they practiced. His eyes followed their movements, noting the effort and the occasional lapse in focus. When Simos approached, wiping sweat from his brow, he glanced at Crelian.

"So, what do you think? Several of them show real promise," Simos said, a note of optimism in his voice.

Crelian's expression remained measured. "They don't seem to be taking the training seriously," he replied, his gaze drifting back to a pair of boys sparring with more enthusiasm than skill.

"Boys their age often need time to focus," Simos said, his tone calm and reassuring. "As we continue our trek, they will keep practicing. By the time we reach Atlantis, they'll be competent in their skills."

Crelian's gaze lingered on the sparring boys. "Let's hope so," he muttered. "These boys have been coddled. A little tough love might be just what they need to survive on this planet."

Simos listened intently, his brow furrowing slightly. "I've noticed Hepluosis's behavior. He's brash and quick to challenge others, and Japster doesn't seem to rein him in. I'll keep a close eye on them."

Crelian's expression hardened. "Good. We can't afford internal conflicts while trying to survive out here. If either of them steps out of line, deal with it immediately."

"I'll make sure they understand the consequences of their actions," Simos assured, his voice steady despite the tension coiling in his gut. "We need unity, not dissent."

Crelian nodded. "If I had known the truth of our situation before you came to rescue us, I would have had you leave those two behind. They're nothing but troublemakers."

"Troublemakers? How so?" Concern flickered in Simos's eyes, his brow furrowed.

"They're power-hungry." Crelian leaned closer, lowering his voice. "They've been sabotaging our repairs at the plant, trying to keep us stranded here longer. If we don't act now, we risk everything. I'm certain of it. Every time we seemed close to completion, something would go wrong. I sent Japster back to Camp Roma with a message, and while he was gone, the repairs were finished without a hitch. Sen was shocked—it was as if he couldn't believe we succeeded. There's a tension between us as well. Their family doesn't associate with anyone else. I wonder if it's jealousy or something deeper."

"I've noticed that too," Simos replied. "I've been meaning to ask you about it."

"We need to keep an eye on them," Crelian said, his tone serious. "Please don't assign them to special tasks unless they're in a large group. And don't give Hepluosis any new skills. He seems too comfortable with that sword."

"He's quite good, I have to admit. Not the best I've seen at his age, but impressive for someone so new to the weapon," Simos remarked, pausing as if carefully weighing his next words. "I'll assign Tevin to be his partner. Tevin will take it easy on him and use basic tactics—we can't let Hepluosis progress too quickly. The last thing we need is for him to become a threat before we fully understand his true potential."

"That would be for the best," Crelian replied, shaking his head. "I fear what he'll become in the hands of the Society."

"Agreed." Simos nodded as they watched the boys drill.

"Great job, boys! Take a break. We'll practice archery soon," Crelian called out, watching as the exhausted boys dropped their swords, some collapsing onto the grass to catch their breath.

"Go cool off in the river; you deserve it!" Crelian told them.

With a whoop of excitement, the boys sprinted to the water's edge, their fatigue momentarily forgotten as they splashed in with renewed energy.

By the time the sun was high overhead, Simos had gathered them once more for the next lesson. He surveyed the group thoughtfully, knowing he needed to assess which weapon suited each boy best to help them develop a skill they could master.

"Archery is not an easy skill to master. It requires a steady heartbeat and a calm hand. Pulling the string back is the easy part. Grab a bow and an arrow. Stand perpendicular to the target, turning only your head to aim. Don't turn your body. Hold the bow with your non-dominant hand—just a relaxed but firm grip. Place the arrow on the string and bring the bow up until the arrow is pointed at the target. Good, just like that. Now, pull the string back until your hand is at your jawbone,"

Simos demonstrated. "The string should lightly touch your face next to the corner of your mouth."

All the boys followed Simos's instructions. Tycho, Cret, Tivadarios, and Hepluosis were the first to pull back their strings correctly. The others struggled to draw their strings and hold onto their arrows, with a couple dropping theirs.

"When you're ready, take a shot."

Cret released his arrow a moment sooner than the others. It soared through the air, and only two arrows struck their targets with a satisfying thud. Tivadarios yelped as the bowstring snapped against the tender skin of his inner arm, causing his arrow to drop to the ground. Hepluosis's shot veered wide to the right. Cret and Tycho exchanged grins, turning to Simos with pride gleaming in their eyes. "Good," Simos said, nodding. "Not a bullseye, but you hit the target. Grab a few more arrows and work on your aim. The rest of you, let's focus on drawing your strings and keeping your arms steady."

Hepluosis scowled at Cret, then glared at the bow in his hands. With a look of frustration, he threw it down and stormed off.

"What's his problem?" Tycho asked Cret.

"We're just better at something than he is," Cret said with a grin. The two boys grabbed a fresh handful of arrows and headed back toward the targets, their confidence growing with                    each                    step. By the end of the day, all the boys were able to hit the target, and Cret and Tycho had each scored a few bullseyes. Simos made a mental note of each boy's developing weapon skills. The two youngest, Sandro and Basileios, would continue training with the staff for now, but as they grew, they could advance to swordplay. Tycho, Vangelis, and Cret showed particular skill in archery, while Hepluosis, Olek, Tivadarios, and Cret also demonstrated promise with the sword.

They had much work ahead, but the basic skills were there.

## ∞ 5 ∞
# First Date

**NEIAPHI** slipped into her family's tent just as Andonis approached outside. She ducked inside before he could see her and moved quietly over to her sleeping brothers. Voices drifted into the tent—Andonis had arrived. Glancing in the mirror, she quickly fixed her hair, studying her reflection.

"Neiaphi, what do you want out of life?" she asked, her reflection, her voice barely a whisper. "You have a handsome boy here who might want to ask for you. What's your problem?" She frowned, letting out a sigh. "Cret, where are you? Will I see you again? Do you still want me?" Tears welled in her eyes, but she shook her head. "Stop this right now," she scolded herself. "Cret isn't here, and you don't know if you'll ever see him again."

She took a deep breath, recalling the woman in her dream. *Choose from those before you.* "You won't marry until your family is settled in a city," she reminded herself. "So, what's holding you back?" She smoothed her dress and hair one last time, stifling a sob as she steadied herself.

Once she had composed herself, Neiaphi stepped out of the tent. Altesse, Cleop, and Net had just finished preparing the evening meal, while Andonis and Neiluios were engaged in quiet conversation by the fire.

"There you are, dear. Can you lend me a hand?" Altesse called.

"Of course, Mother." Altesse handed her two bowls and nodded toward the men by the fire. Neiaphi took the bowls and made her way over to her father.

"Hi, Neiaphi. Let me help you with those," Andonis offered, standing up and taking the bowls from her hands.

"Thank you." She gave him a small curtsy before returning to her mother, who handed her another bowl with a warm smile.

"You should sit next to Andonis, just to be sociable," Altesse whispered. Neiaphi nodded in agreement.

"Ma'am, you look lovely this evening," Andonis said.

"Why, thank you, Andonis." Altesse smiled at the compliment.

Everyone began to eat in silence. After a moment, Andonis broke the companionable quiet. "Did you hear about Neiaphi's new skill, ma'am?"

"No, what are you talking about?" Altesse asked.

"Well, we discovered that Neiaphi is a natural with the bow."

"Really? That's wonderful. But how much of a natural could she be? She's never had any experience with weapons," Altesse replied, still sounding unconvinced.

Andonis recounted the events leading up to Neiaphi's impressive display, carefully leaving out the part where he'd stood close with his arms around her. Altesse's smile brightened as she listened.

When Andonis finished, he glanced at Neiaphi. "Did I miss any details?" he asked. She quickly shook her head, looking away to hide the flush rising in her cheeks. Altesse noticed, her smile widening at their exchange.

"So, I hear you'll be joining your father in Chrysafi tomorrow," Altesse said, gently shifting the conversation.

"Alexa and I both will. I can't wait! Can you join us, Mother?"

"I'm sorry, dear, but I want to rest one more day before we start traveling heavily again."

"Who else is going tomorrow, Sir?" Andonis asked Neiluios.

"Paragon, your father Mace, Net, and I, along with a couple of guards. I'd like to ask you a favor."

"Yes, Sir, anything."

"Can you keep an eye on Altesse and my boys while I'm away?"

"I would be honored, Sir." Andonis bowed his head.

"Thank you. I feel better knowing someone will be around if there's a need."

The meal wound down with light, inconsequential chatter as the sun dipped below the trees, casting a warm, fading glow across the camp. One by one, Net and Cleop excused themselves, retiring to their tent. Altesse and Neiluios lingered by the fire, quietly watching the sky as its colors faded into twilight. Across from them, Andonis and Neiaphi sat in comfortable silence, each absorbed in their own thoughts. Altesse nudged Neiluios gently, giving him a knowing look as she nodded toward their tent. He returned a slight nod and then cleared his throat.

"Well, we're going to turn in for the evening," he said. "Make sure the fire's out before you head to bed, dear."

"Yes, Father. I won't be far behind you." With that, her parents rose and headed to their tent, leaving Neiaphi and Andonis alone in the peaceful quiet of the evening.

After a few quiet moments, Andonis broke the silence. "It was kind of your father to invite me to dinner. I've enjoyed the evening," he said, his tone warm.

"It has been fun," Neiaphi replied quietly.

He hesitated, then spoke again, slower this time. "I don't want to put any pressure on you, but… could we speak openly for a moment?"

Neiaphi sighed, her gaze shifting to the fire's glow. "All right," she replied, her voice barely above a whisper.

Andonis took a deep breath before he began, his tone gentle yet resolute. "I know you still have feelings for this

Cret," he said, raising a hand to stop her from interrupting. "I've asked around, and from what I've heard, he's a good man—someone I'd likely respect if he were here. I don't doubt we'd get along well. But the reality is, he's not here, and I may never have the chance to meet him."

He paused, his eyes searching her face. "I've been enjoying our time together, and I'd like to spend more of it with you—as close friends." Neiaphi remained silent, her heart racing, unable to meet his gaze. "I believe it's possible to care for, even love, two people at once. I know I may never have your whole heart, but having you by my side... that would be enough for me."

Neiaphi looked away, contemplating his words, the firelight casting a soft glow over her face. Finally, she gathered her thoughts and turned to him, finding he wasn't looking at her either. His expression betrayed a trace of nervousness. "Cret is... a dear friend. On Romota, we shared a friendship, but nothing too deep." Her voice softened. "On the ship, we sought each other out for comfort and support, and everything happened so fast—like being hit by a storm. At Camp Roma, customs and propriety kept us apart. And then, just as quickly, he was gone." She swallowed, recalling the letters. "He gave me two letters: one before he left, where he spoke about his feelings for me, and another while he traveled to the Processing Plant. In that one, he told me to forget him. I've been trying to forget; I truly have. However, I dream about him almost every night."

"Do you have any other dreams?" he gently pressed, glancing at her.

"Yes." Neiaphi cleared her throat, hesitating as she considered how much to share. Her shoulders sagged, and she sighed. "The dreams started on the ship, on the way here. I dreamt of a man with grey eyes walking along a path. In the first dream, he didn't speak—he just walked past me. I found him... attractive, which scared me. I've had that same dream many times. It usually starts the same way. Sometimes, he speaks to me and knows my name, but he never tells me his. Eventually, I find myself on a beach when I keep walking down the path in the dream."

Neiaphi paused, collecting her thoughts. "At first, I'm alone on the beach. Then I hear someone calling my name. Later, another man appears, saying he's searching for an island to build a city, where he can be with his love. After I received Cypress and Nexus, they started appearing in the dream too. Sometimes, a wolver blocks my way as I try to return up the path. If I don't wake up, the man on the beach comes to my aid. The dream feels so real... even now, thinking about it, it feels more like a memory than just a dream. Does any of this make sense?"

"Not really, at least not yet. Have you ever met anyone who looks like the man with the grey eyes or the one on the beach?"

"No, not that I remember."

"Well, if you did, I'm pretty certain you would remember them. Any other dreams?"

"Yes, actually. I had another one shortly after meeting you and Alexa. In it, I was standing before you, Aristas, Chartis, Cret, and the man with gray eyes. Chartis was urging me to choose—telling me I had to decide right then. The man with gray eyes promised we'd meet again soon."

"I somehow sent you all away, and then a female voice told me that all my choices would become clear soon and not to fear making a decision. She assured me I wouldn't be married before meeting her. She said I'd be passing near her home soon and that she would meet me in person then. I know it sounds strange," she hesitated, "but I believe her."

"So, you're waiting until you meet this man with grey eyes, see if Cret returns, and encounter this mysterious woman at her home—wherever that might be?"

"Oh, it sounds even worse when you say it aloud." Neiaphi brought her hands to her face, shaking her head.

Andonis gently placed a comforting arm across her shoulders, drawing her close. Neiaphi leaned against him, resting her head on his chest. They remained there for a while, finding solace in the quiet closeness.

Eventually, Neiaphi pulled back slightly, looking up at him. Understanding and concern shone in his eyes. "It feels good to finally share these strange nighttime fantasies with someone. Do you think I'm crazy?"

Andonis held her gaze, his arm still around her. "No, I don't think you're crazy. Is this female voice the same one that said you were destined for great things?"

"Yes."

"I wish the voice had told you where she lived. It would make the wait easier."

"Tell me about it," Neiaphi replied. Andonis gently removed his arm from her shoulders, placing a reassuring hand over hers.

"I can wait. You're worth it. I want you to know that whatever choice you make, I'll support you. I saw the look on your face when your father invited me over tonight—I won't pressure you before you're ready."

"Thank you; that means a lot to me," she said quietly.

"I also want you to know that if, by some chance…" He hesitated, his words unsteady. "I'm not saying this to sway you. I just… need to share how I feel."

"What is it?" she asked, gently placing her hand over his. Andonis looked down at their hands, now clasped together. After a moment, he spoke, his voice unsteady. "If, by some chance, you chose me—and then Cret returned, and your feelings for him were still strong…" He swallowed hard, his throat tight. "I would step aside, if that's what you wanted."

Tears welled up in her eyes, spilling down her cheeks. Andonis reached up to wipe them away, but Neiaphi held his hand, leaning into him. Without saying a word, he wrapped his arms around her, holding her close. Neiaphi let herself cry softly against his shoulder, feeling guilty for putting him through this. He was a true friend, and she regretted how torn she felt. As time passed, her sobs gradually quieted, and her tears dried.

Neiaphi pushed herself back, wiping her face with her hands. "Sorry," she said softly.

"Don't apologize," Andonis reassured her, his voice soft but firm. "You've been through so much in such a short time. Just know that I'll always be here—for you to talk to, to lean on."

She looked down at her hands, a sense of guilt clouding her expression. "This isn't fair to you. My indecision is affecting your life and your choices."

Andonis reached out gently, lifting her chin so she would meet his gaze. "That's for me to handle," he said with a reassuring smile. "I'm here because I want to be. And I'll stay unless you tell me to go. That's what I want—to be with you."

"Oh…," she began to cry again.

"Please, don't cry." Andonis gently wiped away her tears with his thumb. "If Cret comes back, you won't have to ask me to step aside. I'll understand. But until then, let me be here for you. Let me be the strength and the shoulder you need."

He paused, offering her a soft, reassuring smile. "Don't feel like you need to answer me tonight. Go with your father to Chrysafi, and we'll talk later, okay?"

Neiaphi nodded, her voice failing her. Andonis leaned in and kissed her cheek before standing to leave.

But as he turned, Neiaphi sprang to her feet and wrapped her arms tightly around him. "Thank you," she whispered, her voice barely audible. Then, just as quickly, she pulled away and hurried back to her tent.

# ∞ 6 ∞
# CHRYSAFI

**THE** group set out before dawn, the world around them still cloaked in darkness. As the sky gradually brightened with the promise of a new day, the path ahead slowly revealed itself. The horses, eager and full of energy, swished their tails and moved in a steady rhythm. Neiaphi stifled another yawn, which was met by a quiet giggle from Alexa. Nudging her horse closer, Alexa leaned in, her voice a soft whisper meant only for Neiaphi.

"So, how did it go last night?" Alexa whispered.

Neiaphi's cheeks flushed. "We talked for a while. I'll tell you all about it later, okay?" She tilted her head slightly toward her father, signaling the need for privacy.

Alexa smiled. "You'd better."

Their ride took them through the morning hours, the landscape slowly giving way to the clustered rooftops of Chrysafi. When the village finally appeared on the horizon, both Neiaphi and Alexa let out delighted squeals, eager to escape the routine of travel and enjoy the simple pleasures of visiting a town and shopping like regular villagers.

"How long do we have, Father?" Neiaphi asked.

"We can spend most of the day. Your mother isn't expecting us until after dark."

Neiaphi nodded and hummed happily.

"This is going to be a lovely day. What's our first stop?" Alexa asked.

"We need to get some food staples first, then you girls can pick out new dresses," Paragon said.

"Your mother also needs cloth to make more clothes for your brothers," Neiluios added.

"We'll pick something for them—and a beautiful dress for Mother," Neiaphi replied, a smile touching her lips as she spoke with determination.

"We need to stop at the first guard tower, Sir," Greish said to Neiluios. "We'll meet our contact there."

"Do you know who it is?" Neiluios asked.

"His name is Kayson, a member of the Loyals. He'll show us around. The town is mostly friendly, but there are some Society members and spies. Stick together and stay alert."

"Thank you, Lieutenant," Paragon said, eyeing Greish for a moment before glancing at Alexa.

Noticing this, Neiaphi leaned closer to Alexa and whispered, "Is there something you're not telling me?"

"Shhh, later," Alexa whispered.

Neiaphi grinned. "You'd better," she said, mimicking Alexa's earlier tone.

Lieutenant Greish dismounted and approached the guard tower, where the guard greeted him with a skeptical nod. After a brief exchange, Greish entered the building and emerged moments later with a young man in his mid-twenties, walking beside him.

"Good day, and welcome to Chrysafi. How was your journey, Cousin Paragon?" Kayson greeted them warmly, his smile wide.

Paragon, looking slightly confused but going along with it, replied, "Long and tiring. We're looking forward to resting for the day."

Kayson nodded in understanding. "Let's head into town then. A rest sounds well-earned. We'll stop by the bathhouse first so you all can freshen up." Greish remounted his horse, and Kayson joined them on his own mount.

Once they were out of earshot of the tower, Kayson glanced over at Paragon and Neiluios, his voice lowering. "I apologize for the ruse back there. Creating a backstory was necessary, and claiming we'

re relatives seemed like the most plausible cover."

"Understood. Kayson, is it?" Paragon asked.

"Yes, I apologize for not catching all your names. The Lieutenant mentioned yours, Sir, and Neiluios, is that correct?" Kayson gestured toward Neiluios.

"Yes. This is my daughter Neiaphi, Paragon's daughter Alexa, Net, and Leander," Neiluios introduced.

"Welcome. The bathhouses are over here. While you freshen up, I'll tend to the horses; the stable is just behind us."

Neiaphi and Alexa dismounted first, handing their reins to Kayson, who smiled down at them. Neiaphi felt a flicker of recognition but couldn't place where she might have seen him before. Kayson looked equally puzzled. Shaking her head, she turned and walked away.

The two girls headed to the women's bathhouse. Once inside, Neiaphi turned to Alexa. "Have you ever seen Kayson before?"

"Not that I know of. Why?"

"He looks familiar, but I can't place him."

"Come on. I need a drink. Let's see what we can find," Alexa replied.

Neiluios, following Alexa's lead, decided their first stop would be an inn for a meal and a refreshing drink. Soon, they spotted a place called the Pegasus, its sign hanging above the entrance. The weary group entered the dimly lit establishment, greeted by the musty but inviting atmosphere.

They paused in the doorway to let their eyes adjust to the low light. Scattered throughout the spacious room were small tables for two, creating cozy, intimate settings for quiet conversations. Toward the back, a few empty tables were grouped together. Kayson, Greish, and Leander made their way to the bar while the rest of the group chose tables. Neiluios and Paragon settled at one table. Neiaphi and Alexa found another nearby. Net grabbed a third table and pulled it closer to Neiluios and Paragon's.

Kayson joined them at Net's table. "A serving girl will be here shortly. The innkeeper's trustworthy, and he has a room available if we need more privacy."

"Good to know. How are things here in Chrysafi?" Neiluios asked.

"Quiet for now," Kayson answered with a shrug. "We had some unrest last winter, but it's calmed down. An insurgent group tried to take over, but they were held off without bloodshed. How have your travels been so far?"

"We've had our share of unrest, but we are managing," Neiluios said.

"I have a question about the wolves in these parts," Net interjected.

"Wolves? What can I tell you about them?" Kayson asked.

"We encountered some a few days back, and they were larger than any I've ever seen," Net replied.

"We've received reports of extra-large wolf prints, but the wolves to match have not been spotted," Kayson explained.

"We saw several circling our camp, and a few even ventured between our tents in the dark, steering clear of the fires. The next day, we found tracks trailing our group," Net explained.

"Interesting. I'll pass this information along to the leadership so they can keep an eye out. Thank you," Kayson replied.

"Okay, Neiaphi, tell me how last night went," Alexa said softly.

Neiaphi leaned closer. "Andonis is asking for me."

"Well, that's obvious. Is that something you want, though?"

"Yes and no. I'm... unsure." Neiaphi shook her head, sadness flickering in her eyes. "He knows I'm still waiting for news about Cret. He even told me he'd step aside if Cret comes back. He just wants me to be happy, he said."

"That's wonderful news," Alexa said with a bright smile. "Why don't you seem happy, then?"

"On the surface, it is great. I could have companionship now, and if Cret comes back, Andonis would let us be together." Neiaphi paused, her frown deepening. "But I can't imagine doing that to him. Andonis deserves someone who can fully be with him. How can he be okay with being with me for now, only to let me go if Cret reappears?"

"Well, it sounds like he'd rather spend as much time with you as he can and hope Cret doesn't return—or that you might even choose him over Cret if he does," Alexa teased, grinning.

"Thanks," Neiaphi replied, her tone laced with a hint of sarcasm. "Anyway, what's going on with you and Greish?" She shifted the topic, her curiosity piqued.

"Greish and I had a nice talk last night," Alexa said, her voice thoughtful. "I think he likes me, and I know I like him too. But he seems uncertain about something... I'm not quite sure what it is."

"Greish mentioned to me yesterday that he doesn't know if he'd make a good husband or father."

"Oh, is that what he's worried about?" Alexa mused. "No one really knows if they'll be a good partner or parent until the time comes. His unease makes more sense now."

"Your father was watching the two of you. What was that about?"

"I noticed that too. I'll have to ask my father."

"Good day, ladies," the serving girl said with a smile, setting down two drinks and a plate of assorted fruit. Both Neiaphi and Alexa thanked her before eagerly reaching for the juicy treats. They took their time, savoring the sweetness of the fruit, their conversation drifting between lighthearted chatter and the events of the day.

Neiaphi and Alexa followed the men through the village, stopping at various shops along the way. They carefully selected fabric for baby clothes and picked out a couple of dresses for Altesse. After a while, Paragon led Alexa toward a nearby store, leaving Neiaphi standing by herself. A wave of vulnerability washed over her as she glanced around, suddenly feeling alone in the crowd. Her eyes quickly found Greish, who stood a short distance away, observing the bustling activity with a calm, measured expression.

"Hi, Greish," Neiaphi said as she approached him.

"Hi, Neiaphi. Are you enjoying yourself today?" he replied, his gaze still fixed on the people passing by.

"Immensely," she smiled. "Can I ask you a question?"

"Sure, what is it?" He turned slightly, giving her a bit more of his attention, though his eyes stayed alert to the crowd.

"Alexa told me you still haven't spoken about your intentions with her. Have you talked to her father yet?"

Greish turned his gaze to her. "Did she say she would like me to?"

She sighed loudly. "I know she does, and I told you as much. Her father kept looking back and forth between you two on the trip here, and she's confused about it. I thought I'd ask if you knew what was going on."

"I see," Greish replied, scanning the crowd thoughtfully. After a moment, he continued. "Last night, after I said goodnight to Alexa, I saw her father walking around the camp. I asked him if he and his wife had anyone in mind for her, and he mentioned they had a shortlist. I told him I'd gotten to know Alexa over the past couple of weeks and that I often find myself looking for her during my free time. Not only that, but I enjoy spending time with her," he added, his voice softening. "He asked about my rank and future goals, then said he'd speak with his wife. After that, he just walked away. I don't think he likes me."

"When you're a father with a daughter, you'll probably act the same way. Fathers tend to be protective."

"I suppose. Did her father mention anything to her?"

"No, she said she would ask him about you, though."

"Really? But you said she couldn't say anything because it's improper."

"She said it's only proper for you to bring it up first. Once you do, then she's free to discuss it with you, but she can always talk to her father."

Greish shook his head. "If she talks to him about us, then I'll truly know how she feels."

"She hasn't told you?"

"She has, but... I have trouble trusting people," Greish admitted, his gaze distant. "Back at Camp Roma, there was a guard's daughter I was interested in. She told me to speak to her father, and he agreed. But when he told her, she cried and ran off, saying she hadn't been serious. I know it's unfair to compare them, but... once bitten, twice shy." He shrugged, the memory lingering in his eyes.

"I understand. Do you want me to tell Alexa any of this?"

"No, I'll handle it if necessary. It's in her parents' hands for now."

"Well, don't worry about her saying no, okay?"

"If you say so." He smiled and nodded, turning back to survey the crowd.

"Mother would love this dress, Father," Alexa said.

"Do you think so? Then let's get it for her." Paragon wrapped his arm around his daughter's shoulders as they strolled past the street carts.

"A young man spoke with me yesterday evening about you," Paragon mentioned.

"He did?" she replied, beaming up at him.

"So, you know who I'm speaking of?"

"I've only spent time with one man since we joined the Laosans."

"He's your age and a guard. That doesn't bother you?"

"Not at all, Father. Greish is advancing quickly in rank. He's in charge of training the guard dogs and even helps train the younger boys. He's brilliant, Father. I know he'll go far."

"You praise him almost as highly as his commander," Paragon mused, shaking his head thoughtfully. "Is he the one you want to spend your life with? Remember, you might not make it to Atlantis; he could be stationed elsewhere along the way."

"Oh, Father, he's the one I want," she replied, her voice soft but certain. "I dream of seeing the Great City, but as long as I'm with Greish, I'll be happy. I don't want to leave you and Mother, but I love him."

Paragon studied his daughter, a bittersweet realization settling in. She was growing into a beautiful young woman, ready to choose her own path.

"When would you like to marry?"

"Oh, really, Father? Are you saying yes?" She jumped up and hugged him tightly, her excitement overflowing. He nodded, smiling warmly.

"I'd like to wait until we reach Atlantis—or if Greish is stationed somewhere along the way—before we part ways. You and Mother must be there." She was giddy with joy.

"Atlantis it is. I'll do everything possible to ensure you make it all the way."

"Thank you, Father. I'm so happy."

"I've never seen you this happy, and it makes my heart soar." He gazed at his daughter, noticing how much she had changed. In that moment, she seemed five years older. His heart sank just a little, realizing that the little girl he once knew was no longer there. But the woman standing before him, brimming with joy, would always be his sweet Alexa, and his love for her would never waver.

"I have to go tell Neiaphi. Will you excuse me?"

"Of course, dear." She hugged him again before hurrying off.

## ∞ 7 ∞
## ᕼAPPY ᕼEWS

**ᕼEIAPHI** and Greish stood nearby as Alexa left her father's side. Noticing her friend's excitement, Neiaphi made her way over.

"You have a goofy look on your face. What's wrong?" Neiaphi asked.

"He said yes!"

"Oh, that's wonderful!" Neiaphi exclaimed, hugging her tightly. "How are you going to tell Greish?"

"I'm not sure. What were you two talking about?"

"I was just asking him if he'd spoken with your father—I wanted to gather some information for you, but you beat me to it. I say you go right up to him and throw yourself into his arms."

Alexa blushed at the thought. "I can't do that; what would people say?"

"You're about to be married; what could they possibly say?"

"Okay, here it goes." She took a deep breath and stood up straight, squaring her shoulders. Greish wasn't looking her way.

"You can do this: walk up to him, and when he turns around, don't look him in the eyes—just do it," she whispered to herself.

Alexa walked the short distance to Greish, who had his back to her. "Greish," she said softly.

"Alexa?" he replied, turning around. Suddenly, she threw her arms around him and hugged him tightly. He stood there, stunned.

He spotted Neiaphi in the distance, smiling from ear to ear. His attention returned to the girl clinging to him. Gently, he wrapped his arms around her, and she responded by hugging him tighter.

"My father said yes! Oh, Greish, I'm so happy. I love you," she whispered in his ear. Once again, Greish found himself stunned. Her father had agreed, and she still wanted him. He buried his face in her hair, tightened his embrace, and breathed deeply, a faint scent of roses washing over him. She was his.

After what felt like an eternity, Greish pulled back to look at her. Her eyes sparkled, tears streamed down her cheeks, and she glowed with happiness.

"Did your father mention me to you?" he asked, gently wiping a tear from her cheek with his thumb.

She looked at him intently. "Well, he mentioned that a young man spoke to him about me yesterday, but he didn't say your name. I told him I loved you and that I wanted you. Is that what you meant?"

"In a way, yes. So, you truly want me, not just for show?"

"Just for show? What are you talking about? Of course, I want you. I want no one else but you. I love you and only you."

Greish looked deeply into her eyes, still sparkling with joy. He reached for her, and she met him halfway, wrapping her arms around him and resting her head on his chest. She leaned back slightly to gaze up at him, a soft smile lighting her face. As he looked down into her radiant expression, he leaned in and kissed her for the first time.

Neiaphi watched her friend share a tender moment with her future husband, stifling a silent sob as she turned away. She shifted her focus to a nearby cart displaying jewelry, admiring the glimmering pieces.

"Those would look lovely on you," a voice said from behind her. Startled, she turned around to find Kayson standing there.

"Oh, hello," she replied, a hint of surprise in her voice.

"Your friend over there looks quite happy," Kayson said, nodding toward Alexa.

"She should be. Her father is allowing them to marry."

"Oh, that's a joyous occasion. What about you? Are you promised yet?"

"My… you are quite forward. I've met a few like you around here," she responded with a tense smile.

"Oh? So, are you available or spoken for?" he asked again.

Neiaphi eyed him nervously. "It's not proper for me to discuss such things. You should be speaking to my father." The thought of the Taking Practice rushed into her mind. "If you'll excuse me, I, I should be moving on." She began to walk away.

"I can see I'm making you nervous. I didn't mean to frighten you, my apologies. I'll see you later." He bowed at the waist and walked away.

"What did he want, Neiaphi?" Net asked as he approached.

"Net?" Neiaphi jumped. "I didn't notice you nearby."

"I'm always nearby, little miss."

"He was asking if I was promised. Do they practice The Taking here?" Neiaphi asked, her voice wavering.

"Not that I'm aware of. Is that what you thought when he spoke with you?" Net's brow furrowed.

"Yes. I didn't know what to say—I was so scared."

"With The Taking, the man doesn't speak to the woman," Net explained. "He goes straight to the father. Remember, the woman has no say in the matter."

"I see. Good to know." Neiaphi nodded. "Where's Father?"

"He'll be here momentarily. He's picking up one last thing, and then we will leave."

"It'll be good to be back with everyone," Neiaphi said. Net nodded in agreement. He offered his arm, and she took it gladly. Together, they walked back toward the stables.

Soon, everyone gathered at the stables to collect their horses. Net loaded the food and goods into the donkey cart while the others mounted up. Greish assisted Alexa onto her horse.

"Neiluios, Sir." Kayson called out.

"Yes, Kayson?"

"The council has requested that I join you on the journey to Atlantis. I know this area well, and I've been to the Pillars of Hercules. Each group has been assigned a guide."

"Have you been to Atlantis?" Net asked in awe.

"No, sadly, I have not. I reached the Pillars but was not allowed to continue," Kayson explained.

"Where are the Pillars?" Paragon asked.

Far from here," Kayson replied. "The travel time will depend on our travel method."

"Grab your gear and mount up," Neiluios instructed. Kayson ducked inside the stable, emerging moments later with a spirited bay stallion and a smaller brown donkey laden with supplies.

The trek back to camp felt surprisingly brief, and before long, they had returned. As the sun set, casting long shadows across the landscape, the sky darkened, and they dismounted, brushing off the dust from their journey. After a few brief farewells, the group scattered. Alexa and her father made their way to their tent, while Greish and Leander set off to find their commander. Net guided the horses and donkeys toward the corrals.

"You can stay with us tonight, Kayson. We'll be leaving late tomorrow, so there's no need to set up a tent for just one night," Neiluios said.

"Thank you, Sir," Kayson replied, as they walked the short distance to Neiluios's tent together.

When they arrived, Altesse was still awake, sitting by the fire and talking with Andonis.

"Neiluios, Neiaphi, I'm so happy to see you both!" Altesse exclaimed, rushing over to greet them. Cypress bounded toward Neiaphi, casting a cautious eye at the stranger beside them but sensing no immediate threat.

"Is something the matter, dear?" Neiluios asked, his voice full of concern. Altesse glanced over at Andonis, who rose to his feet before speaking.

"The wolves made a daylight appearance, Sir," he explained. "They appeared shortly after you left and lingered at the edge of the forest until midday. They're incredibly fast. The guards fired arrows at any that came closer, but none found their mark."

Altesse visibly shuddered, her voice trembling. "It was terrifying. All I could think about was…" She trailed off, choking back a sob. Neiluios reached for her, and she collapsed into his arms.

"How are my boys?" he asked Andonis.

"They're perfectly safe, Sir. No one was harmed today."

Neiluios nodded, gently leading his wife toward their tent.

"Were they larger than normal wolves, like the ones I heard about?" Kayson asked.

Andonis eyed the newcomer warily before responding. "Yes, they were. I've never seen wolves of that size before." He paused, then added, "And you are?"

"My apologies. I'm Kayson," he replied, extending his hand. "I'll be guiding your group to the Pillars."

Andonis shook his hand and nodded. "I'm Andonis. Neiaphi, may I speak with you in private?"

"Of course," Neiaphi replied, glancing at Kayson. "Please excuse us. Net will be here shortly to show you where you can sleep."

Andonis extended his arm toward Neiaphi, who rested her hand gently on it. Together, they walked away, leaving Kayson behind.

Once they were a short distance away, Andonis turned to Neiaphi. "It's so good to see you again. How was the trip?"

"It was wonderful and relaxing," she replied, a smile spreading across her face. "Oh, and Alexa and Greish are officially promised now."

Andonis smiled broadly. "That's great news. I've seen them together—they're a perfect match." He paused and then reached for her hands. He brought them to his chest and looked into her eyes. "Have you given any more thought to my proposal? Have you spoken to your father?"

Neiaphi's smile faded slightly. "It's all I've thought about, but I haven't told my father yet. I did tell Alexa, though."

"What did she say?" Andonis asked. He lowered her hands, and they started walking again.

Neiaphi waved a hand dismissively. "She's just glad she doesn't have to make this choice. Honestly, she wasn't much help."

"And what about you? What do you think?" He stopped walking again.

Neiaphi hesitated, then met his gaze. "I think… no, I know I need more time. Please, just another day or so."

Andonis smiled softly. "I don't mean to pressure you. Take all the time you require. I'll admit, I'm a bit impatient, but you're worth the wait." His smile lingered as he gently cupped her cheek. Neiaphi leaned into his touch, her eyes fluttering closed for a moment.

"Come on, let's get you back," he said. "You need your rest."

He walked her back to her tent and paused at the entrance. "Goodnight, Neiaphi. I'll see you in the morning."

"Bye, Andonis. Thank you for everything." She smiled as he blew a kiss in her direction before she slipped into her tent.

Kayson stepped out from behind the tent, watching Andonis depart. *So, Andonis is pursuing Neiaphi,* he thought, a smirk forming on his lips. *It seems her father is allowing her a choice—how primitive. I'll have to speak to him and show him the error of his ways.*

"Kayson, the only places to sleep are by the fire or in my tent. Which would you prefer?" Net asked, noticing him standing next to the fire.

"Here is fine, Net. Thank you," Kayson replied.

"Excellent, sir. There's some leftover stew. May I sit with you while we eat?"

"I don't see why not," Kayson said, watching as Net walked over to the pot and served up a bowl for each of them.

## ∞ 8 ∞
## CLOSER TO A DECISION

**THE** camp awoke with the sun the following morning. Neiaphi stepped out of her tent and found Kayson sitting beside a crackling fire.

"Good morning, Neiaphi. Would you like some tea?" he asked, offering her a steaming cup.

"Thank you," she replied, accepting the tea and settling down on the opposite side of the fire. "How did you fare last night?"

"It was a pleasant night, thank you," Kayson answered, taking a sip of his tea. He glanced at her, then back at the flames. "So, you and Andonis… how are things going there?"

Neiaphi's expression hardened slightly. "I've already told you, Kayson. You should speak to my father about such matters," she said, cautious yet firm.

Kayson raised his hands in a gesture of surrender, looking at her earnestly. "Okay, I'm sorry. Yes, you mentioned that. I was just trying to make conversation."

Neiaphi stared at the tea in her hands, lost in thought. She sat in silence until a wet nose nudged her hand. Looking down, she smiled and reached over to scratch Cypress behind the ear.

"That's a handsome dog. What's his name?" Kayson asked, his gaze fixed on Cypress.

Neiaphi jumped slightly at his voice. "Sorry, what did you say?" she asked, blinking as she returned her focus to him.

"I said nice dog. What's his name?"

"Cypress," she replied, smiling down at her loyal companion.

"Good strong name. So, how long have you and your family been traveling?" Kayson asked.

"It feels like forever," she replied, deliberately leaving out details.

Suddenly, Cleop exited her tent, looking startled. "Good morning, Neiaphi! And who is this?"

"Good morning, Cleop. This is Kayson; he's from Chrysafi. He'll be helping us get to the Pillars," Neiaphi explained. "Can I speak with you for a moment? I need some advice."

"Of course, miss. Could you help me get some water?" Cleop asked.

"No problem," Neiaphi replied.

"Please, allow me," Kayson offered, starting to stand.

"That's okay, Sir. It'll give us ladies a chance to talk," Cleop said.

"Please don't call me 'Sir,' just Kayson," he said with a warm smile.

"'Sir' will suit me just fine, Sir," Cleop replied with a playful grin, bowing at the waist before departing the warmth of the fire, Neiaphi and Cypress by her side.

As they reached the stream, Cleop turned to Neiaphi. "What can I help you with?"

"Andonis and I had a long talk the other night," Neiaphi began.

"I saw you two by the fire. If you don't mind me saying, it didn't look like a happy conversation," Cleop remarked.

"It was, and it wasn't," Neiaphi admitted, her voice tinged with uncertainty. "He knows how much I miss Cret and that I want nothing more than to be with him again." Cleop nodded in understanding. Neiaphi took a deep breath before continuing, her voice quivering. "The problem is, I don't know if Cret will ever return to me—or if he even still wants me. His parents might have already promised him to someone else by now." She stifled a sob, trying to steady herself. Kneeling, she dipped the basket into the water, focusing on the task to keep her hands from trembling.

"Did Andonis propose anything to you?"

"His companionship." She sat down on the ground.

"Even knowing that your heart may never be his?" She nodded, her voice trembling. "He said that if Cret ever returned, and we wanted to be together, he would step aside without question. How could he say that? How could he be with me, knowing that one day I might choose to leave him? It's not fair to him. Why would he still want to be with someone like me?"

She nodded, her voice trembling. "He said that if Cret ever returned, and we wanted to be together, he would step aside without hesitation. How could he say that? How could he stay with me, knowing that one day I might leave him? It isn't fair to him. Why would he still want to be with someone like me?"

Finally, she looked up at Cleop, her eyes searching for understanding.

Cleop sat down next to her as Cypress barked and darted off after a bird that had ventured too close. "I can see you're struggling," Cleop said gently.

Neiaphi sighed, contemplating her dilemma.

"I understand your perspective. But let's consider Andonis for a moment. You're focusing on how you feel, but what about how he feels? How would it be for him? Let's pretend you're talking to Cret," Cleop continued. "Now, imagine this version of Cret, pining for another girl whose whereabouts are unknown. Would it be worth it to you to spend whatever time you could with him, or would you simply walk away now and never be with him at all?"

Neiaphi sat in silence, contemplating Cleop's words. "I guess I would choose to be with him, even if it were only for a short time. I never looked at it that way. I've been so focused on how he might feel when I leave. Oh, what am I saying? I don't even know if I would ever leave him. And I don't know if Cret will ever return."

Turmoil was etched across her features, and her eyes shimmered with the onset of tears as the reality of Andonis's feelings began to sink in.

"He's gambling that he will never have to face the pain of losing me," Neiaphi said, her voice trembling. "He doesn't believe Cret will ever return. He's willing to take that bet, even though the consequences of being wrong would be heartbreaking."

Tears began to slide down her cheeks.

Cleop placed a comforting hand on Neiaphi's shoulder. "Don't speak to him today. Avoid him if you can. It's important to talk to your parents about this. And remember, you don't have to marry right away." She smiled reassuringly at Neiaphi.

Neiaphi wiped her face and gave a small smile. "You're right. Thank you. Ugh, I've been crying way too much lately. I need to stop this."

Cleop stood and extended a hand to her. "We should head back; your parents will be up soon."

Andonis lay wide awake, thoughts of Neiaphi swirling relentlessly in his mind. "Stupid, stupid, stupid," he muttered, pushing himself up and slipping out of his tent. *I should just move on, find someone else,* he thought, *but I can't stop thinking about her.* What was it about her that held him so tightly? *Captivating*... Yes, that was the word. She had captured his heart effortlessly—no, quite the opposite. She'd tried to avoid this, done everything to keep him at arm's length, and yet here he was, helplessly drawn to her. *Could I ever look at another girl the way I look at her? He sighed and shook his head, resigned. I'd do anything for her, even if it means letting go—if that's what she truly wants. He added more wood to the fire, slumping down as it crackled and flared, the flames mirroring the storm within him.*

The rising sun found Andonis still staring into the flames.

"Good morning, son," his father, Mace, said. "Why the long face? Let me guess—it's a girl. Neiluios's daughter, right?"

Andonis flinched when his father appeared, but nodded in response.

"She's a pretty girl. I've heard she's graceful, confident, and skilled with a bow."

"You're not helping, Father," he replied grimly.

His father gave him a hearty slap on the back, grinning. "Come now, it can't be that bad. You're my son! You're confident, handsome, smart, a fine marksman, and skilled with a sword."

"Thanks," Andonis replied, still avoiding his father's gaze. "What's the problem? I've seen you talking and spending time with her. Does she like you? Have you spoken with her father?"

"I think she likes me, but the issue is that she loves someone else."

"Who? I haven't seen her with anyone around here."

"He's not here. He's with the group that went to the processing plant."

"Well, she needs to forget him. That group will never make it to Atlantis if the Society has anything to say about it."

"I know it, Cret knows it, and what's even worse is that she knows it too. She's just holding on to the hope that he'll be able to return to her. When he left, he told her to forget about him, but she just can't."

"So, what are you going to do? Are you going to do the same thing she's doing?"

Andonis looked up at his father, who raised an eyebrow, nodding with understanding. "You're right. I'm doing the same thing—holding out hope for something out of reach. I think I understand what she's going through now. Not only that, but I'll need to think on that."

"Do that, son. Now, come help me pack up. We'll be leaving before midday. Today's journey will be shorter, but we've got long days ahead."

They both stood and began gathering their belongings from the tent while his mother and their servant prepared the morning meal. Andonis glanced over at Neiaphi's tent, where she and her servant were returning from the stream, carrying water. By their fire, Kayson sat watching Neiaphi intently; her expression seemed troubled. Andonis knew he needed to speak with her today, though he wasn't sure what he'd say.

Back at their tent, Cleop began preparing the morning meal while Net and Neiluios worked together to load items into the donkey cart. Kayson sat by the fire, his gaze fixed on Neiaphi. She caught sight of him, a spark of frustration flickering in her eyes. *What's his problem?* She thought. *And why does he seem so familiar?*

Feeling unsettled, she went into the tent to find her mother.

"Good morning, dear." Altesse was changing the boys and getting them ready for travel.

"Good morning, Mother. I need to talk to you about Andonis."

"Me, dear? Not your father?"

"You're first, I think. Andonis likes me, and I like him... but..."

"Cret?"

"Yes." Neiaphi sank to the ground beside her mother, picking up Praxis and rocking him gently from side to side. "Andonis says he wants to be with me, even if only for a little while."

"What do you mean, a little while? Is he leaving?"

"No." She shook her head, hesitating. "He said that if Cret returns, and we want to be together, he will leave." Neiaphi couldn't meet her mother's gaze. She held back her tears, but they threatened to escape.

"I see. Oh my, what a choice. What do you need from me?"

"I spoke to Cleop this morning, and she had me put myself in Andonis's place, giving the proposal to Cret. It made me think. I realized I would likely do the same thing. Spending any length of time with Cret would be better than having no time at all."

"Even if it jeopardizes your future happiness?"

"Yes, I think so. Some happiness is better than all misery."

"Then you have your answer. But make sure you're doing this for your sake, not his."

"What do you mean?" Neiaphi looked at her mother for the first time since entering the tent.

"If Cret doesn't return, are you willing to spend the rest of your life with Andonis and have his children?" Neiaphi opened her mouth to respond but then closed it again.

"I see you still have some thinking to do. Spend the rest of today, as we travel, reflecting on that. If Cret doesn't return, you will be with Andonis. Would you be happy? Would you be able to make him... happy?"

"Thanks, Mother," she replied grimly.

"Anytime, dear. Can you help me pack in here?"

"Of course. Mother, can I ask you another question?"

"Yes, dear. What is it?"

"Last night, when Father and I returned, why were you so upset about the wolves? I understand being scared; they are frightening, but you seemed terrified."

Altesse sat in silence for a few moments before clearing her throat. "I never told you what truly happened to your brother back in Romota, did I?"

Neiaphi shook her head.

"It was a beautiful day. You hadn't returned from your classes yet, and your father was still at work. Icarus wanted to play in the courtyard, so I took him outside." She paused, her voice wavering as memories surfaced.

Neiaphi laid a comforting hand on her mother's arm. Altesse offered a soft smile and patted her daughter's hand. "When your father came home, I went inside for a moment. But when I stepped back outside, there was the largest wolver I had ever seen, standing right beside your brother. He wasn't scared—just gently stroking its nose. But when the wolver noticed me, it startled and began to snarl. That's when your brother started to cry.

"The wolver looked from him to me, then grabbed Icarus by his shirt, flung him onto its back, and leaped over the fence. I screamed and tried to climb after them."

"Your father rushed out to see why I was screaming. I told him what happened, but he insisted I'd seen it wrong. He believed the wolver had killed Icarus and carried him off."

"But I know what I saw. The wolver took your brother, and I didn't search for him." She choked back a sob, pressing her hands over her face. Neiaphi wrapped her free arm around her trembling mother.

"I believe you, Mother," Neiaphi said tenderly. Altesse looked up and smiled slightly.

"When those wolves came into the camp last night, it brought everything back. I couldn't help thinking of Icarus, and I panicked. I was terrified for Annas and Praxis—the wolves looked so much like that wolver."

"That's just a coincidence, I'm sure. How could a wolver have gotten to Earth?"

"You're right. I was just being foolish. Andonis was here to protect us—I know that now." Altesse took a deep breath and squeezed Neiaphi's hand. "Thank you for listening. I should have told you sooner. It feels... better, sharing it with you."

Neiaphi placed Praxis down and helped her mother pack up the tent.

## ∞ 9 ∞
## CENTAURS

**AFTER** a much-needed rest by the river's edge, Crelian's group was refreshed and eager to continue their journey. With supplies loaded and spirits high, they boarded the flat-bottom riverboats and pushed off, gliding quietly downstream. The water was calm, and a gentle breeze rustled through the surrounding trees. The favorable weather allowed them to make impressive time, and the stillness of the river felt almost serene. Content with their pace, they decided to spend the first night back on the river, letting the steady current carry them onward as they drifted under a clear, starlit sky.

On the second night, they made camp onshore. After setting up the tents and lighting the fires, the boys retrieved their practice weapons and began their drills.

A few young girls gathered nearby, giggling behind their hands and whispering to one another as they watched.

"Cret, which one do you like?" Tivadarios asked.

"Who?" Cret replied, puzzled.

"The girls over there. I overheard them talking. You seem to be their top favorite," Tivadarios said with a smirk.

"Leda, Iola, Philomena, and Charisma are only a little younger than us. There aren't too many choices," Tycho added. "Who are you going to go after?"

"I don't know any of them. How old are they?" Cret asked, eyeing the giggling group.

"The twins are twelve, and Leda and Iola are ten, I think," Tivadarios replied.

"They're all too young to think about," Cret said dismissively.

"Oh, come on! You're sixteen, and the twins are only four years younger," Vangelis teased, batting his eyelashes. "You have to admit, they're pretty—blonde hair, blue eyes. Who wouldn't want that?"

"I think Cret is more into brunettes," Olek said with a smirk.

"Enough already. If you guys like them, go for it. I'm not interested," Cret replied, waving his hand dismissively.

"Still dreaming of meeting up with Neiaphi?" Vangelis teased.

"We're heading in the right direction, but do you think she won't be promised or married off before we reach them? They think we're lost to the Society, and we have no way to contact her. She has no idea you're coming for her," Tycho said.

Cret ignored their teasing, shaking his head as he walked away. He often wondered if she would still be available when he finally reached her.

Suddenly, movement in the surrounding woods caught his attention. At first, he thought it was a person on horseback, but something about the motion was off—too fluid, too low to the ground. Could it be…? His heart quickened. Quietly, he jogged toward the edge of the trees, peering into the darkness. But the shadows revealed nothing. Instinctively, his hand slid into his pocket, his fingers brushing the flute given to him by King Rees. The familiar sensation grounded him, though his mind raced with questions. What—or who—had he just seen?

Had he seen a centaur here on Earth? Cret's pulse quickened at the thought. He'd long abandoned the idea of ever finding one. The locals didn't even know what a centaur was. He forced himself to slow his breathing, straining to listen. Footfalls? Yes, unmistakable, though faint. Keeping his movements deliberate, he stepped into the woods, his eyes scanning the ground for any sign of tracks. The earth gave no clues. Then, out of the corner of his eye, a flash of brown hide streaked past him. His pulse surged as he spun to face it.

"Wait!" he called out, but it was too late. That had to be a centaur. His heart raced at the realization. How do I get close enough to talk to one? The question echoed in his mind as he weighed his next move.

Another flash, then another. Without hesitation, Cret pushed deeper into the woods, leaving his friends and family behind. He had to find the centaurs and free himself from this burden. The ground trembled beneath the thunder of hooves; he wasn't alone—more than one creature was fleeing from him. "Please! I mean you no harm! I carry word from Romota!" he called, his voice sharp with urgency.

He thought he heard a single hoof strike the earth—just a brief pause. He rounded a large boulder, his lungs burning, but whatever had stopped was gone.

Bent over with his hands on his knees, he struggled to catch his breath. As he lifted his gaze, he froze. A stunning young centaur stood a short distance away. Her coal-black mane and tail flowed with wild elegance, and her sleek black coat contrasted sharply with four perfectly matched white socks on her legs, giving her a commanding presence. She absently touched a medallion around her neck, shifting a cloak of speckled gray rabbit-hide that draped over her shoulders, revealing her golden-tan skin beneath.

She sniffed the air, her eyes sharp and assessing, then shook her head, her mane cascading in silken waves. A sudden stomp of her front hoof broke the silence, and she hesitated, taking a cautious step forward before quickly retreating two steps. Her gaze remained unwavering—wary yet unyielding.

"Please, don't be afraid. I won't harm you," Cret said softly, his voice calm and reassuring. She let out a nervous laugh, her eyes darting around as if expecting someone to appear, but she remained rooted in place. "I'm Cret. What's your name?"

She glanced around as if expecting to be discovered at any moment. Yet, she didn't flee or respond.

"I've come from Romota," Cret said urgently. "The current King of the Centaurs sent me on a mission to find out if Centaurs are still here on Earth. He hasn't received any messages lately and is worried. Are there many of you left?" He paused, hoping for a response. "Please, speak to me."

She studied him intently, but her lips remained sealed. Suddenly, she jumped as if stung by a bee and bolted into the woods, vanishing as swiftly as she had appeared.

"Well, at least one is here. There must be more," he murmured to himself.

"Cret, is that you?" a voice called from the woods.

"Yes, Father! Over here!" he replied.

"Who were you speaking to?" Crelian asked as he stepped into view.

"Myself," he replied.

"Not that part. Before that?"

"Um, how much did you hear?"

"I heard you speaking but didn't quite catch what you were saying. Something about a king?" Crelian eyed him suspiciously.

Cret sighed heavily and recounted his meeting with King Rees during his visit to his grandparents.

"He told me to speak into this flute if I found any centaurs, then toss it into a large body of water. My message will be transmitted to him. He just wants to know if there are any centaurs left here. They lost all communication." Cret handed the flute to his father.

"I've seen you looking at that flute from time to time. I thought you might play it one day. I assumed Neiaphi gave it to you. Are you ready to send your message?"

"I don't think finding one who refuses to speak to me is quite the message he had in mind. Heck, by the time I send this, he probably won't even be King anymore. Chi will likely have taken over."

"What are your plans, son?" Crelian probed.

"Keep traveling to Atlantis; hopefully, I'll find more centaurs along the way. Sorry for running off."

Slowly, the two of them walked back to the camp.

A cold front swept in that night, freezing the river's edge in the shallows. By the time the early morning light broke, grumbles filled the air as people struggled to pack up their frozen camp. The bitter wind stung exposed skin, leaving everyone feeling sluggish and tired.

Day after day, they traveled southwestward, the weather growing colder with each passing day, and the nights even chillier. Simos informed them they would need to find a village to weather the winter, a suggestion nearly everyone agreed with. None of them wanted to face their first winter alone in the forest.

Japster, however, was the lone voice of dissent. "We can't stop. If we do, we'll never reach the others. They'll be stopping too, you know. If we keep moving, we can find them and reach Atlantis all at once."

"This is the second time I've heard you volunteer for hardship. What are you up to, Japster?" Crelian asked openly.

"Whatever do you mean, oh leader, Sir?" Japster replied mockingly. "I only want what's best for us, and being with the others is the best."

"No, we'll soon find a place to stay for the winter. You've all traveled long and hard, and there's no sense in risking anyone's life," Simos stated flatly.

Japster mumbled something, crossed his arms, and stormed off.

"Father?" Hepluosis called, running after him. "What was that all about?"

"Think about it, son," Japster said, a wicked grin spreading across his face. "Sen warned me not to let this group reach Atlantis. What if we joined the others and stopped them too? Just think of the riches they'd shower on us for pulling that off."

Hepluosis laughed and nodded in agreement.

Lyric studied the two strange humans as they made their way back to their encampment. The younger one had spoken to her as if he knew exactly what she was. He seemed unafraid, and strangely, she felt the same. Her entire life had been shaped by warnings to fear the two-legs and stay hidden from them. So why had she stopped and let him see her? Her older brother had kept moving, but she had felt an inexplicable pull toward the young man. She'd nearly spoken to him, her instincts urging her to bridge the gap between them, but then she caught the scent of another two-leg approaching. That was when she bolted—two were more than her nerves could bear.

She trailed them from a safe distance, her sharp hearing catching every word the young one spoke. He mentioned a Centaur King named Rees from a place called Romota—where he claimed they were from. Absently, her fingers traced the charm at the end of the necklace she always wore, her mind racing.

Her mother had given her the necklace on her naming day, a treasured heirloom passed down from mother to daughter for generations. Lyric had always marveled at it when her mother wore it, feeling drawn to its subtle shimmer and intricate design. Now that it was hers, she found herself touching it constantly, as if it held answers she couldn't quite grasp. Her mother had often claimed it was brought to this world by their ancestors, a link to the home they had left behind.

The two-legs had betrayed them long ago, abandoning her people to survive on their own in hostile lands. Lyric's fingers brushed the charm hanging from her neck—a small, flat circle crafted from a strange, smooth material her mother had called "gold." Etched into its surface was a thin crescent moon, with two faint lines reaching inward from its left side. The charm was more than just a keepsake; it was a reminder of her mother's survival.

Her mother had joined the Cedar Clan as a youngling after humans had slaughtered her own clan, leaving her the only survivor. Life was scarcely easier in the Cedar Clan, where the centaurs were constantly on the move, striving to evade the relentless advance of humans that threatened their gathering grounds.

Lyric glanced at the sky, noting the fading light of day; sunset was nearly upon her. She cursed under her breath, realizing she had lost track of time. Swiftly, she broke into a sprint, weaving through the familiar trees, dips, and turns of her homeland with practiced ease. Her family would already be gathering at the evening's meeting point. Each night, the Clan assembled in a small, hidden clearing to prepare for nocturnal foraging—a necessity in a world where it was safer to move under cover of darkness, when the two-legs retreated to their peculiar dens.

"Lyric, where have you been? You were right behind me, then suddenly you disappeared," her brother, Justic, said, his face flickering with concern before settling into a scowl.

"You're too fast for me, brother. I couldn't keep up, and then I turned my ankle on a loose rock," she replied, feigning a limp as she neared their parents. Justic's gaze narrowed, suspicion shadowing his eyes as he shook his head in disbelief.

"Lyric, are you injured?" her mother asked, concern lacing her voice." It's minor, Mother, nothing to worry about," Lyric replied. Her mother nodded, though a trace of worry lingered in her eyes. Lyric's father stood off to one side of the clearing, almost blending into the fading light. He shared her coal-black coat and tanned torso, but without a hint of white. In contrast, her mother's coat was a pure, snowy white, with a lily-white torso to match, her emerald-green eyes striking against the pale fur. She was stunning. When Lyric was born, everyone said she was the perfect blend of her parents: her black coat, white socks, and emerald eyes marked her as a true blessing for the clan—a symbol of good fortune. Her brother, Justic, with his dull brown coat, hair, and eyes, had always seemed envious of her.

"Can I have everyone's attention, please?" called an elderly centaur. All eyes turned to him. Daten, the clan's leader, stood tall despite his years. As the eldest, he had always held this role, and though his coat was now entirely gray, Lyric was certain it had once been as black as her father's. "We will be leaving for the winter gathering soon. This year, the Sage Clan will be our hosts."

"What will our tribute be?" a voice from the crowd asked.

"Do you have any suggestions?" Daten replied. Silence filled the air.

"We have a little time. Let's make it good this year." Everyone nodded in agreement.

Lyric departed the group and headed to the stream. She entered the chilly water and lay down.

"I will never understand you," Justic said. "Bathing in that icy water, and you're not even dirty."

"You should try it, Justic; you could use a bath once in a while," she smirked.

He snorted and walked away. Lyric continued bathing in her favorite spot in the river, where the sandy bottom was nearly free of rocks. As she shifted her weight, something jabbed her foot. Curious, she reached into the icy water, feeling around until her fingers grasped a large stone. Pulling it out, she examined it in the fading light. The rock shimmered in the last rays of sunlight filtering through the trees above. Excited, she jumped out of the river and ran to the Elder.

"Elder, I think I've found something to offer as Tribute," she said, holding out the glimmering golden stone. The Elder took it and inspected it closely. "Very beautiful. It will do nicely. And you, my dear, shall be the one to present it."

She bowed her head, struggling to maintain a serious expression, though she was elated. She would be the one to honor their Clan and present their Tribute. As she looked around, she noticed the other members bowing deeply before her—everyone except her brother. Despite his glare, she had never felt prouder.

"As the Tribute Bearer, you must perform a cleansing ritual," an elder woman announced, stepping forward. "Elia will assist you. The ritual must begin one week before the Giving. Elia, please take Lyric aside and explain what she needs to do."

"Yes, Elder. I am honored," Elia replied, bowing slightly and gesturing for Lyric to follow her.

Lyric's mother smiled warmly, and her father nodded in approval. Justic, however, scowled, arms crossed in defiance.

# ∞ 10 ∞
# New Sparring Partner

**AFTER** another uneventful day and night on the river, they finally set foot on dry land again. Crelian's group gathered their belongings into donkey carts and wagons, bracing themselves for the journey ahead. In the frosty morning light, they began their march inland toward the distant, unseen city.

Simos pushed them hard, allowing few breaks, and they traveled steadily until sunset. Once fires were ablaze and tents were erected, the boys gathered for drills before the evening meal.

In just a few days, most of the boys had already shown improvement. Simos focused their training on the weapons each boy handled best, knowing they would have time over the winter to practice with other arms when there was little else to do.

Hepluosis was sparring with one of Simos's men, his growls echoing in the crisp air. The man's movements were predictable, and Hepluosis claimed victory with ease. "Come on, I've seen you spar better than this," he sneered.

"I don't know what you mean, young sir. Your skills are superior," the man replied with a respectful bow.

"I'm finished with you." He threw the practice sword to the ground and picked up his scabbard a few steps away. "Hepluosis, what seems to be the problem?" Simos inquired.

"Your man here is losing on purpose."

"He would never do that. I assure you he's trying; your skills are simply superior."

"Stop mocking me. I've seen him spar better than that."

"You're mistaken," Simos replied firmly.

Hepluosis scowled and stormed off, leaving Simos shaking his head at the retreating figure.

"Good evening, Sir. Phartar left you a bowl next to the fire," Six said as Hepluosis returned.

"Do you know how to use a sword?" Hepluosis asked.

"I'm fair, I've been told," Six replied. "At the camp, they taught us how to use weapons."

"Good, I'll be sparring with you from now on." Hepluosis sat by the fire, took the offered bowl, and ate silently.

Six bowed his head and returned to the task Phartar had assigned him. Japster emerged from their tent and settled beside his son.

"What's troubling you, son?" Japster asked.

Six stood and left, granting them privacy.

"The man Simos assigned to spar with me is letting me win. He's not challenging me at all."

"Your skills scare them, my son. They wish to slow your progress. Just bide your time; we won't be with them forever. Practice as hard as you can when you can."

"Six says he knows how to use a sword; I'll find out how well tomorrow."

Japster nodded. "Good, good," he said.

Early the next morning, the sound of clashing practice swords echoed through the camp. A short distance away, Hepluosis and Six sparred, their movements fluid yet intense. Though Hepluosis held the advantage, Six was managing to keep up.

From their tent, Cret and Crelian watched the scene unfold. Simos soon noticed them and walked over. "Good morning. Those two are up early," he remarked.

Cret nodded. "I overheard Hepluosis telling his servant, Six, that he thought your man was letting him win. He needed a challenge, and it looks like he's hoping Six will be good enough to provide one."

"My man, Tevin, was holding back," Simos admitted. "Six's skills seem to match Tevin's true ability. That's unfortunate; I'd hoped to keep his practice rudimentary."

As Hepluosis and Six finished their sparring, the camp began preparing to move out. Hepluosis caught Cret's gaze and made his way toward him.

"Do you have a problem, Cret?" Hepluosis sneered.

"I do."

"Wow, looks like little Cret is getting bold."

"I'm not so little anymore. I'm as strong as you and have lost all my fear. Why I was ever afraid of you is beyond me. You're just a spoiled bully—someone who's never made a true friend. The people around you stick around out of fear, not affection," Cret said, waving his hand dismissively.

"I've had enough of you. One day, I'll put you in your place," Hepluosis snapped, spinning on his heel and storming away.

Cret lingered, watching Hepluosis's retreating figure with a wary gaze. Nearby, Six was busy placing the practice swords back in the cart. Cret regarded him thoughtfully, wondering who Six had been before the mind sweep. Simos had questioned each servant to uncover their pasts back in Romota, but had kept many of the details to himself.

All Simos had shared was that some servants had been too dangerous to keep, while others had only minor offenses and could have their memories restored. He'd mentioned that Six's mind had started to recover on its own after some kind of shock, hinting that Hepluosis might have had a hand in it. But why? Cret shook his head, resigned to the possibility he might never know the answer.

He glanced at the bustling camp, where everyone was preparing to move out for the day. With a sigh, he murmured,

"I'm so tired of traveling. I just want to find the others and finally settle down."

Just then, he noticed his mother waving at him. He raised his hand in greeting. "Good morning, Mother. Is there anything I can help you with?" he called.

"Camtis and Corrin have finished packing already. I must admit, all this extra help is a lifesaver."

"That's true. Are they happy working for us, though?"

"They seem to be." His mother shrugged and climbed into the wagon next to Sareen.

Cret mounted his horse, Rees, and joined his father at the front. "Are you ready, my son?"

"As ready as I'll ever be," Cret replied with a nod.

"Have you seen any more signs yet?" Crelian inquired, hinting at the centaurs.

"No, I've been looking but haven't seen anything."

Simos glanced their way, puzzled, but let the question go unanswered. "Everyone, move out!" he shouted.

"How much further until we need to break for the winter?" Crelian asked Simos.

"Depends on our timing. The next town we'll be traveling near is Kranapolis. We have a couple of old technology vessels that will significantly cut our travel time."

"That'll be nice," Crelian replied.

"We should reach Kranapolis in a week if we travel hard."

"Then let's be off." Cret kicked his horse into a brisk trot, and the carts creaked as they began their slow march toward Atlantis.

"Time to start our trek to the Sage Clan and the Winter Gathering," Daten announced.

Lyric checked the pouch around her waist that held the tribute, ensuring it was securely protected.

"Are you ready, my dear?"

"Yes, Mother. How long is the journey to the Sage Clan?"

"I'm not sure. I've never traveled that far to the east," her mother replied. Lyric nodded, her heart racing with anticipation.

Daten took the lead, and the others fell into step behind him. It still amazed Lyric how a group of centaurs traveling together could move as quietly as a single one walking through the forest. Any two-leg settlement they passed would remain unaware of their presence. Lost in thought, Lyric began to hum softly to herself.

"Do you still have the tribute?" Elia asked, walking beside Lyric.

"Yes, elder, It's here in the pouch," Lyric replied, patting it for reassurance.

"Keep it safe. Do you remember all the steps for the cleansing ritual?"

"I think so, but I'm nervous. What if the tribute isn't good enough? What if I mess up?"

"Don't worry, child. Everything will be alright." Elia gave her a reassuring smile and patted her shoulder.

## ∞ 11 ∞
## MAN OF HER DREAMS?

**NEIAPHI** stayed close to her father throughout the day, carefully avoiding being alone. At one point, she noticed Andonis approaching. When he saw her glance his way, he hesitated, and she nudged Nexus closer to her father's horse. Neiluios observed her retreat but said nothing.

Seeing her withdraw, Andonis backed away, leaving Neiaphi watching him from the corner of her eye, her heart heavy. *What am I going to do?* She wondered. Suddenly, a chill ran up her spine, and she looked around, half-expecting Andonis or even Chartis, but neither was nearby. Instead, her gaze landed on Kayson, who gave her a tentative smile and nod. His smile faded, however, when he saw the frown darken her features.

Kayson shook his head as Neiaphi turned away, then noticed Andonis moving his horse toward the rear of the group. "He's interested in her, but she doesn't seem to feel the same way," he muttered. "I should speak with her father."

Andonis kept his distance for the rest of the day, though his gaze drifted to her now and then. Every time he looked, she seemed to sense it and glanced back. When their eyes met, she didn't immediately turn away.

He saw the torment in her eyes, and it tore at him. The pain he was causing wasn't worth his love for her. He had to speak with her. His proposal had been made with the best of intentions—he'd thought she would welcome it. With a heavy sigh, he muttered to himself, "I have to withdraw my offer… stupid, stupid, stupid."

Neiaphi retired to her bedroll early that evening, unable to bear Andonis's constant gaze any longer. It was heartbreaking. She wanted to talk to him, to tell him what he longed to hear—but was that truly what she wanted? She still didn't know. "I need to dream about this, Cypress. It's the only way I can decide." Cypress whined softly, licking her hand. She scratched him behind the ear. "I know it sounds silly, but ever since he made that proposal, I haven't been able to dream. I need guidance. Oh, what am I to do?" She lay down and closed her eyes, willing herself to dream.

"Neiluios, Sir?" Kayson approached, finding Neiluios seated before the fire in front of his tent.

"Yes, Kayson, what can I do for you." Neiluios gestured to the spot beside him.

"I wanted to speak to you about your daughter." Kayson took a seat next to him.

"Neiaphi? What about her?" Neiluios asked.

"Have you chosen her husband yet?" Kayson replied.

"Well, not entirely. It's a decision her mother and I want her to have a say in. There are three suitors currently vying for her affection. We're in no rush; she won't marry until we're settled. Are you asking for her?" Neiluios inquired bluntly.

"Yes, Sir. She's a captivating beauty and from what I've gathered quite intelligent."

"You don't even know her, and she doesn't know you. I doubt her mother would agree to this. I suggest you take the time to get to know Neiaphi; she'll let me know if there's someone else to consider," Neiluios replied.

Kayson frowned. "You don't like what I'm saying. Why?"

"Fathers know what's best for their daughters. Allowing them to choose isn't always in their best interest. I've seen more satisfied marriages when they are arranged between men. Tell me, how was your marriage arranged?"

"I got to know Altesse for a while before asking her father for her hand in marriage. I didn't speak to him until I was certain of her feelings. Like I said, get to know Neiaphi. The choice is ultimately hers."

"Thank you, Sir. Good night," Kayson replied, clearly upset, and left.

"Good night, Kayson," Neiluios said, shaking his head.

Neiaphi tossed and turned, drifting in and out of restless dreams that brought no peace. Frustrated, she sat up, glanced around the tent, and threw the covers aside. With a groan, she lay back down, rolling onto her side. Sleep reclaimed her quickly.

*She found herself alone in a small clearing within a shadowed forest. Wolves howled in the distance. "Hello!" she called, but there was no answer. Nervously, she wandered around the clearing, straining to make out her surroundings. Twigs snapped ominously in the darkness, the sound coming from multiple directions at once. She spun, heart pounding. "Hello?" she called again, her voice edged with fear.*

*Three men stepped into the clearing, their cloaks shrouding their faces in shadow. "Who are you? What do you want?" she asked, terror swelling inside her.*

*One by one, the men lowered their hoods, revealing Chartis, Andonis, and Kayson before her.*

*"We're here for your choice, Neiaphi. Please approach and give us your answer," Chartis said.*

*Neiaphi stepped toward him cautiously. He studied her face, a slight grin forming as he reached out to touch her* cheek. She gently intercepted his hand, shaking her head. "I cannot choose you. You're a good person and a friend, but I don't love you. You'll find someone who will love you as you deserve."

Chartis frowned, and in an instant, he vanished in a blinding flash of light.

She walked over to Kayson, seeking clarification. "You have never been here before. Who are you?"

He looked at her and shook his head. "I've been with you from the beginning. Look closer," he replied.

She did as instructed. He was handsome in a quiet way—perhaps six or eight years older than her, with brown hair and a tall, steady presence. But it was his eyes that held her attention: a striking gray. Gray eyes? She looked again, realization dawning. This was where she had seen him before. "You've been in my dreams from the beginning. You're the man with the gray eyes." She shook her head. "I can't choose you; we've just met. I don't know you." Turning, she started to walk toward Andonis. But glancing back, she saw Kayson still standing there; he hadn't disappeared as Chartis had. She stopped, then turned to face him. "Why didn't you leave?" she asked.

"It's not my time to do so, not yet," he replied, standing his ground.

She continued over to Andonis. He smiled at her. "What say you of me?" he asked.

She looked into his eyes but caught movement behind him. Another man stepped from the shadows—Cret stood at the edge of the clearing, hesitant to enter. Andonis turned, frowning as he saw him. Another man walked out from the shadows; Cret stood at the end of the clearing but did not venture into it. Andonis turned and frowned at Cret.

Neiaphi looked between the two. "Why am I cursed with this choice?" she asked, her voice trembling. As she began to walk toward Cret, he took a step back with each of her advances.

"You cannot go to him, child," a female voice echoed through the clearing.

Neiaphi spun around, searching for the source of the voice. "Where are you? Why are you tormenting me?"

"I'm at my home; you'll be here soon. You're tormenting yourself. It's not my doing, child."

"Where's your home? Please, give me some direction."

"I'm at Krisa."

The scenery shifted, revealing a small village nestled at the base of a large hill topped by a white temple. Neiaphi glanced around, astonished by the sudden change. But in the next instant, the scene transformed again, and she was back in the clearing with Andonis, Cret, and Kayson.

"That's all I can share. Focus on the choices before you. You've already eliminated one, which is a good start. Only two remain. Do not fear your decision; as I mentioned before, you will not marry before you meet me," the voice echoed.

Neiaphi nodded. "Cret, I miss you so much, but please, let me be at peace until you come to me in person. I want you, but you're not here. I must forget you for now. Not only that, but I love you and hope to see you again." Cret bowed and vanished into vapor. After a few moments, Neiaphi turned back to Andonis.

He smiled again. "Will I be happy with you?" she asked.

"I'll do anything I can to make you happy. If you choose me, I'll be the happiest man in the world."

"You cannot choose him yet; you must get to know me first. I demand that you get to know me," Kayson said, striding over to Neiaphi and Andonis.

Andonis stepped between them, holding his hand out. "That's as far as you go."

Kayson drew his sword, pointing it at Andonis.

"Wait!!" Neiaphi cried. "There will be no bloodshed here. Kayson, I do not select you. Go!" she ordered.

He took several steps back, sheathing his sword, but not departing.

Turning to Andonis, Neiaphi sighed loudly. "I choose your proposal if it's still available." He smiled and grasped her hands.

*"It is and will always be available. I'm yours for as long as you want me."*

*She smiled, then closed her eyes.*

Neiaphi awoke in her tent as the sky began to lighten. For the first time since learning of her family's fate on this planet, she felt an odd sense of peace, even as silent tears traced down her cheeks. Wiping her face, she rose and stepped outside, too restless to sleep any longer. She picked up the fire starter by the tent opening and walked to the fire pit. Placing a few twigs in the center, she struck a spark, igniting a small flame. Then, she grabbed a pot of water and set it on a rock near the fire.

She stared into the dancing flames until the water began to boil. Pouring some into a cup, she added a few mint leaves, then resumed gazing into the fire as she sipped her tea slowly. The fire crackled and popped, filling the quiet morning air.

"Good morning. May I join you?" Kayson asked, approaching.

Neiaphi jumped and gasped in surprise. "Oh, you scared me!" she exclaimed.

"My apologies. May I join you?" he asked again.

She nodded, gesturing for him to sit, and handed him a cup of tea. He accepted it without comment.

"Wonderful morning, isn't it? Fall is my favorite time of year. The days are still warm, but the nights are cool and crisp. Do you have a favorite season?" he probed.

She shook her head, distracted. "No, where I'm from, there are no seasons. It's the same year-round, except when it rains," she replied.

Kayson frowned. "One season all year? I've never seen a place like that before. I'll have to visit someday. Where is it again? Someone told me, but they didn't seem to sure."

Neiaphi jolted back to the conversation. "Oh, um..." she stammered. "Laos is far to the east. It's in a secluded area, so it appears to have just one season. I'm sorry; we do have seasons there, but they're very mild with little difference between them," she concluded.

He nodded. "That makes sense." They sat in silence for a few moments before he cleared his throat to get her attention. When she looked up at him, he continued, "I spoke to your father last evening."

She gave him a puzzled look. "What about?"

"You."

"Me?"

"As you instructed, I asked him if you were promised. Do you know what he said?" She shook her head. "He said three men are asking for you, but you haven't decided yet."

She nodded. "That was correct."

"Was? Who has asked for you? Has one or more of them backed out?"

"Someone can back out?" Neiaphi asked, surprised.

"I've heard it done before," Kayson said with a shrug.

"Chartis asked for me first. Aristas asked second."

"Aristas? I haven't met him."

"He's with the group in front of us. He was just asking to protect me."

"Ah, from the Taking Practice." He said nodding his head thoughtfully.

"Who is the third?"

"Andonis, you met him the other day."

"Yes, I remember him," Kayson said, frowning. "You said that was correct. Have you made a choice?"

"Yes," she replied flatly.

"And who is that?"

"I haven't told him yet; he must be the first to hear it."

"Oh, come on! Tell me. I won't say a word. Maybe I can change your mind."

"Why would you want to change my mind?"

"A fourth person is asking for you," he replied bluntly.

"A fourth? You?"

He nodded.

"How so?" she asked. "I only just met you; you don't know me," Neiaphi said, shaking her head.

"I know enough to say I want to get to know you better." She shook her head again. "You won't even give me a chance to prove myself. That's not fair. I might be the better choice for you, you know?"

"Well, I can tell you have an adventurous spirit. Together, we could travel the world and see places you've never even dreamed of. I guarantee you—I'm the man of your dreams."

His last statement caught her off guard. "The man of my dreams, you say?"

He nodded again. "Don't announce your decision yet. Take some time to get to know me first. What's a few more months? If he truly cares for you, he'll wait. If not, then maybe he wasn't right for you."

"I don't think so," Neiaphi replied. "You seem nice enough, but I've already made my choice."

"Well, I'm not going anywhere," he said with a shrug. "And as I mentioned, people do change their minds. I'll be around if you ever decide to give me a chance."

"Thank you for the offer, but I don't think so," Neiaphi said.

He stood, bowed, and replied, "See you around, Neiaphi. Have a good day."

As he walked away, she watched him go. "Straightforward, at least," she murmured to herself. Not wanting to speak with anyone else, she gave a quiet whistle for Cypress.

Cypress lumbered out of the tent, stretching and yawning. "Come here, you silly puppy," Neiaphi called softly. He wagged his tail and trotted over to her.

Together, they wandered into the still-sleeping camp. She weaved between tents, letting her feet guide her without focusing on any particular direction. Suddenly, she found herself in front of Andonis's tent. She wasn't ready to speak with him just yet. The proper steps eluded her, but she figured she should inform her parents of her decision before telling him. She continued walking, deep in thought.

"Am I being foolish, letting a dream guide me?" she murmured to herself. "They feel so real… Could Kayson be right about backing out?" She sighed, shaking her head. "No, I couldn't do that to him."

She stopped by a tree, settled beneath it, and leaned back, closing her eyes. Cypress lay beside her, resting his head on her lap. Before long, she drifted off to sleep.

*Neiaphi found herself walking hand in hand with Andonis along the familiar beach from her dreams. She glanced around nervously, watching Cypress run ahead. The other man had vanished, leaving just the two of them alone.*

*"What are we doing here?" Neiaphi asked Andonis.*

*"You wanted to go for a walk, sweetheart, and you brought me here. Haven't you been here before?"*

*"Only in my dreams," she replied.*

*He stopped and gazed out at the sea. "Is this the beach where the man was looking for an island?" he asked.*

*"Yes. He was standing right..." She glanced around, her eyes widening with surprise. "Right here, actually. We stopped in the exact spot."*

*"That man must have been me, then." He smiled, squeezing her hand gently. She glanced at him and the surrounding area.*

*"Well, you have a sword, and your clothes are similar—though different colors. Are you looking for an island?" she asked.*

*"No," he admitted.*

*"Can't be you, then. I still think that man was Cret," she said softly.*

*"Do you still think about him, sweetheart? You haven't mentioned him in quite some time."*

*"I think about him occasionally. But I'm with you now, and that's all that matters."*

*He smiled and leaned in to kiss her...*

"Neiaphi, what are you doing out here? That's a strange place to sleep," Alexa said, sitting down beside her.

"I couldn't sleep, so I went for a walk. I guess it made me tired again," Neiaphi replied with a grin, trying to stifle a yawn. "How are you and Greish?"

Alexa's cheeks flushed a bright red. "Oh, it's wonderful! He's even more attentive than before. I think he's starting to embrace the idea. I can't wait to be officially married and start a family."

"When are you two getting married?" Neiaphi asked, genuinely happy for her friend.

"We're going to wait until he's stationed somewhere. Father says he'll do everything he can to ensure we make it to Atlantis."

"Then I hope we get there even faster," Neiaphi replied.

"Good morning, ladies," Kayson said, bowing his head as he approached.

"Good morning, Kayson! What brings you around so early?" Alexa asked.

"Just keeping an eye on things that interest me. I'll see you, ladies, later." He smiled at Neiaphi before leaving.

"What was that about?" Alexa asked.

"He asked my father for my hand last night and then spoke to me this morning when I couldn't sleep."

"Oh, bother. You're attracting everyone. You need to get promised, if nothing else, just to stop all this attention."

"I know. It's more trouble not being promised, I think."

"Have you made a decision?" Alexa asked slowly.

"I have. I'm going to accept Andonis's proposal." Alexa frowned. "What?" Neiaphi asked.

"It's the way you said that. You're accepting his proposal, but are you accepting him?"

"Hmm," Neiaphi said, second-guessing her decision again. They sat in silence as the camp slowly came to life. Greish waved to Alexa as he walked the camp perimeter on his rounds.

"I see your point," Neiaphi finally said. "If I knew for sure that I would never see Cret again, I know I could give Andonis my whole heart. With the uncertainty, it isn't easy. I know I can give him most of it right now, though."

"I think that will be enough for him. You can wait to marry until we're in Atlantis as well. We'll marry at the same time. That will be your answer if Cret doesn't show up by then." Her friend smiled broadly.

"That sounds like a good plan. I can give my heart a deadline while making the best of things right now. Thanks,

Alexa. It's so nice to have a friend to talk to." She hugged Alexa.

"Come on, we'd better get back; we'll be leaving soon." They helped each other up and, arms linked, walked back to the main camp.

"Good morning, Father," Neiaphi said brightly.

"Good morning, dear. You seem to be in a good mood today." He beamed at her. He reached down and picked up another crate to put in the cart.

"I am. I've been fighting inner demons, and I think I've finally won."

"Truly?"

"I have. I've decided my future."

Neiluios smiled, turning to face her. "And what's your decision?"

"I wish to become promised to Andonis," she replied.

Neiluios studied his daughter's face for any hesitation. Seeing none, he nodded. "Okay then, consider it done."

"Oh, thank you, Father. Thank you for being so patient with me and understanding. Thank you for everything." She threw herself into his arms.

"Of course, daughter. Have you told him yet?"

"No, I had to get your permission first, right?"

"Yes, good. Now go tell your mother the happy news."

She nodded, a large smile spreading across her face.

Altesse squealed with joy, "Oh, happy day, Neiaphi! I'm so happy for you!" Neiaphi smiled from ear to ear.

Cleop and Net rushed into the tent. "Is everything alright in here?" Net asked, concern etched on his face.

"Nothing could be better. Neiaphi has chosen her husband," Altesse announced.

"Great news, little miss," Net said with a grin.

"Oh, how wonderful!" Cleop added.

Neiaphi's cheeks flushed crimson; she wasn't used to so much attention.

"So, what day has been decided? There's plenty of preparation to take care of," Cleop inquired.

"I'm going to wait until we're settled in Atlantis."

"Why so long to await?" Altesse asked her. "We might not even make it to the city. Your father might be assigned along the way."

"Alexa is facing the same situation," Neiaphi said. "She told me that if Greish is assigned to her before we reach Atlantis, she'll marry before leaving her parents. I want to do the same. I want a home to share with my husband, not a tent." Neiaphi frowned slightly, then grinned.

"What is it, dear?" her mother asked, a hint of concern in her voice.

"I said 'my husband'… it just sounded strange, that's all."

# ∞ 12 ∞
## NIGHTLY WALKS

**AFTER** the camp was dismantled and the journey resumed, Neiaphi searched for Andonis. She scanned the crowd throughout the morning, but he was nowhere to be found.

After the mid-day break, Neiaphi finally spotted Greish. Hoping he might have some answers, she approached him. "Greish, have you seen Andonis?" she asked.

"He volunteered to be a scout today. He went ahead to the second group. He'll be back later," Greish replied.

Neiaphi frowned, puzzled. "Why would he want to be a scout now?" she asked.

"I asked him the same thing," Greish said with a playful grin. "Something about needing a change of scenery. Any idea what that was all about?"

"I'm the scenery he needed to stop seeing," Neiaphi said, her voice wavering. "Oh, I hope I haven't ruined things with him. This is horrible."

"What are you talking about?" Greish asked, frowning.

"Andonis made me a proposal and said I could take my time to decide," Neiaphi explained.

"He actually went through with that?" Greish scowled. "I told him not to rush things. So, are you accepting the proposal?" I told him not to rush things. Are you accepting the proposal then?"

Neiaphi took a breath, then said, "No, I'm accepting him."

"Hmm," Greish paused, considering her words. "Well, the way you put it, I think you two will be happy together. Congratulations."

"Thank you. When you see Andonis, don't tell him I'm looking for him, but could you let me know when he's back?"

"Sure, I can do that. It'll probably be after we stop for the evening."

"I can wait. Thanks, and congratulations about Alexa, by the way."

"Thanks. I think we'll be happy together."

"I know you will," Neiaphi said with a warm smile.

Neiaphi kept scanning the surrounding area for any sign of Andonis as the evening wore on. It was well past dark when Greish walked by and gave her a nod.

"Father, Andonis is back. May I go speak with him?" she asked eagerly.

"Yes, but Net will accompany you and stay nearby if needed." Net gave a reassuring nod.

"Thank you." She grabbed her cloak and wrapped it tightly around herself against the evening chill.

Neiaphi found Andonis brushing down his horse. "Welcome back. Do you need any help?" she asked softly.

Andonis's back stiffened at the sound of her voice. "So, you're speaking to me again?" he asked, without turning around, his tone harsher than intended.

Neiaphi picked up another brush and moved to the other side of the horse. "I don't blame you for being angry," she said, her voice barely audible as her gaze remained fixed on the horse.

He sighed. "I'm not angry with you."

"You should be. I've been acting foolishly," she admitted, her voice trembling. "But I'm ready to have a serious conversation if you still want to."

He moved to her side of the horse and gently took the brush from her hand. Noticing her hands trembling, he asked, "Why are you shaking? Are you cold?" as he began to remove his cloak

"No, I'm fine. Can we sit down?" she stammered. He nodded and led her to a nearby log. "I've been thinking a lot about our last conversation—"

Andonis interrupted, shaking his head. "I should have never placed that burden on you. That was a foolish proposal; please disregard it."

Neiaphi took a deep breath and shook her head. "No, please—let me finish. I've spoken with people I admire and trust, and I've finally reached a decision that I know I can live with—and be truly happy with." She kept her gaze averted, unable to meet his eyes as she spoke.

"And what decision is that?" he asked, his eyes never leaving the trembling woman beside him.

"I accept," she said.

"You accept my proposal?"

She shook her head. "No, I accept… you," she said, finally meeting his gaze. But she couldn't decipher his expression. A few tense moments passed, their eyes locked in silence. "Say something, please," she urged.

He reached down, gently taking her trembling hands and bringing them to his lips, kissing each one lightly. "Are you sure?"

Neiaphi's whole body quivered. She nodded, her voice lost to her. He leaned down and kissed her cheek, and as she looked up, their eyes met again, unblinking. Slowly, he pressed his lips to hers. When she didn't pull away, he deepened the kiss, letting his passion pour into it.

For the next few days, Andonis rode alongside Neiaphi, joining her family for meals and soaking in their easy camaraderie. Each evening, they strolled around the camp

beneath the warm glow of torches, their flickering light casting long shadows along their path, with Net quietly following at a distance. Though Andonis noticed Net's constant presence, he chose to ignore it, focusing instead on the soft laughter and intimate conversations he shared with Neiaphi. "Is something bothering you tonight?" Neiaphi asked, glancing at him as they walked.

Andonis hesitated, his brow furrowing slightly. "I've noticed that Net always seems to be trailing us. Does he follow you everywhere, or is it just me?"

"It's me," Neiaphi replied with a sigh. "Ever since Hepluosis attacked me, Net has become my constant shadow. Please don't take offense; it's just my father being overprotective."

Andonis nodded, a thoughtful expression crossing his face. "I guess I never really noticed how often he's around you."

"He keeps his distance but is always close enough if I need him," she replied, a small smile forming as she glanced back at Net, watching vigilantly from afar.

"I have something for you," he said, shifting the topic. "I've had it for a while but was waiting for the right moment to give it to you. Since that moment hasn't presented itself, I've decided to just give it to you now."

"Really? What is it?" Her face lit up with curiosity.

He smiled, clearly pleased. "I love seeing you happy." He brushed his fingers across her cheek. "It's in my tent. Come on."

They walked the short distance to his tent, and as they approached, Neiaphi noticed it was quiet—his parents were absent.

"Wait here," he said, ducking inside.

Neiaphi stood outside, her mind racing with possibilities about what he could have for her.

He stepped out of the tent, cradling an object wrapped in a large cloth. Neiaphi took it gently, carefully unwrapping it. Her eyes widened in astonishment as a beautifully decorated bow emerged, complete with a full quiver of arrows. "This is stunning! Where did you get it?" she asked, unable to hide her excitement.

"I had your father pick it out in Chrysafi," he explained.

"You're only giving it to me now?" she asked, a mix of surprise and delight in her voice.

"As I said, I was waiting for the perfect moment. I meant to give it to you the day after you returned, but... you were avoiding me," he admitted.

Neiaphi blushed and giggled. "I'm sorry; I had a lot on my mind."

"Before we head off tomorrow morning, let's try it out."

"I can't wait." She stood on her tiptoes and kissed him on the cheek. Taking his hand, she started to head back to her tent, but he hesitated. "What's the matter?" she asked.

He paused, looking down. "I haven't wanted to say anything because these past few days have been the happiest of my life..."

"What is it? You can ask me anything," she said gently.

"I know you say you want me and have agreed to be promised, but... when do you want to get married?" he asked quietly.

Neiaphi stopped, turning to face him fully. "I'm so sorry. With all the excitement, I completely forgot we hadn't talked about that. I told my parents and Alexa, so I didn't realize I hadn't discussed it with you yet." She noticed the hopeful look in his eyes and smiled. "I'd like to wait until we reach Atlantis. Alexa and Greish plan to wait too, unless Greish is stationed sooner. Is that okay?"

"Why wait that long?" he asked, his voice tinged with hurt.

She took one of his hands in both of hers. "Cleop and Net asked me the same thing," she replied, blushing slightly. "I told them I want a real home to share with my husband— not just a tent."

Andonis brushed his thumb gently across her cheek, smiling warmly. "Husband... I like the sound of that," he said. "And I think it's a wonderful idea. I'd like to have a home ready for my wife, too. Once we arrive, I'll secure an official position and find land to start our vineyard. My father had the finest vineyard before we left, and he even brought a few young vines with him. After that, we'll make it official," he added proudly.

"That's exactly what I want," she said, radiating happiness.

Noticing Neiaphi and Andonis approaching, Net returned to the tent. He placed a pot of water near the fire, preparing for Neiaphi's return.

"Good night, sweetheart. I'll see you in the morning. Dream of me?" Andonis asked with a smile.

"You and no other," she replied. He kissed her gently before departing.

Neiaphi walked over to Net, who handed her a cup of tea. She accepted it gratefully.

"Are my nightly walks disrupting what you must do?" she asked him.

"You are fine in what you are doing, little miss."

"That's not the answer I asked for," she said, her tone firm. "Are there other matters requiring your attention that I'm interrupting? Tell me the truth," she said sternly.

"Yes, miss. But it is fine. Really," he pleaded. She softened slightly. "Thank you for being honest with me. Good night, Net. And... thank you."

## ∞ 13 ∞
## KRANAPOLIS

"**WELCOME** to Kranapolis!" Simos exclaimed as the village came into view. A group of guards noticed the approaching travelers and several men rode out at a brisk trot to meet them.

"Halt! Who goes there?" the lead guard demanded.

Crelian stepped forward, a faint smile forming as he recognized the guard. "Captain Lovelle, it's me—Crelian."

"Crelian? By the Gods, it's you." Captain Lovelle dismounted swiftly and clasped his hand. "We feared you were lost for good. How did you manage to escape the Society?"

"These kind people knew what was at stake and rushed us to safety," Crelian said. "How long have you been here?"

"A couple of months now, Sir," Captain Lovelle replied. "They have a sizable lead on you."

Crelian's heart sank. He had hoped they weren't too far behind.

"Are any sailing vessels available to take us to Bacapolis?" Simos asked.

"No, sir. Addident and the others took the vessels. The Society spotted them and destroyed the ships."

"What about the passengers?" Crelian asked urgently. "They left the ships before the destruction. A couple of crew members managed to return to us," Captain Lovelle said with a smile. "Come, let me take you to see the Governor—he may have alternative travel arrangements for you."

"Governor, may I present Crelian from Camp Roma? Crelian was Neiluios' assistant. This group was sent to the Processing Plant. And this is… I'm sorry, sir; I didn't catch your name," Captain Lovelle said, turning to Simos.

"Simos, my friend. It's good to see you again," the Governor said, shaking his hand.

"I've been better, but I'm serving a noble cause now." The Governor nodded.

"So, you were stationed at the Processing Plant?" He turned his attention back to the newcomers.

"Yes, sir," Crelian replied.

"Can you tell me anything about it? What's being processed, and for whom?"

"Can we talk in private?"

"Of course. This way."

"But first, where can my people set up camp, sir?" Crelian asked.

"Captain Lovelle, can you handle that?"

"Yes, sir," Captain Lovelle replied, snapping to attention.

"Go with him, son, and make sure everyone is comfortable."

"Yes, Father," Cret said.

"Simos, would you care to join us?" Crelian asked.

"I'd be happy to," Simos replied.

Captain Lovelle and Cret walked back to the others to start setting up camp.

"How many of you were stationed here? Any officials?" Cret asked.

"Three guards, no officials," he replied.

"Not too many," Cret said with a nod. "How are you adapting?"

"Very well, young sir, thank you. These people have been very accommodating and understanding."

Once in a private room, the Governor asked, "So, what can you tell me about the Processing Plant?"

"First, how much do you know about my people and where we're from?" Crelian asked cautiously.

"Smart man," the Governor replied. "I know you're from our home world of Romota. Do you need anything else from me?" he asked with a smile.

"No, sir, that will do. I just must be careful about what I say, you know." The Governor nodded.

"The plant is receiving shipments of fuel waste from interplanetary ships."

"Interpla... interplan... what kind of ships?" he stammered.

"Interplanetary ships—those that travel from planet to planet," she explained. "I'm not sure what they're getting in return, but they're dumping their waste here on Earth, and the Society is pumping it underground. It seems like more trouble than it's worth, yet they still won't shut it down."

The Governor nodded thoughtfully. "Poseidon established numerous enterprises across the planet—mining, timber, and, I assume, the processing plant. He was selling these goods to unknown parties. The Society has intercepted and shut down most of his operations in this region. I thought the plant was just outdated tech, but we haven't been able to infiltrate it until now," he explained. "The Society must be either earning a fortune or facing serious threats to keep it running. So, why were you sent there?"

"The technology was faulty. They had us trying to repair it by examining the controls without knowing what was actually being processed. When we explained this was impossible, they agreed to let some of us stay behind to address the issue."

"The fuel waste was too dense. The fuel from the ships must have changed over the years. We added a few substances to clear it up and fixed the problem. Once we'd completed the repairs and shown them the process, it seemed they had no further use for us—Simos here saved us."

"My pleasure, sir," Simos said, bowing. "Captain Lovelle mentioned that the Poseidon ships have been destroyed," he added, turning to the Governor.

"Yes, such a pity. They were marvelous ships—the quickest I've ever seen."

"If they were that quick, how did the Society catch and destroy them?" Crelian asked.

"The vessels allowed us to cross the large lake west of here quickly, which helped with trade to Bacapolis. But recently, the Society took control of Bacapolis and learned about our swift transports. Although the lake is vast, there are only so many places the ships could go. Eventually, the Society cornered them."

"That's terrible news; we had hoped to use those vessels. This will set us even further behind," Simos said, and Crelian nodded in agreement. "Don't worry," came the reply. "We have other means of transport. The only challenge is that you'll be traveling over land, making you quite visible. You'll need to move at night and rest during the day. But this should get you beyond Bacapolis's reach within a few days. I can provide you with two Hover Transports and pilots for the journey."

"Hovers, that's wonderful," Crelian said.

"What's a Hover? I've never heard of that," Simos asked.

"It's a large, boat-like vehicle that glides over the land without touching it. It hovers just above the ground and reaches speeds unlike anything we've ever seen."

"Sounds scary. Is it safe?" Simos asked nervously.

"Perfectly safe. No need to worry," the Governor assured them. "I'll send for the hovers, but it will take a couple of days. In the meantime, please make yourselves comfortable in our town—resupply and rest." He then escorted them back to their makeshift camp.

As soon as the sun crested the eastern trees, the sound of wooden practice swords echoed through the camp. Hepluosis and Six were the first to rise, followed by Cret, Olek, and Tivadarios

"You two first. I'll spar with the winner," Cret said.

"Sounds good," Olek replied, while Tivadarios nodded in agreement.

The two boys grabbed their swords and began sparring. Hepluosis paused, watching his competition closely. In a swift move, Six landed a blow on Hepluosis' shoulder. Hepluosis yelped in surprise, growling in response, which made Six hesitate and step back

"Sorry, sir. I didn't realize you'd stopped."

Hepluosis didn't respond; he simply intensified his attack.

Olek and Tivadarios were fairly evenly matched, but Tivadarios eventually gained the upper hand and forced Olek to surrender.

"Great job, both of you," Cret praised. "Let me know when you're ready, Tivadarios." Tivadarios nodded and dropped heavily onto the grass.

"I'll spar with the winner if you dare," Hepluosis sneered. Tivadarios shook his head.

"I'll spar you, win or lose," Cret said, glaring at Hepluosis.

"Deal." Hepluosis sat down, balancing his sword across his knees. Tivadarios and Cret began circling each other. Tivadarios made the first move, and Cret quickly countered. They exchanged blows, volleying back and forth.

Cret slowly began to lose ground. Tivadarios mouthed, *What are you doing?* To Cret, who silently replied, *Just go with it.*

Seizing the opportunity, Tivadarios advanced again. Cret slipped on the dewy grass and fell onto his back. Tivadarios made a striking motion toward Cret's head.

"I surrender!" Cret exclaimed, releasing his sword.

Tivadarios smiled and helped Cret to his feet. "You're getting better, my friend," Cret praised.

"Are you ready for me?" Hepluosis chuckled. "Why don't I save you the embarrassment and just tell everyone it was a close match, but I prevailed?"

Cret looked at his practice sword and spun it around. "No, I think I'll beat you. On your feet."

"I don't want to rush you; take your time. I'm not in any hurry," Hepluosis admonished.

"I'm fine, unless you're scared?" Cret mocked.

Hepluosis snarled and rose to his feet. Cret got ready and slowly backed away from him.

"Running already? And I haven't even done anything yet," Hepluosis taunted. "Why don't you just admit defeat now?" Cret shook his head as Hepluosis lunged, slashing at him. Cret sidestepped and swiftly countered the blow

At first, they seemed evenly matched, but Cret gradually started gaining ground. No longer backing away, he made steady progress toward Hepluosis.

Hepluosis seemed to be tiring as he lunged again. Cret slapped him on the back with the flat of his sword, causing Hepluosis to nearly lose his footing. He quickly recovered and spun around, finding the point of Cret's sword at his throat.

Hepluosis didn't say a word; he glared at Cret and then stormed away. Six stood watching silently, then bowed his head to Cret before following his master. They moved to the other side of the camp and began sparring again. Cret laughed as he glanced over at Olek and Tivadarios, who were rolling on the ground with laughter.

"That has to be the funniest thing I've ever seen! I've never seen him speechless," Olek said, struggling to contain his laughter.

Crelian sat by the fire with Camtis, watching the boys spar.

"I've never seen Tivadarios beat your son before," Camtis remarked.

"Me neither," Crelian agreed.

The next matchup was between Cret and Hepluosis. "This should be interesting," Camtis commented. "I've seen Hepluosis spar, as well as Cret, and I think they're pretty evenly matched."

"I was thinking the same thing," Crelian replied, watching the match with great interest.

Cret seemed to win easily, while Hepluosis and his servant stormed off in frustration.

"I think I'd better get Cret a sword. Please let him know I went to town and will return shortly."

# ∞ 14 ∞
# QUICK TRAVEL

**THE** silent hovers glided effortlessly above the dark terrain. The moon was obscured by thickening clouds, and thunder rumbled in the distance. Occasional flashes of lightning briefly illuminated the sky and ground, revealing a dense forest of dark green evergreens interspersed with trees adorned in bright red and orange foliage. Although the scenery was inviting, the cloak of darkness brought a severe drop in temperature, causing families to huddle together for warmth.

They traveled under cover of darkness each night, resting during the day. While the children could sleep on the hovers, the adults remained alert, constantly scanning the distance for any signs of glowing fires. On the second night, they had to reroute around a hunting campsite

By the third day, they set up a makeshift camp to wait out the rain. The men took turns watching the surrounding forest for any signs of movement. The pilot informed them they were close to Turber Village, where scouting activity was likely to increase.

The heavy rain that had grounded the travelers overnight gradually turned into a freezing drizzle as the hours passed. Cret sat beneath a tree on night watch, listening to birds singing in rhythm with the rain pattering on the leaves as the sky slowly brightened. He yawned, looking forward to a few hours of rest in a warm bedroll.

Suddenly, his head snapped around at the sound of crunching leaves and the crack of a twig. He sat as still as stone, sensing someone moving in the trees behind him. A thud followed by a muffled curse reached his ears. Cret tightened his grip on the hilt of his borrowed sword. To his right, he caught a flash of movement and the glint of the rising sun on a blade. Quietly, he stood, scanning the area—if there was one intruder, there could be more. He crept around a tree, positioning himself to flank the intruder sneaking into his camp.

The intruder crouched behind a bush, murmuring to himself. Cret slowly and quietly crept up behind him. Suddenly, the intruder turned and cried out in surprise at the sight of a sword at his throat. "Please don't kill me!" he shouted, panic evident in his voice.

Crelian and Simos burst out of their tents, alarmed by the shouting that shattered the morning's quiet.

"Don't move, and no harm will come to you," Cret warned the intruder. The man dropped his sword and raised his hands. He squinted in the early morning light. "Cret, is that you?"

Cret lowered his sword slightly. "Who are you?" The man slowly lifted a hand to his hood and removed it.

"Akronis?" Cret exclaimed as he fully lowered his sword. Simos and Crelian rushed to his side.

"Akronis? Good to see you," Crelian said.

"You know this man?" Simos asked.

"Yes, he's a guard. Were you stationed at Turber?" Cret inquired.

Akronis relaxed at the sight of their smiling faces. "Yes, I was, along with nine others. How did you escape from the Society?"

"We had help," Crelian replied, gesturing to Simos.

"You should come to the outpost with me; everyone will be so happy to see you."

Crelian shook his head. "No, we need to keep moving. We're trying to catch up with the others."

"They have a significant head start. How do you plan on catching up to them?"

Simos shook his head. "We have our ways; please excuse us if we don't disclose them."

Akronis nodded. "I understand. I won't report any findings from this morning. I should be going before I'm missed. Also, I wanted to let you know that I was tracking a horse and rider. I think it was a woman, but I only saw her once and found very few tracks once I got here. Do you have anyone riding deeper into the forest?"

Crelian shook his head. "No, but thanks for the warning. We'll keep an eye out for her."

Cret glanced around. *A woman on horseback out here?*

Everyone was on high alert for the rest of the day and into the evening. The Hovers resumed their almost invisible flight as soon as it was deemed safe.

As the sky brightened on the fifth day since finding the Hovers, they landed again and set up camp. "I need a few volunteers to scout a two-mile perimeter," Crelian announced. Several boys raised their hands, despite their mothers' protests.

Simos raised his hand to calm everyone. "Please, calm down. We need everyone's help, and these boys are brave enough to volunteer and deserve commendation. You will travel in groups: Olek and Tycho will head north, Basileios and Tivadarios will go west, and Cret, Hepluosis, and Vangelis will go south."

"Why are three of us going south? I can do it by myself," Hepluosis said with a scowl.

"Bacapolis is to the south. I want extra eyes there; that's where the most danger is."

"Then shouldn't an adult go with them?" Cret's mother, Sephi, asked.

"Good idea. Any volunteers?" Six raised his hand; he was the only one. "Thank you, Six." Sephi didn't look pleased with the choice. "Mount up, boys. Look for tracks, watch for smoke. Be quiet and return quickly."

Cret walked over to Rees, but his mother touched his arm before he could mount. "Please be careful, my son. I don't trust Hepluosis and his servant."

"Neither do I, Mother. Neither do I."

"Cret, take this. I hope you don't need it, but it's yours." Crelian handed him a sword. Cret took the sword and unsheathed it.

"This is beautiful, Father. Thank you." He sheathed the sword and belted it at his waist after removing the one he had borrowed for the evening watch. Once mounted, his father patted Rees's slick neck.

"Be safe, my son. I'll see you soon."

"Thanks, Father. I will." Cret nodded and then rode off with Hepluosis, Vangelis, and Six.

The foursome made their way south, occasionally splitting up to scout game trails. When they were just over a mile out, Cret motioned for everyone to stop.

"Why are we stopping?" Hepluosis sneered.

"I think we should give the horses a break," Cret said as he dismounted

"Oh, thank you. My legs could use a good stretch," Vangelis replied.

"The longer we take getting to the two-mile mark, the longer we'll be gone," Hepluosis said, frowning.

"We've been traveling for over two hours. A rest is in order," Cret countered.

"Two hours at a snail's pace," he grumbled, glancing at Six, who merely shrugged. Reluctantly, he dismounted and handed his reins to Six.

Cret pulled some dried meat, wrapped in a cloth, from his pack and offered some to Vangelis. Vangelis nodded in thanks and sat down next to a small stream. "Hepluosis, Six?" Cret called, holding up the meat for the other two.

"Nothing but a waste of time this whole trip is turning out to be," Hepluosis scoffed, turning his back on Cret. Six shook his head and followed his master.

"We'll be back before the evening meal, I'm sure, Sir," Six replied.

"I don't care about that," Hepluosis snapped. "What I care about is wasting my time. I should be drilling, not riding through this damp forest looking for who knows what."

A twig snapped loudly, startling a bird into flight nearby. All heads turned, and the sound of swords being drawn shattered the eerie silence. Cret stood and gestured for everyone to stay put as he cautiously approached the disturbance. No other sounds followed; the forest seemed deathly still, as if all the birds and insects were holding their breath. Only a gentle breeze rustled the vibrant red and orange leaves.

Cret inched closer to the bushes, his sword at the ready. He scanned the area but saw no signs or tracks; whatever had snapped the twig was nowhere to be found. Looking back at his travel companions, he shrugged.

"Who said you were in charge? I won't take orders from you," Hepluosis spat.

"Fine. Which way do you want to go?" Cret replied curtly.

"I'll go west, but not because you said so." He mounted and kicked his horse into a brisk trot.

"I'll head southwest, Sir," Six said with a slight nod.

"Thank you, Six. Let's meet back here in two fingers of time. Take your time and keep your eyes open."

For the next finger of time, Cret kept Rees at a slow pace, carefully navigating the dark, damp forest. He surveyed the stillness for any signs of movement, but everything felt eerily quiet.

Crack... Snap...

Something up ahead stirred in the underbrush, then fell silent. Cret halted, waiting for it to move again. Suddenly, a piercing scream shattered the quiet. Startled, Cret spun Rees around and galloped toward the sound, leaving the unknown creature behind.

Cret burst into a clearing just in time to see Hepluosis galloping toward him, fear evident in his expression, with Six close behind.

"Hold up!" Cret shouted, raising his hands in a placating gesture. "What happened? Who screamed?"

"We encountered some men sneaking through the forest," Six said urgently. "They jumped Hepluosis from behind and knocked him off his horse. I managed to drive them away, Sir."

"He wasn't addressing you," Hepluosis sneered, crossing his arms. Six dipped his head and backed his horse a few steps.

"I was startled, but I didn't scream," Hepluosis insisted.

"Well, I heard a scream, and you two are the only ones I see. Have you seen Vangelis?" Cret asked, scanning the surroundings.

Hepluosis fell silent.

"Six, have you seen him?" Cret pressed.

"No, Sir," Six replied.

"How many men did you see?"

"Two, Sir."

"Which way did they go?"

"South, Sir."

"Okay. Vangelis went east; let's head that way and find him."

"Why should we? He went east and didn't run this way like you did. He must be too far away to have heard anything. I'll just wait here for him to return in about a finger of time." Hepluosis crossed his arms and nodded curtly.

Cret shook his head. "No, if two men jumped you, and you screamed that loudly, and Vangelis didn't come to your aid, then something must have happened to him. We'll head east and fan out but stay close together."

"Humph," Hepluosis mumbled.

Six nodded in agreement.

The trio turned to head east, picking up Vangelis's trail. They followed a game path, occasionally veering off into the surrounding forest. After a short time, Cret noticed the trail veering south.

"Why did he start heading south?" Hepluosis asked, frowning.

"He must have heard something," Cret observed. "Keep your eyes open."

By midday, the sun had reached its zenith, casting long shadows over the tracks where Vangelis's trail intersected with those of four mounted strangers. Signs of a struggle marred the ground, and all five sets of tracks veered south.

"This doesn't look good. Vangelis is gone," Hepluosis said flatly. "We need to head back and warn everyone to keep moving."

"We're not leaving without Vangelis," Cret said firmly.

"Face the facts. There are at least four assailants, and we're only three. He knew the risks when he volunteered. Six and I are going back; you can do what you want." Hepluosis spun his horse around and trotted off briskly.

"Six, please inform everyone where I'm going. I'll scout further south to see where they took him. I'll return before attempting a rescue."

"Yes, Sir." Six spurred his mount into a canter, quickly catching up to his rapidly departing master.

# ∞ 15 ∞
# RESCUE

CRET pressed on southward, following the tracks left by Vangelis and his captors as the sun dipped lower, casting deep shadows through the forest. Twilight settled around him, and with it, the evening chill crept in. Suddenly, the unmistakable rhythm of hoofbeats sounded from up the trail. Cret guided Rees off the path, sinking low into the thick brush. From his concealed vantage, he watched as a black horse emerged, its pace unhurried yet purposeful. The horse carried an air of striking elegance, its four perfectly matched white socks glowing faintly in the dim light as it passed along the trail.

"Those legs look familiar," he whispered to himself.

The horse stopped. Had the rider heard him? He strained to see higher up the mount, needing a glimpse of the rider.

"You can come out, human; I can smell you hiding there," a female voice called. "Show yourself if you wish to save your friend."

Cret emerged from the shadows and approached the centaur filly he had met briefly before. "Do you know where they took my friend?" he asked.

She nodded. "Follow me." She set off at a quick trot. Hopping back on Rees, Cret followed her further south.

A short time later, the centaur slowed and raised her hand. "They took him there." She pointed to a makeshift camp with three tents. "He is in the middle cave over there."

"Cave?" Cret looked at the centaur filly, perplexed.

"Yes, the middle cave where you humans live," she replied, mirroring his confusion.

"We call them tents, not caves," he explained. She shook her head and sighed.

"What they're called isn't important. Your friend was taken into that one. How are you going to get him out?"

"I don't know yet. How many other men are in the camp?"

"Three that I saw, but I can smell at least five different ones have been here, plus your friend."

"You can smell the difference between people?"

"Of course! Can't you?"

"No." He shook his head, grinning. "I guess centaurs have a better sense of smell. Let's find a place to hide and watch the camp until dark. I want to see if the others you smelled arrive."

"Agreed." She walked over to a large bush and lay down out of sight. Cret, leading Rees, joined her. She looked at Rees and nickered softly. He responded with a gentle snort and lay down next to her.

"You can speak to horses?" Cret asked, settling down beside Rees.

"In a way. Horses don't communicate the same way we do," she replied, turning her attention back to the camp.

Cret glanced up at the sky. "Not much longer until dark. Do you know if my friend is injured?"

The centaur filly shook her head. "I saw them jump him and tie him to his horse. His condition is unknown, but I don't smell any blood."

"That's good to know. My name is Cret, by the way."

"I remember," she replied.

"What's your name?" he asked.

She turned toward him. "You want to know my name?"

Cret laughed softly. "Of course! I don't want to just say, 'Hey, centaur.' I'd like to know your name; you have one, don't you?"

She returned his smile and turned her gaze to the camp. "Of course I do. I'm Lyric."

"That's a beautiful name for a beautiful filly."

"I've never spoken to a human before. You say the strangest things." She tilted her head to one side and glanced at him.

"What did I say that's strange?"

"You called me beautiful. How could you find me beautiful? It would never work out between us." She shook her head.

"Just because I find someone beautiful doesn't mean I want a relationship." It was Cret's turn to shake his head.

Lyric flipped her head, returning her attention to the camp.

Suddenly, a scream ripped through the air, and Cret leaped to his feet. Lyric grabbed his cloak, trying to hold him back. He glared down at her.

"There's nothing you can do rushing in there right now. Stick to the plan. Let's hope he can survive a little longer."

"How can you say that?" he asked, shocked.

"Think about it. Why would they kill him now and not when they first captured him? They need him for something; they won't end his life just yet."

Cret didn't move to leave, but he refused to sit down either. He glanced up at the sky, praying to whatever gods were listening that he had made the right choice by waiting.

Hepluosis and Six returned just before nightfall, the last patrol to arrive. Crelian rushed over, eager to hear their report, but he halted abruptly, scanning the area for signs of Cret and Vangelis. They were nowhere to be found.

"Where are Cret and Vangelis?" Crelian asked.

Hepluosis stared at Crelian but remained silent.

"I'm asking you a direct question, young man," Crelian said sternly.

"He was careless and ran into someone. He's missing. Cret stayed behind to look for him," Hepluosis finally replied.

"And you and your servant just strolled back to camp, leaving Cret and Vangelis alone? You should have rushed back here so we could organize a search party! But no, you return as if you don't have a care in the world. Now it's almost dark—too dark to be of any help. At first light tomorrow, you and your man will lead us to where you last saw him. Now go to your tent and stay there!"

Crelian glared at Hepluosis, nearly spitting the last sentence at him. Sephi approached her husband, placing a trembling hand on his arm. As Hepluosis and Six made their way to their tent, Crelian turned to Sephi and embraced her as she sobbed openly.

"I understand your concerns for your son's well-being," Simos said cautiously, "but is it wise to mount a search party? You must consider the safety of everyone in the group, not just those two boys. We need to keep moving for everyone's sake."

Sephi stiffened in Crelian's arms but did not look up. "We will leave no one behind," Crelian stated flatly. "If they've been captured, they may be forced to reveal our location."

"Which is why we need to keep moving, Sir," Simos replied.

"They may also reveal our mode of transportation and where we acquired it, Sir," Crelian mocked.

Simos sighed. "They're your people. We're only here to help you; it's your call."

"Thank you. We will leave at first light: myself, Hepluosis, Six, and four others." Simos nodded and then departed.

Crelian somberly led his sobbing wife to their tent.

Lyric and Cret listened impatiently as Vangelis screamed and pleaded for his life. Lyric was right: five men held Vangelis captive—three were in the tent with him, while two stood guard. More than once, Cret felt the urge to charge into the camp, but each time, Lyric gently stopped him with a hand. "Getting yourself captured or killed won't save your friend," she reminded him. It was well after dark before the camp fell silent.

Cret stealthily crept through the hostile camp, staying hidden in the shadows. Two assailants occupied the first tent, two were at the last, and one sat by the fire. In the middle tent, Vangelis was alone, tied to the central support pole.

Cret circled to the back of the middle tent, searching for an entrance. Unlike the others, this tent's sides were sewn into a leather floor. Finding no way in without slicing a hole, he slowly returned to Lyric.

"What did you find out?" Lyric asked.

"There's no way into the tent except through the front." He hung his head.

"Then we must find a way to lure them out of the camp so we can rescue your friend," she said flatly.

"Any suggestions?"

"I have an idea. Let's rest for the night, and I'll share it with you then."

"Tomorrow? Why not tell me now?"

"No, tomorrow will be better." She leaned against a tree and closed her eyes.

Cret shook his head at his peculiar new friend, baffled.

The sky softened with the approaching dawn as Crelian exited his tent, leaving his wife and daughter still sound asleep. Several campfires crackled in the early morning air. Camtis was saddling the horses while Corrin packed food for them. He glanced toward Hepluosis's tent; Six was busy saddling their horses, but Hepluosis was nowhere to be seen.

"Good morning, sir," Joranios said as he approached.

"Good morning. Are you ready to leave?"

"Yes, sir," Joranios nodded.

"Good. We will leave as soon as Simos's appointed men are ready."

"The horses are ready, sir."

"Thank you, Camtis."

Two men leading their horses approached Crelian. "We're ready, sir."

Crelian nodded. "Camtis, please inform Hepluosis that we are ready to leave."

A few moments later, everyone was mounted and waiting. Hepluosis glared at Crelian but said nothing. Crelian motioned for Six to take the lead.

"Please retrace your steps to where you last saw Cret." Six nodded and began.

As the sun's early light brightened the eastern sky, Lyric gently nudged Cret's foot with her hoof. He bolted awake, sword in hand.

"Calm yourself," she said. "It is time." Cret noticed a rope tied around Lyric's midsection.

"What's with the rope?" he inquired.

"You'll create a distraction east of the camp, then head north and west. I'll rescue your friend and take him south. There's a large lake where I can lose any pursuers. I'll find you this evening."

"Are you sure about this? How will you find me?"

"I can track you easily. Don't worry. I can travel faster than any horse through this dense forest."

Cret nodded. "When do we begin?"

"Head east now and create a distraction to lure them away from the camp. I'll find you this evening." Cret saddled Rees and rode toward the eastern edge of the camp.

"Distraction, distraction. What should I do?" he whispered to himself. Soon, he came upon a small rock outcropping. Climbing to the top, Cret gathered several large rocks and fallen logs, stacking them near the edge of the outcropping.

"Well, here goes nothing. I hope this is loud enough." Cret grabbed a long branch and wedged it under the pile. After three failed attempts to shift the debris, he braced himself and put all his weight into it. A bellow escaped his lungs as the pile finally toppled down the small summit with a satisfying crash. Quickly mounting Rees, he rode north, leaving a trail to lead them further away.

Lyric waited for Cret's distraction, hoping it would draw everyone away from the camp. Suddenly, a thunderous crash echoed through the forest, sending the camp into chaos as men tumbled out of their tents. Three dashed toward the sound on foot, while a fourth prepared a couple of horses and followed a few moments later. The fifth grabbed his sword, glancing nervously into the trees as he approached the edge of the camp's clearing, peering into the encroaching darkness.

Lyric moved to the back of the prisoners' tent. "Whatever happens, try to stay calm and don't shout. You're being rescued, but this might hurt a little," she whispered.

"What? What's going on? Who are you?"

"Questions later. Please brace yourself," she replied. Taking a deep breath, she bolted south. The rope around her midsection tightened and then became taut. The tent slumped to the side before finally pulling free from the ground. Lyric raced through the forest, the tent trailing behind her.

She glanced back to ensure her passenger was still with her. The man inside the tent grunted and groaned as it bounced along the forest floor. A sharp cry escaped him as she sped through the trees. The last ambusher scrambled onto his horse, trying to pursue, but she easily outdistanced him. Before long, she reached the water's edge.

"Please hold your breath; we're entering the water!" she shouted back to the man before plunging into the chilly lake. She swam swiftly to the other side of the narrow finger. Emerging from the water, she dragged the tent-wrapped man into the bushes and hurriedly removed the tent from around him, untying him from the pole. He sputtered and coughed.

"What was that?" he asked, looking around, sputtering and coughing until his lungs were clear.

"That was a rescue," she replied.

"Rescue? I thought you were trying to kill me."

Lyric shook her head. "Well, I'm glad you're still in one piece, mostly.

"Thank you. You're a centaur!" He said, surprised when he finally looked at her, "I didn't know there were any left on Earth."

"Please, we need to get moving. We have to meet up with Cret before nightfall. We can talk later."

"Cret? How do you know him?"

"I met him a few weeks ago. Please, we need to move out. Can you walk?"

"I don't think so. They broke my leg to keep me from escaping." He used a nearby tree to pull himself up and tested his weight on his left leg. "Nope, that won't work," he said, stifling a cry.

Lyric walked over to him. "Carefully, get on my back. I'll see if I can carry you."

"I don't think I can."

She looked at him, leaning heavily against the tree. Slowly, she lowered herself to the ground. Vangelis carefully sat on her back and swung his uninjured leg to the other side. It took her several moments to stand under his added weight. Grunting with effort, she took a few steps to steady herself.

"Am I too heavy?" he asked.

"I'm just unaccustomed to carrying someone. I'll be fine." She gradually adjusted to the change in weight and balance. After a moment, she broke into a trot.

"Whoa, watch those low branches! That one almost hit me. My head is above yours," he said. She twisted her torso to face him.

"So, I see. I'll be more cautious."

"Where are we meeting Cret?" Vangelis asked after a few moments. He felt utterly lost, but they seemed to be making good progress.

"North of here. I'll find him; do not worry."

"How will you find him in this forest?"

"When we get close, I can smell him and his horse."

"I had no idea centaurs had that ability. My experience with centaurs is limited, though."

"Please get down," she said, stopping in a small clearing.

"Did I offend you? I'm sorry, I didn't mean to."

"No, you didn't offend me. I just need a short break. Carrying someone is very taxing." She chuckled. "I'm glad I'm not a horse."

Vangelis slid off and collapsed to the ground. Lyric stretched her legs and then settled beside him.

"My name is Vangelis. What's yours?"

"I'm Lyric. Are you from Romota?"

"Yes. Do all centaurs here on Earth remember Romota?"

"No, Cret told me about it. We've been taught about a planet we came from, but the two-legs betrayed us, leaving us stranded here. Have you met centaurs before?"

"Me? No, I've only seen them from a distance. Centaurs usually keep to their own settlements; most don't come into the cities. I'm sorry you were stranded here. We're in the same position." He glanced down at his hands.

Six led the search party to the spot where they last saw Cret. He pointed out signs left behind. "His trail leads this way," he said.

"How careless of him to leave a trail," Hepluosis sneered.

"That's enough, young man," Crelian said sternly. "Cret was wise to leave a trail for us to follow. He's tracking Vangelis; if someone ambushed Vangelis, he wouldn't worry about them following his trail. Let's see what we can find."

Soon, they spotted signs indicating that Cret had met up with another rider, and the trail now included tracks from several horses. By midday, they arrived at what appeared to be Cret and his companions' campsite from the previous night.

Ahead lay a clearing with the remnants of another camp. Crelian circled the area. "Looks like there were three tents set up here," he observed, "and one of them has been dragged away."

"Over here, sir," one of the men called out. "There's an obvious trail leading east. It looks like three people followed it."

Another voice chimed in, "Two followed the dragged tent south."

Crelian nodded thoughtfully. "It seems Cret and his companion attempted a rescue. Let's hope it was successful. We'll head back north and set up camp. Tomorrow, we'll fan out to the east and west as we return to the main group. Hopefully, that's where they're heading, too."

Cret guided Rees across the rugged forest terrain, his steps steady despite the uneven ground. *Lyric and Vangelis should be close by now,* he thought, glancing up at the sky visible through the gaps in the thick canopy. The sun was sinking lower, casting long shadows, and soon the forest would be swallowed by darkness. The quiet rustling of unseen creatures scurrying through the branches was the only sound breaking the heavy stillness.

"Cret, I'm here," came a whispered voice, barely audible.

Cret spun around, scanning the dim forest but seeing no one. "Where are you, Lyric?" he called, tension tightening his voice. Just then, emerging from the fading light, Lyric appeared, Vangelis draped over her back. Without hesitation, Cret sprinted toward them. As he reached them, Vangelis slid off her back, and a heartbeat later, Lyric collapsed to the ground, unconscious.

"What's wrong with her? Is she injured?" Cret asked, gently placing a hand on her forehead, feeling for any signs of fever.

"I don't think so," Vangelis replied, his voice strained. "She just wore herself out carrying me. Those men who attacked me broke my leg to keep me from running." He gestured to his injured left leg.

"This looks like a good spot to set up camp for the night," Cret decided. "Stay here; I'll get a small fire started."

Vangelis managed a sad smile. "I couldn't move even if I wanted to."

He and Cret took turns keeping watch throughout the night, but no signs of pursuers appeared.

"I'm sorry. I've never slept like that before."

Cret jumped slightly at the sound of Lyric's voice. "That's quite alright," he reassured her. "From what I heard, you had a tiring day. We'll be leaving shortly, but I wanted to make sure you were okay before we did. Also, thank you for all your help."

"It was the right thing to do. I also must be on my way. My family will be missing me soon."

"What are you doing over here?" Cret asked, curiosity lacing his tone.

"We're traveling to the Winter Gathering," Lyric explained. "Sometimes we travel together, but we separate to avoid drawing attention when we're near two-legs. I need to hurry to reach our next stopping point. Thank you for keeping watch last night."

"My pleasure. I couldn't have rescued my friend without you."

"You're resourceful; I'm sure you would have figured it out," Lyric replied with a faint smile.

Cret shook his head. "I need to ask you something." Lyric nodded in response.

"The King of the Centaurs on Romota is worried. He was supposed to receive a signal that all was well here some time ago, but it never came. He asked me to find the centaurs and ensure that you're all right.

"He gave me a special flute to send him a single message, but… I'm not sure what to say. I need to understand why the signal wasn't sent. Perhaps some technology was damaged. Do you know anything about it?"

"I don't," she replied. "My mother came from a clan that knew about our home planet, but my father's clan did not. When the two-legs attacked, her clan was wiped out—she was the only survivor and still very young. She received this necklace, which she said represents our planet." She removed the necklace and handed it to Cret.

"Yes, this symbol is ancient," he said, examining it closely. "I learned about it in a history lesson. Long ago, people used symbols to communicate before written language existed. This was the symbol for Romota." He handed the necklace back to her. "That's a very old symbol. Keep it safe."

Lyric nodded and placed it around her neck again.

"I'll ask my mother about messages to Romota, but I fear she was too young to know much," Lyric said as she stood, shaking leaves out of her hair. "If I learn anything, I'll try to find you. Where are you headed?"

"To a great city called Atlantis, somewhere east of here."

"I'll find you, my friend. Safe travels."

"Safe travels to you as well, Lyric. I'm glad to have met you." Lyric nodded and took off at a quick trot.

Suddenly, Vangelis shot up. "What was that? Did they find us?"

Cret shook his head. "No, Lyric just left. Come on, let me help you onto Rees; we need to get back to the others."

Crelian and the others rose early, spreading out from east to west as he'd suggested, methodically working their way back toward the group. He and Camtis took the west side, while Six and Hepluosis moved through the center. Joranios, Fane, and the two Loyals, Eburos and Petros, covered the east.

With each passing step, Crelian's hope of finding his son and Vangelis dwindled. Whoever had set up that camp had surely captured them, likely taking them to Bacapolis. He'd need to organize a search party in the city, with or without Simos's approval.

Suddenly, a horse snorted to Crelian's right, snapping him back to the present. He froze.

"Father, is that you?" Cret called out.

Crelian sighed with relief. "Over here, son. I'm so happy to see you. Is Vangelis okay?" Cret emerged from the bushes to find his father's smiling face.

"His leg is broken, but he's alive." Cret led Rees out of the trees, Vangelis on his back.

"How are you holding up, Vangelis?"

"Hanging in there, sir. I'll just be glad to be back with my family." Crelian patted his arm reassuringly.

"Let's get back."

# ∞ 16 ∞
## WOLVES

"**I** can see the other groups up ahead. I hope all is well," Alexa said, a hint of nervous excitement in her voice.

"Welcome to the Chief Sea, ladies. We'll need to travel by ship for the next leg of our journey—almost to The Pillars and then on to Atlantis," Kayson added.

Neiluios's group of weary travelers let out a loud cheer. Smiling faces and waving hands greeted them as they neared the shores of the Chief Sea.

"I don't see any ships. When do you think they will arrive?" Andonis asked Kayson.

"I'll find out. Excuse me." Kayson looked at Neiaphi and bowed his head.

Andonis leaned over to Neiaphi. "What was that?" he whispered.

"He's still asking for me," she whispered back. Rage flashed across his face for a split second before he replaced it with a Stoic expression.

"Is everything alright?" she asked, eyeing him cautiously.

"Everything will be fine. This is something that's handled between men. Don't worry yourself about it." He shot her a brief smile that didn't reach his eyes. "I'll be back." He kicked his horse and followed after Kayson at a full gallop.

"What was that about?" Neiaphi asked Alexa. "What did he mean, 'this is something handled between men?'"

Alexa glanced at Neiaphi, then at the backs of Andonis and Kayson galloping away. "When a woman is promised, she might as well be married. It's inappropriate for another man to pursue her. Kayson's actions aren't unheard of, but most men will not stand by and quietly accept them. I fear this will not end without a fight."

"Am I destined for nothing but turmoil in this world?" Neiaphi hung her head. "I have enough battles within myself; now I have to witness two men fighting over me. I made my choice—why won't Kayson leave me alone? He doesn't even know me."

"I fear this is not something you can stop. I've seen men killed over a woman when neither would back down."

"I have to try," she replied sternly.

Kayson rode his horse at a brisk trot through the crowd, his gaze sweeping over faces as he searched for someone in charge. Near the shoreline, he spotted a tall, imposing man standing next to two men he recognized.

"Kayson, my boy! It seems the gods are smiling on you," said the older man as he drew near.

"Thank you, Cletus." Kayson swung his right leg over the horse's neck, dismounting smoothly before stepping toward the men.

"This is Addident, the leader of the Laosans," Cletus said, nodding toward the man. Kayson bowed his head in acknowledgment. "And this is Kayson; he has been leading the third group."

Addident extended his hand, and Kayson clasped his wrist in greeting. "My group's leader would like to know the status of the ships, sir," Kayson said respectfully.

"We're expecting them any day now. Have your group set up camp—we'll spot the ships about a day before they're close enough to board," Addident replied.

"Excellent, sir. I'll instruct my group," Kayson replied. "Do you know how long the next leg of the voyage will take?"

"Several days. We'll make landfall and camp for the winter."

Kayson frowned. "Is something the matter?" Addident asked.

"I was hoping we would go straight to The Pillars and set up camp there."

"There are things these people need to learn before reaching The Pillars," Cletus said. "And there are a few things we can learn from them as well."

Addident eyed him cautiously, "What information can we provide you?"

"Relax, my friend," Cletus replied with a smile, giving Addident a friendly slap on the back. "Get your people settled; we'll speak tonight."

"With your leave, then," Kayson said, awaiting permission. Cletus nodded in approval.

Andonis sat tall on his horse, watching as Kayson approached. "Hello, my friend. I have news for the others," Kayson said, a smile spreading across his face.

Andonis frowned. "I need to speak with you."

Kayson's smile widened. "Later, please. I need to share the news with Neiluios first."

"Is there any danger?" Andonis asked, his tone serious.

"None that I know of, my friend. Let's get back to the others, and we'll talk later," Kayson said.

Andonis fell in beside him, his expression darkening. After a few moments, he spurred his horse forward, cutting off Kayson's path.

"What's the matter, my friend?" Kayson asked, his tone steady.

"We are not friends," Andonis spat. "I'm here to tell you that your advances toward Neiaphi must stop. She is spoken for, and I won't tolerate any further intrusion."

Kayson narrowed his eyes, "I don't think your claim on her is valid."

Andonis's eyes widened. "How so?"

"She has already told me that two others have spoken for her to protect her from The Taking. I believe you are doing the same." Kayson held his arms out wide. "I, on the other hand, have genuine intentions of making her mine. Her father is allowing her to choose." He scowled, shaking his head. "I am the man for her; she just doesn't know it yet."

Andonis unsheathed his sword, pointing it at Kayson. "She is mine. I won't tolerate your advances. Leave her alone, or you will feel the bite of my sword."

"Threat acknowledged. This is over for now, my friend," Kayson replied with a smile, then urged his horse forward, quickly moving past Andonis.

Once again, a temporary camp was erected. Neiaphi stood to stretch her back, glanced around at the bustling camp, and sighed.

"Something bothering you?" Altesse inquired.

"I'm just looking forward to a permanent home," Neiaphi replied, bending over to help her mother lash the tent rope to a stake.

Altesse patted her arm and smiled. "Soon, dear, very soon. Your father says we will reach the winter camp shortly. Once we're settled there, it will feel more like a permanent home."

Neiaphi grinned from ear to ear. "I can't wait!"

"Would you like to have a house of your own with Andonis when we arrive?" Altesse asked.

Frowning, Neiaphi replied, "You and Father would allow this? What would the locals think?"

"Oh dear, you'd have to be married first, of course."

"Oh no." Neiaphi shook her head. "Alexa and I will be married in Atlantis."

"Why wait so long? We may never reach The Great City, dear. Besides, winter weddings are always lovely, or so I've been told."

"I'll handle that when the time comes, Mother. Right now, I just want to focus on reaching The Great City."

Altesse nodded sadly, "Your father left this decision up to you. Why don't you go say goodnight to Andonis? I'll finish up here."

Neiaphi stood and brushed off her dress, glancing around the camp. She saw Cleop tending to the twins while Net finished preparing the evening meal. In the distance, her father was speaking with Addident and several other men. Curiosity piqued, she decided to walk toward them, hoping to catch a bit of their conversation.

Cypress stirred from his nap by the fire and started to follow, but she gestured for him to stay. He sat back down, whining softly.

Slipping between the hastily erected tents, Neiaphi crept closer to the men. After a few moments, she found herself standing just behind the tent next to them.

"How many were seen this time?" one of the men asked.

"At least a dozen for certain, maybe more, sir."

"I've never heard of wolves acting like this. It's as if they're looking for something. Keep the fires well-lit tonight, and everyone must travel in pairs. I want the guard watch doubled as well," Cletus instructed.

"Agreed. Captain, please make it so," Addident said.

"Yes, sir." Captain Hue bowed and departed.

"My wife and Andonis mentioned that it seemed the wolves were stalking my tent. We're the only ones with newborns—could they be looking for them? I overheard some locals saying that wolves have been known to steal children in the middle of the night," Neiluios added.

Cletus nodded, "I've heard those stories, but they're often told to keep children indoors at night—made up by mothers to corral their unruly broods."

"So, there's no truth to the stories?"

"No, my friend. I've never heard a credible account."

"All the same, I would like a guard placed near my wife at all times, please, sir," Neiluios pleaded with Addident.

"See to it," Addident replied, nodding.

"Thank you, sir." Neiluios noticed some movement in the shadows behind a tent. He stared intently for several moments, but seeing nothing else, he bid goodnight to Addident and returned to his family.

Neiaphi stepped slightly deeper into the shadows, careful to stay hidden as her father's gaze drifted briefly in her direction. When he looked away, she turned and headed toward Andonis's tent.

She walked along the edge of the camp's boundary, making sure to respect the privacy of those gathered around the evening fires. Glancing off into the distance, she gazed toward where she believed Atlantis lay, lost in thought.

A flicker of movement snapped her out of her reverie, and she froze mid-step, straining to focus on the source. It moved low to the ground, advancing on all fours. Neiaphi shook her head, convincing herself it was nothing, and resumed her path toward Andonis's tent.

Suddenly, a deep, throaty growl echoed from the darkness. Her heart pounded in her ears, drowning out her ability to pinpoint the direction of the sound.

The growling grew louder, closing in from the right. She swallowed hard, her breath coming in short gasps. No one knew where she was; no one would come to her aid. Another blur of movement appeared to her left.

A large shape blurred past her, taking a protective stance in front of her. It was Cypress, his hackles raised, mirroring the low, menacing growl directed toward the hidden threat. The creature crept closer, its gaze fixed on Neiaphi, seeming to ignore Cypress altogether. Cypress shifted closer to her, his eyes never straying from the wolf.

Neiaphi took a few tentative steps to her left, inching toward the camp. But another growl and the sound of footfalls stopped her in her tracks. There was a second threat behind her now. Cypress flicked his head toward Neiaphi, his gaze urging her to run, but her legs felt glued to the ground.

She had never felt such fear—not even on the ship with the Society bearing down on them. Back then, she was surrounded by family and friends, a weapon in her hand. But now, she was utterly alone, save for Cypress. He might manage one wolf, but two, or more lurking in the darkness? It was impossible.

"Please don't hurt me. Please leave me alone," she whispered, barely audible. "I won't harm you, I promise." The growling continued, unmoving. Neiaphi's legs trembled, and her arms quaked. "Cypress, hold steady, boy. The wolvers won't attack if you don't move."

The growling stopped abruptly. The wolf in front of her took a step back, cocking its head in curiosity. Neiaphi's heart steadied just a little. Did it respond to her voice, or was it something else? "Are you a wolver?" she asked timidly. The wolf sat back on its haunches. "I didn't know there were wolvers on this planet. How did you come to be here, I wonder?" Just then, a second wolver emerged from the shadows and settled beside the first.

Cypress whined, glancing anxiously at Neiaphi. "Easy, boy. It's okay... I think." The wolver behind her moved back, circling with cautious steps and giving Cypress a wide berth.

It stared intently at the first wolver, bowed its head, and then darted off into the night. The two remaining wolvers stepped closer, their postures tense. Cypress stiffened and began growling again. The leader barked, its tail wagging, yet it held its ground, hesitant to advance.

Shouts echoed in the distance, drawing the wolvers' attention. Several men sprinted toward her position, weapons at the ready. An arrow whistled through the air, embedding itself in the spot where the lead wolver had stood just a heartbeat before. The creature leaped aside with astonishing speed, its reflexes almost cat-like. Neiaphi glanced back toward her approaching rescuers and saw Kayson at the front, with Greish and Net just steps behind. Greish's patrol dog dashed to Cypress's side, settling into a protective stance. Neiaphi turned back toward the shadows where the wolvers had been—they had vanished into the night. Kayson rushed up to her. "Are you alright?" he asked, genuine concern in his eyes as he placed a hand on her shoulder.

"Neiaphi, are you harmed?" Net almost screamed at her.

"Oh, Net," she sobbed, grabbing hold of him. "I'm so glad you all saw me. I didn't know what to do."

"What happened? How many were there?" Greish asked.

"Um, um… three that I saw. I—I…" she stammered.

"Greish, with your leave, I'd like to take her home. You can question her more later," Net said.

"Agreed. I will scout out and see if more are lurking near camp. Kayson, you're with me." He pointed to Net, "As soon as she's home, please find Captain Hue and tell him what we know." Greish set off the way the wolvers had gone at a cautious pace. Kayson lingered a moment longer, staring at the Net leading Neiaphi away, then hurried to catch up to Greish.

Greish and Kayson walked silently, scanning the camp's perimeter for any signs of movement. They turned their heads left and right as they peered into the darkness.

After circling the entire perimeter and seeing no movement in the dark, looming forest, they finally stopped.

"What do you want to do now?" Kayson whispered.

"Let's stay here a moment, then retrace our steps. Maybe they'll circle back." Kayson nodded in agreement.

"While we wait, can I ask you something?" Kayson asked softly. Greish nodded.

"What's going on between Andonis and Neiaphi?" Kayson asked.

"Not sure what you mean. They're promised. What more do you want to know?" Greish replied.

"Well, they weren't when I first met your group. It seemed to happen all of a sudden. Are they both serious about it or is this just a move to appease their parents?"

Greish shook his head. "You're new here, so I don't blame you for being confused. Andonis has been courting Neiaphi for months, ever since he met her. Neiaphi, on the other hand, had her heart set on someone stationed elsewhere.

It was hard for her to let go and even harder to open her heart to someone new. But they're a good fit together. I just hope no one tries to come between them," he said, looking squarely at Kayson.

"Oh, yes, me too. Newfound love is fragile, though. You never know where the heart might lead," Kayson said.

Greish harrumphed. "Let's make another circle around the camp."

"Yes, indeed."

Net led Neiaphi back to their tent, walking quickly with his arm wrapped around her. When Altesse saw them approaching, she hurried over; concern etched on her face.

"Net, what happened?" she asked.

"Several of those large wolves surrounded her. Why were you walking alone?" Net asked Neiaphi.

"I was on my way to say goodnight to Andonis," she replied, her voice still shaky.

"Come here, dear. You need to sit down," Altesse said, guiding her inside the tent. Neiaphi nodded and allowed her mother to lead her.

"Tell them I'll be back. I need to find Addident and Neiluios," Net said to Cleop.

"Yes, of course." Cleop grabbed a couple of cups of tea and headed into the tent.

"I swear, Mother, those weren't just wolves. They were wolvers," Neiaphi said, her voice trembling. "I asked them if they were wolvers, and their attitude changed. They sat down and just looked at me. They even sent one away."

Altesse pondered her daughter's words for a moment. "I believe you, but let's not mention it to your father just yet."

"You want to hide this from him?" Neiaphi's face twisted in surprise.

"Just for now. I don't see any harm in it," Altesse replied. "Your father is a smart man, but he didn't believe me about your brother. I know what I saw then, and I believe you now. But your father needs to see things for himself. Others saw the wolves too, didn't they?"

"Well, yes, but Mother, they were much farther away than I was. They didn't look into their eyes like I did. Those eyes weren't the eyes of an animal. I know that sounds strange."

"They had intelligent eyes, knowing eyes... almost like there was a soul behind them," Altesse said distantly.

"Yes, that's it. Eerie and comforting at the same time." Altesse nodded in agreement.

Cleop remained silent while they spoke quietly. When a pause in the conversation presented itself, she approached and handed them the tea.

"Thank you, Cleop," Neiaphi said gratefully.

"Cleop, please keep this conversation private," Altesse added.

"Yes, ma'am, of course," Cleop replied, bowing her head.

Net and Neiluios hurried back to the girls. Outside the tent, the fire was slowly dying, left untended. Neiluios ducked inside, and Cleop bowed to him before stepping out. Neiaphi and Altesse looked up, smiling in greeting.

"How are you, dear?" Neiluios asked Neiaphi.

"Fine, now, Father. Those wolves were enormous—almost twice the size of Cypress."

"I'm so relieved you weren't harmed," Neiluios said as he hugged her before sitting beside Altesse. "From now on, everyone in camp must travel armed and in pairs, day and night."

"Even during the day?" Altesse asked.

"It's for the best. Other groups have spotted the wolves during the day as well. We'll also have a guard posted near you at all times," he said to Altesse.

"Near me? Why?"

"I fear the wolves might be targeting the boys. The locals say those stories are meant to keep children inside at night, but I'm not so sure."

"If you think it's necessary."

"I do. Let's get some sleep."

# ∞ 17 ∞
# Doubts

**ANDONIS** sat before Neiaphi's tent, stirring the fire in the cooking pit when Net emerged.

"Good morning, Sir," Net said politely. "How long have you been here?"

"Most of the night. I couldn't sleep. How's Neiaphi?" Andonis asked quickly, standing up.

"She was visibly shaken last night but unharmed. I haven't seen her since."

Andonis raked his fingers through his hair and sat back down. "I shouldn't have delayed coming to see her. She was on her way to see me when she was ambushed. This is all my fault." He hung his head, resting his elbows on his knees.

"You can't blame yourself, sir. This has never happened before; no one could've predicted the wolves would attack like that." Andonis said nothing, only shook his head. "Why don't you go back to your tent and get some sleep? I'll come get you when Neiaphi wakes, sir."

"No, I need to see her."

"As you wish. Tea?" Net offered, handing a cup to Andonis, who nodded and accepted it.

A short while later, Neiluios and Neiaphi emerged from the tent. Andonis sprang to his feet.

"Good morning, Andonis," Neiluios greeted.

"Good morning, Sir. Good morning, Neiaphi," Andonis replied.

Neiaphi smiled. "Good morning, Andonis. I didn't expect to see you so early."

"I had to see for myself that you were okay. How are you?" Andonis asked, concern edging his voice.

"Better this morning, thank you." Neiaphi offered a small smile.

Andonis gently took her elbow and guided her to a spot near the fire, where Net had set a bowl of fruit. "Here, eat something," he said, handing her the bowl.

"Thank you," she murmured, accepting it.

"Can you tell me about the attack?" he asked, his tone soft but insistent.

Neiaphi stared into the fire, her silence stretching for several moments. Just as Andonis was about to change the subject, thinking she wasn't ready to discuss it, she took a breath and began speaking.

"I was on my way to see you, to wish you a good evening," she said, her voice barely above a whisper. "I tried to give everyone some privacy, so I stayed near the outskirts of the camp, where the light from the fires barely reached." She paused, shuddering at the memory. "Then I heard it— movement in the dark, followed by a low, menacing growl. I froze.

"Cypress appeared beside me, his growl echoing through the darkness," she continued, her voice trembling. "There was a wolf in front of me—huge, the largest I've ever seen—and another one closed in from behind. But it was strange... almost like they understood me." She paused, wringing her hands. "I... I started talking to them, asking them not to hurt me."

"What is it?" Neiluios asked, his voice tinged with concern.

Neiaphi hesitated, glancing away. "I don't know. It sounds silly in my head, and I'm afraid you'll think I'm crazy."

"It's okay," Andonis said, his tone gentle as he reached out, slowly placing his hand over hers. "You can tell us."

Neiaphi cleared her throat, her voice wavering slightly as she continued. "I told Cypress not to attack the wolvers. The one in front of me just... sat down and stared. It was like it was waiting for something. I asked if it was a wolver, and it responded with a low whine, almost as if it understood. Then it barked at one of the others, and that one just took off into the woods without hesitation."

She paused, gathering her thoughts. "Then, out of nowhere, an arrow whistled through the air and struck the ground where the wolver had been. It darted away—impossibly fast, like nothing I've ever seen. It moved more like a cat than a wolf." Neiaphi's voice trembled. "I glanced back and saw Greish and Kayson running toward me, but when I turned back, the wolvers—or…um… wolves—were gone. Vanished." She fixed her gaze on the ground, too afraid to meet her father's or Andonis's eyes.

Andonis gently squeezed her hands, his gaze steady and reassuring. "I don't know what those animals were, but I believe you. The way they behaved—there was definitely something unusual. What matters most is that you're safe."

Neiaphi glanced up at him, a faint, grateful smile forming on her lips.

Neiluios listened in silence, his expression thoughtful. "Do you believe me, Father?" Neiaphi asked, searching his eyes for reassurance.

He looked deeply into his daughter's gaze, memories of Altesse's description of the wolver flooding back—how she spoke of it after their son's death. "I don't know what those wolves are or what they want from us," he finally said, his voice heavy with uncertainty.

"But, Father, you must believe Mother about what happened to Icarus. Whatever those creatures are, I see intelligence in their eyes."

Andonis shook his head gently. "Why don't you get some rest? You've had a trying evening."

Neiaphi shot him a disbelieving look. "You don't believe me, do you?"

He hesitated, searching for the right words.

Andonis spoke first. "You're just tired, Neiaphi. Your mind might be playing tricks on you. After some rest, you'll see things more clearly and remember better."

Neiaphi stood abruptly. Andonis reached out and grabbed her hand. She paused but didn't meet his gaze. Tears streamed down her face, hurt pulsating in her eyes. "After everything I've confided in you, I thought you understood me better than this."

"It's not about believing or not believing. You just need more rest, that's all. Let's talk this evening." Neiaphi shook off his hand and returned to the tent without looking back.

Andonis sighed, running a hand through his hair. "I'm sorry, sir. I could have handled that better."

"No, my boy. You did fine," Neiluios replied, his voice steady but tinged with sadness. "I didn't know what to say to her, so I let you handle it. The truth is, I'm not sure what to believe at this point. I already doubted my wife, and if I doubted my daughter as well, it would only create more tension in our lives." He offered a sad grin, the weight of uncertainty heavy on his heart.

Andonis chuckled, raking his fingers through his hair once more.

By midday, the camp buzzed with activity. On the distant western horizon, sails emerged—a promise of adventure. Only one more day remained before they would set sail again.

Near the shoreline, a group of young men had gathered, the sharp sound of practice swords thwacking against one another filling the air.

Andonis and Greish circled each other, swords poised. Greish lunged forward, aiming a quick slice at Andonis's head. Andonis dodged the strike effortlessly, spinning behind him. In an instant, Greish mirrored his movement, and their swords connected with a resounding thud. The two were evenly matched, each anticipating the other's moves with impressive agility.

"Come on, you two! You've been at this forever. Can one of you just win already?" Aristas teased, a playful grin on his face.

Andonis raised a hand, signaling for a pause, and Greish stepped back, yielding. "Why don't we make this interesting? How about you and Bacceon spar against Greish and me?"

"Two on two? What do you say, Bacceon?" Aristas asked, glancing at his brother. Bacceon stood, stretching his back with a grin.

"Sounds like fun," he replied, enthusiasm lighting up his eyes. The brothers grabbed practice swords and went through a few drills to loosen up, their movements quick and fluid.

"Are you two ready yet?" Greish prodded, a smirk playing on his lips.

"In a hurry to lose, I see," Bacceon shot back, his confidence unwavering.

"No, I'm just eager to spend some time with a beautiful woman who came to see me," Greish replied, gesturing toward Alexa and Neiaphi as they approached.

Andonis glanced over at the girls as they slowly approached. Neiaphi was smiling, radiating good spirits, but when she caught his eye, her expression shifted to one of determination.

Greish slapped Andonis on the back, returning his attention to the moment. "I need you to focus here and now. My reputation is on the line."

"I'm focused, don't worry," Andonis replied, brushing off the concern.

Meanwhile, Kayson, sitting a short distance away, couldn't help but let a faint smile creep across his face as he observed the unspoken tension between Andonis and Neiaphi.

Greish and Andonis squared off against Aristas and Bacceon, the four of them circling each other, waiting for someone to make the first move.

Aristas lunged toward Andonis, his blade slicing through the air. Bacceon glanced in his brother's direction, momentarily distracted, and that was all the opening Greish needed. He advanced swiftly, closing the gap between them.

Bacceon barely managed to block Greish's swift slice aimed at his head. Seizing the moment, Bacceon advanced, pushing Greish back a few steps. A confident smile curled at the corner of Bacceon's lips as he pressed forward, forcing Greish to retreat once more.

"I thought Greish was better than this," Neiaphi whispered to Alexa, a hint of disappointment in her voice.

Alexa smiled knowingly. "I've seen him practice this move with some of the other guards. Just wait and watch."

Greish looked winded as he retreated a few more steps, spinning out of the way just in time to avoid a quick chop aimed at his left arm. Bacceon grinned broadly, reveling in the moment. "Not so confident when you're being bested, are you?" he provoked.

Greish didn't respond; instead, he intently tracked Bacceon's every motion, his eyes narrowing as if locking in place, a glazed look hinting at his focus.

Andonis and Aristas sparred back and forth, lunging and thrusting with practiced precision. When Andonis let his right shoulder slump for a moment, Aristas seized the opportunity, striking at the exposed area. But Andonis parried effortlessly, sliding his blade down Aristas's until their hilts locked. In a swift motion, Andonis spun Aristas's sword in a tight circle, disarming him in an instant.

Meanwhile, Bacceon pressed his advance on Greish, who continued to retreat, deflecting each strike with gritty determination. Bacceon's movements began to slow as he exerted himself. Sensing his chance, Greish stepped forward, thrusting his sword toward Bacceon's midsection. Bacceon faltered momentarily but managed to block the attack just in time.

"Now that Bacceon has worn himself out, it's Greish's turn to attack," Alexa whispered, a hint of excitement in her voice.

The tables quickly turned, with Greish advancing while Bacceon began to retreat. The match was decided in mere moments when Bacceon lost his footing, and Greish delivered a swift slap of the flat of his sword across Bacceon's shoulder blades.

"Now that was a workout," Greish said, a smile spreading across his face as he extended a hand to Bacceon.

"That was a nice trick you played on me, letting me think you were beaten to wear me out," Bacceon replied, accepting the hand.

"I've been working with some of the junior guards," Greish explained. "I want to give them an advantage if they ever encounter a better swordsman."

"That'll do it," Bacceon said, catching his breath.

"Andonis, my friend, you've improved greatly since we last sparred," Aristas praised genuine admiration in his voice.

"I've had a great teacher," Andonis replied, nodding toward Greish.

"And motivation not to embarrass yourself, I would imagine," Bacceon added with a playful smile, glancing over at Neiaphi. Her cheeks flushed red, and she hung her head, a mix of shyness and embarrassment washing over her.

Andonis glanced at Neiaphi but said nothing.

"How about you, Kayson? Need any practice?" Aristas asked, shifting his focus.

Kayson smiled sheepishly. "Oh, I think I'm good for today. You all look pretty tired, and it wouldn't be a fair match."

Greish walked over to Alexa, extending his hand. "Neiaphi, do you mind if I steal my love for a while?"

"Of course not, Greish," Neiaphi replied, avoiding Andonis's gaze. "Aristas, would you mind walking me back to my tent?"

Aristas glanced between Neiaphi and Andonis, then nodded. "Um, of course, Neiaphi. Here, let me help you up." He extended his hand to her.

After a brief moment, he looked at Andonis, who gave a subtle nod before turning away and walking off.

Aristas and Neiaphi walked in silence for a few moments, the tension hanging heavy in the air. Finally, Aristas cleared his throat, attempting to break the silence. "So, I heard about your brush with the wolves last night—that must have been terrifying."

Neiaphi nodded but said nothing, her expression distant.

"This is ridiculous," Aristas said abruptly, coming to a stop. He grabbed Neiaphi's shoulder and spun her around to face him, his eyes searching hers for answers.

"What's wrong?" she asked, stunned, rubbing her shoulder.

"How old are you?"

"Sixteen. Why?"

"Sixteen? I would have guessed you were no more than ten based on how you're acting."

"What are you talking about? How am I acting?"

"Like a child. You're pouting and moping around just because Andonis doesn't believe your account of the evening."

"You're giving him the silent treatment. Put yourself in his shoes: imagine someone telling you they SPOKE to a wolf, that it responded, gave instructions to another wolf, and then vanished without a trace. Greish and Kayson claim they saw the wolf right in front of you, but when they searched, they found no trace—no prints coming or going. You have to understand that this whole situation is strange. Sulking because your story is being questioned isn't helping."

Neiaphi had been hanging her head while he spoke. Slowly, she looked up at him. "How am I supposed to act? As if nothing happened? Like my memory isn't being challenged? Like none of this ever occurred?"

Aristas placed both hands on her shoulders. "Of course not. Something happened, and that's a fact. What exactly occurred isn't essential right now. The most important thing is that you are safe and loved. Don't push everyone away just because they questioned you. It's crucial to keep our loved ones close, despite our differences. We're in unknown territory, and we're getting closer to those who have tried to harm your people more than once."

"I'm not saying Andonis couldn't have handled his conversation with you better this morning, but you shouldn't take his words to heart. Let's agree to disagree on this and move forward."

Neiaphi began to walk again. "I'll think about it," she finally said. Aristas let the topic drop and continued the short distance to her family's tent.

"Thank you, Aristas," Neiaphi said with a smile. "Have a good night."

Andonis watched as Aristas walked Neiaphi back to her tent.

"Hey, want to talk about it?" Bacceon asked.

"No," he replied flatly.

"Want to spar some more to clear your head?"

Once again, Andonis shook his head, scowling.

"I hope everything is okay between you two," Kayson said cheerfully as he got to his feet.

"Everything is fine. There's no need to get all giddy like a little girl. She had a rough night and just needs some space," Andonis growled.

Kayson held up his hands in surrender. "Whoa, no need to get touchy. Just an innocent comment from a concerned friend."

"We're not friends, as I've said before. I know you've asked about her. Just stay away from both of us, and everything will be fine." Andonis threw his practice sword with the others, grabbed his cloak and sword, and stormed away.

Bacceon retrieved the practice swords and followed Andonis.

"I'll just have to see where her heart lies now," Kayson whispered as he made his way toward Neiaphi's tent.

Neiaphi sat by the fire, mesmerized by the dancing flames. Her eyes slowly glazed over as her gaze remained fixed on the fire.

"May I join you?" Kayson asked. Neiaphi jumped at the sound of his voice.

"I'm sorry. Did I startle you?"

"A little. What do you want?" she replied coldly.

"Everyone seems so joyful today," he said mockingly.

Neiaphi sighed. "Sorry, what can I do for you on this fine, crisp evening?" she asked, forcing a smile.

"Much better. May I join you?" he asked again.

She gestured to a log on the opposite side of the fire. Kayson settled in a little closer than she had indicated. She frowned but said nothing.

"Do you want to talk about last night?"

"No."

"Talking about what troubles you can help. You'll feel better."

"I doubt it."

"Let's try this. After Net took you home, Greish and I searched the entire camp and found no sign of the wolves, even though I knew they were standing right next to you. It puzzles me how they could enter and exit without leaving any prints. Cypress and the other dogs' prints are everywhere, but there's nothing from those wolves."

Neiaphi looked up at him, confusion etched on her face. "Are you asking for my input or my opinion?" Kayson nodded. "How do you know that the prints you saw, which you assume are dog prints, don't belong to the wolves?"

"Oh, I considered that for a moment," Kayson replied, "but I remembered how big those wolves were. An animal that size would leave a print much larger than even our biggest dog."

"That makes sense. However, the wolves were incredibly light on their feet. Maybe they don't leave deep prints. Did you check again this morning?"

"We conducted another search at first light but still came up empty. Can you share anything else about your encounter that might shed light on why they were here?"

"I've told everyone everything that happened. I don't want to keep reliving it—I just want to forget and move on. We'll be heading out again tomorrow, away from this shoreline. I just want things to get back to normal."

Kayson reached over and placed a hand on Neiaphi's knee. "It will. You'll see." Neiaphi moved her leg away from his hand and shook her head.

"No, I'm afraid nothing will ever be the same again. Please excuse me." With that, Neiaphi stood.

"Whenever you need to talk, just remember I'm here to listen. I'll always believe you," Kayson called after her. She glanced back briefly before ducking into her tent.

Once she was gone, Kayson kicked dirt over the fire, then leaned back, gazing at the stars. "She'll be mine; it's only a matter of time. Time and patience."

# ∞ 18 ∞
# Ðaco

CRELIAN, Cret, Vangelis, and the rescue party returned to the others before dark.

"I'm glad to see you back safely," Simos said. "How many assailants were there?"

"Five that I could see, sir," Cret replied. "They broke Vangelis's leg after capturing him to ensure he couldn't escape."

"How did you rescue him?" Simos inquired.

"I had help from a friend," Cret said.

"A friend? Who?"

"They wish to remain anonymous, sir. I'm just glad I ran into them out there. I don't think I could have rescued him without their help." Simos's eyes urged Cret to say more, but Cret only shook his head.

"We'll be leaving as soon as the sun has completely set. Please be ready," Simos said before walking away.

Several men and women approached Vangelis. The men carried him to his family's tent while the women gathered branches and bandages to help set his leg.

A cry of pain echoed from Vangelis's tent as his bones were realigned.

Crelian and Cret returned to their tent to start packing.

The Hovers took off at blurring speed once the horizon fully concealed the sun.

"How much longer do we have until winter hits?" Crelian asked Simos.

"We'll need to stop in a few weeks to establish a more permanent camp before winter sets in," he replied. "There's a spot near a town called Chrysafi. We have many friends there."

Crelian nodded. "That's good to hear. Resting for a few months, even if we're not to Atlantis, will be welcome for everyone."

"I agree. It won't be long now. Sit back, relax, and let these wonderful machines do all the work." He slapped Crelian on the back.

Dawn found the weary travelers making camp once again. The men were assigned to watch duty while the women and children rested and cooked.

Two evenings later, as Crelian's group searched for a suitable place to camp for the night, they were unknowingly being watched. A small scouting party hid within the tree line near a large clearing, having set up a cold camp to remain concealed from unknown riders.

A young scout kept watch, huddled under his cloak in a vain attempt to stay warm on the brisk autumn night. With only his eyes peeking out, he sat still; anyone glancing in his direction would see only a boulder nestled against a tree.

Suddenly, the Hovers entered the clearing. True to their name, they hovered above the small pond at its center. The scout's eyes widened, and his whole body trembled with fear. He knew he should wake his commander, but he felt rooted to the ground. What were those strange flying objects? He could see people moving around atop them and hear a donkey braying nervously. The objects themselves were silent, gliding effortlessly through the air. After a few moments, they slowly descended, settling on the ground in a cloud of dust.

Slowly, the scout regained his composure and roused himself.

"Sir, sir. You need to see this," Andros whispered as he shook his commander.

"What is it, Andros? You'd better not be seeing things again," Giles grumbled, shuddering as he removed his warm bedroll.

"Look, sir. Those crafts flew into the clearing and then landed over there," Andros said, pointing to the strange objects.

"Flew?" Giles sneered. "You must have been sleeping again."

"No, sir. They flew in and landed, I swear it." Just then, one of the Hovers lifted off the ground, glided toward the opposite tree line, and landed again. "See? I told you they flew!"

"Quiet down. Wake the others. We need to get deeper into the woods before we're seen." Andros nodded and did as he was told. They quickly broke camp and fled into the forest's darkness as quietly as possible, watching the strangers set up camp and relax for the remainder of the day.

"Who are they, sir?" Alec asked.

"They aren't ours, and that's all I care about. After dark, we'll disable their flying boats."

"How, sir? We don't even know what they are. How can we disable them?"

"We'll find a way," Giles replied.

"We have a problem, sir," Petros announced to Simos as the sun began to dip below the horizon.

"What kind of problem?"

"Hover #2's balance system was damaged when we hit that rock trying to land this morning. It'll need repairs before we can load it."

"Wonderful," Simos replied sarcastically. "How long will it take to fix?"

"A day, two at most."

"Well, then get on with it. Everyone, it looks like we'll be staying here a bit longer."

Very few travelers seemed displeased by the news. Fires were rekindled, and some people ducked into their tents for a bit more rest.

Crelian approached Simos. "Is this a safe place for us to be?"

"As safe as any, I suppose. Bacapolis isn't too far; I just hope we're far enough from it." Simos smiled, patting Crelian on the shoulder. "Get some rest, my friend."

Back at his tent, Crelian sank heavily next to the fire. Cret sat nearby, lost in thought.

"Looks like we get to rest a bit longer," Crelian finally said after a few moments of silence.

"I heard. It'll be good for everyone. We've been on the run so long; stopping feels nice. I'm eager to reach Atlantis, but we could use a break." Crelian patted Cret's knee, then fell silent.

Two men raced into the cover of the trees just moments before the fires raging over the Hovers ignited a fuel source and exploded. Everyone leaped from their tents, weapons at the ready. Several men circled the area, but the assailants were nowhere to be found.

Crelian and Simos gazed glumly at the wreckage; both hovers were utterly destroyed. "How far is it on foot to our winter holdout?" Crelian finally asked.

"Too far," Simos replied. "Everyone, start packing; we leave at daybreak." Without another word, Simos stormed into his tent.

Crelian's weary group of travelers trudged slowly across the increasingly cold landscape for several weeks. They journeyed from sunrise to nearly sunset six days a week, reserving one day to hunt and catch up on rest. Each night, the ground froze, only to soften slightly by day, making their progress slow and laborious.

Simos led the way, speaking little, and pushing them all with determined urgency. He was set on putting as much distance as possible between them and Bacapolis before winter forced them to establish a more permanent camp. Though Chrysafi was their intended destination, he knew they'd never reach it on foot. The Hovers had let them cover greater distances in less time than Cham's group, and Simos had calculated they could meet up with them before reaching The Pillars. But now, that hope was gone.

For the past few mornings, frost had blanketed the grass and trees, melting only by mid-morning. The first snowfall, however, was only days away.

They had to find somewhere safe to camp.

The following day, Simos sent two scouts out early to see if they could find a suitable place for them.

Late that evening, the scouts returned, their faces weary yet resolute. They approached Simos, who had been waiting by the fire, his expression tense. As the scouts dismounted, one of them stepped forward, his voice low. "We've scouted the path ahead," he said, glancing around at the tired travelers now stirring from their rest. "There's movement near the next valley—could be bandits or a rival group."

Simos nodded, his eyes narrowing. "Then we'll need to adjust our route," he replied. "Do you have any good news?" Simos asked.

"Yes, sir," they replied in unison.

"There's a small town up ahead that should be friendly enough. No loyalists, but no organized society either."

"Well, that's a start. Did you speak to anyone there?" he inquired.

"I spoke with the town leader; his name is Danic. He said we're welcome to set up camp in the forest outside of town and that he welcomes any trade we may have to offer."

"That's good news. How far ahead is it?"

"We should reach it in two days at the wagons' pace."

Simos nodded. "Rest up, everyone; we'll stop for the winter in two days."

The small town of Daco, nestled beside a wide river, appeared just ahead, bringing a wave of relief over Cret as he noticed several figures standing at the town's edge, visibly unarmed.

They veered away from town and headed toward a stand of trees a short distance away. The scouts had reported suitable trees that could be felled to construct more permanent structures to withstand the winter. Cret overheard some villagers saying it would get cold and that the snow would become deep.

Cret and many others had never seen snow before. Back in Romota, it only snowed on the highest mountaintops, and the city never experienced snowfall. The prospect of the first snow coming soon was exciting and unnerving.

That night, hasty tents were erected, and everyone settled in early. Although they had stopped traveling, their work was only beginning.

The weeks blurred together as the days stretched on. The men labored each day, cutting trees, debarking them, and assembling lean-to-style huts—one for each family. Each hut featured a large central room with a fire pit beneath a roof vent to allow for ventilation. Elevated sleeping pallets were built for each family member, with space below for hot stones to warm the beds through the night.

While the men constructed the huts, the women crafted heavy clothing and cloaks from materials purchased in Daco. Older boys split their time between helping with construction and hunting, gathering as much game as possible to build a stockpile of smoked meat for winter.

Though Daco, a riverside town known for its fishing, could supply food, no one wanted to rely solely on it. Better safe than sorry.

"That's the last of the huts! Excellent work, everyone," Crelian praised as the final structure was completed.

"Now your family can finally get out of that tent," Georgios remarked with a grin. "You really should have taken the first one, you know."

"I didn't feel right taking the first one. Drawing straws was the fairest method for distributing them—no favorites, no fights."

"Well, it didn't stop every fight," Georgios replied.

Crelian couldn't help but smile at the memory of Japster throwing his fist in the air and storming off, claiming the drawings were rigged. Ironically, he hadn't won a single drawing and had received his hut just before Crelian. "It was worth it, if only for that moment," Crelian mused.

"Welcome home, my family," Crelian said as Sephi and the others approached.

"It'll be nice to have walls and a roof for a while," Sephi said, her face lighting up with a smile. Beside her, Sareen bounced slightly, her grin stretching from ear to ear.

"Well, go on in," Crelian urged, stepping aside to let his family enter the hut. He closed the door gently behind them, the sound a comforting reminder of their newfound shelter.

## ∞ 19 ∞
## PERSISTENCE

**As** the camp stirred to life, cookfires crackled to life, and people began their morning routines. Neiaphi sat by the fire, her gaze fixed on the approaching ships. They drew closer with each passing moment, and by later that day, they would reach the shore.

Neiaphi glanced over at Andonis's tent and sighed when he emerged from behind it. She knew she needed to speak with him and offer forgiveness, but finding the right words seemed impossible. As he walked to his fire and sat down, he raked his hands through his hair and let his head hang low.

Neiaphi sighed again and stood up, grabbing her cloak. "Net, are you busy?"

Net stepped out of the tent, a hint of curiosity in his eyes. "What can I do for you, Little Miss?"

"I need to speak to Andonis. Can you walk me over there?" Neiaphi asked.

Net hesitated. "Can it wait until we board the ships?"

"I thought about that, but what if he gets placed on a different one?"

"He won't do that," Net reassured.

Neiaphi sighed. "You're right. I'll wait. Sorry to bother you."

"Are you sure?" Net asked.

Neiaphi nodded and sat back down. She glanced toward Andonis and noticed him looking her way. She gave a small smile and waved. He waved back, a puzzled expression on his face. Neiaphi quickly buried her face in her hands, staring down at the ground.

When Neiaphi composed herself and looked up again, Andonis was gone. Tears welled up and streamed down her face. *What a stupid little girl I am*, she scolded herself. First, Cret had been taken from her, and now she was pushing Andonis away—all because he'd questioned what she said about the wolves when, deep down, she didn't even know what really happened that night.

Net noticed Neiaphi's turmoil and quietly slipped away from the camp while she wasn't looking. He headed toward Andonis's tent and greeted him as he approached.

"Good morning, Sir," Net said.

"Good morning, Net," Andonis replied, glancing in the direction Net had just come from. "How's Neiaphi this morning?"

"She's…confused, it seems. She asked me to bring her to you but changed her mind, and now she's crying. I don't know if there's anything you can do to cheer her up."

"Thanks for letting me know," Andonis said.

"She did mention being afraid you might end up on a different ship than hers," Net added.

Andonis frowned. "Does she really want that?"

"No, Sir." Net shook his head. "She doesn't."

"Good, that would be unbearable. Thank you, Net."

Net bowed and returned to Neiluios's tent. Andonis turned and walked toward the shoreline. He would speak to Neiaphi on the ships, after they both had more time to think and compose themselves.

The ships arrived just before dark, their decks aglow with lanterns and sails rippling in the wind. It would take several days to cross the Chief Sea. A meeting was called for all men, and the families were divided among the boats.

The following morning, tents and belongings were stowed away quickly. First, the animals and supplies were loaded, followed by families eager to board and escape the watchful eyes of the wolves in the forest.

As usual, Neiluios's family boarded last. While waiting, Neiaphi searched for Andonis or Alexa, but with so many people moving around, she couldn't spot either of them.

Once on board, Neiaphi hurried to the main deck to look for her friends, but no one was in sight. The ship seemed nearly empty, carrying only a few crew members, some single Loyal men, and the animals.

"Father, why were we assigned to this ship?" Neiaphi asked.

"The luck of the draw, I guess," her father replied. "Why don't you go below deck and get some rest."

"I've been resting for days. I was hoping to speak with my friends," Neiaphi said, glancing around the nearly empty ship.

"I'm sorry, dear," he said gently. "We'll reach the other shore and set up our winter camp in a few days. There will be plenty of time to socialize then—plenty of time. All winter, in fact." He gave her a reassuring smile before heading over to speak with the captain.

Neiaphi went to the railing and looked at the other ships. "I wonder what ship he is on?" she muttered.

"The first one, I believe."

Neiaphi jumped at the sound of Kayson's voice. She spun around with a hand raised to her mouth.

"I'm sorry, I didn't mean to startle you so." He bowed slightly.

"What are you doing on this ship?" she asked, narrowing her eyes slightly.

Kayson straightened up from his bow, a faint smile tugging at his lips. "The same as you, I suppose. Traveling across the sea and hoping for a smoother journey than the one we've had so far."

Neiaphi's eyes remained wary. "But why this ship? There are so many others."

"I was going to ask you the same thing. This ship is meant for animals and travelers without families." He shrugged casually.

"Then who made the mistake and put my family on board?"

"I'm sure it was just an oversight or luck of the draw, I suppose. Or perhaps, fate. Either way, the Gods must be smiling on me today—now I have a chance to speak with you and get to know you better." He smiled broadly.

"I'm not in the mood to talk." She turned her back to him.

Kayson glared at her back. *How dare she dismiss me like that! She needs to learn her place.* He steadied himself, took a deep breath, then placed a hand gently on her shoulder. She tensed and glanced at his hand. *She is a strong-willed girl. She will need to be taught gently, like breaking a young wild horse,* he thought with a smile.

"It's not polite to turn your back on a man who's speaking to you," he said, his voice tightening with impatience.

"Please, just leave me alone," she whispered, her voice trembling. Kayson's grip on her shoulder tightened as he forced her to face him. "What do you want, Kayson?" Her eyes searched his face for an answer.

"I just want to have a nice conversation with a nice woman," he said, his tone unnervingly calm.

"Well, I don't want to speak to anyone right now." She tried to turn away, but his grip tightened, holding her in place. "Let me go."

His eyes began to glaze over, a distant look creeping in. "Please," she pleaded, a slight whimper escaping her lips. Slowly, his fingers released their painful hold on her shoulder.

"There, now that was polite. I'll see you later." He spun on his heels and walked away.

Neiaphi shuddered, watching him retreat. That encounter brought back memories of her unsettling meeting with Hepluosis many months ago.

Neiaphi, Altesse, and Cleop remained below deck all day, tirelessly sewing more clothes for the two growing boys. The task felt never-ending, a constant reminder of their needs.

Cleop hummed softly as she worked, her needle dancing through the fabric. Altesse glanced at her daughter, noticing Neiaphi with her head bowed, staring blankly at the shirt in her hands instead of sewing.

"We'll see everyone else very soon, dear. These next couple of days will fly by, you'll see."

"I know, Mother," Neiaphi replied, her voice tinged with sadness.

"When was the last time you spoke with Andonis?" she prodded.

"The morning after the attack."

Altesse paused, contemplating. "I saw you and Alexa walking over to the boys later that day. Wasn't he with you?"

"He was," she replied flatly.

"And you two didn't speak then?"

"No. I was stupid—I acted like a spoiled little girl and ignored him. Now he's justifiably mad at me, and it hurts." Tears began to leak from her eyes, glistening as they rolled down her cheeks.

"You're not a spoiled little girl. You were hurt, and you lashed out. At least you didn't hit him," Altesse teased gently.

"Mother, that's not helping," she replied, keeping her gaze fixed on the fabric in front of her.

"Sorry, dear. How can I help?"

"I don't think you can. I need to get back to him and talk to him—if he even wants to speak to me again."

"Why wouldn't he want to? He doesn't seem like the type to shy away from a conversation."

"Yesterday morning, I waved to him from our fire. He waved back but looked confused as if he didn't understand why he was waving, and then he was gone. I think I might have ruined whatever was starting to take shape between us."

"I'm sure you didn't. Why don't you take a break before bed and get some fresh air? Just don't stand too close to the railing."

"Okay, I won't be gone long." She stood and smoothed her dress, trying to shake off the weight of her worries.

The air was cold and crisp, each breath refreshing against her skin. Water sprayed off the railing with every passing wave, its chill biting at her cheeks. The moon hung full in the sky, illuminating the scene, while the stars twinkled brightly, undimmed by any clouds in the night sky.

Neiaphi made her way to the front mast and sat down, leaning her back against it. She wrapped her cloak tightly around her shoulders, closed her eyes, and listened to the ship's symphony—the wood creaking with each subtle movement, the sails flapping gently in the breeze, the water lapping rhythmically against the vessel's sides, and the faint sounds of animals stirring below deck.

She opened her eyes at the sound of approaching footfalls. Someone came from behind and passed by on her right, continuing until he reached the railing. It was Kayson.

Neiaphi sighed quietly and closed her eyes again, trying to lose herself in the ship's soft, soothing sounds.

"Peaceful night, isn't it?" Kayson finally broke the silence.

"It was," she replied curtly.

"You don't like me much, do you?" He turned to face her, his expression curious.

She opened her eyes and met his gaze. "No."

"That's not fair, you know. You don't even know me." He paused, a hint of a smile tugging at his lips. "Let's make a deal. Tomorrow, we'll sit and talk all day, and if by the end of it, you still don't like me—not even a little—you'll never have to speak to me again."

"All day?" she echoed, a hint of reluctance in her voice.

"One day is all I ask for."

"Fine." She stood up, not bothering to say goodnight, and walked back to her cabin without looking back.

"Do you need me for anything today, Mother?" Neiaphi asked, a hint of eagerness in her voice.

Altesse shook her head gently. "I don't think so, dear. Why don't you head up top and see if you can spot any land?"

Neiaphi hesitated. "Are you sure? I could sew something or comb your hair… anything." Her eyes searched her mother's face, almost pleading.

Altesse chuckled, a warm smile spreading across her face. "Go on, away with you."

"Fine," Neiaphi grumbled, though she did as her mother asked. Once on the top deck, she scanned the area for Kayson, half-hoping he'd assume she was still in her cabin and wouldn't come looking. When she didn't see him, she slipped toward the ship's rear and settled between two crates, positioning herself to stay hidden. Cypress followed her lead, lying down beside her.

By mid-morning, her backside ached from sitting, and she knew she'd soon have to stand and stretch. Glancing around cautiously for any sign of Kayson, she rose to her feet. Just as she was about to lower herself back down, Kayson emerged from behind a stack of crates, catching her off guard.

"There you are! What a beautiful morning, wouldn't you say?" Kayson exclaimed, his eyes bright with enthusiasm.

"Just lovely," she replied, offering a smile that didn't quite reach her eyes.

"It truly is," he continued, seemingly oblivious to her lack of enthusiasm. "Would you like to take a walk around the deck for a bit?"

As they walked side by side, Cypress trailed silently behind them. After completing a lap around the deck, Kayson broke the silence. "So, what was life like in Camp Roma?"

"It was primitive but clean," she replied, her tone measured, as memories flickered through her mind.

"Primitive? Wow, was it really more so than the tents we've lived in for so long?" Kayson asked, raising an eyebrow.

"Compared to back home," she replied, her gaze drifting away.

"Back home? Tell me about it," he pressed, curiosity lighting his eyes.

Neiaphi hesitated the weight of his question settling heavily on her. "I'm supposed to forget about that place. I'll never go back there and shouldn't dwell on it."

"Surely remembering it won't cause any harm," Kayson said, watching her closely. Neiaphi remained silent, her thoughts locked away.

"Well, if you aren't going to share, I'll tell you about my home," he offered, attempting to lighten the mood.

After a couple more laps around the deck, Neiaphi felt the need to sit while Kayson droned on about his childhood. She was only half-listening to his tales, her mind drifting elsewhere. Thoughts of Andonis filled her head—*what was he doing? Was he missing her? Did he still want her?*

"And that is how I ended up with your wonderful group of people," Kayson concluded, a proud smile on his face.

"That's fascinating," she replied, her tone polite but distant, still lost in her own thoughts.

"It is, isn't it? So, what do you want out of life, Neiaphi?" Kayson asked, his gaze earnest.

Neiaphi stared at him blankly, relieved she had been paying attention when he finally posed a question. What did she want? Cret? Andonis? To be left alone? "I don't know," she admitted, her voice barely above a whisper. "Everything has happened so fast. I just want time to breathe and think."

Kayson nodded thoughtfully. "Life is short. You have to act quickly and seize opportunities, or they pass you by. So, how about it?"

His enthusiasm was palpable, but Neiaphi felt a knot tighten in her stomach.

Neiaphi looked at him, puzzled. "How about what?"

"Grabbing opportunities with me," Kayson replied, his eyes sparkling with enthusiasm. "I can show you the world! I've shared stories about all the places I've been, and we can explore even more together. I can't see you sitting at home tending to children. No, you need room to run and explore. Adventure awaits—and it awaits with me."

"But I'm promised," she said, shaking her head.

"Not really," Kayson countered, his tone firm yet gentle. "You're promised to someone your heart doesn't want, and your heart is tied to another you'll never see again. I can see it in your eyes when you look at him. You don't love Andonis. As for this Cret fellow, he's lost to you. I'm the man of your dreams; you just haven't realized it yet." He took both of her hands in his, holding them against his chest.

Wide-eyed, Neiaphi stared at their hands, then quickly looked up at his face. Startled, she jerked her hands back as if she'd just been bitten, but Kayson held on tight. In her attempt to escape, she inadvertently pulled him closer. He leaned in, aiming for a kiss, but Neiaphi, unable to free her hands, reacted instinctively. She brought her knee up sharply, making solid contact with his groin.

Kayson doubled over with a huff, finally releasing her hands.

"I love Andonis, and yes, I still long for Cret." She shook her head and took a few steps back. "Andonis is the one I choose to be with, not you. Never you. Leave me alone." With that, she spun around and hurried back to her cabin.

Kayson glared after her, a dark look crossing his face. "It seems the competition needs to have a convenient accident," he sneered, his voice low as he watched her disappear below deck.

"Land ho!" came the call from one of the crew.

Excitement rippled through the ship as everyone rushed to the railings to catch a glimpse of the distant shore.

Andonis moved to the back of the ship, glancing over at Neiaphi's boat, hoping to spot her looking forward. But she was too far away, and he couldn't distinguish which figure on the deck belonged to her.

The past couple of days had been agonizing for Andonis. He hadn't felt ready to speak to Neiaphi before the ships departed, but he never wanted to go this long without seeing her. Just the other day, when she waved to him, he had considered walking over to her, but hesitation held him back.

At that time, he hadn't known what to say and feared what her response might be. Now, all he could do was relive that moment every night, letting his imagination craft the ending. Would she have jumped into his arms, apologizing for her strange behavior, or would she have slapped him across the face, refusing to see him again? No matter how the scenario played out in his mind, he always woke in the middle of the night, drenched in sweat.

They would make landfall the following morning, and he resolved to approach her, though he still didn't know what he would say. Should he just stand there and let her do the talking? Perhaps that would be for the best.

He had been told that they were the only Laosans on the ship. How had she gotten separated from everyone? Had her father arranged it on her behalf? He shook his head—it didn't matter. What mattered was that he needed to be near her again and speak to her, regardless of the outcome.

The ships were unloaded one at a time. Andonis found himself on the first vessel, while Neiaphi remained on the last. He kept busy helping to load and unload the rowboats, ferrying supplies to shore, his mind drifting in anticipation of seeing her again.

As Neiaphi's ship drew closer to shore, the crew began lowering the animals into the water, one by one, coaxing them to swim to land. Next came the wagons and carts, followed by the remaining passengers, who were finally allowed to disembark.

Neiaphi perched at the bow of the rowboat, poised to leap off as soon as the water became shallow enough to stand.

Kayson sat in the middle, helping to row the boat toward shore, his scowl fixed on the back of her head.

Neiaphi's eyes scanned the beach, searching for familiar faces. She spotted Alexa and Greish standing next to Aristas, Bacceon, and Kayo, but Andonis was nowhere in sight. When Alexa saw her, she waved enthusiastically, and Neiaphi returned the gesture with a smile.

As the boat's bottom began to scrape against the sand, Neiaphi spotted Andonis standing off to one side, alone. Though she couldn't make out his expression, his posture was rigid, almost tense. Without hesitation, she leaped from the boat into the chilly water, gasping at the sudden shock of the temperature as she sank to her knees.

She trudged through the freezing water, her wool dress quickly absorbing the chill and weighing her down. Once she reached dry ground, she ran toward Andonis as fast as she could.

Andonis watched her leap from the boat and struggle to reach the shore. He started to move in her direction, uncertainty gripping him. Was she coming for him, or was she trying to escape?

It appeared she was running right for him.

Neiaphi struggled to move through the soft sand, her soaked dress dragging heavily behind her. Tears streamed down her face, but she wouldn't meet his gaze; instead, she kept her eyes fixed on his chest, avoiding the connection she desperately needed.

As she neared him, Neiaphi slowed slightly before crashing into him, burying her face in his chest and hugging him tightly.

Andonis was momentarily stunned but quickly recovered, wrapping his arms around her protectively and burying his face in her hair, savoring the familiar scent that calmed him.

"What's the matter?" he asked after a moment, his eyes catching Kayson glaring at them. He scowled back, protective instincts flaring. "Neiaphi, what happened? Are you alright? Did he do something to you?"

Neiaphi shook her head. "Shhh." She lifted her gaze to his eyes, then dropped it to his lips. Lost in the moment, he leaned down and kissed her deeply, pouring all his concern and longing into the embrace.

When they parted, she hugged him tightly again. "I'm sorry for how I was acting. I was wrong to push you away. Please forgive me," she whispered, her voice trembling with emotion.

Andonis chuckled. "There's nothing to forgive. I should have been more supportive." He tightened his hold on her, lifting her off the ground and spinning her around with a grin. "Let's go to your family's tent. I've already set everything up for you," he said, gently placing her back down. Grabbing her hand tightly, he led the way, a sense of joy bubbling between them.

After one more day of traveling, the group of Laosans and Loyals finally arrived at their winter camp. The settlement was largely abandoned, but it would serve as their home for the next couple of months. A few villagers remained year-round to assist travelers passing through, whether on their way to speak to the Oracle or journeying to Atlantis.

Andonis had traveled alongside Neiaphi's family all day, never leaving her side. He even requested that their families be placed next to each other for the winter, wanting to ensure she wouldn't have to go far to visit him whenever she wished.

Neiaphi smiled brightly upon seeing how close their winter homes were to each other. When Andonis noticed her joy, he instinctively drew her closer, sharing in her happiness.

"I love you," she whispered, her eyes shining with sincerity. Andonis met her gaze, warmth flooding through him.

"I love you too," he replied, his voice steady and filled with conviction.

# ∞ 20 ∞

# THE SAGE CLAN

**LYRIC** stepped into a vast clearing, feeling the weight of countless gazes upon her. A wave of nervousness washed over her; she had never been the center of attention for so many people before. This was the largest gathering she had ever witnessed, marking the farthest east her Clan had ever ventured for a winter gathering.

She held the Tribute before her, cradling it as if it were the world's most precious object—because, to her, it truly was. Lyric paused before the Elder of the Sage Clan, a proud and ancient centaur. The Elder's pure white form stretched from her hooves to her eyes, which were blind yet somehow still capable of sight—magic, as the stories went.

Lyric swallowed the lump forming in her throat as she approached the Elder. She bowed deeply, raising her hands above her head in a gesture of reverence.

"Oh, great Elder of the Sage Clan, the Cedar Clan presents this Tribute to you as our humble expression of gratitude for the honor of joining this winter's gathering."

The Elder stepped forward, then paused. She lifted the shimmering rock high for all to see, bowing her head as she retreated. Lyric stood and began to step back.

"Hold, Child!" Lyric's heart raced. Had she done something wrong? Had she disgraced her clan? "Where did you get that?" The Elder pointed a crooked, wrinkled finger at Lyric's necklace. Instinctively, Lyric's hand shot up to her throat.

"My necklace, great Elder?" Lyric stammered. "My mother gave it to me."

"Where did she get it? Who is this child's mother?" The Elder's voice rose, sharp and demanding.

Lyric's mother, Aileena, stepped forward. Standing shoulder to shoulder with Lyric, she bowed. "I am her mother," she replied.

"Where did you get this?"

"From my mother. When I was very little, my Clan was attacked by the two-legs, and I was the only survivor that I know of. I was wearing it when the Cedar Clan finally found me. Do you know what it is?"

"Come." That was all the Elder said before turning away from the gathering.

Whispers erupted among the crowd; this was highly unusual.

The Elder led Lyric and Aileena to another clearing, where two male centaurs guarded the sole entrance.

"May I see the necklace, please?" the Elder asked.

Lyric glanced at her mother, who nodded. Carefully, Lyric removed the necklace and handed it to her.

"It has been many, many years since I last saw this. I was not much younger than you, child," the Elder said, nodding at Lyric. "We were at our winter gathering when the bearer of this necklace fled into the night. She was chosen as our representative to Romota."

Lyric's eyes widened in surprise. "You've heard of Romota, Child?" she whispered in an accusing tone.

"Just recently," Lyric replied, her voice barely audible. Aileena stared at her daughter in disbelief.

"Where did you hear about it?" Lyric hesitated. "It's okay, dear one. Let me tell you both a story. Please." The Elder gestured to the ground and settled herself comfortably on the lush grasses of the clearing.

"We're not from this planet. Our home is called Romota. We were once allies with the two-legs—humans. They brought us here in star-traveling ships, asking for our help in establishing colonies on this planet. It was a great honor to be included."

"As the years passed, we distanced ourselves from the humans and established our own settlements. Each year, we reported to them and offered assistance when needed, while also maintaining contact with those back on Romota.

"More years went by, and soon our contact with the humans dwindled to the point where we only saw them when they were hostile. It seems they forgot who and what we were. We live longer than they do, so many more generations have passed for them than for us.

"Soon, we couldn't trust anyone we encountered. We fled our settlements to live in the wild like animals, hunted like beasts, and remained forever on the run.

"Even though we lost contact with the two-legs, we maintained communication with Romota. This," she said, holding up the necklace, "is the key to our technology for sending and receiving messages. I last saw it around the neck of the chosen one. She was an adventurous filly, too young for such responsibility. Intrigued by the two-legs, she constantly sought them out. Her father caught her speaking to one right before the Tribute offering and chastised her in front of everyone. In her shame, she fled from that spot and was never seen again.

"Some believed she fled to live with her two-legged lover; others thought he killed her after she fled and stole her necklace. She looked just like you." The Elder pointed at Aileena.

Aileena's eyes widened. "My mother told me I resembled my grandmother. She died when I was very young."

The Elder nodded. "Have you ever heard this story before?" she asked Aileena.

"I was told it was always passed down from mother to daughter, representing our home planet. However, I never believed the stories."

"Then please tell me, child, how have you come to hear of Romota?" the Elder prodded Lyric.

Again, Lyric hesitated. "It's okay, dear. I will tell no one."

Lyric cleared her throat. "Before I found the Tribute and left to come here, Justic and I ran into a two-leg." Her mother gasped. "He heard us and chased us. I don't know why, but I stopped and let him catch up. He claimed he was from Romota and was supposed to report to the king of the centaurs. He knew what I was." She shook her head. "I almost spoke, but then I smelled another approaching. I fled into the trees. The first man told the second a story about how the Centaur King had given him an important mission: to search for centaurs in this world and send back word that they were okay."

The Elder pondered Lyric's words for a moment. "Have you spoken with him since?"

"Yes," Lyric replied quietly.

"Lyric, how could you? You know to stay away from them!" Aileena spat.

The Elder held up her hand. "It's quite alright, dear. I'm certain this one means us no harm. Do you think you could find him again?"

Lyric needed time alone to absorb all that the Elder had told her. With winter approaching, the Elder wanted her to leave the safety of the gathering to find the two-leg—the human—again. She went to the creek to think, the necklace securely around her neck once more.

"I am not that adventurous," she told herself aloud. "But he was cute," she whispered, "for someone without a tail," she added.

Even if she wanted to, could she? She knew he was traveling roughly in this direction, but what if he changed course? She had found him before; she recognized his scent. "Where do I begin? I could travel back to where I helped him. No, he's on those flying things. I won't be able to pick up his scent or that of his horses while he's in the air."

"Lyric? Are you here?"

"Over here, Justic," she called.

"I just had a strange conversation with Mother and Father. I'm supposed to help you find some two-leg and bring him back here alive. What is this all about?" Lyric stared at her brother. They had never gotten along, but he seemed serious and a little curious. She told him about her conversation with the Elder and her encounters with the human. Justic listened without interrupting.

"I was wondering what was taking you so long. You're always wandering off." He narrowed his eyes at her. She grimaced, bracing for a lecture. "It's about time," he said smugly.

"What is?" she asked, confused.

"It's about time the prophecy about you came true, and mine as well, it seems."

"Prophecy? What are you talking about?"

"Shortly after you were born, a wanderer came to the Clan. He pulled Father aside and spoke of a prophecy. After my naming day, Father told me about it. The wanderer claimed you were destined for greatness and that you would one day do something to save all centaurs from certain death."

"I was destined to protect you on that journey, but only if I stayed close to you. You were to be given the necklace Mother wore, and I was never to leave your side, or the prophecy would fail. Mother was never told about the prophecy, at least not until today."

"Oh, how I hated you growing up…"

"I've always known, but I never understood why," she said sadly.

"It wasn't really you I hated; it was how carefree you were. You always ran off by yourself. I would try to follow, but you always evaded me."

"I thought you were trying to stop me and would tell Mother and Father where I was going."

"I just wanted to be close to you so that whatever the prophecy was, it wouldn't fail."

"I wish you had told me."

"I swore to Father that I wouldn't. The wanderer said you had to find your own path without prodding. When you found the Tribute, I was crestfallen; I thought that was the prophecy and couldn't see how I would be involved or how it would save all centaurs from certain death."

"But then the Elder saw your necklace, and I realized that the shimmering rock was only the first step. If you hadn't found that rock and presented it to the Sage Clan Elder, she might never have noticed your necklace and demanded that the two-leg be brought to her. He must be the one who will save us."

Lyric gazed at her brother with newfound love. He did care for her. She had always thought he was just jealous of how Father let her wander off on her own. Now, she realized her father was trying to make the prophecy come true. "I'm sorry for not including you. My adventures would have been more fun with company."

He knuckled her shoulder. "It's okay now. Come on; we have a trip to pack for."

"All packed?" Justic asked.

"I think so," Lyric replied, adjusting her backpack, which held a heavier cloak and some dried food.

"How long do you think this is going to take?"

"I don't know. Those things he rode in travel with great speed, and I have no idea if he changed directions. I don't think we'll ever find him, Justic."

He laid a hand on her shoulder. "We will find him; this is your destiny." She smiled, though she was not reassured.

They said their goodbyes to their parents and the Elders of all the clans. As the sun disappeared from sight, they set out. "I guess we should head in the direction I think he went; maybe we'll run into him. If we make it back to where I helped him, we can see if we can pick up his trail and follow it."

"Sounds like the best plan we have."

They traveled through the night and rested during the day in thick bushes.

On the fourth night, they encountered a human town. As they skirted around it, they stumbled upon another settlement with crude shelters by human standards.

"Is this normal? Two groups so close to each other yet separated?" Justice asked.

"I don't know. Come on, let's go wide around this one as well," Lyric replied

They picked their way through the woods, careful not to break any twigs that might alert the men on watch.

"Wait a minute." Lyric shot her hand up to stop Justic. "I know that scent. He's here in this camp."

"Are you sure?"

"Yes, I see his black horse over there." She pointed to one of the corrals.

"Okay, let's find somewhere to stop and wait for morning. Have you thought about how to approach him or what to say?"

"Not yet." She bit her lower lip in thought.

Cret emerged from his family's hut earlier than usual, troubled by strange dreams of centaurs hunting him and a city on fire. He drew some water from the large bucket in the back of a wagon that served as the community's water supply. After taking a drink, he splashed some on his face. He noticed some of the horses were agitated, with Rees kicking and bucking. He ran over to see if a predator was nearby.

"Shhh, easy boy, it's okay," he said as he approached Rees. The horse settled down but continued to snort. "What is it, boy? What do you smell?"

"Me," a familiar voice said from the shadows.

"Lyric, is that you?" Cret asked. Lyric stepped forward slowly, looking around.

"Can we talk?"

Cret looked around to ensure no one saw him and followed her into the woods. He tracked her footfalls for a few minutes, moving farther from the camp. She rounded a large boulder and stopped next to another centaur. He was significantly larger than she was, with his arms crossed over his chest. A large club and a bow were strapped to his back. He scowled at Cret but didn't say anything.

"Why are you here? It might not be safe." The other centaur sniffed the air but remained silent.

"I need your help, Cret."

"My help? Sure, anything!" he exclaimed.

"I need you to come with me to the winter gathering and speak to the Elders."

"You need me to do what?"

"I need you to come with me…." He raised a hand to stop her.

"Sorry, I heard you, but I guess I should have asked why?"

"This," she said, holding up the necklace, "is a key to some technology we used to have that enabled us to communicate with those on Romota. It's a long story, but somehow, our fates are intertwined. I need your help to save all centaurs from certain death."

"Huh, well, wow. That's a lot to take in and something to ponder. Um, how—um—are you sure? Wow," he stammered.

"This is the one who is going to save us," the other centaur said with a huff.

"I'm sorry, I'm Cret. And you are?" Cret held out his hand in greeting. The centaur looked at his hand but made no move to shake it.

"I am Justic, Lyric's brother."

"Nice to meet you, Justic. Now, Lyric, can we start this conversation over? Let's go back to the time we last met."

Lyric nodded and began the story.

"Well, I must say that's not much clearer. There's more information, but I'm still confused. I'm not sure how I'm supposed to help you. You said yourself that you're not in any immediate danger. I don't know where this lost technology is or how to operate it if we find it. I have this flute; I speak into it and then throw it in water. It sends a short message back to Romota, letting everyone know if any centaurs still live on this planet."

"Maybe they can send help," Justic said.

"Hmm, maybe."

"All I know right now is that I'm supposed to bring you back so the Elders can meet you."

"You don't live in a city, do you?" he chuckled.

She looked at him crossly. "Of course not. Why?"

"It would make a dream I just had all too real. Wait here; I must inform my parents that I'll be going. Can I bring anyone? How many days until your gathering?"

"Four days if you ride your horse. You may bring someone if they can be trusted." Justic whispered something to her, but she held up her hand and shook her head.

Cret walked back to the camp, searching for his father. He was usually among the first to rise in the morning and always took over the watch.

"Father, I need a word."

"So serious, so early in the morning. Of course, son, come sit." He patted the stump beside him.

Cret sat down. "Father, I have a journey I must take. I'll be leaving shortly."

"A trip? Where and with whom?" he asked, surprised.

"The centaur filly and her brother are in the woods behind us. They said I need to speak to their Elders, claiming I'm the only one who can save them from certain death."

"What does that mean? Are they under attack?"

"They are not currently threatened," Cret said, shaking his head. "I don't understand it either, but she helped me, and now I feel obligated to help her. We wouldn't have found Vangelis without her."

Crelian and Cret sat in silence for a few moments. Cret waited patiently for his father to make up his mind. He knew he would leave without his father's approval, but receiving it would set his mind at ease.

"Alright, but take someone with you to watch your back. I'll think of something to tell everyone about where you two went."

"Thank you, Father. I'll be leaving first thing. What should I tell Mother as I pack?"

"The truth—all of it. I'll have to explain it to her later anyway; it will make my life easier if she hears it from you." Cret nodded and headed back to his hut.

At midday, Cret and Tivadarios quietly mounted their horses, pretending it was an extended hunting trip. They rode north of the camp into the thick woods.

"This way," a female voice called.

"Is that her?" Tivadarios asked.

"Shhh, later." They rode in silence for most of the day. As night approached, the two centaurs came into view.

"Oh, she's beautiful," Tivadarios whispered.

"Thank you," she replied, tilting her head to one side.

"Oh, um, you heard that? Um, you're welcome." His cheeks turned bright red.

"Centaurs have excellent hearing," Cret informed him.

"Yeah, I see that now," Tivadarios replied coyly.

"We'll stop here briefly, then continue once it's fully dark."

"But we can't see in the dark," Tivadarios pointed out.

"And we can't travel safely during the day," Justic countered.

"Well, how about you travel at night and leave a trail for us? We'll remove the trail as we go during the day to catch up," Cret suggested.

Lyric and Justic exchanged a look. Justic shrugged and lay down.

"We'll try it. Let's rest for a bit, then continue. You can follow our trail in the morning. I'll bend the branches like this when we change directions."

Cret nodded. They settled down for the evening, with Cret taking the first watch. Once darkness enveloped the woods, Lyric and Justic set out. They planned to follow at first light, hoping to reunite before continuing their journey.

They maintained this pattern for three days, and on the fourth day, Lyric was waiting for Cret and Tivadarios when they arrived. "I want you to stay here for an additional day. We will speak with the Elders to determine where they want to meet with you. I don't think it would be wise to walk you through the middle of the gathering."

"I don't think that would be wise either," Cret agreed.

"What do they want with you?" Tivadarios whispered.

Cret shrugged his shoulders, unsure of the answer.

"Why haven't they left yet? There's nothing here," Hepluosis said, peering at Cret and Tivadarios, who were still sitting beside their nightly campfire.

"They must be waiting for someone," Six replied.

"But who? They don't know anyone here. They've never left the group before to meet anyone," Hepluosis questioned.

"It seemed like they were following someone," Six noted.

"Make yourself comfortable; we'll wait, too," Hepluosis replied.

Cret and Tivadarios caught a couple of rabbits and lounged around the fire as they cooked. They took turns napping and keeping watch. When the sun sank completely below the horizon and the distant howls of wolves began to echo through the night, Lyric emerged from the shadows.

"Are you two ready?"

"I guess," Cret replied. "What am I expected to do?"

"I wasn't told. I think the Elder just wants to speak with you."

"Alright, let's go," Tivadarios said, springing to his feet. ~Ω~

"Can you see who they're speaking with?" Hepluosis asked, straining to see into the growing darkness.

"I think it's a woman. She hasn't dismounted from her horse," Six replied.

"They're going with her. Let's go."

They finally reached their destination just before sunrise. Lyric slowed as three large male centaurs armed with spears approached them.

"Halt!"

"The Elder has requested that I bring these two to her," Lyric said, holding her hands up.

"Follow us." They turned to the right, went wide around the gathering, and took them to the clearing where Lyric met the Elder.

Lyric led the two humans into the empty clearing.

"What now?" Cret asked.

"We wait, I guess," she replied, making herself comfortable on the ground. Cret and Tivadarios dismounted and loosened their saddles.

The sun was high in the sky when The Elder finally arrived. Buckets of water were brought in for the horses and Lyric, but Cret and Tivadarios were not offered anything.

"Remove those saddles from those poor creatures," The Elder spat, clearly upset. Cret and Tivadarios jumped up and quickly complied.

The Elder settled herself on the lush grass, scowling at the two humans who stood before her, visibly uncomfortable.

"Here is the human I spoke to you about, Great Elder," Lyric broke the silence.

"Why are there two of them?"

"I am sorry, ma'am...," Cret began.

The Elder raised her hand, silencing him, and turned her gaze to Lyric.

"He requested a companion for the journey, Great Elder. I didn't think it would be a problem; I take full responsibility." She bowed low.

The Elder turned her scornful gaze upon the two humans, examining them in complete silence.

Cret and Tivadarios exchanged worried glances but remained quiet.

"Why have you come to this planet after so many years of searching for us?" she finally asked.

"We didn't come here looking for you. I don't think anyone even knows you are here. My group was sent to help those in the City of Atlantis. King Rees of the Centaurs on Romota asked me to locate any centaurs I could find to ensure you were okay. He said he hadn't received an update as expected," Cret replied.

"King? They have a king? Why hasn't he come back for us?"

"I don't know, ma'am. That's all I was told. He said he received regular reports, and those who were left behind were happy where they were."

"How were you supposed to send a message back to him?"

"I have a special flute," he replied, pulling it from his pocket. "I'm to speak a short message into it and then throw it into water. Once submerged, it will send the message back."

"When you met Lyric, why didn't you send the message then?" she pressed.

"I didn't have anything concrete to tell him. I still don't know why the messages stopped or if you need help. I didn't want to waste my only message just to say that Centaurs still live on Earth. I want to give them a full, meaningful message since I'm friends with the King's son."

"On your world, do centaurs and humans live side by side?"

"In some areas, I think, but not near the capital. The city of Romota is populated solely by humans. The centaurs have a settlement a day away. King Rees came to Romota once when I was very young, though. Our King held a week-long celebration in his honor."

"What is their settlement like? Do they live in houses?" she asked with a hint of disdain.

"I'm not sure," Cret replied. "I've never been to their settlement. King Rees's son, Chi, would visit me at my grandparents' house. When he mentioned that King Rees wanted to see me, he took me to a clearing in the forest, much like this one. I never thought to ask what their houses looked like."

The Elder nodded thoughtfully.

"May I see the flute?" she asked. Cret nodded and stepped forward to hand her the flute. One of the male centaurs blocked his path with his spear and growled at him. Cret threw his arms up and held the flute out for the centaur to take. The male centaur glared at both the flute and its human holder. The Elder cleared her throat loudly, causing the male centaur to jump slightly. Reluctantly, he took the flute and handed it to the Elder.

The Elder examined the flute intently before standing and departing.

"Wait! I have to finish my mission, please," Cret called, starting to follow her. But once again, he was blocked by the guards.

"You will stay here," one of the guards commanded, pointing at Cret and Tivadarios. "You will leave," he said, gesturing toward Lyric.

She nodded. "I will return. Do not be afraid."

The guards followed Lyric out of the clearing. One turned to look back, nickered to the horses, and they raised their heads to follow.

"Wait! We need our horses to return home. Come back here!" Tivadarios yelled. "What is going on?"

"I'm not sure, but I have a bad feeling about this," Cret replied.

The two scanned the perimeter of the clearing, searching for a way through. The undergrowth was so thick with brambles that even a rabbit would struggle to find an opening. Two guards stood firmly, blocking the path into the clearing, leaving them trapped.

"What do we do?" Tivadarios asked nervously.

"Wait, I guess. I'm sorry for getting you involved."

He slapped Cret on the back. "I've got your back; this was my choice."

Shortly after, a young centaur emerged in the clearing, carrying a basket. As soon as Cret stood up, she gasped and took a startled step back.

Cret raised his hands in a calming gesture. "It's okay. I won't hurt you. What's your name?"

Her eyes widened in fear, and without a word, she dropped the basket and bolted away. The nearby guards cast sharp glances at Cret but did not intervene.

Cret retrieved the basket and returned to his seat. Inside, he found an assortment of berries and nuts, two gourds filled with water, and their bedrolls.

"It looks like we'll be spending the night here," he said, glancing at Tivadarios. Tivadarios grunted in agreement.

"What should we do now, Sir? They went with the Centaurs," Six asked, his voice tinged with uncertainty.

Hepluosis glanced in the direction they had gone. "Let's wait here and see what happens," he replied calmly

# ∞ **21** ∞

## 𝕂IDNAPPED

**KAYSON** kept his distance from Neiaphi and Andonis for the rest of the week, observing them from the shadows. Gradually, the camp settled into a routine: the women tended to the children and gathered in small groups to gossip, while the men focused on repairing the few remaining houses and hunting whenever they could. Like the others, Kayson was assigned to the night watch, blending into the rhythm of camp life.

The days grew colder, with snowfall expected any day. The first snow finally arrived, and the Laosans greeted it with delight. Boys piled up mounds of snow to hide behind, launching snowballs at each other in playful mock battles. Laughter filled the air as children darted through the village, stretching out their tongues to catch the delicate snowflakes.

Kayson sat on a log, huddled under his cloak, finishing his watch shift when something smacked the back of his head. He spun around, drawing his sword in a flash.

"Sorry, sir!" two little boys shouted as they bolted away, laughing and flinging more snowballs over their shoulders. Kayson shook his head, a sigh escaping his lips.

Over the past week, Kayson had been consumed by dark thoughts, plotting an accident for Andonis. Once Andonis was out of the way, Neiaphi would need someone to turn to for comfort, and Kayson was determined to be that person. He envisioned persuading her to leave these people behind and travel with him. The thought of resuming his adventures filled him with eager anticipation.

Kayson stood and stretched his back, then cast one last glance at the surrounding woods before retreating to his hut for a moment of respite. Suddenly, movement in the shadows caught his eye. He approached the trees, shielding his eyes from the rising sun.

The sun rose higher, casting long shadows across the ground. Another flash of movement caught Kayson's eye, prompting him to edge closer to the trees, scanning the area for the source.

"Halt! Go no further," a gruff voice growled softly. Kayson froze in place. "Come closer and sit on the log in front of you. Don't draw attention to yourself," the voice ordered.

Kayson obeyed, heart racing. "Who are you? Show yourself!" he demanded with bravado.

The voice ignored Kayson's demand. "You are different from the others, and I know what you truly are. You do not belong here. Where are you from?" it demanded.

"I asked you first," Kayson shot back, trying to assert himself.

"You are in no position to dictate the direction of this conversation. Answer me!" the voice growled again, low and threatening.

Kayson took a deep breath. "I am Kayson."

"Where are you from?" the voice growled.

"From across the Chief Sea."

"Why are you here?"

"I joined these people a short time ago to lead them to The Pillars."

"The Pillars?" the voice echoed, curiosity mingling with suspicion. "You mean the way to The Forbidden Floating City?"

"Yes." As the word left his lips, deep, throaty growls reverberated through the woods.

"Enough!" the voice barked, silencing the growls. "Why do these people travel there?" it demanded.

"I'm not sure; I was told they are needed there. That's all I know. I was ordered to guide them, and then I'm free to depart. Neiluios or Addident are the ones you need to speak to—they seem to be the leaders here."

"No, you will do, as you are one of us. We will need a diversion soon. I will find you when the time is right. Go, and speak not of me."

Kayson rose, scanning the trees, but he saw and heard nothing. A sense of unease washed over him as he quickly retreated to his hut. *I will not continue to be used by those who think they hold all the power. I will be free,* he thought.

Andonis approached Neiaphi, leading their horses, a smile brightening his face as he handed Nexus' reins to her.

"Where are we going?" she asked, returning his smile.

Andonis grinned and pulled a pure white cloak from his saddle, draping it around her shoulders. Neiaphi rubbed the soft fur against her cheeks; it was made entirely from white hares.

Still silent, Andonis helped her mount her horse before swinging onto his own. "Where are we going?" she repeated, curiosity lacing her voice.

Andonis smiled at her, waved to her father, and nudged his horse into a slow trot. Neiaphi hesitated, then shrugged, waved to her father, and followed him out of the settlement.

For several minutes, they rode in silence. Neiaphi's gaze shifted between the landscape and Andonis, trying to read his expression, but he remained focused ahead, eyes scanning the horizon as though they were not alone.

Neiaphi opened her mouth to ask again where they were going when Andonis finally spoke. "Since we boarded the last boats, I've had the same dream," he said, his voice low. "I dream of a temple on a mountain, with a small village at its base. Inside the temple, there's only one occupant—a beautiful woman, a priestess."

Neiaphi listened intently; Andonis rarely shared his dreams with her. "In this dream, I meet the priestess, and she tells me I will lead a great expedition with an unusual group. I tell her I'm already on a great expedition, but she only laughs and says this one will surpass even the Laosans' journey. It will take me far from home and from most of those I love." Andonis hesitated, and Neiaphi nudged Nexus closer, placing a hand on his arm. For the first time since setting out, he turned to meet her gaze. "I ask the priestess if you'll be with me on this journey. She smiles and tells me the answer will be revealed soon.

"I think I understand now how your dreams must feel," Andonis said quietly, holding her gaze. "I've had the same dream every time I sleep. It's mostly unchanged—until recently." He paused, taking a deep breath. "Now I see giant wolves surrounding the temple, and strange half-human, half-horse creatures…"

"Centaurs," Neiaphi interjected.

He blinked, taken aback. "Excuse me?"

"The creatures—they're called centaurs. They're from Romota. Groups of them came to Earth with Poseidon and the replacements. I didn't know any were still here."

"I've never heard of them or seen them before," Andonis murmured, almost to himself. "Anyway, in my dream, the centaurs chase the wolves, and a few men on horseback join them. You and I run to the temple and take shelter there." He hesitated, his expression thoughtful. "That's when I always wake up. I only had this version of the dream once, several nights ago, and now… I find myself missing it, like I was left without an ending."

Neiaphi nodded, listening closely. "So, where are we going?"

"The other day, I was sent further out to scout," Andonis began. "I came across an area that looked just like the one from my dream. I wanted…" He trailed off.

"What is it?" Neiaphi glanced around, suddenly on edge. Had he seen something?

He shook his head slightly, then continued, "I wanted to see if you'd recognize it too."

"Me? Why would I? I've never been here before," Neiaphi replied, furrowing her brow.

"I don't know," Andonis said, rubbing the back of his neck. "But something about this dream and the priestess reminds me of your dreams."

"Oh." Neiaphi scanned the surroundings more intently. "The temple on the hill that you describe sounds familiar. I think that's where the voice in my dreams lives. But here, nothing and everything feels familiar," she sighed. Andonis gave her shoulder a reassuring pat.

"It's okay; come on, the view is beautiful up here." Andonis urged his horse into a trot. Neiaphi grinned, whipping Nexus into a gallop.

"Hey, wait up!" Andonis called, kicking his horse to follow.

Laughter bubbled up from Neiaphi as the wind whipped through her hair, tugging at her cloak. Nexus surged up the hill, her powerful haunches propelling them forward. As Andonis's horse drew closer, she glanced over at him, her eyes sparkling and her features soft and relaxed.

Andonis couldn't recall ever seeing her this happy and at ease. A smile spread across his face as he urged his chestnut stallion for a little more speed when the slope leveled off. The horse complied, effortlessly edging past Nexus. Andonis glanced back, giving Neiaphi a playful wink.

Neiaphi leaned forward onto Nexus's neck, a grin on her face. "Come on, girl, you can beat that beefy stallion! You're slick and nimble. Let's win this!"

Nexus whinnied, shaking her head but picking up speed. Slowly, she closed the gap until they were neck and neck with Andonis's horse. Suddenly, he raised his hand and pointed ahead; they were approaching the edge of a cliff. Both riders quickly reined in their horses, bringing them to a halt just in time.

Both horses were lathered and breathing heavily, their heads hanging low. Andonis dismounted and raised his hands to help Neiaphi down. She swung her legs over and slid down, and he caught her waist, gently lowering her to the ground.

They walked the short distance to the cliff's edge, where the valley floor stretched out before them, an endless expanse of trees blanketing the landscape.

"This is breathtaking," Neiaphi said softly. Andonis placed his hand on the small of her back.

"I thought you would like it." She leaned into him, resting her head against his chest. He wrapped his arms around her, holding her close, savoring the moment together.

The clouds in the western sky blazed like a roaring fire as the sun hovered just above the horizon. Neiaphi dismounted Nexus in front of her hut, handing the reins to Andonis. "See you soon," she said, and he nodded, leading the horses away.

"Hello, Mother," she called as she entered.

"Did you have a good ride?" her mother asked.

"Oh, the best! What can I assist you with?"

"Go clean up. The evening meal is almost ready."

"Sorry I was gone so long," Neiaphi said, and Altesse smiled, shaking her head.

"Hello, Andonis," Altesse greeted as he approached the fire.

"Ma'am," he replied, bowing his head respectfully.

"Hello, my son. Where have you been all day?" Miry teased Andonis, her eyes sparkling.

He kissed her on the cheek. "Out on the best ride ever. Neiaphi's little mare is quick, and Neiaphi is a skilled rider." Miry patted his arm and returned to their shared cookfire.

Evening meals were always spent this way, with the two families sharing the work and enjoying the benefits of good food and friendly conversation.

Altesse, Miry, and the servants were always the first to retire for the evening, followed closely by Neiaphi. Neiluios, Mace, and Andonis remained behind, sharing the moonlight and the crisp evening air as they prepared for their night watches.

Andonis walked slowly around the outskirts of their settlement with his sword belted at his hip. He hugged his cloak tighter against the chill and rubbed his hands together for warmth. Reaching into a pocket of his cloak, he pulled out a pair of rabbit fur-lined mittens that Neiaphi had made for him. Slipping his hands into the soft fur offered a small comfort against the cold.

The moon had vanished, leaving the night shrouded in darkness beyond the flickering firelight. Owls hooted in the trees, and the occasional howl of a distant wolf pierced the stillness, but overall, the night was eerily quiet.

As Andonis completed his third round, a series of piercing screams shattered the night. The watchmen jumped, rushing back to the huts, while men still in slumber bolted outside into the chaos. Several giant wolves stood like sentinels in front of Neiluios's hut, their eyes glinting in the darkness, and cries echoed from within.

With his sword drawn, Andonis sprinted alongside Neiluios, both of them moving cautiously as they neared the hut. The wolves growled menacingly, their hackles raised in preparation for a fight. They lowered their heads, spreading their front legs slightly, ready to pounce.

Andonis charged forward, swinging his sword from side to side to scare the wolves away. One of the wolves lunged into the hut and evaded his blade, blocking the entrance. A moment later, three wolves exited the hut, sprinting at full speed. They leaped impossibly high over the heads of the attacking men, vanishing into the inky darkness beyond.

Neiluios and Andonis rushed into his hut to find Altesse and Neiaphi sobbing and clinging to each other.

Neiluios grabbed his wife, "Are you two okay? What happened?" he demanded.

"The boys... they took the boys. The wolvers took the boys," Altesse cried, crumpling into Neiluios's arms.

Andonis moved toward Neiaphi, who reached out for him and pressed her face into his chest. He placed a comforting hand on the back of her head. "The wolves killed the boys?" he asked softly, dread creeping into his voice.

Neiaphi shook her head, tears streaming down her face. "No, they took them. Two of them grabbed the boys by their bedding and ran off with them," she sobbed. "We tried to stop them, but they snarled at us, and then a third wolf came in, cornering us away from the boys. They didn't even cry." Overwhelmed, she shook her head and slumped to the floor.

Neiluios hugged Altesse tighter. "We will hunt those wolves down and kill them for what they have done. My boys will not have died in vain."

Altesse pushed away from him, her eyes blazing. "No, you will pursue those wolvers and rescue our sons," she said sternly.

Neiluios shook his head, patting her arm gently. Altesse stood, brushing his hands off her. "You will not deny or dismiss what I'm saying. Two WOLVERS," she shouted, "entered this hut and walked over to the boys. They whined at them, and the boys giggled. I screamed! Neiaphi started throwing things at them, trying to scare them away.

"They ignored us completely; they only looked at the boys." Neiluios stared at his wife, silent, processing her words. "Then another wolver entered, growling at Neiaphi and backing her up against me. The first two grabbed the boys so gently, and then all three fled."

"Mother is telling you the whole truth, Father. I don't know what those creatures are, but they're not simple animals. There's intelligence in their eyes. They communicate with each other, coordinating their actions."

Andonis turned to Neiluios. "Your orders, Sir?"

Neiluios gazed at his wife and then at his daughter. "It's too dark to see anything right now. At the first light of dawn, we will find my boys. Arrange teams of three, and make sure each team has a dog."

Andonis nodded, placing his hand on Neiaphi's shoulder and gently squeezing. She put her hand over his and looked up at him. "Find them," she whispered. He bent down, kissed her cheek, and then departed.

Before the first light of dawn brightened the predawn sky, several groups of three assembled outside Neiluios's hut. Greish approached Andonis, who stood off to the side. "Just the two of us?" he asked.

"I'll join your group," Kayson said as he approached.

Andonis squinted at him. "Why?"

"I want to help find those two helpless boys."

"Fine, you're with me. All right, everyone. The wolves were seen leaving the settlement in that direction." He pointed to the west. "Most of us will go that way, but they could have fled in any direction once cloaked in darkness." Everyone nodded in agreement.

Neiluios approached Andonis, his expression grim. "Find them and bring them home safely, son," he said.

"I will, Sir." Andonis bowed his head in acknowledgment. "Those riding—mount up. All others, head out. If you don't find any tracks by midday, return here. Those that find tracks, keep following them, and leave sign for the rest of us to follow your trail."

Andonis, Kayson, and Greish mounted their horses and began riding west.

When the sun rose fully above the horizon, Greish spotted what appeared to be wolf tracks. He dismounted to examine them closely.

"The tracks look fresh. They're headed southwest. Should we follow?" he asked.

"It's the first sign we've seen. Let's follow," Andonis replied.

Greish mounted his horse and signaled to his dog, who took the lead. They followed the faint tracks for a short while, noting that several more prints had merged with the original. Greish estimated that five wolves were ahead of them.

As dusk fell, the three men continued trailing the wolves. When it became too dangerous to travel further, they set up a cold camp. Greish handed Andonis and Kayson a bar of dried meat, along with some fruit and nuts. They ate in silence, the weight of their mission hanging heavily in the air.

"I'll take the first watch; you two get some sleep. Kayson, I'll wake you for the second watch," Greish said. Kayson nodded in agreement. Greish stood and walked over to the horses, double-checking that their leads were securely tied.

Finding a suitable spot, he settled in to keep watch. After a short while, he stood and made a slow circuit around the camp. The moon hung high overhead, casting a silvery light that illuminated the surroundings.

A rustling sound caught Greish's attention. He moved cautiously toward it, straining to hear the source. Breathing, a soft rubbing sound, and then a horse snorting reached his ears. Crouching, he widened his stance and slowly drew his sword, preparing for whatever lay ahead.

"Show yourself, and you will not be harmed," he said almost under his breath, his voice steady despite the tension in the air.

No answer.

"I know you're there; this is your last chance," Greish warned.

"It's me, Greish. Don't hurt me," Neiaphi said meekly.

"Neiaphi? What are you doing here?" he asked, lowering his sword slightly.

Neiaphi crawled out from the bush where she had been hiding, brushing herself off as she emerged. Cypress stood by her side. "I couldn't just sit back there waiting. I have to help."

"Come on, let's get you closer to the others," Greish urged, gesturing for her to follow.

Neiaphi started heading back to where she had left Nexus. "I'll get her in a moment; come on."

They walked the short distance to where Andonis and Kayson were lying. Greish pointed to a spot near Andonis, and Neiaphi settled down there. He gave Cypress a hand signal, and the dog lay his head on his paws beside her. Neiaphi leaned against him for warmth, grateful for his comforting presence.

After ensuring Nexus was secure with the other horses, Greish woke Kayson. Kayson blinked, taking in the sight of an extra person sleeping near Andonis. He turned to Greish, raising an eyebrow in question.

"Another searcher following the wolves' tracks. I told them they could join us," Greish explained.

Kayson nodded and began a slow patrol around their camp, scanning the surroundings for any signs of danger.

Andonis checked on the horses one last time before returning to wake the others and uncover the identity of the mystery person. He had a strong suspicion about who it was, but hoped he was wrong. Whoever had joined them was riding Neiaphi's horse.

He just hoped it wasn't her. The sky was brightening, but the earth remained cloaked in shadows.

He woke Greish first. "Who is that?" he asked, pointing to the figure huddled under a blanket with a dog.

"I'll wake them and let them tell you," Greish replied, a hint of hesitation in his voice. Andonis scowled at the thought.

Greish walked over to Neiaphi and nudged her with his foot. She peeked out from underneath her blanket and glanced up. "Time to get moving?" she asked quietly.

He nodded, and she slowly wrapped the blanket around herself as she stood.

Andonis was busy packing his blanket into his pack, his back turned to her. Neiaphi approached quietly and tapped him on the shoulder. He spun around, his eyes hard as steel, surprised by her presence.

Neiaphi jumped and swallowed hard when his eyes locked onto hers. She dropped her gaze, wringing her hands. "I'm sorry if I've made you angry," she managed to choke out.

Andonis continued to stare at her, his silence weighing heavily in the air.

"Please, say something. I couldn't just sit there and do nothing, knowing nothing. It was killing me." Still, he remained silent. "I—I left shortly after everyone else.

"I snuck away when my father was preoccupied with my mother. I traveled most of the day before I came across the wolf tracks and intercepted your trail. I... I was going to approach you this morning. Please, say something or yell at me. Just do something."

Andonis dropped his gaze to his pack, and Neiaphi's heart plummeted. He reached inside and pulled out a couple of pieces of dried meat, holding one out for her and tossing the other to Cypress. Neiaphi grabbed it with a trembling hand.

As she grasped the meat, Andonis caught her wrist with his other hand and squeezed. Neiaphi whimpered slightly, feeling the pressure. But then he let go abruptly, wrapping his arms around her in a fierce hug.

"I didn't mean to hurt you. I'm sorry," Andonis whispered in her ear.

Neiaphi shook her head. "You have nothing to apologize for. I should never have left the settlement. I'm sorry."

Andonis pulled away and gently wiped the tears from her cheek.

"Your eyes sparkle when they're wet, but I hate seeing you cry," Andonis said softly. Neiaphi blushed and wiped her eyes. "Just thinking about you being out there alone yesterday, with gigantic wolves roaming around, frightened me."

"I'm sorry; I didn't mean to make you worry."

"Mount up, you two," Kayson sneered from atop his horse. "We have wolves to find."

After midday, they came to a river.

"Do you think the wolves crossed?" Neiaphi asked.

"No, look!" Greish pointed downstream. "The tracks follow the river."

After several moments, the wolf tracks split into two groups.

"Greish and I will follow the group along the river," Kayson said. "You and Neiaphi should head inland."

"Sounds good to me," Andonis nodded. "We'll set up cold camps again tonight. If we don't find anything by tomorrow night, we'll meet you back at the river the following day."

"Nyx and Cypress will be able to find each other when we need them. Good luck," Greish replied.

Andonis and Neiaphi turned to follow the three wolves that moved inland, still tracking the river. The surrounding forest was quiet, with countless birds flitting from branch to branch, observing them. A rabbit bolted as they approached, darting from one bush to another.

Andonis kept a watchful eye on the trees, noting that nothing significant moved about.

"Do you think we will find them?" Neiaphi whispered.

He didn't respond immediately, glancing at her from the corner of his eye. Her head was down, and her shoulders slumped forward.

He nudged his horse closer. "I don't know if we will." She lifted her gaze. "But I promise you I won't give up looking. I wish I could be more hopeful. We don't even know if they're still alive or if they're being carried by the wolves we're tracking."

Neiaphi's eyes hardened. "The wolves were looking for my brothers specifically. I don't know why, but they didn't seem to want to hurt them. I've never seen an animal act like that. They carefully and impossibly wrapped the boys in their blankets with their mouths and then picked them up by the blankets. My brothers were quiet and unafraid. I wish I could have been that brave. Wherever they are, I know they're okay.

"Were they looking for just babies, or for my brothers specifically? Why are my brothers always taken? First Icarus, and now Annas and Praxis. My poor mother." She shook her head.

"We'll find them."

Andonis and Neiaphi set up camp when the tracks became too faint to follow.

Another cold night passed in the wilds. Andonis took the first watch while Neiaphi slept soundly. Suddenly, a chorus of wolf howls tore through the night. Neiaphi and Cypress jolted awake.

"Do you see them?" Neiaphi shouted over the deafening noise. Andonis shook his head, gripping his sword as he circled around her. Just as suddenly as it started, the howling stopped.

"What was that about?" Neiaphi asked.

"I'm not sure," Andonis replied.

The rest of the night was quiet.

Though the sun had risen, no light pierced the thick, dark clouds above. Shadows cloaked the countryside as the wind picked up, and the temperature dropped sharply.

Neiaphi huddled under her cloak, face shielded from the biting wind. Cypress plodded alongside Nexus, head down. Suddenly, a thunderous crash echoed through the trees ahead. Andonis drew his sword, stepping protectively in front of Neiaphi as the noise grew louder. She reined in Nexus, urging her to back away slowly.

Kayson burst through the trees on horseback, moving as swiftly as possible. Andonis stepped forward. "Where's Greish? What's going on?" he asked.

Kayson, scratched and bloody, was too winded to reply. He slid from his saddle, landing heavily with one foot caught in the stirrup, his leg twisting at an unnatural angle.

Neiaphi gasped, her hands rising to her mouth. Andonis dismounted, pulling Kayson free from the panicked horse. Neiaphi rode closer, taking the reins and working to calm the stallion. "Is he okay?" she asked.

Andonis checked him over quickly. "I think so. Nothing broken, nothing serious. Let's rest until he comes to."

Neiaphi led the horses to a nearby tree, tying them securely but leaving their saddles on in case a quick retreat was necessary. Andonis poured a small amount of water into Kayson's mouth. His eyes fluttered open, and he coughed, sputtering as he came to. Andonis steadied him, helping him sit up. "Are you okay?" he asked.

Kayson looked around nervously. "How many were following me?" he asked, visibly shaken.

"Wolves?" Andonis replied. "We haven't seen any. It's been quiet out here."

Kayson sighed with relief. "Oh, good."

Neiaphi leaned forward, her voice tense. "Where's Greish? What happened?"

Kayson took another drink, steadying himself before he spoke. "They attacked just after the howling stopped. The silence was... too quiet. Five wolves emerged from the shadows. Greish's horse broke free and bolted. Three wolves went straight for Greish and his dog; the other two came for me. I heard a splash—Greish's dog was just... gone. Greish screamed, and then all five wolves turned on me. I got on my horse and fled. Thank the gods I found you." He glanced around, lowering his voice. "We need to move. It's not safe. Let's get back to the others."

Neiaphi's face fell as she sank to the ground. *Greish was dead? Poor Alexa. How would she cope?* Neiaphi stared at Kayson, but his words were muffled, distant. Andonis was speaking too, but she couldn't make out a thing. Everything seemed far away, as if she were underwater.

Andonis gently grabbed her arm and shook it. "Yes?" she asked, her voice distant.

"We need to get moving. Back to the settlement," Kayson said, mounting his horse with urgency.

Andonis helped Neiaphi to her feet, leading her to Nexus. He steadied her as she mounted, his grip firm and reassuring.

"Come on; we have to get back! We have no time to lose," Andonis urged, turning his horse in the direction they had come from.

"No," Neiaphi said softly, shaking her head.

"What?" Kayson and Andonis replied in unison, surprise etched on their faces.

"We're not leaving without word of my brothers. We must find them," she insisted, her voice steady despite the fear coursing through her.

"If those wolves find us first, we'll never know what happened to them—or what will happen to us," Andonis said, his voice firm. "We need to return, gather more men, and leave you in a safe place."

Neiaphi glared at him, her determination unwavering. "I'm not leaving now that I'm so close to them. I've encountered these wolves before and emerged unharmed. They're harassing my family for some reason, and I won't abandon their trail. You're both free to go gather more men if you wish, but I'm moving forward." She took the reins and spun Nexus around. "Cypress, come!"

Andonis stared at her for a moment before jumping onto his horse and riding up beside her. Kayson remained on his horse, a shocked expression plastered across his face. *How dare a woman speak to men like that?* He quickly masked his surprise with a look of distaste and fell behind them.

Andonis looked back at Kayson. Kayson wore an amused smile that he smoothed to a look of concern.

"Are you coming with us?" Andonis asked,

"I'm not leaving the two of you alone to fend off the wolves," Kayson replied

Andonis shrugged.

Andonis took the first watch that night. Wolves howled in the distance, their cries echoed by others closer in, but it was nothing like the night before. He raked his hands through his

hair, the weight of Greish's absence heavy on his heart. Two little boys were gone—who would be next?

He walked over to Kayson and kicked his foot. Kayson bolted upright. "Your turn," Andonis said, tension creeping into his voice as he retreated to his bedroll.

Kayson slowly got up and made his way to the edge of their cold camp, peering into the darkness. He glanced back at Andonis's still form, a sense of weight hanging in the air. "Tomorrow, my friend. Tomorrow," he murmured, a vow echoing in the silence.

At midday, the three searchers paused for a brief rest. Kayson slipped away, his heart racing until he found exactly what he was looking for. He climbed a rock outcropping. "Perfect," he muttered. "Andonis!!" he shouted, his voice echoing off the stones. "Come quick! Hurry!!"

Neiaphi and Andonis jumped at the sound of Kayson's scream. "Stay here; I'll go help him."

"Don't leave me here alone," she pleaded, fear creeping into her voice.

"Cypress will stay with you," he assured her, placing a sword in her hand. "I won't be gone long. I promise I'll be back."

She gulped and nodded. Andonis took off running toward Kayson's frantic cries.

Kayson called for him a few more times. As Andonis reached the rocky hill, he saw Kayson battling something, but he couldn't hear any growling or see any other wolves nearby.

"Hurry, I can't hold them off!" Kayson yelled down to him.

Andonis sheathed his sword and climbed the rock outcropping. As he reached the top, he pulled himself over, only to find Kayson standing with his sword pointed at him.

"What are you doing?" Andonis raised his hands to shield his face just as Kayson lunged, striking him across the head. Andonis lost his footing and fell backward.

He landed hard on his back, his head bouncing off the rocky ground. Kayson looked down; Andonis lay still, not moving. A smile crept across Kayson's face as he drew his dagger, slashing it across his own skin in several places.

Suddenly, Kayson caught a flicker of movement behind him. Cypress burst from the trees, leaping at Kayson with a fierce snarl. Kayson raised his hands, deflecting the dog's charge. Cypress was launched over the cliff's edge, landing beside Andonis in a heap.

Kayson sneered as he gazed down at the two motionless forms. "That was easier than I thought it would be. Now for my prize." He climbed down and jogged back to find Neiaphi.

Stopping behind a tree, he peered out. Neiaphi sat on a rock, gripping the reins of all three horses with one hand while struggling to hold a sword before her with the other, her eyes darting around nervously. He retreated slightly and then took off running as fast as he could.

Neiaphi jumped when he exploded through the trees. "Mount up, quickly!" Kayson yelled at her.

"Where are Andonis and Cypress?" she asked.

"No time, mount up now!" he bellowed. He grabbed his reins from her and mounted his horse. She complied, looking around for the other two.

"Quickly, follow me." Neiaphi fell in behind him, leading Andonis's horse along. They rode further inland, away from the river but still downstream. After a few moments, Neiaphi halted.

Kayson glanced back, frowning. "What are you doing? We need to keep moving to stay ahead of the wolves."

"But what about Andonis? What about Cypress? We can't just leave them here. I won't leave them!"

Kayson sighed. "I didn't want to tell you just yet. While I was scouting, I ran into a pack of wolves. Andonis and Cypress came to my rescue, but... they didn't make it." Neiaphi's hands flew to her mouth as she gasped. "I'm sorry, but it's just the two of us now. We need to keep moving and put as much distance as we can between us and that pack. We'll figure out our next steps tomorrow morning."

"What if they're alive? We have to go back and find out!"

"No," Kayson snapped, his scowl deepening. "I told you they're gone. I saw it with my own eyes."

Neiaphi crossed her arms defiantly. "I didn't see anything."

Kayson glared at her defiance. "I see. When you say you saw something, you expect everyone to believe you, yet you don't trust others." He shook his head, staring at the ground. Slowly, he raised his gaze, his eyes glazed and fixed. Neiaphi flinched and lowered her own. "I'm sorry for your loss, but we must leave unless you wish to join them. NOW!" He growled the last word.

She nodded and mounted Nexus.

They rode hard for the rest of the day. Neiaphi kept her eyes downcast, silent tears tracing her cheeks as they traveled.

The next morning, she rose early, saddling the horses before Kayson even stirred. Walking over to him, she nudged his foot with determination.

"It's time to keep searching for my brothers."

Kayson huffed and sat up, brushing the dirt from his hands. "I think it's time to abandon this fool's quest. How many more lives have to be lost for the sake of finding two little boys?"

Neiaphi's eyes narrowed. "How dare you."

He scoffed. "How dare me? Your defiance—and the defiance of every woman in that settlement—is the root of your problems. In time, you'll realize your mistake and understand how things are meant to be."

Neiaphi glared at him, her voice steady and defiant. "Never. I will never submit to your ideology. I thought you were a Loyal, but now I see you for what you are—a Society sympathizer, a wolf in sheep's clothing. Go your way, Kayson; I'll go mine." Neiaphi shook her head and turned her back to mount Nexus.

Kayson sighed, shaking his head. He unsheathed his sword and hit her in the head with the pommel. She crumpled to the ground with a groan.

Kayson stood over her, breathing heavily as he watched Neiaphi lying motionless on the ground. "A wolf in sheep's clothing indeed," he chuckled dryly. "You'll come around eventually," he muttered and then sheathed his sword, grabbed Nexus's reins, and began preparing the horse, his movements precise and cold.

After a moment, he bent down and lifted Neiaphi's limp form. "I don't know why I thought this would be easy. My fault." He shook his head. "You will submit; you will."

He tossed Neiaphi over Nexus's saddle and secured her. He mounted his own horse and cast a final glance at the path she'd hoped to take. Then, with a grim smile, he turned them both in the opposite direction and rode into the gathering shadows.

Neiaphi woke to a splitting headache. Attempting to move, she realized she was bound across Nexus's back like a freshly hunted deer. She squinted against the midday sun, groaning softly as she took in her surroundings. Up ahead, Kayson led Nexus, guiding them forward. She let out another moan as Nexus stumbled over a rock.

"Hello again," Kayson greeted her with a broad smile.

"Where are you taking me?" she snarled.

"We're heading west. Don't worry; I know the way. Just sit back and relax."

She squirmed against her bindings. "Can I at least sit up?"

Kayson paused, frowning, then sighed and stopped. "Fine, but don't try anything." He untied her from Nexus, sliding her to the ground while keeping her hands bound behind her back. After letting her stretch, he lifted her back into the saddle and tied her hands securely around Nexus's neck.

"Is this really necessary?" she asked, gesturing to her bound hands. "And where's Andonis's horse?" She looked around frantically.

"I let him go. No point in hauling an extra mount without a rider."

Tears slipped down Neiaphi's cheeks as Kayson grunted and mounted his horse. She turned her eyes toward the sky, sending out a silent prayer. *If there are any divine beings up there—or out there, anywhere—please, help me.*

# ∞ 22 ∞
## INTO THE WOODS

"CRET, Cret. Wake up," a deep voice whispered from the darkness.

Cret jolted awake. "Who's there?" he whispered back.

"Hurry—gather your belongings, and then wait."

Cret nudged Tivadarios, who, without a word, began rolling up his bedroll.

They settled by the faintly smoldering fire, waiting in silence. Several long moments slipped by, each one stretching the tension.

"This way," the voice hissed from behind them.

Cret and Tivadarios quickly gathered their packs and moved to the edge of the clearing. There, they spotted a small opening in the branches.

"Through this hole."

Tivadarios stared, wide-eyed. "We can't fit through that hole!"

"Fine," the voice huffed. A sword was drawn, its blade slicing through the air before crashing down into the bushes, hacking and chopping at the branches.

"That's good," Cret shouted over the noise. "Hurry, everyone's going to hear that!"

The boys pushed through the underbrush and emerged to find Lyric, Justic, and five other centaurs waiting for them. Lyric held the reins of their horses, ready to flee.

"Here, hurry! We have to leave now," she urged, thrusting the reins into Cret's hands. He nodded, and they both mounted quickly.

The seven centaurs and the two boys on horseback fled the area as swiftly as possible. Confused voices echoed in the distance but soon faded away. No sounds of pursuit followed them.

They maintained their breakneck pace until the sun crested the horizon.

Cret and Tivadarios slowed their lathered mounts to a brisk walk, allowing them to cool off.

Lyric glanced back. "Come on, don't fall behind! We have to keep moving," she urged.

Cret shook his head, feeling Rees's neck. The horse was breathing hard, foam covering his neck and haunches. He dismounted and signaled for Tivadarios to do the same.

The centaurs halted, eyes narrowing. "What are you doing, two-leg? I will not be caught—not now," one of the males said, his coat coal black from mane to tail.

"Our horses can't keep going at this pace. They need to rest, or they'll die."

The male snorted but didn't respond.

"Do you think anyone is following?" Tivadarios asked nervously. The same male nodded his head.

"What was going to happen to us?" Cret asked.

Lyric sighed. "We need to keep moving as fast as your horses can manage." They all began walking, with Cret and Tivadarios still on foot. "The Elder used me. She claimed she only wanted to speak with you and learn what you knew about our home world. She hoped you had access to the ship. I've heard from others that she has always dreamed of returning to our true home—away from two-legs."

"When you told her that centaurs were not the ruling beings on Romota, she was crestfallen. The idea of returning home only to be subject to the whims of two-leg rulers did not sit well with her. I begged her to let you both go, but she refused. She intended to take you to Atlantis and bargain with them for a safe place where we could live and rule on our own."

Cret shook his head. "No one there knows me or would care about what happens to me."

Lyric shrugged. "That was brought up. What if they refuse to bargain? The Elder said you would be executed before them, and then it would be war." That statement sparked much yelling, and three clans, including theirs, left the gathering early. "Justic and I couldn't sit back and let her kill you. It's my fault you're in this mess to begin with."

Cret and Tivadarios mounted their horses once they began to breathe normally again. The nine four-legged companions broke into a quick, ground-covering trot.

"When we learned these two would help you escape, we decided to join in. The prophecies surrounding them are too intriguing to ignore. My name is Ambrite; these are Peleros, Bal-air, Simandro, and Myreia."

"Nice to meet you all, and thank you. Where are we headed now? We need to get back to our people."

Ambrite shook his head. "That's the first place they'll look for you. Lyric is young and not used to betrayal. It's not her fault she revealed the location of your families."

Tivadarios gasped.

"Calm yourself," Ambrite said. "My brother and several others I trust have volunteered to assess the threat your party poses to us."

"They won't find any threat when they report back. However, others will be looking for you now. If you're seen going back, they'll take that as a threat. We'll travel west for a while and then circle back to hopefully intercept their path this spring when they start moving again."

"Spring? I can't be gone that long. My father will send out a search party if he hasn't already."

Ambrite raised a hand. "I've sent a message with my brother to your father, assuring him that you are safe and will see him in the spring."

"You can write?" Cret asked.

Ambrite started to laugh.

"Sorry, I didn't mean to offend," Cret added quickly.

"No offense taken. Yes, I can write. My clan wasn't as sheltered from two-legs as others. We traded with them and even schooled alongside their children. I've had many human friends. Come, your mounts look refreshed. Let's get moving—I want to put as much distance as possible between us and the gathering before we stop for the night."

"Halt or you will be killed, two-leg!"

Hepluosis growled, spinning his horse around, sword at the ready, only to find an arrow notched and aimed at his chest.

"Drop the sword and raise your hands above your head," the centaur ordered.

Six unsheathed his sword and threw it to the ground. Hepluosis hesitated momentarily before complying.

"State your business on these grounds!"

Hepluosis crossed his arms over his chest and scowled at the four centaurs surrounding him and Six. The one with the bow advanced a few steps. "Speak, two-leg, or you will never speak again," he said.

"I am on the trail of two 'two-legs,' as you call us."

"What are your plans for them? To join them and kill us?"

Hepluosis barked out a laugh. "I didn't even know there were centaurs on this planet. I have no fight with you."

"Then what are your intentions?" the centaur snarled.

"When I find Cret, I plan on ridding this planet of him. He's a thorn in my side."

Two of the centaurs nodded to each other. "You can join us in the hunt, then."

"No, thank you. We'll be fine on our own."

The centaur shook his head, glaring. "Unacceptable. Travel with us or leave this trail. We won't have you getting in our way."

Hepluosis glanced at Six, who shrugged. "Fine, but you won't stop me from killing him myself."

"We have a use for him first; then you may do as you wish."

Ambrite found a cave to shelter from the increasing wind and the threatening storm. Cret gathered some wood while Tivadarios built a small fire in the cave's rear. Rees and Tivadarios' horses were tied near the mouth of the cave. The centaurs gathered with the humans around the fire, creating a circle of warmth. They spent the evening quietly reflecting on the events of the past day and the months to come.

"I'll take the first watch," Cret said, breaking the silence.

"Not needed. Centaurs don't sleep much; get some rest. We'll handle the watches. Lyric, you and your brother have the first watch. Wake me for the second."

Lyric and Justic walked over to the horses and lay back down.

Cret and Tivadarios unrolled their bedrolls and crawled in. After a few moments, Cret realized he wouldn't fall asleep anytime soon. He got up, walked over to Lyric, and sat beside her.

"Problem?" she inquired.

"Can't sleep yet. Are you all sure you want to risk everything to help two boys? You could just leave now and say you saw us escape and chased us but lost us."

Justic shook his head. "That would never work. No, this is the right thing to do."

"What's this prophecy that Ambrite talks about?"

Lyric looked at her brother, silently urging him to tell the story. "After Lyric was born, a wanderer told my father that she would save all centaurs from certain death and that I needed to stay close to her for her to succeed. We don't know what she will do, but her necklace is the key."

"The necklace with the Romota symbol on it?" Cret asked.

Justic nodded.

Cret pondered his words before responding. "Whatever you're destined to do, if I can help in any way, I would be honored to assist you."

Lyric sighed. "I don't know what I'm supposed to do or when. We'll continue as planned. We'll find a safe place to winter and then seek your people in the spring. We'll have plenty of time to get to know each other. If I do something that saves all centaurs between now and then, you'll be here to assist. Otherwise, you'll rejoin your families, and I'll return to mine."

"Sounds good. I think I can sleep now. Goodnight."

Cret and Tivadarios woke to the enticing smell of meat roasting over the fire.

"Oh, that smells wonderful," Tivadarios said as he stretched.

"We have plenty for everyone. Bal-air was able to find a boar last night. It's almost done," Myreia replied.

"I didn't know centaurs ate meat," Cret said.

"What did you think we ate? Grass, like a horse?" she spat.

Cret coughed. "I never thought about it. We were only fed nuts and berries back at the gathering."

Myreia hung her head. "That was the Elder's doing; she punished you for crimes you didn't commit. You two will have the first share; I'm sure you're starving."

"I could eat the whole thing; I'm so hungry," Tivadarios said, his mouth watering.

After they finished eating, they headed out, deciding to travel until midday, rest, and continue after dark. They planned to switch to a nocturnal travel schedule until they found a suitable place to stop for the winter and store provisions.

They continued this pattern for several days before spotting large wolf tracks in the freshly fallen snow.

Simandro growled at the tracks. "The monsters are lurking in these shadows."

"I haven't seen their kind in ages," Bal-air replied.

"How many?" Peleros asked.

"I see at least five," Simandro said.

"What are these monsters you speak of?" Cret asked.

"Large wolves. Intelligent, cunning, and devious. We've been at war with their kind for as long as any centaur can remember."

"Can we avoid this pack?"

"Let us hope so."

They changed course, heading slightly south to steer clear of the wolves.

After a few more nights of travel, they found themselves pursued by the monsters every night. The howls echoed eerily close, pressing in on them. The wolves slept during the day, allowing the weary travelers to continue until midday, but each night, the wolves were right on their heels. It felt as if the creatures were deliberately driving them ever southward.

Cret and Tivadarios rode with the centaurs at night. With their superior night vision, the centaurs could travel swiftly without stumbling. The horses also fared better at night, without their riders second-guessing their footfalls. Each male centaur took a shift carrying the two humans while Lyric and Myreia scouted the best trails for them to follow.

"I don't know how much longer we can keep this up," Tivadarios said after dismounting at midday. "I know you're all as tired as I am."

"We have to keep going; we don't have enough numbers to fight what's behind us," Justic replied.

"It's growing colder by the day, and game is getting scarcer. We must stop and store enough food, or we'll surely starve before spring."

"You're right, young one," Ambrite said. "We need to find a place to make a stand. Let's hope we discover a suitable location in the next few days. If we continue down this path much longer, we may never find your people again."

"I've been thinking about that. As long as we can reach a town that knows the way to Atlantis, we'll meet up with our families there. I'd prefer to travel with them so they know I'm alright, but I'll be fine as long as I see them again," Cret reflected.

"You are wise beyond your years, Cret. I'm glad to know you," Ambrite replied.

# ∞ 23 ∞
## WINTER

GREISH limped through the trees, searching for tracks—horse, dog, or man. Finally, he stumbled across his horse and sighed with relief. At least his foot travel was over. The horse nickered a greeting, tossing its head slightly and trying to move toward him, but its reins had become tangled in a bush. Greish untied the reins and led the horse to a small pool of water.

"You must have been here a while. Sorry about that, boy. When we find that traitor, he will pay for everything he's done. Come on; we need to find Kayson and make sure Andonis and Neiaphi are okay." He mounted and rode in the direction where he had last seen Andonis and Neiaphi.

Greish slowed his horse when he heard a snort ahead. Dismounting, he walked stealthily toward the sound. It was Andonis's horse, its reins caught around its front legs. He didn't see any other horses or hear anything else. Quietly and slowly, he approached the frightened animal.

"Easy, boy, easy now. It's going to be okay." He held his hand up and inched closer. The horse snorted and shook its head. Greish moved his hand to the horse's head and quickly grasped the bridle near the bit.

The chestnut stallion jerked his head with a shriek but relaxed as Greish's grip remained steady. "There you go; everything's okay. Where's your rider, boy?" He stroked the horse's nose and then untangled its legs.

After remounting, Greish quickly spotted three sets of horse tracks, which merged into two, but there were no dog tracks. He searched the area for any sign of Cypress or Andonis but found nothing indicating wrongdoing. Deciding to follow the trail back, he hoped to piece together what had happened.

He traveled for the rest of the day before stumbling upon a campfire and tracks belonging to three horses and two people—one male and one female. He searched the immediate area for any sign of Cypress and Andonis.

"Well," he sighed, "let's camp here tonight and start fresh in the morning, boys," he addressed the horses, "What do you say?"

As soon as there was enough light to make out the tracks, Greish set off. He followed them back to a small clearing, where he found Andonis's and Cypress's prints. Greish surveyed the area, piecing the scene back together.

"Three horses and a dog entered and stopped," he muttered to himself. "Everyone dismounted, and one headed into the woods—looks like Kayson. Neiaphi walked over here with Cypress and sat down. Andonis went toward the river, but then rushed back and continued after Kayson." He tied both horses to a tree, unsheathed his sword, and followed Andonis's tracks into the trees.

"Kayson and Andonis entered, but only Kayson exited." He growled and quickened his pace. Reaching a large rock outcropping, he noticed the tracks disappeared at its base. He scaled the side to the top. "There appears to have been a struggle up here. But what happened?"

He scanned the area but found nothing. Sighing, he looked down at the ground. "What happened down there?" Climbing back down, he stood in the middle of an impression on the ground and knelt to examine it. Broken twigs and blood scattered the earth. "ANDONIS! ANDONIS!" he yelled, desperation lacing his voice. "CYPRESS! ANDONIS!"

"Greish, is that you?" a weak voice called out.

"Andonis, where are you?" Anxiety laced his voice.

"Over here!" A rock flew from his left. Greish rushed toward the bushes and found Andonis huddled underneath. He reached in and helped Andonis out.

"What happened?" But before Andonis could answer, a growling, snarling dog knocked Greish off his feet.

"Cypress! Down!" he commanded. The dog instantly stopped, sitting with a whimper. "Glad to see you again, too."

"I'm so relieved to see you. Kayson said wolves ambushed you, that you and Nyx were killed."

Greish growled, "We didn't encounter any wolves. Kayson claimed he spotted something in a ravine; when I leaned over to look, he pushed me. Nyx probably attacked him. Shortly after I landed in the water, I heard another splash, but nothing surfaced. I'll find Kayson, and he'll pay."

Andonis bolted upright. "How long have I been here? Did you find Neiaphi?"

Greish handed him a waterskin. Andonis gratefully accepted it, drinking deeply. "I'm not sure how long I've been separated from you all," Greish replied, shaking his head. "Your tracks appear to be a day or so old."

"Kayson and Neiaphi's tracks headed east and then turned north. They took your horse with them for a while, but let it go. I found him," Greish said urgently. "Come on; we must get on their trail before the weather erases it. What are your injuries?"

"I twisted my knee and smacked my head when I fell, but I'll be okay."

Greish held out a hand, and Andonis grabbed his wrist, standing on shaking legs.

"Come on, Cypress, let's go." Andonis leaned heavily on Greish, using him as a crutch.

Once back at the horses, Greish assisted Andonis in mounting his steed. They rode until the tracks faded away beneath them.

For three days, Greish and Andonis pursued Kayson and Neiaphi. By the night of the second day, Andonis finally felt well enough to ride hard for the first time since the accident.

On the evening of the third day, a storm rolled in. They arranged their bedrolls into a makeshift tent to shield themselves from the biting wind, snow, and sleet. When they awoke, the ground was coated with two inches of pure white snow. Greish stared in astonishment. "I've never seen so much snow before."

Andonis patted him on the back. "We'll see more before winter. But now we have a problem."

"No tracks," Greish finished for him.

"If we're lucky enough to get close, we should be able to track them easily, but…" He trailed off.

"I say we keep heading in the direction we last knew they were going."

Andonis nodded. "Agreed."

Kayson urged Neiaphi onward, riding from sunrise until well past sunset each day.

"Where are you taking me?" she asked, every few hours, but received no answer.

"What are your plans for me? I deserve to know."

Again, silence met her inquiry, prompting her to huff in frustration.

Neiaphi tucked her hands under her cloak, hunching her shoulders as if shivering from the cold. She flexed her wrists and fingers, working them back and forth in an effort to loosen her bindings. Today, she had managed to create a bit of wiggle room, and with a stroke of luck, she hoped to free her hands before they stopped for the night.

Nexus stumbled once more over an unseen rock or log. Neiaphi squinted into the darkness, straining to guide her around the debris on the ground. Suddenly, she faltered again, and she fell to her knees. Neiaphi cried out, startled by the jarring motion. With a quick reflex, she clutched Nexus's mane, managing to stay mounted despite the rough tumble.

"Quit fooling around back there!" Kayson snapped.

"I didn't do anything," she shot back. "We can't see! Nexus is going to break her neck—and mine along with it. Where are you in such a hurry to get to? No one is following us; you made sure of that."

Kayson halted abruptly, causing Nexus to bump into his horse. "What do you mean, I made sure of it?"

"Nothing," Neiaphi replied, her voice flat.

"NO! What are you saying? I told you what happened to Greish and Andonis!" he yelled, frustration lacing his words.

Neiaphi fell silent, refusing to respond.

Kayson dismounted and seized Neiaphi, yanking her off Nexus and tossing her to the ground. "Don't move from that spot," he growled. He led both horses a short distance away and tied them to a tree.

As the small fire crackled, Kayson skinned a rabbit he had caught earlier in the day. Neiaphi's mouth watered at the scent wafting from the cooking meat. The dried rations Greish had provided ran out two days ago. After eating his fill of the rabbit, Kayson tossed the remainder and a sleeping roll into her lap.

"Get some sleep; we'll be moving out again soon." Neiaphi glared at him, unsure if he could see her expression in the meager light of the campfire. Despite her defiance, she was fast asleep within moments of curling up and closing her eyes.

Neiaphi jolted awake, her wrists throbbing as Kayson tightened the ropes. He scowled down at her, his voice soft yet menacing. "Can't have my bride-to-be getting any foolish ideas in that pretty little head of yours."

"I am not going to marry you," Neiaphi spat.

"You have no choice, my dear," Kayson sneered. "You're of marrying age, unwed, and no longer promised to anyone."

"I am still promised, you fool."

"To whom? A dead man?" He scoffed. "I think not."

"Aristas asked for me even before Andonis did," Neiaphi stated firmly. "The moment I see my father, he'll know I choose Aristas—and that I would never choose you."

Kayson shook his head as he moved closer to the fire. "I don't think so."

"What do you mean?" Neiaphi demanded. "My father would never allow me to marry you."

Kayson gave her a sly smile. "I know."

Her eyes narrowed, words dripping with disdain. "Then enlighten me."

Kayson's smile widened. "I have no intention of asking your father. Where I'm taking you, my dear, you'll never see your family again. The only way to keep some fat old man from claiming you in the next village is if we're already married. In fact, maybe I'll say we are now and start enjoying the benefits of married life."

Neiaphi's hands flew to her mouth as a sob escaped her lips.

"Enough!" he snapped. "I saw the look in your eyes when we first met. You wanted me then, and now there's no one here for you to keep up this act of disinterest."

He stalked over with a slow, confident swagger, stopping just inches from her. Hovering above with his hands on his hips, he looked down at Neiaphi, who curled into a ball, her face stricken with terror as she tried to edge back. "Well, I know what I saw," he said, a scowl darkening his expression. "Your thoughts are just… clouded. In time, you'll accept my decision."

"All women do; it's your nature to do as your man says. That's how the world works. Get up; it's time to move on."

Neiaphi rose slowly, gathering her sleeping roll and trudging over to Nexus. The horse nickered softly, nudging her chest. She leaned close, whispering, "I know, girl, you're tired too. We'll rest soon… but first, we need to find a way out of this."

Snow fell gently throughout the day, the slight warmth a small mercy against the previous day's biting wind. Yet by midday, the accumulating snow on Neiaphi's cloak began to soak through, seeping a bone-deep chill. She pressed on, focusing on the slow, deliberate movement of her wrists, working them back and forth to loosen the ropes that bound her.

Kayson urged them forward, pressing on into the dim, fading light. In the distance, Neiaphi noticed the faint outline of a small hut nestled in a valley beside a quiet stream. There was no trace of firelight or smoke rising from it. Kayson halted, scanning the forest and ground for any fresh tracks, before dismounting and tying Nexus to a nearby tree. He extended his hand sharply. "Give me your hands." Neiaphi kept her gaze fixed on the hut, but his voice cut through, harder this time. "Now!" he growled.

Neiaphi's gaze dropped slowly, her glare sharp, but she reluctantly complied. Kayson looped another rope around her wrists and tied her securely to the tree. "Stay here!" he snarled. She watched as he crept toward the hut, his movements tense, head swiveling as his eyes darted around the clearing. Sword in hand, he peered through a small window, then circled the hut, vanishing from her view.

A few moments later, Kayson reappeared, standing tall and alert. He hurried to her and quickly untied the ropes binding her to the tree. "Get down," he ordered, his voice sharp. Neiaphi hesitated, scanning her surroundings with wide eyes, nerves twisting in her stomach.

"Is it safe? Do you think they'll be back?"

Kayson shrugged, his gaze darting around. "No one's been here in a few seasons—except for rats." Neiaphi shuddered at the thought, her imagination running wild with images of the filthy creatures scurrying about.

Kayson grabbed the rope tied to her wrist and secured her to the hut before leading the horses to a small corral with a lean-to shelter. Once he settled them in, he vanished into the forest, only to return moments later with an armful of wood.

That night was a welcome respite, sheltered from the wind and frost, with a warm crackling fire. It would have been perfect if only Andonis and Greish were back and there was something to eat. Neiaphi hunched her shoulders, staring into the flames, lost in thought.

"I'll go hunting tomorrow," he said, nodding as he surveyed the hut. "I think this is a great place for us to stop for the winter. We have shelter and fresh water, and no one should stumble upon us."

Neiaphi kept her gaze downcast, lost in thought, as tears slid slowly down her cheeks.

"Why are you tormenting yourself?"

She lifted her gaze slightly, looking at him through her glistening eyelashes.

"You will answer me when I ask you a question. Do me a favor and cooperate; it'll make your life easier and mine more pleasant. Just like all obedient women, you'll find your life pleasurable and carefree."

"Doing as you're told and being obedient is easier than you think; just try it. You might even like it." He winked at her. She glared back but remained silent. "Fine, be that way. You'll come around eventually. I just hope it doesn't take all winter."

Kayson left early the following day, tying Neiaphi to the central pole of the hut. "I won't be far, and I'll be keeping an eye on you. Don't try anything foolish; you won't like the consequences. And make sure to clean this place up while I'm gone." She glared at him but remained silent.

He stormed out of the hut and slammed the door. Neiaphi glanced around the tiny space, wrinkling her nose at the dust and filth. She walked to her bedroll, sat down, leaned against the wall, and folded her arms across her chest.

Several hours later, Kayson returned with three rabbits, two squirrels, a handful of raspberries, and a couple of strange-looking roots. He tossed the rabbits and squirrels into her lap. "Clean these and cook them." Startled, Neiaphi jumped up, knocking the bloody animals to the ground.

"You do it!" she spat.

Kayson strode over, slapping her across the cheek with the back of his hand. "Don't speak to me in that tone!" he growled. "Now clean those before they spoil."

Neiaphi lowered her voice, but it still dripped with disdain. "I don't know how."

"My, how you've been spoiled. You've had servants your whole life, haven't you? It must have truly been hard traveling for so long. I bet you've never had a hard day in your life until now."

He waited for a reply, but Neiaphi merely glared at him with her chin raised. Frustrated, he snatched up the animals. "Fine; I'll be back with processed meat. I hope you can figure out how to cook them." With that, he stormed out of the hut.

Neiaphi gathered the raspberries and the curious roots, then walked the short distance to the fire pit, scanning her surroundings for something to cook with. She spotted a dented pot and a couple of bowls. After retrieving her clean shirt from the bedroll, she wiped the pot and bowls as best as she could.

Kayson returned with the cleaned meat and a bucket of water, then quickly came back with an armful of wood. In no time, a fire crackled to life in the pit. Neiaphi poured some water into the pot and bowls, placing them over the flames to boil. "What are you doing?" he asked.

"I'm cleaning these," Neiaphi replied.

"You're wasting water."

"I refuse to eat from bowls that have been sitting here for who knows how long, with who knows what crawling in them. Now, I need a knife."

"Whatever for?" he asked.

"To slice the rabbits and chop up this root you brought. It's edible, right?"

"Of course! I wouldn't go through all this trouble just to poison you. It's called celeriac. I will slice it for you."

"Don't trust me not to cut myself," she sneered.

"I don't trust you not to cut me, my dear."

While he worked, she skewered the squirrels onto a stick and positioned them over the fire to cook. She wiped out the bowls and refilled them with water and raspberries to steep, then added the rabbit and celeriac to the pot to make a soup.

"If only we had some mint, the tea would be better," she muttered to herself.

They ate in silence. Neiaphi retired early, still exhausted from their recent journey.

Andonis and Greish pressed on, hoping they were heading in the direction Kayson had taken Neiaphi. All signs of their trail had vanished with the snowfall, and their spirits were beginning to wane.

Finally, they reached a small, quiet village. Dismounting their horses, they made their way to the town square, relieved to find a modest inn with an adjacent stable. After settling their horses, they stepped into the cozy inn, where the aroma of roasted meat and the warmth of twin fireplaces on either side of the room greeted them.

"Good day to you, gentlemen! How can I be of service?" asked a plump woman with rosy cheeks.

"Good day, ma'am. We're looking for two people and hope they passed this way," Andonis replied.

"Who might you be looking for?" she asked.

"A man and a woman," Greish replied. "The man is about my height, with brown hair. The woman is yay high," he added, holding his hand to indicate Neiaphi's height, "with light brown hair and blue eyes."

She shook her head. "Haven't seen them. But can I offer you a place to rest for the night?"

"That would be wonderful. And two servings of whatever that delightful smell is," Andonis replied.

The woman smiled broadly and gestured to a table near one of the fireplaces.

Both men removed their cloaks and sat down heavily with a sigh. Cypress, their loyal hound, settled himself closer to the fire with a huff.

A moment later, the woman returned, carrying two large bowls of stew, a plate of cheese and bread, and two cups of wine. She tossed a large, meaty bone to Cypress, who caught it eagerly. "Thank you," they both said before diving into their food.

Once they'd finished, Andonis asked, "Do you think we got ahead of them?"

Greish shook his head. "No, they must have turned off somewhere."

"Let's wait out this storm, then fan out, backtrack a bit, and see if we can pick up their trail."

Greish nodded grimly.

# ∞ 24 ∞

## CRASH

SEVERAL exhausting nights later, Cret, Tivadarios, and the centaurs waded through a small river, planning to stop for the night on the other side. As they moved halfway through, a fireball streaked across the sky, illuminating the entire forest. With a deafening roar, the ground shuddered, sending sound crashing into the trees ahead. The centaurs ducked underwater for cover, while the horses screamed in fright.

"Come on, Darios! Let's see if they need help!" Cret shouted over the noise. Tivadarios nodded and hurried after him.

"Wait! Come back!" one of the centaurs called after them.

Cret rushed ahead, recognizing the shape—a spacecraft. But who was piloting it, and why had they come? The ship didn't appear too badly damaged; it looked like a cargo vessel of some kind. Suddenly, the side door chimed and began to open slowly. Cret and Darios slowed their pace and dismounted. A figure emerged from the doorway, obscured by smoke and blinking lights, making it impossible to discern what type of being it was.

Cret breathed a sigh of relief as a man, dressed in clothing similar to that of the crew from the ship that had brought them here, slowly descended the ramp. Cret raised his hand in greeting, but the man stopped short, retreating a few steps before hesitating.

"It's okay. We won't harm you. Are you from Romota?" Cret asked.

The man's expression went slack. "How do you know that name?"

"It's a story I'd be glad to share once we set up camp. Will you join us? Is anyone else with you?"

"I'm all alone now," he replied softly.

Three men and the centaurs sat quietly around a sizable crackling fire near the fallen ship. Ambrite and Simandro walked around the camp, surveying their surroundings.

"I don't like this," Simandro said. "We should keep moving. The monsters will surely surround us and ambush us." Ambrite nodded in agreement.

"I think we need to stay here and find out what happened to our new friend," Cret said, gesturing to the pilot.

"M-m-monsters?" the pilot stammered.

"Just large wolves—nothing more," Tivadarios reassured him.

Myreia huffed as she pulled an arrow from her quiver, checking the sharpness of the stone tip. The pilot's eyes darted nervously toward the dark woods.

"Be at ease," Cret said. "My name is Cret; this is Tivadarios, Ambrite, Justic, Lyric, Simandro, Myreia, Bal-air, and Peleros." Each centaur nodded in acknowledgment as their names were spoken.

"My name is Pelagios. Where are you from, and how do you know where I'm from?"

Cret launched into their story, keeping it brief and focused on the essentials. So much had happened to them in their short time on Earth that by the time he finished, the moon was no longer visible.

Pelagios nodded. "I've heard a tale of a doomed ship with many souls lost in space, never to be heard from again. It must have been you and your group." He shook his head. "Why did they say you were lost when you clearly made it here?"

"Like I said, the Society intercepted our message and changed our drop point. When the ship returned, they must have learned the truth. Instead of searching for us, they simply declared us lost." Cret shook his head and ran his fingers through his hair. "To our families left behind, I suppose 'gone' means just that. We can't return."

Pelagios looked at him, puzzled. "Why not?"

"In the time it took us to get here and how long we've been here, over ten years have already passed on Romota, maybe more. There won't be anyone left to return to," Tivadarios explained.

"Who told you that?"

"The King gave a letter to Addident, stating we would never return."

Pelagios's jaw dropped. "The King lied to you! Why would he lie?"

"What do you mean?"

"The trip here for large cargo vessels like yours is five years in stasis. Ships like mine make it in less than one."

"Okay, but I don't see the lie yet. Romota and Earth age at different rates. For every year we're here, five pass on Romota."

"That's not true. I've made three trips here in the past decade, and I even stayed for an entire year once.

"Other than my age slowing while in stasis, I haven't noticed any difference between my family and me. You've been gone for less than six years so far, and that's all the time that has passed here and back home."

Cret and Tivadarios were speechless. Finally, Cret found his voice. "I can't believe the King did this to us just to eliminate a rival for the throne—one who doesn't even have a son."

Pelagios nodded in agreement. "The capital held a grand funeral and celebration of life for all of you just before I left. It was a week-long holiday. Your names have been recorded in the Hall of Heroes."

"That's little consolation for stranding us here. This is no life to live, especially given the hardships we've faced and will continue to face on this harsh, technology-free planet," Tivadarios said with disdain.

"We'll survive and thrive on this planet, my friend," Cret replied.

"What if I don't want to? I'm sure others would wish to return home."

"To what? We have more opportunities here, and these people need our help and knowledge," Cret argued. Tivadarios thought for a moment before nodding.

"Come, since we're stopping for the night, we all require rest. We'll keep watch in pairs tonight."

"Everyone is welcome inside my ship. No one and nothing can get in once the doors are shut."

The centaurs exchanged glances before reluctantly agreeing. Pelagios smiled broadly and led them to his ship. Cret, Tivadarios, their horses, and Lyric, stepped onto the ramp without hesitation. The other centaurs hesitated, staring at the strange surface. Ambrite placed a hoof on it and flinched at the metallic ring it produced.

"It's okay. It won't bite you," Lyric called with a chuckle.

Justic shot his sister a glare, quickly mounted the ramp, and entered the ship.

Simandro was the last to step inside. He glanced around the strange interior and snarled. "I do not like this."

"We'll be safer in here from the wolves and the elements," Cret remarked.

"Hmm, I don't think they'll fit through the doorways," Pelagios said, eyeing the centaurs' imposing size.

"We'll sleep in this cave area, then," Ambrite replied.

"In the cargo hold? That won't be comfortable," Pelagios frowned.

"It's no different from a cave and warmer than sleeping under a tree. We'll be fine for the night."

"Alright, I'll show you two to some crew quarters." He nodded to Cret and Tivadarios.

"Goodnight, friends. See you in the morning," Cret said, bidding them goodnight.

Cret found it difficult to sleep on the crew cots. He chuckled to himself; they felt too soft, whereas he once thought they were too hard.

He made his way through the ship, and eventually found the command deck. Pelagios was already there, studying the many gauges on the control panel.

"Mind some company?" Cret asked, clearing his throat.

"Not at all. Do you know anything about cargo ships?"

Cret shook his head. "No, sorry, but I don't mind taking a look." Pelagios gestured for him to approach.

"So, what happened to your ship? What were you carrying?"

"We transport ore and lumber from here to Romota. It was a strange night; we had just arrived in orbit and were planning a few days of shore leave on the moon."

"The moon?"

"Oh yes. A great place to stop—some of the best food around." He cleared his throat. "Well, we were asking for permission to disembark when we were told to continue to Earth. We complied, though gloomily."

"When making our final approach, we received new instructions to offload waste first, but not at our regular station. They told us to come to this side of the planet. When we landed at the new station, men in cloaks were waiting for us as we disembarked. I'm always the last one to leave the ship; it was my job to start the waste transfer.

"After completing it, I went to the cargo hold and looked out. It was horrifying; three of my crew were dead on the ground, and two men were holding my Captain. A third man approached him and stabbed him in the stomach. He sagged in their arms, and then they let him collapse to the ground. A man with a sword decapitated him..." Pelagios's eyes were glazed over, and his voice cracked.

"I rushed back up and initiated the preflight. I sealed the cargo hold and took off as quickly as I could. I didn't realize they'd attached grapples to the ship, and the waste lines were still connected. I broke free and shot into the sky. Someone must have been trying to disable the engines when we landed; I managed to fly for a while before the engine caught fire, forcing me to land here."

"We saw the fire," Cret said.

Pelagios nodded. "Then you found me."

"What are your goals now?"

"Get the ship flying again and make it to another station for deeper repairs, I guess."

"The Society keeps intercepting our communications. I'll see how I can help you get this ship operational. But I fear any station in this area will be controlled by the Society."

"Any suggestions?"

"I think you should come with us to Atlantis. They'll know what to do."

"What about my ship? I can't leave it here," he said, horrified.

"Agreed. If we can get it flying, we'll take it as close to Atlantis as possible and hide it until we figure out where you can get it repaired for the trip home."

"What if we can't get it flying?"

"We'll have to cover it here, but let's not dwell on that."

"I suppose this is as good a spot to stop as any. We'll have more than adequate shelter and protection," Ambrite said to Cret.

"That's what I was thinking, too. We can winter here, and if Tivadarios and I can help Pelagios with the repairs, we should be able to continue in the spring and reach Atlantis with ease." Ambrite discussed it with the other centaurs, and everyone agreed it was the best option they had.

Tivadarios rummaged through the ship, finding dozens of blankets and portable heating units to make the cargo hold more comfortable for the centaurs.

Meanwhile, Peleros and Myreia spent several days hunting and scouting the area for any nearby two-legged settlements.

Daily routines began to take shape, fostering a growing sense of camaraderie among the group.

"I've found them; they're up ahead near some sort of strange structure," the scout reported.

"What do you mean, 'strange structure'?" Hepluosis sneered.

"I don't know, two-leg. I've never seen anything like it before," the scout shot back, his expression defiant.

"Show me!" Hepluosis demanded.

The scout glanced at his leader, who nodded. "Show him. Let's see if he knows what it is."

The scout led the three centaurs and two humans on horseback into the woods. After some time, they slowed as they approached a large scorched patch of land. They followed the path until they finally came across the source of the scar on the ground.

"Well, I didn't expect to see that!" Hepluosis exclaimed.

"What is it?" one of the centaurs whispered.

"It's a cargo ship." When the centaurs exchanged puzzled looks, he added, "It flies through space between planets."

"Can it take us back to Romota?"

"If it isn't broken, yes. You said they're staying inside it?"

"Yes, they're using it like a cave."

"Looks like they're planning to winter here. We'll attack tonight." Everyone nodded in agreement. They retreated into the shadows of the dark forest to wait for nightfall.

As darkness fell, night creatures stirred to life. Cret, Tivadarios, and Pelagios sat around the fire, engaged in mild conversation. Two centaurs patrolled the perimeter of the downed craft, while the other three hunted and foraged nearby.

Unbeknownst to them, two humans and four centaurs watched from the cover of the trees, waiting for the right moment to strike.

"When do we attack?" Hepluosis whispered.

"When they're all present," the leader hissed.

One of the hunting centaurs returned with a large deer, and moments later, the other two returned with their kills.

"Now?" Hepluosis breathed.

The leader raised a hand, signaling for silence.

He scanned the eager faces around him, all waiting for his command. His gaze shifted back to the craft, where the centaurs sat in a small group, processing their catch while the three humans conversed.

He slowly lowered his hand, signaling his centaurs to creep forward. Suddenly, the quiet of the night shattered with a chorus of howls. His group froze in place; their prey tensed in response. Growls and heavy, raspy breathing echoed from the shadows.

He motioned for his group to back away slowly; the wolves seemed more interested in the centaurs than in them.

A low growl escaped his gritted teeth as his prey retreated to their craft, closing the doors just as the wolves stepped into the firelight.

"Monsters! We need to flee!" one of his centaurs whispered urgently.

The monsters circled the craft, one of them striding toward the fire to lift its leg over it, causing the flames to hiss and crackle. The beast let out a throaty growl that almost sounded like a laugh. One of the females glanced at him and shook her head, a look of amusement in her eyes.

Crack!

One of his group stepped on a small twig, which sounded like a log in the still air. The monsters whirled around, sniffing and growling as they caught the scent.

"RUN!" the leader yelled urgently.

Everyone took off as fast as they could, racing toward the river. Monsters were slowed by water; it wouldn't stop them, but it would provide the much-needed distance between them and the death that now hunted them.

# ∞ 25 ∞
# THE HUTS

**ANDONIS** walked into the Shabby Tree Inn that had served as his home for the past few days. Each day, he and Greish scoured the woods for any sign of Kayson or Neiaphi. He approached their usual table and sat down heavily.

Roslyn spotted him and quickly brought over a few slices of roast boar, a large piece of bread, and an assortment of boiled roots. She smiled broadly before departing.

He stared at his food but made no move to eat. Greish sat down next to him and grunted in greeting. Andonis nodded in response. Roslyn appeared a moment later with more food.

"I think we should winter here," Greish said. "I've been talking to others and learned that there are about a dozen scattered hunting huts in this area.

"During the fall, the waterfowl and deer migrate through here in large numbers, attracting many seasonal hunters. A trader mentioned he'll have a map of their locations for me when he returns in a moon cycle. We can keep searching and speak to any travelers we meet. I'm sure Kayson found one of those huts and is bedding down for the winter."

Andonis grimaced at Greish's choice of words and then nodded in agreement. "We'll need to find work then," Andonis said grimly.

"I've secured us night watch six nights a week."

"What would I do without you?" Andonis asked, a hint of gratitude in his voice.

"You'd be running around the forest like a chicken with its head cut off, screaming Neiaphi's name until you were hoarse."

Andonis chuckled. "Yeah, probably." He raked his hands through his hair. "I just hope he's keeping his hands off her."

"I'm sure she's fine. I get the feeling he really likes her. I don't think he would harm her."

"I'm just afraid of how much he likes her."

Greish grimaced. "I'm going to retire early. We start our watch tomorrow at dusk." Andonis nodded. Greish stood and patted him on the shoulder before heading out.

Cypress looked up, and Greish motioned for him to stay. The dog laid his head back down.

"What do you think, Cypress? Do you think she's okay?" Cypress whined softly. "Yeah, I miss her too. Come on, boy."

Andonis and Greish settled into a monotonous routine. They were on watch from dusk to dawn. Greish would head in for a few hours of sleep while Andonis patrolled the surrounding houses to see if anyone had noticed anything suspicious. When he returned, he would wake Greish, who would then question the shop owners and traders while Andonis rested for a few hours. As dusk fell, the whole process would begin anew. On their nights off, they ventured further from the village.

Finally, the moon cycle passed, and the trader returned with the map they had requested. They met at the Inn, at their customary table, to plan their route for the next night off.

"I say we hit these first," Greish said, pointing to a cluster of five huts located furthest from the village to the southwest.

Andonis nodded. "We'll tackle the farthest ones first and work our way back. We can search these five and then those three."

"Agreed. The day after next, we'll head out. I'll let the Governor know we might not return."

Neiaphi spent her days and nights tethered to the center pole of the hut. The rope around her ankle dug painfully into her skin. Kayson checked the cord several times a day, ensuring it was tight and secure, but he never commented on the wound.

On the second day in the hut, she attempted to loosen the rope and was met with a slap across the face, followed by two days without food.

He told her she was lucky he was a kind and caring person; otherwise, he would have beaten her unconscious for her defiance. After that, she didn't try to loosen the rope again.

Her only expectation seemed to be cooking for Kayson whenever he managed to find something for them to eat, and keeping their home clean. He would eat his fill and allow her to have whatever was left, if anything remained. When she questioned him, he reminded her that he was the provider and insisted he couldn't share anything unless he had full strength.

On the fourteenth day, he took her outside and led her down to the stream. Neiaphi stopped at the edge, inhaling deeply as she stretched her back and raised her hands to the sky. Despite the cold air and the snow-covered ground, the warmth of the sun on her face felt wonderful.

She sat down and dangled her legs in the stream, gasping slightly as the frigid water made contact with her skin and the growing, festering wound on her bound ankle. Without letting Kayson see, she carefully rinsed the dried blood from her skin, allowing the icy water to numb the pulsing pain.

"You should fully submerge," he said with a smirk.

She glared at him, refusing to respond.

"I'm serious. A full bath in the icy water is refreshing. I bathed earlier and feel invigorated." A sly smile crossed his lips.

"I will not undress in front of you." She scowled at him, hate seething in her eyes.

"Fine, remain dirty," Kayson shot back.

Neiaphi slowly stood and walked back to the hut with a slight limp.

"Stop trying to elicit sympathy from me. That limping will only earn you an empty stomach and sore ribs."

She stiffened her back and slowed her pace, attempting to minimize the limp, but she winced with each step.

"This place is looking shabby again. Be a dear and tidy up while I'm gone," he said with a broad smile before leaving to check his trap lines.

Neiaphi walked to the window to ensure he had left the clearing. Once he was out of sight, she approached the dying fire and added a few logs, stoking the flames. Then, she moved the cooking pot filled with water over the fire.

Limping slowly around the hut, she tidied up as best she could. She refolded the sleeping rolls, restacked the firewood pile, and smoothed the dirt floor with a pine bough. When the water began to steam, she partially undressed and washed herself as best as she could. She repeated this routine every day when she was certain Kayson was gone for a while. After rinsing her washcloth in the water, she let it come to a boil again; Kayson would expect tea when he returned. A small smile curled the corner of her lips as the water started to boil.

The sky darkened, and Kayson still had not returned. She wiped her eyes again; some days, the tears wouldn't come, while on others, they seemed never-ending.

At some point, she drifted off to sleep beside the crackling fire.

Bang...

The door swung open, and Kayson strode in. Neiaphi jumped at the sudden break in silence. He motioned with his head behind him, and she looked outside to see a large deer. Sighing, she stood, favoring her bound ankle; she knew what he expected her to do.

She grabbed the bone knife he had made for her, checking its edge absentmindedly as she shuffled out of the cabin. The blade barely sliced through the meat of the deer.

He had taught her how to gut and skin the deer, and now he expected her to do it every time, regardless of the hour, day, or night.

Kayson checked her bindings, then collapsed onto his bedroll, quickly snoring loudly.

Neiaphi finished with the deer just as the sun peeked above the treetops. After dragging the meat inside, she hung the strips on the drying lines throughout the hut and placed a large steak near the fire on a hot rock. She left the hide outside to dry; tanning was the only task Kayson insisted on handling himself.

After cleaning up, she collapsed onto her bedroll. Just as her eyes closed, Kayson kicked her feet.

"Stop lazing about. You're going to burn my breakfast."

She moaned but complied. Shuffling over to the fire, she flipped his steak and sat down heavily beside it.

"You know, if you started acting like a wife instead of a disgruntled slave, I might consider getting you some help around here," he smirked. Neiaphi kept her eyes downcast, glaring at a rock near the fire.

"Fine. Give me my food," he snapped.

He ate in silence, and when he finished, he left the hut without a word. Neiaphi quickly found her bedroll again and fell into a deep, troubled sleep.

Weeks blurred together in a monotonous routine.

"Nothing but deserted huts. Where should we look tomorrow?" Andonis asked, huddling around a small fire with Greish as they studied the trader's map.

Greish marked a large X over the huts they had searched with a piece of charcoal. "Hmm… I think we should try these three next."

Andonis nodded in agreement.

"I hope we don't search every hut and still not find them."

"I'm sure they found a place to shelter. No one in any direction has seen them," Greish reassured him.

"What if they were caught out in the storm and never found shelter?"

"Don't think like that. We will find them my friend, and we will make sure he pays for what he has done," Greish said sternly.

Four days later, Andonis and Greish came up empty-handed once again.

Greish started a fire while Andonis gathered more wood. When he approached the fire, he threw the wood down with a thud, making Greish jump in surprise.

"Whoa, calm down."

"Sorry, I'm just so frustrated," Andonis scowled.

"I know, I know. We'll find her," Greish reassured him.

"I don't think so. I've been thinking—what if those wolves found them? With the storm, we'll never find any sign of them. This is hopeless." He sank down beside the fire.

"So… what do you want to do? Give up and go back to tell her parents that all their kids are gone?" Greish replied, his voice laced with anger.

Andonis looked at him, shock and grief etched on his face.

"I'm sorry. I'm frustrated too," Greish said, lowering his voice.

"I know, and I'm sorry. No, we have to keep looking. I need to find some sort of sign, good or bad."

Greish patted him on the shoulder. "I still feel in my gut that we'll find her safe and sound."

"I hope so."

They were on the move as soon as it was light enough to see. They reached the first hut before the sun fully crested the horizon—empty, like all the others.

By midday, they neared a stream marked on the map. According to the map, a string of huts lined the creek. The first two they checked were vacant.

Suddenly, Cypress yipped once. Greish turned to see what he had found. Rushing over, he discovered a rabbit caught in a snare.

"Andonis, over here!"

Andonis spurred his horse over to him.

"Do you think the snare is fresh? Maybe someone set it when they were here in the fall," Andonis said.

"It looks fresh and is well-placed. I don't think it could have survived that storm and then last another two months without being tripped. Let's split up and move silently."

Andonis and Greish spotted a hut with smoke curling from the roof, each from opposite sides of the clearing. Using hand signals, Greish instructed Andonis to wait and watch. A conspicuous figure moved around inside.

Andonis's heart thundered in his chest as he quietly approached the lean-to at the back of the hut. Two horses were fenced in—Kayson's and Neiaphi's. His heart raced and his thoughts swirled. She's here—after months of searching, he had finally found her. She was within reach at last.

He crept around the clearing and slid up next to Greish. "Their horses are in the back."

Greish nodded grimly. "How should we proceed? What do you want to do?"

"I don't think I'm in a rational frame of mind. I'll defer to your military training," Andonis replied.

"Okay, we'll wait through the night. I'd prefer to get Neiaphi and leave without a fight. I don't want her to be injured." Andonis nodded in agreement. "Hopefully, Kayson will leave in the morning to check his trap lines. You'll rescue Neiaphi and head back to the Shabby Tree. I'll stay behind to deal with Kayson."

Andonis pursed his lips. "Are you certain you want to confront him alone?"

"What do you suggest?"

"Everything you said, but we'll take Neiaphi a short distance away. When we see Kayson approaching, you and I will move in together."

Greish shrugged. "Your call, but I think I can handle him myself."

"We've never seen him spar. Think about it—he's always respectfully declined any offers but watched us intently."

Greish's mouth dropped. "You're right. I didn't think of that. We'll do what you suggest. Can we keep Neiaphi far enough away?"

"I hope so. I just hope she won't try to interfere."

"Get some rest; I'll take the first watch."

The sun was high overhead when Kayson finally emerged from the hut, smiling and stretching his back. "I'll be back, wife. Make that wonderful stew tonight. I'm going to be hungry."

Andonis growled and began to rise, but Greish placed a hand on his shoulder to hold him back.

"Not yet; stick to the plan," he whispered. Andonis growled again but settled back down.

Kayson headed south, away from the hut and Neiaphi's liberators. Greish stood and quietly followed him for a short distance to ensure he was genuinely leaving the area. Moments later, he returned. "He's gone; let's go."

They stayed in the cover of the trees and circled back around to the lean-to before approaching the hut.

Andonis swiftly approached the door and opened it slowly. Neiaphi squeaked and quickly pulled a blanket up to cover herself. Her dirty, knotted hair shielded the left side of her face, and her eyes went wide when she saw him.

"A-Andonis… is that you?" she whispered. He hurried over to her, grabbing her and crushing her to him.

"It is you. He said he killed you. How, how, how?" she mumbled between sobs of joy. He hugged her tighter, then swung her legs up to carry her, starting to walk toward the door.

She cried out, grabbing at her leg as the rope around her ankle tightened.

Andonis stopped and set her down. "He tied you to the hut?" She nodded, pushing her hair from her face.

Andonis grabbed his knife and severed the rope, leaving a piece still attached to her ankle. He looked up at her, smiling, but the expression quickly melted into a scowl as he gently touched her cheek, feeling the dark, angry bruise surrounding her left eye.

She dropped her gaze, leaning into his hand and nuzzling it. "Come on, let's get out of here." He picked her up again, and though he couldn't tell if it was his imagination or not, she felt lighter in his arms.

"Wait, I need my bag." Neiaphi pointed to a small pack in the back of the hut. Andonis quickly retrieved it and then exited the cabin, making his way back to the lean-to. Greish had brought their horses and had tethered Kayson's horse to his. He smiled broadly when he saw them approaching, Neiaphi's face buried in Andonis's shoulder.

"Can you mount Nexus on your own?" he asked, gently placing her feet on the ground.

"I think so," she whispered. When she looked up and saw Greish, tears filled her eyes again, and she reached out for him. Limping visibly, she walked the short distance and hugged him tightly. "I'm so happy to see you."

Greish pushed her back to look at her. "Did he hurt you?" Greish asked, rage flashing across his face.

She nodded. "Later. He won't be gone long; we need to get away from here," she said, fear lacing her voice.

Andonis helped her mount, and the three of them rode north. Once deep in the woods, they stopped.

"Wh-what are we doing? We have to keep moving! He'll find us for sure here."

"We can't just run from him. We have to stop him here and now, or we'll always be looking over our shoulders," Greish said firmly.

"Oh, no. Let's just keep going. I can't lose either of you again," she pleaded, her voice trembling.

Andonis placed his hand over hers. "This is how it has to be. Trust us—neither of us is going anywhere without you." She nodded, but tears streamed down her cheeks.

Greish hurried to the hut and gathered as much dried meat as he could carry. Just as he returned, a chilling howl echoed through the silent forest. Neiaphi's eyes widened in alarm, and she instinctively grasped the reins, preparing to flee.

"Stay calm; that's just Kayson approaching," Andonis said firmly. "Stay here, no matter what." Neiaphi nodded, but her fear only deepened. He patted her leg reassuringly before jogging off to catch up with Greish.

Kayson froze at the sound of the howl piercing the silence. He glanced around, unease settling in—too close for comfort. That howl sounded familiar. Not spotting any movement, he headed toward the hut and flung the door open with a loud crack, relishing the way it kept Neiaphi on her toes. But she was gone. Spinning around, he returned to the clearing to find Andonis and Greish standing there, swords drawn. Cypress joined them, growling menacingly with his hackles raised. Kayson dashed to the lean-to, determined to retrieve the sword he had hidden away.

His challengers followed him cautiously.

"Where is she?" Kayson snarled, brandishing his sword.

"Safe," Andonis shot back. "What were your intentions?"

"Like you don't know. You've seen her. What man wouldn't want her? She's my wife now, and I'm the envy of every man."

"You won't be leaving here alive, my friend. You'll never lay a hand on her and hurt her again," Greish said.

Kayson laughed, "It's you, my friends, that will not be leaving here alive."

"Two against one," Cypress growled, stepping forward. "Make that three against one. This isn't going to end well for you," Greish added, his voice steady and firm.

Kayson chuckled softly, "You two are no match for me. I've watched you spar; I know your weaknesses, but you don't know mine. I don't have one," he said with a gleeful smile. "Show me where you've hidden her, and I'll let you leave unharmed. Trust me, Andonis, she won't make you happy. She's tainted now, no longer the blushing bride-to-be. I... made her a woman. But just between us, I've had better. If I didn't have so much invested in her, I'd gladly hand her over."

"Enough!" Andonis yelled. "You'll never lay another hand on her again."

Kayson slowly crept toward them, prompting the three of them to start a slow circle around him.

Andonis advanced first, with Greish coming in from the opposite side a split second later. Kayson deftly blocked Andonis, then spun around to intercept Greish in a blur of lightning-quick movements. He moved impossibly fast, his defenses holding strong against their attacks.

Greish whistled, and Cypress jumped to his feet, leaping into the fray, ready to join the fight.

Kayson's eyes widened with concern as he retreated, positioning the lean-to behind him to keep his attackers in view.

"Give up, and we'll spare you," Andonis offered, his voice steady despite the tension in the air.

"Ha, like I believe that," barked Kayson. He lunged forward and sliced Andonis across the chest, his sword biting into nothing but clothing. "I'm the better man for her, and you know it," Kayson taunted, his voice dripping with arrogance. "Where were you when the wolves attacked her in the dark? Hiding in your tent while I was protecting my interests. I came to her rescue, not you. But you think she has chosen you," Kayson sneered, dodging another strike. "Or so you believe."

"What do you mean, 'so I believe?'" Andonis demanded, confusion flashing across his face.

Kayson smirked, "I've had plenty of time to talk to her, just the two of us. She's mentioned Cret—how she can't wait for his return so she can leave you."

Andonis laughed, "And yet you still pursue her. If she wants to leave, she'll find a way to do it, just like she would with you."

"That's where you and I differ, my friend. I'm willing to kill for what I want." With that, Kayson lunged forward in a spinning attack, slicing Greish across the cheek and catching Andonis in the arm with the same swipe of his broadsword. Cypress jumped forward and latched onto Kayson's non-sword arm. Kayson roared in pain and frustration at having let his guard down for a moment. With the hilt of his sword, he clubbed Cypress on the head just before he swung around to block Greish's next strike.

The air filled with the deafening howls of wolves, echoing through the trees and sending a chill down Andonis's spine. Cypress, shaking off the blow, hurried to Greish's side, his eyes scanning the darkening forest. Andonis felt a surge of panic. *Neiaphi!* He screamed her name silently in his mind, fear gripping his heart.

Ignoring Greish's urgent command to stay, he sprinted into the trees, desperation driving him in the direction he had left her. Each step echoed with the fear that he might be too late.

As he sprinted through the trees, he spotted two massive wolves. They startled at his sudden appearance but allowed him to pass. When he reached the clearing where he had left Neiaphi, he found her surrounded by a larger pack of wolves. They sat in a loose ring around her, while the horses stood calmly by her side.

He slowed to a stop. "Are you okay?" he called.

"Yes, they haven't hurt me. I think they're protecting me."

The wolf closest to Andonis stood and moved aside, allowing him to enter the ring. He cautiously stepped forward, sword still in hand. Neiaphi reached for his hand and dismounted as he approached.

"Is it over?" she asked quietly.

"I don't know. When the howling started, I came straight here."

"You left Greish alone?" she asked, mortified.

"Cypress is with him. I'm sure he still has the upper hand."

"I'm fine here; go back, help Greish."

"Are you sure?" Neiaphi grabbed his arm and squeezed, and he winced at the sudden pain.

"You're—you're hurt!" she cried, concern flooding her voice.

"I'll be fine."

"Go, then, and come back to me quickly." She kissed him on the cheek. Nodding, he sprinted off.

Greish, Kayson, and Cypress watched as the wolves entered the small valley, howling and growling as they slowly closed in. The pack circled them, their terrifying cries echoing off the trees.

The wolves halted ten paces away, snarling and baring their teeth. The largest of the pack stepped forward, its presence commanding and fierce.

The wolf whined and barked once, catching Cypress's attention. Cypress tilted his head, responding with a whine of his own. The wolf leader sat and barked again, asserting its authority.

Cypress, undeterred, wagged his tail and gently tugged at Greish's cloak, trying to pull him away.

"Cypress, release," Greish commanded, but Cypress continued to insistently tug him further from Kayson.

"Where are you going? Are you leaving me to fend off these wolves on my own?" Kayson asked, a hint of frustration in his voice.

"It looks that way. The wolves seem to have instructed Cypress to remove me, and I think I'll comply," Greish replied with a calm demeanor.

"Coward," Kayson snarled. "You and that fool Andonis don't deserve the women who have chosen you."

"Sorry, but I think I'll live to fight another day. Goodbye, Kayson," Greish replied, a steady resolve in his voice. Kayson glared at him, taking a step forward.

The lead wolf sprang to its feet, hackles raised, and a chorus of growls erupted from the pack. Kayson retreated a step, and the wolves fell silent, their eyes fixed on him. He growled, scowling at the wolves as they circled slowly, their intent clear.

Greish shot a glance at the wolves as he passed, realizing he wouldn't be able to take his revenge on Kayson with them around. Suddenly, a loud crashing sound echoed through the forest, and he braced himself for a confrontation. Moments later, Andonis burst through the underbrush and skidded to a halt beside him.

"What's happening?"

"The wolves surrounded us and ordered Cypress to remove me. They're still closing in on Kayson, but he doesn't seem frightened by them, only angry."

"Told Cypress?"

Greish shook his head. "I'll explain later."

They jogged back to Neiaphi, several wolves trailing behind them.

Neiaphi sighed with relief as she spotted the three of them jogging toward her. Cypress barked and raced ahead, leaping and twisting in the air. Tears streamed down her cheeks as she smiled and opened her arms wide. He tackled her to the ground, whining and moaning. "I'm happy to see you too," she laughed. Once she composed herself, she embraced Greish and Andonis in turn.

"So, is Kayson…?" she asked, trailing off.

Greish shook his head. Her eyes widened in fear.

"Wh-what happened?" She glanced around nervously.

"Let's move a bit farther away. We can talk about it tonight when we stop."

"Agreed," Andonis said.

The forest was silent that night. The fire crackled, and the scent of pine boughs smoking in the flames helped clear her head. Greish passed around some dried deer he had taken from the hut. She eagerly accepted a piece, soaking it in her tea for a moment before tearing off a mouthful.

Greish recounted what had happened after Andonis left. Andonis shook his head, keeping his eyes downcast. Neiaphi glanced at him from the corner of her eye. These wolves exhibited the same peculiar behavior as the ones she had encountered in the camp, what felt like a lifetime ago.

Andonis reached over, took her hand, and squeezed gently, still avoiding her gaze. Her heart fluttered. *Did this mean he finally believes me?* She wondered.

"We should get some sleep. If we travel hard tomorrow, we can make it back to the village," Greish said, stifling a yawn. "I'll take the first watch."

Andonis nodded. Neiaphi curled up in her bedroll and closed her eyes.

*Neiaphi walked through the woods, the forest feeling both foreign and familiar. Carefully navigating the ground litter and deadfall, she inhaled deeply, savoring the sweet scent of pine. Surprisingly, she felt a sense of peace, even in her uncertainty about where she was.*

She entered a clearing and froze in fright. The hut where she had been held captive stood before her, the front door swinging slightly in the breeze. Two deer drinking from the stream noticed her, their heads rising in alarm before they bounded away, tails flicking. Neiaphi scanned the clearing, but it seemed deserted. "How did I get back here?" she murmured to herself.

With slow, deliberate steps, she crept closer to the hut. Her heart hammered in her chest, and her breathing was ragged, as if she had just finished sprinting. Her head swiveled, eyes darting around, anticipating Kayson to leap from the shadows and capture her once more. "Don't be silly; the wolves got him," she chided herself.

She peered into the hut. It was empty; everything she had left behind remained in the same place, untouched.

Suddenly, movement caught her eye. She spun around to see a wolver standing in the middle of the clearing. Swallowing the lump in her throat, she stepped to the edge of the porch. The wolver sat down.

"Um, hello," she said.

The wolver whined and then lay down.

She took a few steps closer. "What do you want? Why am I here?"

"I needed to speak with you, so I brought you to a place familiar to both of us," a female voice echoed in her mind.

Neiaphi shook her head and rubbed her temples.

"Are you speaking to me?"

"Yes, child. I don't have much time. Please, sit." The wolver gestured with its head toward the ground in front of it.

Neiaphi hesitated.

"Please, child, I will not harm you. If I wanted to attack, I would do so in the waking world, not come to you in a dream."

"Okay," she said, still unsure but complying. She sat on the sun-warmed grass a few steps away from the large wolver.

The wolver nodded her head. "My name is Mara. I've come to give you news."

Neiaphi leaned forward. "What news?" She took a deep breath.

"Your brothers are safe."

"What?" She jumped to her feet. "Where are they? Are they close? I have to find them."

"Calm yourself. You cannot reach them yet, but do not fret; they are safe. I wanted you to know this so you can ease your spirit."

Neiaphi frowned. "Why did you take them?" she asked quietly.

Mara huffed. "We didn't take them. We are not the only pack on this planet. There are others, and not all are friends. We intercepted the ones who stole your brothers. They are safe with our cubs. We will find you and return them, but not yet. We'll be bedding down for the winter; we'll seek you out this spring."

"Spring? No! My parents cannot wait that long. I cannot wait that long."

"Everything will be fine. Your brothers are too young to be brought to your parents in this cold. We only travel at night; they wouldn't survive the journey."

"I'll go with you, and then I can bring them back. Please," she pleaded.

"No," Mara said sharply. "I will contact you when it's time." She stood up.

"Ummm..."

"Yes, child?"

"What did you do to Kayson?"

"Kayson?" Mara asked, tilting her head.

"The man who was holding me here. He called himself Kayson."

"He has returned to his kind for punishment."

"You let him go? How could you? You stopped Greish from killing him! Now he will find me again. There will be no punishment from his kind. Men on this planet control their women with an iron fist," Neiaphi snarled.

"He was fallen and lost for a long time; he will be punished greatly for his transgressions. What he did is not allowed. Do not worry; he will never harm you again.

*"I am deeply saddened that he broke so many of our laws. He should never have contacted you that first time before you arrived on this planet. He will never Dream Walk again, nor will he leave this planet. So many laws have been violated. Be at ease, child; justice will be served."*

*"What do you mean, fallen? What will happen to him?"*

*Mara said nothing more and trotted into the forest, disappearing from view.*

*"MARA, COME BACK!!" Neiaphi yelled.*

"Neiaphi, wake up. It's okay, you're safe," Andonis said, shaking her slightly.

She bolted upright, panting.

"Are you okay?"

She nodded and reached for her water skin. After a long swallow, she wiped her mouth with a shaky hand. "Just a dream." Andonis looked her in the eyes, "You don't believe that, do you?"

She shook her head slowly.

"Tell me about it."

Again, she shook her head. "Not yet. I need to mull it over for a while."

He nodded, patted her shoulder, and stood to resume his watch.

"Stay close, please," she said quietly.

"Of course. I'm never leaving you again." He settled back down beside her. Bundled in her blankets, she nestled closer, pressing her back against him. He smiled down at her, resting his hand gently on her side.

She sighed softly. "Thank you," she whispered.

"Welcome back, boys! So glad to see ya again. And who do we have here?" Roslyn bounced with joy as she rushed over to them.

"Roslyn, this is Neiaphi," Andonis introduced her.

Roslyn's mouth fell open in surprise.

"Is this the girl you've been searching for?" Andonis nodded. She slapped him on the shoulder. "You said she was pretty. Nay, she ain't pretty." Neiaphi hung her head, glancing at her tattered clothing before trying to smooth her matted hair. Andonis narrowed his eyes.

"She's beautiful. Come here, dear; you must be frozen." Neiaphi glanced up, warmth rising in her cheeks. Roslyn grabbed her hand and led them to their usual table in the back of the inn, near one of the twin fireplaces.

She left them and returned a moment later with three steaming mugs and a large meaty bone. "Stew or roast?" she asked.

"Stew, please," Greish replied, taking the mugs and handing them out. Andonis nodded, holding up two fingers. Roslyn quickly nodded and hurried off.

Neiaphi eagerly accepted the mug from Greish, feeling the warmth on her frozen fingers as she breathed in the sweet-spicy steam. "What is it?" she asked.

"They call it Raki; it's like mulled wine with honey." Neiaphi took a sip, and the spicy warmth slid down her throat, settling heavily in her stomach and warming her from the inside. She sighed and took a larger swallow, closing her eyes in delight. Suddenly, she jumped as a bowl thudded onto the table in front of her.

"Feeling better, dear?" Roslyn smiled.

Nodding, Neiaphi replied, "Yes, thank you."

"Are you okay? Unharmed?" Roslyn prodded.

"Yes, ma'am."

Roslyn narrowed her eyes and harrumphed. "I'll find you some respectable clothing, and if you need anything—anything at all—let me know." She looked Neiaphi up and down, then glared at the two men beside her.

"Really, I'm fine now. These two rescued me."

Roslyn nodded sharply, then turned her attention to a drunk patron calling her name.

They ate in comfortable silence. Halfway through her stew, Neiaphi's eyelids began to droop. Greish elbowed

Andonis and nodded at her. He looked over and nudged her as her head started to bob.

"Oh, sorry," she muttered.

"It's okay. Let's get you some rest."

"Good night, Greish," Neiaphi said. He patted her hand and smiled.

Andonis helped her up the stairs, guiding her carefully as she favored one leg. She limped beside him as he led her down the dimly lit hallway to the last room. He picked up the lantern outside the door and lit a candle. As the room brightened, a table with a washbowl, a chest, and two pallets came into view in the otherwise small, bare space.

Neiaphi froze in the doorway. "I hope you don't mind if we share a room," Andonis said quietly. Neiaphi shook her head and stepped inside. She sat on the pallet, pulling her cloak around her a little tighter. Once a fire crackled merrily in the small fireplace, she shed her heavy cloak and moved to the window.

"Are you okay?" Andonis asked as he hung up both of their cloaks to dry by the fire.

"I'm fine," she replied meekly.

"No, you're not."

A knock on the door interrupted them. Neiaphi glanced at the door, fear flickering in her eyes. Andonis stepped forward and called out, "Who is it?"

"Roslyn mentioned there might be an injured person in need of care," came the reply. Andonis opened the door and peered into the hallway. An older man stood a few paces away, holding a bag in his hand.

"I am the village healer. Is there anyone that needs tending?"

"Yes, please come in." Andonis backed away and opened the door fully.

The healer looked between the two and noticed the dried blood on Andonis's sleeve. "How bad is that wound, young man?"

Andonis waved his hand dismissively. "It can wait. Please tend to Neiaphi first."

The healer looked up at her and motioned for her to sit. Neiaphi settled on the chest, pulling her skirt up slightly to reveal a hastily bandaged ankle. The healer immediately got to work, unwrapping, cleaning, and re-bandaging her wound. Neiaphi's heart hammered as she tried to avoid making eye contact with him. She hoped he wouldn't ask what had happened; she just wasn't ready to speak about it yet.

After Andonis's arm had been tended to, the healer handed him a small container of ointment along with instructions on how to care for Neiaphi's ankle before departing.

Neiaphi returned to staring out the window. Andonis approached from behind and placed a hand on her shoulder, but quickly withdrew it when she flinched.

"I'm sorry," she said quietly.

"It's all right," he said gently. He backed up and sat on one of the pallets. "Please, sit and talk to me. You haven't said more than four words at a time since your nightmare."

Neiaphi sat down beside him, keeping her eyes cast down.

Andonis lifted her chin, turning her head to face him. Tears streamed down her cheeks. "Please speak to me. I want to help," he said, gently wiping her tears with his thumb.

She dropped her gaze again, her lip quivering. She tried to shake her head, but he held her chin firmly.

She opened her mouth, but no sound came out. Andonis pulled her in, pressing her against him. She wrapped her arms around him tightly, sobs racking her body. "Shhh, it's okay now. Everything will be okay." He stroked her hair and rocked her gently. "You're safe now. No one can harm you here."

He held her tightly until her sobbing subsided and she relaxed in his arms. After a few minutes, she fell asleep, and he gently laid her down, tucking her under the blankets. Her breathing became even and calm.

He added a couple more logs to the fire, blew out the candle, and flopped down on the other pallet. Sleep found him quickly.

Andonis rose with the sun, feeling the chill in the air. A quiet knock echoed at the door. Neiaphi stirred and rolled over, but didn't fully wake.

He opened the door a crack to find Greish standing on the other side. "How is she?"

Andonis stepped into the hallway, closing the door behind him. "Still sleeping. She cried herself to sleep but is refusing to talk."

"Just give her time. She's strong; she'll come around."

"I don't know. I've never seen her like this before. She seemed fine before that dream; I've never seen her so shaken."

"Go down and get some breakfast for both of you. I'll keep watch here."

The smell of mint tea coaxed Neiaphi out of her deep slumber. The heavy feeling in her head had lifted, but her muscles screamed with every movement. She groaned as she stretched her arms and legs.

"Good morning," Andonis said brightly.

"Good morning."

"Feeling any better?"

She shrugged and took the tea he offered.

"Still not talking?"

She shrugged again, bringing the cup to her mouth to hide a grin. Closing her eyes, she savored the warmth of the tea sliding down her parched throat. "Feeling better now," she said softly.

"What do you want to do now?" he inquired.

"Go back to the winter village, to our families."

Andonis's jaw dropped. "You want to give up on your brothers?" he asked, astonished.

She shook her head. "No, I'm following the instructions given to me."

"Your dream?"

She nodded and began to tell him about it. He sat in silence, listening intently as she recounted the details. Neiaphi kept her eyes down, staring at the cup in her hands.

She was still too nervous to look at him when she finished. Andonis stood and paced around the small room with his hands clasped behind him. He eventually stopped and sat down beside her, lifting her chin with his index finger. Although she raised her head, she kept her eyes downcast.

"Neiaphi," he said quietly, "please look at me." She slowly raised her eyes to meet his. "I don't know what your dreams hold, but I know you are remarkable. Are you sure you want to travel now? It might be better to wait until spring."

"No, I can't be away from my parents that long. The uncertainty must be killing them right now. I need to ease their minds if I can."

"Okay. Let me tell Greish. It might take a day or so to get everything ready to leave. Is that alright?"

Neiaphi tilted her head. "Of course. Why wouldn't it be?"

He stroked her cheek with his thumb. "I don't want you to get impatient and leave without me."

"Oh, I wouldn't do anything so rash," she said with a grin.

"Riiight, you never do anything rash," he chuckled.

"Thank you."

"For what?"

"For believing in and supporting me. I'm so happy you found me. I thought you were dead. I was so scared. He…he…" She hesitated.

Andonis pulled her into a tight hug. "It's okay. Don't relive it. You're safe now."

They sat in silence for a few moments. "Did you bring anything to eat?"

Andonis pulled back. "Of course, but it's only for happy people."

"Well, then load up my plate," she replied as cheerfully as she could. "And then…" She glanced down at herself. "How about a bath?"

Andonis laughed. "Of course. Food first, though."

## ∞ **26** ∞
## RETURN

"**ANY** signs?" Ambrite asked.

"No, sir. It looks like we were followed by four plus two two-legs. The monsters took off in pursuit, and none have returned."

Ambrite nodded. "Good. How are the repairs coming?" he asked Cret.

"Good," Cret replied. "But I've never fixed a cargo ship before. I still think it'll take most of the moon to finish."

Pelagios slapped him on the shoulder. "I never would've guessed you'd get it done that quickly. You've got a real talent for troubleshooting. If we can fire up the engines this afternoon, we'll know for sure."

"Good, good," Pelagios said, a smile creeping across his face. "That's what I like to hear."

The new moon came and went, leaving a blanket of snow covering the ground and crisp air that bit at exposed skin. As the engines choked and sputtered, birds took flight, startled by the noise. Pelagios walked beneath the craft, listening intently as the engines settled into a steady hum. Nodding to himself, he muttered under his breath.

At the edge of the tree line, five Centaurs stood in a small group. "It's okay to get closer," he called to them.

"We're fine," Simandro replied.

Pelagios walked to the front of the craft and signaled for Cret to kill the engines. As the roar of the engines faded, the centaurs approached.

"We'll take a test flight tomorrow morning," he informed them.

"Why not now?" Lyric asked, curiosity glistening in her eyes.

"Just in case we go down again, I want to make sure we have enough daylight to settle in."

"You two-legs surprise me almost daily," she chuckled.

"How do we surprise you?"

"You're much more intelligent than I originally gave you credit for."

"Well, thanks, I guess."

"You're welcome," she replied as she trotted away.

The sun glinted off the cargo ship as it broke through the tree canopy. The vessel rocked slightly from side to side. "Is everything okay?" Tivadarios asked, clearly concerned.

"I'm not a very good pilot," he admitted with a grimace. "I'm almost getting the hang of it. Yes, there, that's better." He leveled the ship and hovered just above the treetops. "Here we go." He pushed the controls, and the ship sped forward. He maneuvered in a serpentine pattern, then a figure eight, before finally circling back to land in the same clearing.

Ambrite was the only centaur brave enough to join them on the maiden flight. "That was amazing! I've never felt anything like that before."

"I felt the same on my first flight, but it's even more thrilling from the command deck," Cret said. "Will you be joining us again?"

"I go where Lyric goes."

"Did someone say my name?" Lyric called as she came up the ramp.

"I was asking Ambrite if you all would be joining us. We can drop you off at your winter gathering before heading back to our camp."

"No," she replied, shaking her head. "I feel connected to this craft, but I'm also drawn to continue south."

"Then this craft needs to take us south," Justic said, joining them. "We'll take you back to your families first, of course, if Pelagios is willing to head that way." Lyric nodded in agreement.

"I'm in. As long as I'm here and no one knows where I am, I want to explore more of this planet—and I'd love to see Atlantis."

"Then it's settled. We'll drop you off with your families and then continue south."

"No." All eyes turned to Cret. "I think I'll travel with you for now. I have a feeling I need to stay close. What about you, Darios?"

Tivadarios shrugged. "I go where you go, my friend."

"Then it's settled: we'll head south to Atlantis tomorrow," Pelagios said.

"No, we need to leave tonight. It's better to travel under the cover of darkness so no one sees us," Cret stated.

"Agreed," several voices replied in unison.

Cret stood on the command deck, gazing at the distant horizon. The dark trees blurred by as the craft sailed through the inky blackness. Hold on, Neiaphi, I'm coming.

"Riders coming in!" Leander shouted as three figures appeared on the horizon. Several men rushed to his side, weapons at the ready.

One of the riders broke away from the others at a slow lope, his hand raised in greeting.

"Leander! Greetings! May we enter the camp?"

"Greish? Is that you? Oh, thank the gods, we thought you were lost! Who's with you?"

"Andonis and Neiaphi. We have news about the boys—good news, we believe."

"NEILUIOS!!" Leander shouted as loud as he could. "NEIAPHI HAS RETURNED!!"

Cheers erupted throughout the camp. Neiluios and many others rushed toward them, while a woman sprinted from the other side of the camp. She reached the men and pushed past them, heading straight for Neiaphi.

Neiaphi spotted her mother rushing toward her and climbed off Nexus as quickly as she could despite her injury. Altesse grabbed hold of her, sobbing. They crumpled to the ground, tears streaming freely from both of them. Neiluios enveloped them in his arms, joining in the joyful reunion.

"Hello, Father," Andonis greeted.

"So glad you made it back. What happened out there? Where's Kayson?" Mace inquired.

"I think we should tell everyone at the same time. It was quite an adventure."

"Did you find those wolves or the boys?" he asked after a moment's hesitation.

"Yes and no, Father. Most of this story needs to be retold by Neiaphi—when she's ready."

Another woman cried out loudly as news of their return reached the far side of the camp. Alexa came running, sobbing openly. Greish saw her coming and met her halfway. He picked her up and held her tightly.

Neiaphi, Andonis, and Greish sat together close to a large bonfire in the main square, all eyes on them. Around them, everyone huddled in small clusters around dozens of smaller fires.

Neiluios stood. "Thank you all for coming this evening. As you've undoubtedly heard, three of our missing have returned. I know many of you have been asking what happened to them during their absence, and I appreciate your understanding and patience. We felt it best to tell the story just once. Who would like to begin?" He turned to the three standing before him.

Greish cleared his throat and began the tale from when they first left the camp in search of the wolves. After Greish finished recounting his dive into the icy river, Andonis picked up the story, sharing his interactions with Kayson. The two of them tag-teamed the rest of the narrative until they reached the part where they spotted the hut where Kayson had kept Neiaphi.

"Do you feel up to telling your tale?" Andonis asked her.

"I think so…" she stammered, hesitating. After a moment of silence, she began. Several women gasped and openly cried as she recounted Kayson's abusive behavior. Neiluios scowled, pounding his fist into his hand.

Andonis grabbed her hand and gently squeezed. She hadn't shared everything Kayson had done, and it seemed she was still leaving out a few details. *Hopefully, she'll open up to me in the future,* he thought.

When they reached the part of the story where they had rescued Neiaphi and left her in the clearing to confront Kayson, they fell silent, looking at each other.

Addident stood. "Is there something wrong?" he asked.

"Not exactly, Sir," Greish replied. "It's just, um, we're not sure how the rest of this will be received."

"Please, just listen to what we say and how we interpret what happened. It may sound strange and is hard to explain," Andonis said slowly.

They continued telling their parts of the story, detailing their interactions with the wolves. The audience listened silently, seemingly holding their collective breath.

"You just left Kayson there? What if he escaped?" an unseen voice called from the crowd.

"What news of the boys?" someone else asked.

Neiaphi hung her head. She had told very few people about her dreams. Would they be supportive, or would they ridicule her? What choice did she have? She cleared her throat, keeping her eyes cast downward, and shared her dream, the news of Kayson's fate, and her decision to cease the search. When she finished, she kept her head down. Andonis placed his arm around her shoulders but said nothing.

After a tense moment of silence, someone near the back spoke up.

"It's nothing but a dream of hope. We must face the harsh truth. I'm sorry to say this: six were lost, and three have returned. We need to be thankful for what we have."

Neiluios stood and faced the crowd. "I am beyond grateful that these three have returned, but my heart is heavy knowing my boys are still lost. If my daughter says this is true, then I believe her." He raised his hand to quiet the murmurs.

Neiaphi's heart soared at her father's words; she looked up at him, tears glistening in her eyes. He met her gaze with a silent question, and she nodded in response.

"My daughter had another dream—a dream that saved us all. She foresaw an attack during one of our ship crossings, warning us of the danger and allowing us to arm ourselves before The Society could strike."

Being the only other dream she had shared with her father, Neiaphi knew that was what he wished to convey. All eyes returned to her, and as her cheeks blazed, she hung her head once more.

Addident approached Neiluios. "What do you say we do, young lady?" he asked her.

Neiaphi looked up, surprised by his intense gaze. She steadied herself before answering, wringing her hands in her lap, grateful that Andonis had not removed his arm from her shoulders.

"Mara said she would bring the boys back to us. I hate to wait. I don't know what these dreams are, but..." She hesitated. "I feel confident that this one will come to pass, just like the others."

"Others? You've had dreams beyond these two?" someone shouted.

Neiaphi shook her head and muttered to Andonis, "She's tired. I'm going to take her to get some rest. Thank you, everyone."

Murmurs spread through the group as they all retreated to their huts.

"Thank you. I couldn't answer any more questions."

"My pleasure." He smiled warmly at her and led her back to her hut.

## ∞ 27 ∞
## NEW ALLY

"**CURSE** those monsters. They let our prey escape."

"What are your intentions now?" Hepluosis asked.

The lead centaur paced angrily back and forth in the clearing where the ship had once occupied.

Hepluosis, Six and the centaurs had stayed almost consistently on the move for several days after the large monstrous wolves had attacked them. They found a large cave to shelter in and ward off the attack. After about a week, the wolves grew tired of their resistance and had retreated into the forest. They stayed there for several days before slowly making their way back to where they had last seen Cret and the others

"Can you track them?" Brutus demanded.

"Not in the sky," Hepluosis huffed. "That ship will leave a smoke trail, but it's only visible for a short time. How long do you think they've been gone?"

"A couple of days at most."

"I think they've evaded us then," Hepluosis said, shaking his head.

"Unacceptable," the centaur replied, folding his arms across his chest.

"Then what do you suggest we do, Brutus?" Hepluosis growled.

"Watch your tongue, two-leg." Brutus took a few steps closer, jabbing an arrow near his face and nicking his cheek. Hepluosis jumped back with a scowl, blood trickling down his face. "We'll find them somehow. We'll camp here tonight and head out at dawn."

Hepluosis and Six had the last watch, sitting on opposite sides of the fire with the flames at their backs to protect their night vision. Wrapped tightly in their cloaks, they hoped the sun would rise soon.

Hepluosis's eyes began to droop when suddenly the wind picked up, thunder roared overhead, and debris swirled around them. Everyone jumped to their feet, weapons at the ready.

"What manner of demon is this?" Talite yelled above the roaring thunder.

"We should head to the trees," Pena said, whirling around in search of the enemy.

"Everyone to the trees! Take cover!" Brutus ordered.

From the shelter of the trees, they watched as a ship landed directly on their campfire.

"Is that them? Did they return?" Brackus asked.

Hepluosis shook his head. "No, this one is different."

The ship settled in a cloud of dust with a loud grind and a deafening screech.

Huddled in the darkness, they watched as the door opened, and six armed men exited the craft. They fanned out, standing sentry, while two additional men walked down the ramp.

"Any signs?" one of them asked.

"Horses were here just moments ago, sir. We must have scared them off."

"Horses! I don't care about horses. Any signs of him?" the apparent leader snapped.

"Nothing fresh, sir. He was here but has moved on."

"Spread out and find me clues about where he went," he snarled.

As the men fanned out to search the area, the centaurs and the two humans tried to melt into the shadows, but it was to no avail.

"Halt! W-w-what are you? OVER HERE, I NEED HELP!" The men converged on the man's scream.

Pena scowled at the man, pointing his sword at her chest. "What are you?" She folded her arms and said nothing. The other men arrived with weapons drawn and mouths agape.

The leader squared his shoulders and approached the prisoner. "What are you?" he demanded.

Pena's lips thinned, her arms still crossed, but she remained silent.

"I don't think it can speak, sir," said the one who found her.

"Then kill it and continue searching," the leader snapped.

The rest of the centaurs flooded into the clearing, flanking the humans.

"You'll do no such thing," Brutus sneered, nocking an arrow and aiming it at the leader.

All the humans turned to confront the new threat. Pena took advantage of their distraction and grabbed the man closest to her, wrapped her arm across his shoulders, and held her dagger to his neck. He gasped, swearing in surprise.

The leader turned his head sharply, then faced her again. "What manner of beast are you?"

"We are centaurs. Have you never seen our kind before?" Brutus asked.

He shook his head. "Where do you hail from?"

"I think you're in no position to ask questions. You will answer ours. Who are you searching for?"

The human leader glared, hesitating before answering. "A man stole a ship. We need it back."

"One of those flying things?" Brackus asked.

"Yes, one of those flying things," he mocked. "So, you have seen it?"

"We're tracking the centaurs and two-legs who joined the one you're looking for."

"Maybe we should join forces, since we're searching for the same thing," Six suggested.

"No," Brutus and the human leader said in unison.

"If I may, sir?" Hepluosis interjected. "More eyes and feet on the ground will make the search easier." Both leaders scowled.

"You're searching for the pilot, while we're looking for the other two men. They've teamed up. We share a common goal; it would be best to work together so we don't impede each other's efforts."

"What's your name, young man?" the human leader asked.

"Hepluosis, sir."

"Where are you from?"

"Hmmm. That's not something I can reveal at this time. However, if we work together, I might be inclined to share my story."

"I don't like being forced into a decision," the leader growled. "But having more men searching could be beneficial. We'll try it, but don't get in our way or slow us down." He pointed his sword at them for emphasis.

"What say you?" Hepluosis asked Brutus.

"I don't like associating with so many two-legs, but I'll agree for now."

"Then it's settled; we have a shaky alliance," Hepluosis replied, nodding his head.

The forest darkened long before the sky under the canopy of trees. Two campfires flickered to life—one surrounded by centaurs and the other by humans. Six and Hepluosis sat off to the side, uncertain which fire to approach. As outcasts from both groups, their place felt uncertain.

"Hepluosis, over here!" one of the humans called. "Join us."

One of the men passed around bowls of steaming stew and Hepluosis, and Six each took one with murmurs of thanks.

"Where are you all from?" Hepluosis asked between mouthfuls.

"We're from the north."

"But where specifically?" he pressed. No one spoke. "I know you're not from any village or town around here. No one has technology like that." He nodded toward the ship. "Are you members of the Society or Loyals?"

The leader stood and approached him, stopping directly in front of Hepluosis and looking down. Hepluosis met his gaze but made no other movement.

"What do you know of the Society and the Loyals?"

"I know that all of us," he gestured to the humans and centaurs around them, "are not from this planet. At least, not originally."

"Are you feeling more inclined to share your story now?"

"Perhaps," Hepluosis nodded. "But first, Society or Loyal?"

"We are members of the Society." The leader extended his hand in invitation for Hepluosis to begin, then retook his seat.

"Can we start with your name, sir?" Hepluosis asked.

"I am Captain Rirmell."

After a pause, Hepluosis began retelling his story, carefully highlighting and embellishing his father's successes while downplaying Addident's and Neiluios's and enhancing their failures. Captain Rirmell and his men listened quietly, occasionally chuckling and nodding in agreement.

"Well, young man," Captain Rirmell said slowly after Hepluosis finished his tale, pausing from sharpening his dagger, "that's quite a story." Although every detail was true, it was significantly embellished. "I'm not sure if I fully believe you."

Hepluosis opened his mouth to protest, but Rirmell held up his hand. "However, since I have no one to collaborate your story and verify its validity, and you know things that only someone from the Society would know, I'll believe you for now. If, however…" He pointed his dagger at Hepluosis, "You are lying; I will personally cut out your tongue." Hepluosis nodded, keeping his face as neutral as possible while his heart thundered in his chest.

"I have no fears, Sir. I've told you the truth." Rirmell nodded and returned to his sharpening.

"Who do I need to speak with about joining your outfit?"

Rirmell snapped his eyes up. "Why, me, of course. I handpicked all my men—only the best for my missions. If you want to join us, you'll need to prove yourself. You'll have plenty of opportunities soon."

"We will not enter that thing," Brutus said, arms crossed over his chest.

"Then you'll be left behind," Captain Rirmell replied, mirroring his stance. The two leaders glared at each other. "This thing," he gestured behind him, "is our only means of travel for this mission."

"Where do you expect us to ride in that thing?"

"We have horses on board for when the need arises. You can ride with them; there are a few extra stalls," he replied scornfully.

All the centaurs closed in around their leader at the insult. "We are not horses."

Rirmell held his hands out in surrender. "I meant no disrespect. I'm just saying that's the only space in my ship large enough to accommodate you and your crew." The corners of his lips curled into a slight grin.

"We will decide for ourselves if these accommodations meet our needs. Lead the way," Brutus snarled.

Rirmell guided the centaurs to the stable compartment before heading to the command deck.

"Where to, sir?" the pilot asked.

"Where do you think the one you're chasing is going, young man?" Captain Rirmell replied, directing the question at Hepluosis.

Hepluosis rubbed his chin. "Well, my first thought was that he would return to his family, but he hasn't shown any signs of doing that so far. I think he's going after her."

"Her who?"

"Neiluios's daughter, Neiaphi. He's been pining for her since he was assigned to the processing plant. We were informed that her group has a slight lead on us and is most likely almost to Atlantis. We should head in that direction."

"Do you know where Atlantis is?"

"No, Sir. I was hoping you did."

"It's a closely guarded secret," he growled. "I know the general direction, and I'm aware it lies beyond The Pillars. I can get us there. If we miss them by then, we may never find them. Head to The Pillars—everyone, keep your eyes on the sensors. We need to locate them."

The search continued for several days until they finally discovered a recent campsite, no more than a day old.

"We're close now," Rirmell announced. "We'll risk a few hours of travel in daylight. With any luck, we'll catch up to them tonight."

"That looks like a good spot for the day," Cret said, gesturing toward a small lake. "I don't see any firelight nearby."

"Looks good to me," Pelagios replied. He maneuvered the craft into the clearing and set it down a short distance from the water's edge.

Once on steady ground, the centaurs headed straight for the water. Myreia waded in until her torso was submerged, glancing back at the others with a playful smile before diving under.

"What is she doing?" Tivadarios asked, alarmed.

"She does this all the time. Don't mind her," Bal-air replied with a huff.

"I didn't know centaurs could swim underwater!" Tivadarios exclaimed.

"Most can't," Simandro remarked with a scowl.

"Have you ever tried?" Bal-air asked, a smirk on his face.

"No! I can't swim underwater."

"How do you know if you've never tried?" Bal-air challenged.

Simandro ignored him and headed toward the tree line.

"Can you swim?" Tivadarios asked Bal-air.

He shook his head. "Myreia tried to teach me once, but…" He trailed off. "No intentions of trying again."

Tivadarios smiled but let the conversation drop. Myreia reemerged, holding a large fish at the end of her dagger.

"Here you go, two-leg," she said, handing the fish to Tivadarios.

"What am I supposed to do with this?" Tivadarios asked, staring at the fish.

"Those who hunt, hunt; those who don't, clean," Myreia replied with a grin.

"I'll help. Come on," Cret said, stepping forward.

A short time later, Simandro returned, proudly holding a couple of grouse.

"Where do you think we are now?" Pelagios asked Cret as the grouse and fish sizzled over the fire.

Cret squinted up at the clouds drifting past the sun at its zenith. "Not sure. I've never seen a map of this area. I was told Atlantis is an island, so I guess we keep heading south until we reach the water, and then…" He shrugged.

"I hope we find the ones you're looking for," Pelagios replied.

"Me too."

Pelagios sighed heavily. "I have some bad news."

"What's the matter?" Cret asked, concern in his voice.

"Something's wrong with that blasted engine again."

"Can we fix it?" Cret inquired.

"I'm not sure yet."

"Not a bad place to spend the rest of the winter, if it comes to it" Lyric replied.

"Agreed," Ambrite echoed.

"If we have to head out on foot, might need to camouflage the ship, though," Tivadarios chimed in.

"I have a few ideas," Cret said, rubbing his chin in thought.

Neiaphi sat in front of her hut, her cloak wrapped tightly around her as she warmed her hands by the small fire. Beside her, Alexa mirrored her silence, both women lost in thought. With an armed escort now a necessity, the men were too busy to watch over them, leaving the two of them to pass the time alone. Since Neiaphi, Andonis, and Greish's return, the village had tightened its defenses. No one walked alone, and no one dared venture outside the village boundaries.

Alexa studied Neiaphi as she stared into the fire, her expression grim. "Do you want to talk about it?" she asked gently.

Neiaphi shook her head. Alexa moved closer, wrapping an arm around her shoulders. "You need to talk about it. It might help you feel better."

"Maybe..." Neiaphi paused, a sob escaping her. "But I can't," she whispered, barely audible.

"If you can't talk to me, how about Andonis?" Alexis suggested, but Neiaphi tensed. "Okay, how about your mother?"

Neiaphi took a deep breath. "No, I think I can tell you. It's just hard."

Alexis sat quietly, ready to listen. Huddled together, Neiaphi began to share her story in a barely audible whisper. Alexis leaned in closer, offering silent support as she listened intently. When Neiaphi finished, they sat in silence for a moment, absorbing the weight of her words.

Alexa sighed and hugged Neiaphi again. "Thank you for sharing that with me. I'm here for you."

"Thank you, Alexa. I do feel a little lighter."

Nodding, Alexa shifted the topic. "Do you know when we'll be moving again?"

Neiaphi shook her head. "I haven't heard anything, but I don't think my parents will leave until spring."

"Do you believe the wolves will bring your brothers back?" she asked quietly.

"I hope so." Neiaphi closed her eyes. "I hope so."

After his watch concluded, Greish found Alexa and Neiaphi sitting together. Alexa stood as he approached and walked over to him.

"Is she okay?" Greish asked, concern flickering in his eyes.

Alexa shrugged. "She will be, I think. She finally told me what truly happened..." Her voice trailed off as she wrapped her arms around herself, lost in thought.

Greish nodded slowly, sensing the weight of Neiaphi's story. "That's a good step. Sometimes just sharing the burden helps."

"Yeah," Alexa replied, looking back toward the hut. "I just hope it eases her pain."

"Let's take a walk. Maybe the fresh air will do us both some good," Greish suggested, gesturing for her to join him.

Greish wrapped his arm around her, concern in his eyes. "Can you share any details?"

Alexa shook her head, then shrugged. "I think I should tell Andonis, though. I know she won't tell him, but I believe he should know."

"I'll take you to him," Greish offered.

"No." She shook her head. "Not yet. Soon, though."

# ∞ 28 ∞
## SPRING

**NELAPHI** stood with her eyes closed, facing the mid-afternoon sun, savoring its warmth on her face. A small smile tugged at the corners of her lips.

"That sun feels good, doesn't it?" Andonis asked as he wrapped his arms around her waist. She tensed for a moment but soon relaxed, leaning into him with her eyes still closed.

"It does. This is the warmest sun I've felt since fall. Is spring far away?"

"No, it's just starting. Before long, the grasses will turn green, flowers will bloom, and the trees will begin to bud."

"Oh, I can't wait! Winter is such a dreadful time of year. It comes every year, doesn't it?"

Andonis laughed as he spun her around. "Yes, winter comes every year, but it has its perks. Once we're married, we can spend those long nights by a crackling fire, sharing warmth and stories."

An emotion flickered across her face. One Andonis couldn't quite decipher before a smile settled in. "Hmm, that sounds nice. Have you heard when we'll be leaving?"

"Your father doesn't seem to be in a hurry. From what I can see, the other two groups will leave first; we'll be the last. I think the first is set to leave in a few weeks, with the second two days later, and then it'll be our turn." He paused, holding his breath for a moment.

"What is it?" Neiaphi asked softly, placing a hand on his cheek.

Andonis placed his hand over hers, guiding it to his lips. He kissed her palm gently. "I'm sure your brothers will be back before we leave."

She closed her eyes again and nodded. "I'm certain of that, too."

He pulled her close and hugged her tightly. "I need to tell you something."

"What is it?" she asked, returning the embrace.

"Let's sit down first." She looked up at him, then nodded and settled onto a log near the dying fire.

"Alexa spoke with me this morning."

"What about?" Neiaphi asked, grabbing his hand with both of hers.

He glanced down at their hands before lifting his gaze to meet hers. "She hopes you won't be upset, but she told me what really happened…"

Neiaphi's body went rigid, and she pulled her hands away. He reached for her again, bringing her hands to his chest, but uncertainty washed over him. He struggled to find the right words.

"I'm sorry. I'm so ashamed of what happened…" she started to say.

He gently placed a finger on her lips to silence her. "You have nothing to be ashamed of. What he did—what he tried to do—was not your fault. I've been so relieved to learn he didn't go as far as I feared. It's been tearing me apart, imagining what could have happened to you. What he said he did to you."

"Oh! I didn't know he told you anything," she said softly.

"He was trying to manipulate me into making a mistake. I didn't believe him at first, but then I saw how shaken you were—the condition of your clothing, little more than torn rags. I feared the worst."

"I'm so sorry." She leaned over and wrapped her arms around him. "I should have told you. The beatings and shamings have been so hard to relive. He only allowed me to wear clothes when he wasn't around. I fought at first, but then he started tearing my dress. I feared he'd ruin it completely, and then I wouldn't have anything to wear."

He hugged her tighter. "My feelings for you would remain the same, no matter what. I'm just grateful you weren't hurt more than you were. When we finally found you, he was calling you his wife, and I feared the worst."

"I think it was only a matter of time before he acted on his threats. He seemed to be waiting for spring for some reason."

"Well, there's plenty to celebrate now. Come on—your mother asked me to take you to the town hall. Spring is just around the corner, and it's time for a feast." Andonis stood and gently pulled her to her feet.

"Another ceremony?"

"Each season brings many reasons to celebrate, and we must give thanks."

Neiaphi glanced at him from the corner of her eye. "Do you believe in the gods?"

Andonis paused. "I was raised to believe in them," he said with a shrug. "I never questioned it until I met you. Even if the names I pray to are made up, I still feel there's something greater than me, greater than all of us."

"Well, I think I can agree with that," Neiaphi said.

The town hall buzzed with laughter, filled with the rich aroma of roasted roots and meat. Neiaphi couldn't help but smile as small groups of children wove their way through the mingling adults, chasing each other and the many new puppies scampering about. Spotting her, Alexa waved enthusiastically.

"Pleasant day; the gods are smiling on us today," Alexa said with a bright smile.

"I can't argue with that." Neiaphi hugged her tightly. "So, who are we honoring today?"

"Dionysus, the goddess of fertility and wine. I've never been able to join in on the nightly festivities before. I can't wait! Normally, this is a three-day festival, but since we didn't have a harvest last fall, we're only doing it tonight. Hopefully, Dionysus won't be offended."

"I'm sure it will be fine," Andonis replied.

"So, how is this festival celebrated?"

"Day one is the Opening of the Jars and Sampling of the Wines. Day two is called Pitchers."

The men would participate in a drinking contest, and even the children would be given a small taste of wine. On the third day, cooking pots filled with vegetables and seeds would be left out for any wandering spirits. At the night's end, the villagers would drive those spirits away from the village.

"My favorite part is watching all the plays. Our village had two excellent playwrights, and it was always a tough decision to choose which one would put on the best performance," Alexa said with a smile.

"So, how are we celebrating this year?" Andonis asked, curious.

"We have a small supply of wine, and a few of the servants have been rehearsing a play to present tonight," Alexa explained, her eyes sparkling with excitement.

"Sounds like a fun evening," Neiaphi replied, a smile spreading across her face.

"Looks like someone's already on stage; come on, let's get closer!" Alexa tugged Neiaphi and Andonis along, weaving through the crowd.

The girls found a spot to sit on the ground near the stage. Andonis's mother, Miry, stepped on stage. Miry was a slender woman with sandy brown hair and striking green eyes. She was joined by Aner's wife, Iris, a plump woman with greying blonde hair.

Together, they recited a poem about two women being pursued by Zeus simultaneously, and how they tried to sabotage each other's chances with him. Alexa and Neiaphi laughed at the antics they described.

After the first play, Andonis returned with three cups of wine. More individuals and groups took turns reciting poems and acting out short stories, adding to the lively atmosphere.

As the sun sank lower in the sky, fires ignited around the village square, casting a warm glow over the scene. Large trays of food were brought out, and a few servants played instruments and sang, their melodies blending with the laughter and chatter of the villagers as everyone enjoyed their meal.

"Having fun?" Andonis asked Neiaphi.

"Oh, yes. This has been a wonderful evening."

"Come on," he said, extending his hand. She hesitated before placing her hand in his.

"Come dance with me."

She jerked her hand away. "What's the matter?"

She cast her eyes down. "I don't know how to dance."

"Now, how is that possible?" he asked with a chuckle.

"Well, okay, I know how to dance, but I don't know how you… dance," she replied, meeting his gaze.

"Oh, come on, just follow my lead," he encouraged, guiding her to an open area.

The celebration continued late into the evening, filled with food, drink, and dancing. The night was calm and clear; the moon shone brightly above, and the stars twinkled, appearing even more vibrant as their spirits lifted. As the night wore on, the crowd gradually thinned as people began to retire. Greish and Andonis kept their partners on the dance floor until both girls finally pleaded for a break.

"I'm so dizzy," Alexa said, plopping down hard at one of the tables. Greish quickly handed her a cup of wine.

"Oh no, water, please! My head is spinning," she replied.

"Me too," Neiaphi chimed in, feeling her own head swim. She stumbled slightly, and Andonis grabbed her elbow to steady her. "Thanks. Does wine always do this to your head?"

"If you drink too much, yes," Greish replied with a chuckle.

"Well, then, I will never drink this much again," Alexa declared, and Neiaphi nodded in agreement, instantly regretting the motion.

"Do you think you can walk?" Andonis asked.

"I think so," she replied, though doubt flickered in her eyes.

"Let's get you to bed." She nodded slightly and attempted to stand, but her knees felt weak. After a moment, she tried again, only to slump back to the ground, giggling.

Andonis smiled and scooped her up effortlessly. She grinned at him as he cradled her in his arms, leaning into him for support.

"Please, don't let me drink that much anymore."

"Aww, I like you like this—completely and totally dependent on me."

She shot him a glare, but it quickly faded into a smile. "Don't get too comfortable; you'll never see me in this position again."

"If you say so," he teased, a playful grin spreading across his face.

Neiaphi emerged from the cozy darkness of her family's hut into the blinding light of midday.

"Hello, sunshine!" Andonis called cheerfully.

Neiaphi grimaced. "Oooh, not so loudly, please. How can you be so chipper this morning?"

"It's past midday!" he replied with a grin.

"Really? I've never slept in like that before."

"You've never drunk like that before. You need to be careful."

"And I never will again."

"Feel up for some archery practice?"

"Not today, please."

"Grab your bow."

"I said not today," she groaned.

"If we need you, it doesn't matter how you feel; you still have to perform."

Neiaphi groaned again but complied.

Andonis led her to the village archery range. She took an arrow from her quiver and notched it on the string, taking a steadying breath. Her head still spun slightly, and her heart hammered in her chest. After a few more breaths to clear her vision, she released the arrow. It sailed down the range, missing the painted target entirely.

"Try again," Andonis urged as she reached for another arrow. This time, it sailed true and struck the target. "Good, good, again." Neiaphi continued until her quiver was empty.

"Feeling any better?" he asked.

Neiaphi hesitated for a moment before replying, "I do!"

"Sometimes, just getting your mind off things helps," he smirked.

"Thanks, but now I'm starving," she said, rubbing her stomach.

The engine groaned and creaked as it tried to turn over—Snap, Crack, Boom, followed by a cloud of smoke and then silence.

"Blasted engine!" Pelagios exclaimed, emerging from beneath the ship.

"What's wrong with it?" Lyric asked, concern etched on her face. Pelagios wiped his hands on his pants, frustration clear in his eyes.

"It's broken," he said flatly.

She rolled her eyes. "That I can see. What's broken? And please don't just say the ship."

"I don't know yet. I'm a transfer engineer; I'm not very good at fixing what I fly in," he admitted, shaking his head in frustration.

"I'm sure, between you and Cret, you'll figure it out," she reassured him.

"I don't think so, not this time. I'm afraid we might have to continue on foot," Pelagios said, a hint of defeat in his voice.

Lyric frowned. "That's not ideal for Cret. I know he's in a hurry."

Did someone say my name?" Cret asked as he approached.

Lyric nodded slightly. "Pelagios thinks the ship is beyond repair."

"That's bad news. Are you sure? Do you want me to take a look?"

"I'm pretty sure you can take a look, but we broke something when we nestled into these trees. I think we just need a replacement."

"Something? What's broken?" Cret asked.

"I don't know the name. Let me show you." They crawled back under the ship. "This part here—I don't see how we can fix it with what's on board."

"You're right. I don't recognize it either, but it definitely looks beyond repair."

"What do you think, Cret?" Lyric asked as they emerged.

He shook his head. "It's broken," he replied flatly.

"So, what's next?"

Cret scratched his chin thoughtfully. "I'll head south again. I just hope I'm not too far from the water and that I can reach the crossing before the others. What about you two?"

She hesitated before replying, "I'll continue with you. We may have only known each other for a short time, but I feel like our paths are intertwined."

"Sounds good. What about you?" he asked Pelagios.

"Well, I'm not staying here by myself, but I'm not looking forward to walking," he admitted.

"Who's going to have to walk?" Ambrite interrupted. Cret recapped their conversation for him and Simandro.

"Sounds like you're walking, two-leg," Ambrite teased.

"I'll carry the human," Simandro said with a smirk.

"A-are you sure?" Pelagios stammered, glancing nervously at the centaur.

"You don't seem too heavy. I think I can handle you," Simandro said with confidence.

"It's harder than it looks," Pelagios replied. "They move and throw you off balance."

Lyric huffed in agreement, "Makes you pity horses even more."

Cret chuckled as he walked by, playfully slapping her on the rump. She squealed in surprise and kicked at him, but he quickly dodged out of reach, laughing at her reaction.

"Everyone, rest up. We'll leave in three days," Cret announced.

Neiluios paced in front of Addident's tent, anxiety knotting in his stomach. He knew he needed to speak to him but didn't know how to begin.

"Can I help you?" Addident asked, approaching from behind. Startled, Neiluios jumped and spun around.

"Yes, Sir. I—I need to speak with you."

"Come in; no one's home at the moment," Addident said, stepping aside.

They entered the dimly lit hut, where Addident sat and gestured to the only other chair for Neiluios.

Neiluios sat down, clearing his throat. "You aren't ready to leave yet, are you?" Addident asked, anticipating his concern.

"Um, yes, Sir. We can't leave—not yet. We must wait."

"For how long? What if they never come?"

"That's something Altesse and I have discussed at great length. We'll stay behind, just the two of us. Neiaphi will travel with Andonis's family. If they don't show by summer, we'll follow."

"You're set on this decision?"

"Yes, Sir."

"Well, then, good luck. I hope to see you following us soon. I'll send a scout back occasionally to look for you." Neiluios stood. "Thank you, Sir. I was afraid you would force us to leave."

Addident shook his head. "I put myself in your position, and if your wife is anything like mine, it wouldn't matter what I said."

"Thank you, Sir." Neiluios left, feeling a weight lifted from his shoulders.

He found Altesse and Neiaphi sitting by the fire in his hut. They looked up at him, their eyes filled with questions.

"We can stay," Altesse sighed, relief washing over her.

"Do I really have to leave you?" Neiaphi asked, her voice tinged with concern. "Can't I stay as well?"

"Yes, dear. You need to continue. This is something your mother and I must do. It's not your obligation. We'll follow behind you by summer at the latest."

Neiaphi hung her head, accepting the truth. She just hoped her dream was real and that they wouldn't have to separate after all.

Three days later, the first group set out, followed by the second two days after. On the morning the final group was scheduled to leave, a massive snowstorm descended, blanketing the camp in white before anyone could rise.

As they emerged from their huts, biting snow and hail assaulted them, pelting the ground with such force that it felt as if the hail was coming up from the earth instead of falling from the sky. The storm raged throughout the day and into the night. When morning finally arrived, the sun shone brightly, but the deep layer of snow and fierce winds created treacherous travel conditions.

"Looks like everyone's staying put for at least another day, Sir," Net said, peering out the door.

"I'm glad," Neiaphi replied. "More time together," she mumbled as she retreated deeper into their home.

Sometime in the night, the wind finally subsided, replaced by the haunting chorus of wolves howling at the moon and calling to one another. Little sleep was had by many in the village that night.

As soon as dawn broke over the horizon, Altesse hurried out of their hut to start a fire, performing her daily ritual of checking around the house for any signs of nighttime visitors. Finding nothing amiss, she walked back to the fire, her heart heavy as she warmed herself against the chill of the morning air.

She rounded the last corner, her eyes downcast, and nearly bumped into a giant wolf sitting by the fire. Startled, she jumped and stifled a scream. The wolf remained still, its yellow eyes fixed on her. There was something unnerving about those eyes—they were unlike any wolf's or any animals she had ever encountered.

She swallowed hard a few times and wet her lips with her tongue. "Greetings," she finally said. "Do you have word about my boys?"

The wolf let out a low growl, prompting Altesse to take a cautious step back. In response, the wolf stood, turned, and bounded away. Altesse watched it disappear into the trees, her heart heavy as she lingered, staring long after it was gone.

A soft cooing sound drew her attention back to the fire. Altesse rushed forward, shaking with anticipation, and lifted the blanket to reveal two little boys sound asleep inside. Dropping to her knees, she sobbed with relief.

Annas stirred, yawning and stretching, before opening his eyes and smiling up at her. He reached a chubby hand toward her, giggling. She grasped his hand and pressed a kiss to his tiny fingers. At that moment, Praxis stirred and began to cry.

"Shush now, little one, Mother's here," she whispered, cradling Praxis in her arms. He settled down instantly.

Within moments, the entire hut was crowded around Altesse and the boys. Neiluios knelt beside the basket and gently lifted Annas. The little boy reached up and playfully grabbed his nose, causing everyone to laugh.

"They seem healthy, ma'am," Cleop observed. "Well-fed and happy."

"They do indeed; let's get them inside," Neiluios said. Everyone filed back into the hut, their spirits lifted by the sight of the boys. Altesse settled on the floor, wrapping the blanket tighter around them as she gazed lovingly at her sons. The warmth of the fire and the joy of the reunion filled the space, dispelling the lingering chill of the storm outside.

At daybreak, the last group of travelers set out, undeterred by the wet and muddy conditions. With determination in their hearts, they began their journey toward the Pillars, their sights ultimately set on Atlantis. Each step forward felt like a promise of new beginnings, despite the challenging terrain beneath their feet.

After three days of traveling, Cret and his group sought shelter from a late spring storm that raged for most of the day and night. When the tempest finally subsided, they resumed their slow trek southward on foot, the damp ground underfoot a reminder of the storm they had endured.

"I really wish that cursed ship hadn't broken. I'm not used to this mode of travel," Pelagios remarked. Simandro huffed, shifting under his weight. "No offense, my friend, but I'm sure riding you is more agreeable than any horse; my behind just isn't accustomed to this kind of abuse."

Simandro chuckled. "My back isn't used to this, either."

"I can walk for a while if needed," Pelagios offered.

He shook his head, his hair whipping back and forth. "No need. I'm fine for a while longer."

"Have you ever been to the Pillars?"

Simandro shook his head again. "No, I've never ventured so far from home before. I never thought I would, either. How far from your home are you?"

Pelagios ran his fingers through his hair, frustration etching his features. "Further than you can imagine. My ship…" he gestured toward the sleek vessel behind them, "travels at many times the speed of light. It took a considerable journey to reach this planet."

"Speed of light? Journeying through the stars? You two-legged beings are truly fascinating," came the reply, a mix of intrigue and disbelief in their voice.

"Centaurs have journeyed through the stars; that's how your ancestors arrived here, you know."

"I've learned that recently, but it's still difficult to grasp. Did we have our own ships? Did we operate them ourselves?"

"No, my friend. Your kind was always the passengers."

"That's a relief."

"Why is that?"

"I would hate to think we've regressed and lost skills we once possessed."

"I'm certain that anything forgotten could be relearned with relative ease."

"Report!"

"I located a camp where they sheltered during that storm over there. They're about a day ahead of us on foot."

Captain Rirmell nodded, his expression steely. "Mount up. We'll find them tonight," he growled, determination lacing his words.

The ship roared to life once more, lifting slowly above the treetops. After a brief moment to stabilize the engines, it shot forward in a blur.

"Do you think those people will find them tonight?" Six asked Hepluosis in a hushed voice.

"I hope so. I'm eager to prove my worth," Hepluosis replied.

"You'll get your chance, Sir."

Hepluosis nodded, his gaze fixed on the passing trees, a scowl etched on his face. He closed his eyes, steadying himself against the dizzying blur outside.

# ∞ 29 ∞
# CONVERGENCE

"**COME** on, hurry up! RUN!" Ambrite yelled, his voice cutting through the chaos. Everyone sprinted through the dense forest, their feet pounding the ground. Curses escaped lips as each stumble sent them sprawling into the dark underbrush.

Wolves howled and bayed, closing in from behind. With each passing moment, their cries grew louder and more frenzied, echoing through the trees.

"Where are we going?" Tivadarios screamed above the terrifying howls.

"I don't know—just keep running!" Ambrite shouted back.

They finally burst through the trees into a clearing, their speed increasing as they raced across the open ground. In the distance, a small hill silhouetted against the sunset beckoned.

"Make for high ground!" Cret yelled, his voice rising above the din. "Maybe we can find a place to make a stand!"

Everyone veered to the right, centaurs, and horses straining for breath as they raced through the twilight. As they approached the hill, a small village came into view. Several men, alerted by the howling wolves, stood at the perimeter, swords drawn.

"HOLD!" one of them shouted, his voice firm.

"Please, we seek refuge! Please!" Cret yelled, raising his hands in a gesture of peace.

"Turn and stand your ground. What's chasing you?" the apparent leader demanded. The other men gaped in astonishment at the centaurs, clearly having never seen one before.

"Wolves—lots of them," Ambrite replied, urgency in his voice. One of the villagers squeaked in surprise at his words, taken aback by the sight before him.

Cret leaped from Rees while he was still running, tucking into a roll before springing back to his feet. Tivadarios and Pelagios allowed their mounts to come to a halt before dismounting.

"How many do you think are out there?" the apparent leader asked, scanning the trees.

"Unsure, Sir. They started chasing us a while ago, but we didn't stop to count," Cret replied, breathing heavily.

"It seems they've stopped pursuing you now."

Cret nodded, glancing back. "Still baying, but at least they're keeping their distance in the trees."

"Fires are surrounding the village tonight; every man is on watch!" the village leader yelled, rallying his men into action. "My name is Stavros. I must say, you are a curious party—not from around here, I presume."

Ambrite stepped forward, bowing his head in respect. "We are from the northwest. I am Ambrite, the leader of this small group of centaurs." One by one, everyone introduced themselves to Stavros, and the tension of the moment began to ease.

"What brings you to our village?" Stavros asked, his gaze steady.

"Just passing through, Sir," Cret replied.

"Well, we can offer you a night of standing watch in exchange for your story—and a hot meal in the morning," Stavros proposed, a hint of a smile on his lips.

"That sounds like a fair offer, Sir. We'll take it." Cret extended his hand, sealing the agreement.

"Find a fire," Stavros instructed, "and we'll speak further during the morning meal."

As the new sun rose, the wolves remained hidden, finally falling silent. The watch-fires were extinguished, giving way to cook fires, and younger boys, took the place of the weary men who had kept watch through the night.

The newcomers ate in silence, huddled together, utterly exhausted from their harrowing night.

"Do you feel like sharing your stories now?" Stavros asked as he approached, his expression curious and inviting.

"Can I ask you a question first? I see the village here, but I also see structures up the hill. What's up there?" Cret inquired.

"That is our holy temple. Our priestess resides there, speaking to the gods. Our purpose is to ensure she is well cared for while performing her duties," Stavros explained.

"A noble mission," Cret acknowledged. "But there isn't much to tell you about us."

"I find that hard to believe," Stavros countered, a hint of a smile on his lips. "Three humans with two horses traveling alongside seven centaurs—a creature I didn't even know existed until last evening."

"Tivadarios and I were assisting Lyric and Justic when we encountered the other five centaurs. Along the way, we met Pelagios, who had lost his mount. He agreed to help us in our search."

"Search for what?" Stavros asked, curiosity piqued.

"The centaurs are searching for something to aid their race," Cret replied cryptically, leaving the details hanging in the air.

"What exactly are they searching for?" Stavros pressed, his brow furrowed.

"We don't know what we're looking for," Justic answered, a hint of frustration in his voice.

"If you don't know what it is, how will you find it?" Stavros asked, confusion evident.

"When I find it, I'll know," Lyric replied, his tone enigmatic.

"Well, I asked for a story, and I received one. There's clearly much more to it than you've shared." Stavros paused, studying their faces. "But I will respect your privacy. Where to now?"

"Not sure. Have you ever heard of The Pillars of Hercules?" Cret inquired, a spark of hope in his eyes.

"Yes, you're quite far from them. The quickest way to get there is by boat," Stavros said, noting the collective groan from the centaurs. "Not fond of water, I see?"

"Centaurs prefer to keep their hooves on solid ground," Simandro grumbled, his expression dark.

"Well, that option is still available, but it will take many more moons," Stavros replied. "I can help you arrange passage if you wish."

"That would be very helpful, thank you," Cret said, relief evident in his voice.

"Good, good. However, I'm afraid you'll be here for a few days. A merchant from Krisa trades with us; he's the one who can arrange your passage. We expect him in a few days."

"Well, if you don't mind our company, we'd welcome the rest," Cret replied, a hint of a smile on his lips.

"Wolves are chasing them. Is this a common occurrence? Wolves chasing centaurs?" Captain Rirmell asked, his gaze fixed on the scene below as they flew high above the trees. Seven centaurs and two horses raced across a clearing, pursued by a large pack of wolves.

Brutus crossed his arms, his expression grim. "Only the largest variety, which we call the Wers. We've never gotten along; we compete for territory and food. They're unusually smart and calculating, and they usually avoid two-legs like you."

"There's a village up ahead, Sir," one of the soldiers reported.

"Where?" Captain Rirmell snapped, scanning the landscape.

"There, Sir! They're headed right for it."

"By Zeus, we've lost them again. Circle around the village. We'll find a place to land away from the wolves and keep watch. Once they leave the village's safety, we'll capture them once and for all."

"Cret, Cret!!" Tivadarios called from the entrance of Cret's hut. "Get out here!"

"What is it?" Cret emerged, sword in hand.

"Whoa, stand down! There's no danger, but look at what's coming." Tivadarios pointed to the north, where a large group of travelers was making their way toward them.

Cret's heart stopped, and a lump formed in his throat. Could that be Neiaphi? He raced to the holding pens and leaped onto Rees's bare back, urging the horse forward. He trotted briskly through town before spurring Rees into a gallop.

Several men broke from the group to intercept the approaching rider.

"Addident, Sir! It's so nice to see you again," Cret said, coming to a stop.

"Cret, my boy! Where's your father? How did you beat us here? Did everyone make it safely?" Addident asked in a rush, his voice filled with concern.

Cret raised his hand with a smile. "That's a long story. Have you had trouble? Your group looks a little small."

"This is only a third of us. We split up to avoid looking like an invading army," Addident replied with a chuckle.

"Great idea." Cret strained his neck, peering past Addident. "Is everyone else far behind?"

"She's not with us," Addident replied.

"Oh," Cret said, wincing.

"Don't worry; she's with the third group. It'll be several days before they arrive. Do you think this town will mind us resting for a few days?"

"Let's go ask, and then I'll answer your questions," Cret suggested.

They rode back to the village together.

"Stavros, this is Addident," Cret called as they approached. "He's the leader of our group, and I haven't seen him in some time. He would like permission for his group to rest here for a few days."

Stavros fell silent for a moment, then lifted his gaze to the temple. "We must ask Pythia; only she can permit so many to stay at the base of Pytho."

"Pythia? Who's that?" Addident asked, curiosity evident.

"Our priestess. Come, we'll go ask."

They walked the winding path up the hill to the temple in silence, the surrounding atmosphere both calming and surreal. Cret glanced around, reminded of a visit to an ancient temple back on Romota with his grandmother; it had the same sacred feeling.

As they approached, two priests emerged from a small building to the right of the main temple structure. Dressed in long white robes, both men had their hoods raised, casting their faces in shadow.

The priests bowed to Stavros. "These men request an audience."

"You know that is not allowed at this time. Come back on the seventh day of the next moon. These two have plenty of time to perform the cleansing before then. Good day." Both men turned to leave.

"Let them come," a sing-song voice called from within the temple. One of the priests rushed to the entrance and bowed deeply. "Addident and Cret, please join me," the woman thundered, her tone both commanding and inviting. The two men exchanged startled glances.

Tentatively, they approached the temple. Once at the entrance, they hesitated.

"Please, gentlemen, I will not bite. Join me; we have much to discuss," she urged, her voice warm yet firm.

They entered the temple and found a beautiful woman seated on a simple chair in the center of the room. She wore a flowing white dress, and her sandaled feet were crossed beneath the chair, her hands resting lightly on her lap.

"Welcome. I have waited for many moons to meet you. I am Pythia," she said, her voice serene.

"Thank you for agreeing to meet with us. As you seem to already know, I am Addident." He bowed his head slightly. "May I ask how you know who we are?"

"Let us go somewhere more private. Stavros, please remain here or return to the village," Pythia replied, gesturing toward a door at the back of the temple.

Stavros entered behind them silently, bowing before retreating to give them space.

Pythia stood gracefully and led them deeper into the temple, down a spiral staircase. At the bottom, they encountered a hole in the ground with a tripod chair positioned above it. Behind the chair, a hidden entrance led to a small, dimly lit room.

"Please, have a seat," she offered.

"Thank you, ma'am—um, Pythia. I'm not sure what to call you," Cret stammered, feeling a mix of awe and nervousness.

"Pythia is fine," she replied with a warm smile.

"What do you do here, if that's not too bold to ask?" Addident inquired, curiosity lighting his eyes.

"What the people here believe has been changing lately," Pythia explained. "In the past, they believed I listened to Gaia and spoke for her. Now, they think this temple belongs to Apollo, one of the new gods in their religion."

Addident and Cret exchanged confused glances. "Where are you from?" Addident asked, his curiosity deepening.

Pythia smiled shyly. "I was born in the village below. Very few of them know our true origins. When I was chosen to be the next Pythia, I was educated in our true history."

"Do you really speak to the gods?" Cret asked cautiously, his eyes searching hers.

"My dear Cret, you know the answer to that," she replied with a knowing smile.

"Then how do you know who we are?" he pressed.

"We have technology that I use in this room, which allows me to perceive people's thoughts," she explained.

"I've heard of such technology, but it's illegal to possess it on Romota," Addident stated, a hint of concern in his voice.

"Well, I'm glad I'm here then," Pythia continued. "As soon as I learned about your impending voyage, I followed you and tried to help in any way I could. I'm limited in what I can do and how far my reach extends, but you are an amazing group of people—determined and wonderfully kind. I want to ensure that you reach your destination safely. I have several boats on their way; they'll arrive at our port in less than a moon. Your entire group will be welcome here until then."

"That's wonderful news. Where will we be heading?" Addident asked.

"Directly to the Pillars," Pythia replied. "I would send you all the way to Atlantis, but if you bypass the Pillar without Royal permission, you'll be sunk before you even see the city. I'm afraid there are limitations to what even I can do."

"My Lady, the assistance you've provided is more than appreciated, and you have my greatest admiration," Addident said sincerely.

"Addident, third in line to the Royal Throne of Romota, please do not thank me just yet. Your journey is far from over and still fraught with peril." Addident bowed his head in acknowledgment. "I am honored to have met you both. You may take your leave."

Addident and Cret stood, bowed, and turned to leave.

"Cret, please stay for a moment," Pythia called. Both men stopped in their tracks. "I have information only Cret needs to hear. He'll only be a moment behind you." Addident nodded and stepped out.

"Cret, please sit again," Pythia urged.

Cret sat, his gaze fixed intently on her. "Neiaphi is well. Put your mind at ease," she said, her voice soothing.

His mouth dropped open in disbelief. "Is she close?" he asked softly, hope lacing his words.

Pythia dropped her gaze, her expression somber. "She has been delayed by the recent storm. You'll be gone before she arrives, I'm afraid. You must leave immediately; you are needed."

"By whom?" Cret asked, confusion flickering across his face.

"Atlantis," she replied, her voice steady.

"Atlantis? We're still far from there; you said so yourself. And they don't even know me. How could they need me?"

"All you say is true, but trust me, you are needed," Pythia insisted.

"Okay. What do I need to do?"

"I'll have Stavros take you to our port. You will meet with Captain Matteas."

"What about the others I traveled with?"

"Tivadarios can decide for himself. His future is not tied to yours. Please send the others to see me. I wish to meet with them before nightfall."

"Yes, ma'am." He hesitated, then added, "Are you sure I can't stay and see Neiaphi just for a few moments? Just so she knows I'm okay."

Pythia shook her head. "I don't understand. What harm could come of it?"

"You and Neiaphi's futures are tied together, but not yet. You must each go your own way for now."

"But we'll be together in the future?" he pressed, hope flickering in his voice.

"Cret, my dear boy, I cannot tell you your future. It must unfold naturally. I've seen you together, and I've seen you apart. I've seen you happy in both cases, and I've seen you miserable in both as well. Your future is yours; just live it."

Cret hung his head, raking his fingers through his hair, feeling the weight of her words.

"I know that's not what you want to hear," Pythia said gently.

Cret swallowed hard. "Have her parents chosen for her yet?"

"They are allowing her to choose."

After a moment's pause, he asked, "Has she chosen?"

Pythia studied him for a few moments, then sighed. "I've instructed her to make a choice, but she won't marry until she reaches Atlantis."

Cret released a breath he didn't realize he was holding. *She has chosen; she is promised. Would he be able to win her back? How would he reach her before she got to Atlantis if he didn't go straight there?* "Do you know who she chose?"

She nodded. "You don't know him. He's a good, caring man, very protective of her. Don't worry; she thinks of you often. All hope is not lost." She held up a finger. "But do not shut your heart to the opportunities that present themselves to you."

"What do you mean?" Cret asked, a frown creasing his brow.

"I've said all I can. Please send the others to see me. I have information Lyric needs."

Cret stood, feeling the weight of her words. "Thank you for your guidance," he said, then turned and departed.

As Cret walked back down the hill to the village, his thoughts drifted. Pythia had mentioned instructing Neiaphi. How had she done that? "I should have asked her," he mumbled to himself.

"Should have asked who what?" Lyric said, appearing beside him. He jumped at the sound of her voice. "Sorry, didn't mean to startle you."

"Oh, you're just the centaur I was coming to see," Cret replied, recovering quickly. She raised an eyebrow. "The

Priestess Pythia wishes to see all the centaurs right now. She says she has important information for you."

Lyric broke into a canter back to the village, glancing over her shoulder. "Thank you! I'll go get the others!" she called back.

"Take Pelagios with you, please!" he yelled after her.

"Welcome, noble centaurs and Pelagios of Romota. Please enter," a voice called from within the Temple. The gathered group exchanged nervous glances before stepping inside.

They approached Pythia, who smiled warmly at them. "Lyric, my child, it is so nice to meet you at last, all of you. I've been looking forward to this moment for some time. Your journey is just beginning. As the prophecy foretold, centaurs are in grave danger. You'll soon meet someone who will be the key to your salvation."

"Who?" Lyric whispered, her curiosity piqued.

"I cannot tell you his name. He'll be driven to help you; you must accept his assistance."

"Why so cryptic?" Justic asked, furrowing his brow.

She shrugged. "Sometimes my visions are not clear."

Ambrite stepped forward. "Are we all needed on this journey?"

"Two of you are not needed; two will continue with Cret."

"Which two?"

"Speak with him tonight, and the choice will be made known."

"So Cret is leaving?" Lyric asked, concern etching her features. "I thought he was essential to my quest."

"He was up to this point; his path is changing. He'll be leaving tomorrow. You must stay until the rest arrive."

Justic crossed his arms. "More two-legs?"

Pythia laughed lightly. "Yes, I'm afraid this planet is filled with us, which is your problem."

"What about me?" Pelagios asked, his brow furrowing.

"Your future is now tied to that of the centaurs, but do not fret. You'll see Romota again if you desire it." He let out a sigh of relief. "Now go; you have much to discuss."

Cret and Tivadarios sat around a campfire in a secluded part of the village, the sun dipping below the horizon as they engaged in quiet conversation.

"May we join you?" Lyric asked, her voice soft.

"Of course! You don't have to ask permission," Cret replied with a warm smile. He offered her a cup. "How did it go up there?"

Lyric settled beside him, taking the cup with a sigh. "It seems our paths are parting, my friend."

Cret nodded. "I figured as much. Where are you headed?"

"I'm staying here, at least for a while. I'm supposed to meet someone who will save the centaurs. What about you?"

"To a ship, I think. I'm meant to help Atlantis somehow." He shook his head in frustration.

"I see she left you in the dark as well."

"Yeah, it's very frustrating."

"What about you, Pelagios? Did she have any advice for you?"

"My future is tied to Lyric's for now, it seems," he said.

"Tivadarios?" Lyric asked.

"I'll be staying with Cret," he stated.

"Really? I thought you would want to see your family again," Cret said, stunned.

Tivadarios smiled and, with a couple of firm but friendly pats on Cret's back, said, "Nay, I go where you go. That's what friends do."

"Thanks, my friend. I welcome your company."

"I'll be joining you as well," Bal-air said.

"As will I," said Myreia.

"You will?" Cret asked.

"Pythia said two of us would be joining you and that the decision to do so would just come to us. This just feels like what I am supposed to do," Myreia replied.

"I feel the same. Traveling by ship doesn't sound enjoyable, but I feel compelled to stay with you, Cret," Bal-air added.

"Well, thank you. We leave at sun-up. I have a letter to write for my parents. I'll see you then."

"Cret, wait up!" Lyric called, trotting after him.

He turned to see her catching up. "You mentioned writing a letter to your parents. I'd be honored to deliver it for you."

"That would be great. I'll have another one for you to deliver, too, if that's all right."

"Of course, no problem. Who's the other letter for? Her?"

"Yeah. I'm not sure what to say, though."

"Did you find out anything today?" She gestured toward the temple with her head.

"A lot of words, but not many answers. I'll see you later."

# ∞ 30 ∞
## PYTHIA

CRET waved goodbye to Lyric and the others as his small group made their way toward the port south of the village. That night, he slept little, wrestling with the letters he needed to write to his parents and Neiaphi. He had no idea what to say. Why had he chosen to leave instead of staying, especially with Neiaphi so close? He missed her deeply—would she believe his reasons? Was it even logical to go when he knew she was nearby?

He must have started and discarded a dozen letters, always pausing at the same line. *Who was she promised to? Why hadn't she waited? But was it fair to ask her that?* As far as she knew, he was still back at the processing plant, and she might never see him again. Of course, she had to move on. Was it right to show up and make her choose? Could she even select? Would she pick him?

Maybe he should have told Lyric to pretend he was missing. Would she have done it? But lying wasn't an option; she deserved to know how he felt and where he had gone. She would either love him for his honesty or hate him for leaving, and he wouldn't be there to find out which.

"There she is!" Stavros exclaimed as sails appeared on the horizon, breaking through Cret's spiraling thoughts. "I'll take Cret to the ship first and then return for everyone else." The group nodded in understanding—there was no need to draw attention to the centaurs.

"Do you know where she's headed?" Cret asked, a knot tightening in his stomach.

"I do not. Captain Matteas will inform you of that, I'm sure."

"Well, then, let's meet this Captain," Cret said, a mix of eagerness and apprehension in his voice.

"Eager to be on your way, I see," Stavros remarked, but Cret remained silent, focused on the ship ahead.

The vessel was tied to the dock, gently rocking on the choppy water. "Hello, the ship!" Stavros called out, his voice carrying over the waves.

"Hello, the dock!" came the cheerful reply from aboard.

"I have business with Captain Matteas," Stavros announced, stepping forward.

"What business is that?" a burly, sour-looking man demanded, his eyes widening in surprise. His mouth fell open, then snapped shut. "Come aboard," he said quickly. Cret and Stavros exchanged curious glances.

"Hurry up, young man! I need to get your cargo on board and set sail," the captain bellowed.

Cret rushed up the gangplank, confusion flickering in his mind. "You knew I was coming?"

"The Priestess spoke to me," the captain replied, his tone now more serious. "She told me to expect you and to take your special cargo with me."

"Where are you headed?" Cret asked, curiosity etched on his face.

"She didn't tell you?" the captain replied, raising an eyebrow.

Cret shook his head. "She mentioned I was to help Atlantis, but that was it."

"Interesting. That nymph speaks with a forked tongue, I swear." The captain spat on the ground, grunting in irritation. "I can't discuss it here. Let's push off and retrieve your cargo. But I can't fathom why you left it east of here, on the other side of the knoll."

Cret shrugged. "That's where I left it. Stavros will be staying here. Let me say goodbye, and then we can be off."

Stavros looked at Cret, confusion etching his features. Cret led him back to the gangplank. "Do you know the place the captain mentioned?" he asked quietly.

"Yes, it's not far from here, but it's secluded."

"Pythia thought of everything." He chuckled. "Can you get the others there before this ship arrives?"

Cret considered for a moment. "Shouldn't be too hard. I'll leave immediately. Good luck to you, Cret. May the gods smile on you always."

"Thank you, my friend."

Just before sundown, the ship finally set sail. "How long until we reach my cargo?" Cret asked. Captain Matteas stood at the bow, gazing out at the rough water.

"Before sunrise. You can use my cabin if you need to rest."

"No, I think the sea air will do me good. I'll find a quiet spot to rest." The captain nodded.

Cret bolted awake, startled. He hadn't meant to doze off. The sky was lightening with the rosy hue of dawn, and sailors moved about the ship, pulling on ropes and calling out orders. Several were working the lines to ease the mainsheet, slowing their forward momentum.

"So, what is this cargo we're retrieving?" Captain Matteas yelled at Cret from across the deck.

Cret peered into the darkness, scanning the shoreline. He spotted Tivadarios astride his horse near a large outcropping.

"You'll see soon enough," he replied.

Matteas scowled. "I don't like all these secrets."

"When you see my companions, you'll understand."

"Companions? I wasn't told I'd have more passengers; I was only informed about cargo and stock."

"Well, the stock are my companions," Cret replied, chuckling as the captain raised an eyebrow. "You'll see soon enough."

"Can they swim?"

"I know one can."

"Lower the dinghy," the captain yelled gruffly.

Four sailors rowed the small boat with Cret and the captain toward the shore. Tivadarios dismounted and helped pull the craft ashore. "Didn't take you long to get here!" he said.

"Not at all. Is everyone ready to go?" Tivadarios nodded and then whistled.

Myreia and Bal-air approached, leading Cret's horse. At first, as they emerged from the bushes, they appeared to be two people guiding another horse. But as they drew closer, the reality of their size became apparent. Two of the sailors gasped, one made a sign across his chest, and the captain swore, backing up a couple of steps.

"What in the name of all the gods on Mount Olympus are those?"

"We are centaurs," Bal-air said coldly.

One of the sailors jumped into the water and swam back to the waiting ship.

"Are you demons?" one sailor whispered.

Myreia scoffed. "We are not demons; we are flesh and blood like you, and we have feelings."

"Please forgive him," the captain said, clearing his throat. "We've never seen the likes of you before, and I'm afraid we overreacted."

Bal-air nodded, while Myreia frowned but remained silent. "How are we to board your ship?" Bal-air asked.

"We have a flat raft we can send out. You should be able to lie on it while we hoist it aboard. Can you keep the horses calm during the trip?"

"Shouldn't be a problem," Bal-air replied.

"Good." The captain turned to face the ship and waved his hands in the air. Moments later, a raft was lowered into the water and rowed to shore.

"Where are we headed now?" Cret finally asked the captain.

"We're supplying Atlantis's naval force. We'll rendezvous with them in a few days. Will you be joining them?"

"I think so; Pythia said I was needed to help Atlantis."

"Have you been to the Great City?" he asked, slightly in awe.

"No," Cret shook his head, "but I've been heading there."

"You're a strange group," the captain harrumphed.

A small village at the base of a large hill came into view. Neiaphi gazed at the temple atop the hill, her eyes wide and her jaw slightly slack.

"What's the matter?" Andonis asked, riding beside her.

"I've seen that temple before," she replied quietly.

Andonis frowned. "Me too! This is the one from my dream I told you about."

Neiaphi nodded in agreement.

"Do you think the voice lives here?" Andonis asked.

"I hope so. I'd like to meet her and have her stop bothering me while I'm sleeping." She frowned at the thought.

"Are you still having trouble with nightmares?"

"I have the same dreams most nights; only a few of them are nightmares."

Several riders approached from the village. Greish nudged his horse into a trot and motioned for Andonis to join him.

They broke into a canter. As they neared, Andonis spotted Addident riding out to greet them.

He smiled broadly and raised his hand in greeting. "Andonis, my boy! Glad that storm didn't slow you down too much. Is that Neiluios and Altesse I see back there?"

Andonis nodded. "Yes, sir. The twins have been returned."

Addident's jaw dropped. "Truly?"

"Yes. The morning after the storm broke, the boys were left in a basket outside their hut." They turned around and headed back to the slow-moving wagons.

"Glad to see you, Neiluios," Addident said. "Head east of town; you'll find our camp. You're all welcome to visit the town proper whenever you like. I'll be calling a meeting tonight. We have some news to share."

"Good or bad, sir?"

"Good news, good news!"

The sun slid below the horizon in a fiery glow, and voices filled the night as everyone gathered to hear the news Addident had.

Neiaphi and her family huddled with several women hovering over Altesse and the twins. "Neiaphi, can I have a word with you?" Addident asked.

She nodded, and Andonis stood to follow. "Just Neiaphi, please," Addident added. Andonis slowly sat back down, nodding.

"I wanted to tell you what I'm about to share with everyone else first."

Neiaphi stared at him. "Why?"

"It will affect you more than anyone, and I don't think it would be fair to surprise you with it. Cret arrived here before we did," he said slowly.

Neiaphi's eyes went wide as she frantically searched the crowd.

"He's not here now, but he was, and now he's on his way to Atlantis."

Neiaphi furrowed her brow, trying to grasp what he was saying. "Why did he leave?"

"I believe he left a note for you. I'll make sure you get it tonight."

She nodded and somberly headed back to her family.

"What's wrong?" Andonis asked. She shook her head but remained silent.

Addident stood next to the fire and slowly raised his hand. Everyone turned to face him, quieting down.

"I am so warmed to see all these smiling faces tonight. We have a few new faces with us, and we'll soon have many more." Murmurs broke out among the gathered crowd. He held his hand up until they fell silent.

"When we first arrived here, we were greeted by two old friends and, along with them, a few unexpected ones. Cret and Tivadarios beat us here." Andonis glanced at Neiaphi; she was looking down, wringing her hands.

"The rest of their group managed to flee the processing plant safely, thanks to the Loyals. They wintered not far from where we did, as far as we could tell. We will stay here, sending out patrols daily to search for them. We'll continue to Atlantis once our family is complete again."

Cheers erupted from the crowd. Addident raised his hands once more.

"Cret and Tivadarios have continued on, but they left us some new friends. I'd like to introduce you to Pelagios. He's a transport crewman from Romota." Questions erupted from the crowd. Addident smiled and waved for quiet again.

"And these are his friends: Lyric, Justic, Ambrite, Peleros, and Simandro." A hush fell over the crowd as the centaurs emerged from a tent. "These five, along with the two accompanying Cret, were born here on Earth. I know everyone has lots of questions, but please keep them to one at a time. We don't want to overwhelm our new friends."

Neiaphi kept her eyes downcast and slipped away silently.

Andonis noticed her departure and turned to follow, but Neiluios grabbed his arm and shook his head. "Leave her for now," he said. Andonis stopped, staring after her fleeing form.

"Trust me; she has a lot to think about right now. Talk to her in the morning." Neiluios nodded. "By then, she'll be thinking clearly again."

Pelagios and the five centaurs filtered through the crowd, answering questions. Lyric headed in the direction Addident had instructed her. She spotted two women, each holding a baby. That must be Altesse; she needed to find Neiluios. There he was—this man fit his description.

Nervously, she walked through the throng of people, several children smiling up at her. Before meeting Cret, she had never seen a two-leg; now, she was swimming through a sea of them.

"Sir, may I speak with you?" she asked Neiluios.

"Lyric, is it?" She nodded. "I'm Neiluios. How can I help you?"

"I have a couple of letters for you from Cret."

"Cret? I see." He took the letters from Lyric, noting that one was addressed to him and the other to Neiaphi.

"Cret said you may read the one for Neiaphi, and then you can decide." She frowned. "What are you to decide?"

"Cret has written a couple of letters for Neiaphi. He lets me read them first so I can determine if she's emotionally able to handle their contents. I've let her read all of them so far." He placed the letters in his pocket. "How did you meet Cret?" He gestured for her to walk with him.

They strolled slowly through town as Lyric recounted how she met Cret and shared their adventures together. "That's quite a story. Thank you for sharing it. I'd better find Neiaphi. I'm sure I'll see you again soon."

Neiluios made his way back to their new camp. The sound of crying led him to their tent. Altesse and Cleop were consoling the twins, Net was repairing a basket, and Neiaphi was nowhere to be seen.

"Where's Neiaphi?" he asked.

Altesse's eyes went wide with fear. "I thought she was with you. Andonis was here a few moments ago looking for her as well." She covered her mouth with her free hand to stifle a sob. "Don't worry, I'll find her."

"I'll help too, sir." Net stood and followed him out of the tent.

The full moon hung high overhead, and the stars twinkled brightly. A warm breeze flowed gently through the camp, lifting the loose edges of the tents.

"I'll go this way, sir." Neiluios nodded and headed in the opposite direction.

He moved quickly through town, peering down every alleyway and behind every house. Where could she have gone? She knows better than to wander alone. Fear bubbled up inside him. All streets led to the base of Temple Hill. As he approached, he spotted Andonis standing at the bottom, staring up the path. "Do you think she went up to the Temple?" Neiluios asked, stopping beside Andonis.

"That's the only place I haven't checked yet," he replied.

"Shall we?" Neiluios gestured toward the Temple.

"Do you want me to join you, sir?" Net asked as he rounded a corner.

"Net, please go back to the tent and let Altesse know where I've gone."

"Yes, sir."

The Temple was a modest structure set atop the hill, with a couple of smaller buildings standing off to one side. Torches flickered in the darkness, illuminating the entrance.

"Please enter, my friends," a female voice called from within. They exchanged glances. "I have information for you both."

They stepped into the dimly lit Temple. "Hello!" Neiluios called out.

"Hello, gentlemen. It's a pleasure to meet you. I am Pythia." A woman in a pure white gown emerged from the shadows.

"Hello," they said in unison.

"You said you have information for us?" Andonis asked.

"But first, may I ask who you are?" Neiluios inquired.

She smiled. "I told you, my name is Pythia."

"Yes, you did. But who are you?"

"I am the Priestess here at Apollo's Temple."

"I've heard of this place," Andonis said. "You can foretell the future."

"Truly?" Neiluios whispered.

Pythia shook her head. "No, not really."

"That's not what I've heard. I've heard many tales of your predictions."

"All the stories you've heard are true to a point. We have technology that allows me to read minds, and in that way, I can influence someone's actions to make their future come true."

"But what about Neiaphi's dreams? There's no way you could have just molded those predictions," he said, skepticism evident in his voice.

She smiled. "Well, sometimes I get lucky." Andonis crossed his arms with a frown.

"Where is my daughter?" Neiluios interrupted.

"She's safe. She was here, and I sent her home with one of my acolytes." Neiluios stood. "Please stay. I have important information for you."

She paused for a moment. After he sat back down, she continued, "I know you have many questions; everyone does. As for you, Neiluios, you are on the right path. You are needed in Atlantis, but you won't stay long. Your sons are destined to help form a new nation—one that will rival Atlantis but will be accepted on this planet. They will become the technological leaders here without appearing foreign."

"Rasenna!" he whispered under his breath.

"You have already dreamed of it," she smiled. "Your boys, with your guidance, will lead those who need to flee Atlantis to a new land. You'll make your home there and flourish. However, the journey to that point will be difficult, but nothing worth having is ever easy."

"Why would anyone want to flee Atlantis?" Andonis asked.

"War is coming. Sooner than anyone would like."

"And I must take my family to Atlantis and survive a war?" Neiluios asked, astonished.

"You will survive; those you meet and befriend may not—at least not all of them. Life's lessons are never easy. This is an important step in the rearing of your twins. You may leave now and join your family. I wish you all the best that I know is coming your way. You and yours will be fine; take heart in that."

"What about me?" Andonis inquired.

"What I have for you is for your ears only."

"I will leave you then. Good night, and thank you, Pythia." Neiluios patted Andonis on the shoulder.

As he hurried back down the winding path, his thoughts raced. His little boys were destined to start a new civilization; it was beyond belief.

Neiaphi sat next to Net, staring into the fire that crackled merrily in front of their tent.

"Good evening, sir," Net said as Neiluios arrived.

Neiluios settled down next to Neiaphi, draping an arm around her shoulder and nodding to Net.

Neiaphi sighed and leaned into her father, but her eyes remained fixed on the flames.

"Do you want to talk about it?" he asked after a few moments. She shook her head.

"I have a letter from Cret for you," he said, holding it out for her.

Neiaphi stared out of the corner of her eye at the letter in her father's hand. Slowly, she willed her hand to move and took the letter, holding it gingerly and feeling the weight of the paper in her fingers.

"Are you going to read it?" he pressed.

"I will, but not now."

He nodded. "Pythia told me something interesting." At this, Neiaphi finally tore her gaze from the fire and looked up at him. "Your brothers will be helping to form a new nation when they get older."

"So… you will not be going to Atlantis?" Neiaphi asked.

"Oh, we will still go. I'm meant to raise the boys there, and after the war starts, we'll flee with others, marking the beginning of the new nation."

She breathed a shaky sigh. "Good. I don't want to go to Atlantis alone."

"We would never leave you; you know that."

She nodded, fiddling with the letter in her hands.

"Can you tell me what Pythia said?"

"I'm still processing what she told me. I need more time."

"Andonis, I have asked you to stay behind because what I have to tell you may be something you do not wish to share," Pythia began. Andonis nodded, his lips thinning into a grim line.

"I see several paths for you. Each holds its peril and its pleasure. No one path is better than the other. I have seen you choose one and then change to another."

"That doesn't sound very promising," he said with a hint of sarcasm.

"I wish I had an easier answer for you. Would you like me to continue?"

"Does it matter? If there are several paths, each filled with good and bad, what's the point in knowing them? Maybe I'd be better off not knowing my choices at all."

"You make a valid point; if that's your choice, so be it." She held up a hand to stay him. "However, I believe you should hear what I have to say regardless. Knowing your choices before entering the water, so to speak, is only fair."

Andonis thought for a moment, scratching his chin. "Okay, I will listen," he finally said.

The early morning sun found Andonis walking in circles around the perimeter of their camp.

After his conversation with Pythia, he had returned to his family's tent, his heart racing, knowing that sleep would elude him for some time. He stoked the fire and sat for a while, but that didn't help. So, he started to walk—just a few laps around the camp should calm him down and prepare him for sleep.

Yet hours later, with legs that screamed for rest, he still found himself strolling around the camp.

He stopped at the edge of the camp, furthest from his tent, and turned to face the rising sun, letting its warmth wash over him.

Suddenly, thundering hooves crashed through the trees, startling Andonis and sending him scrambling for the sword at his hip. A black horse burst from the underbrush, nearly colliding with him. The horse veered at the last moment, pivoting to face him. Andonis jumped aside, sword raised, pointing straight at the creature. As his blurry, sleep-deprived eyes focused, he realized it wasn't a horse at all. It was one of those centaur beings—the one with the striking green eyes.

"My apologies. I didn't see you until the last moment," she said, panting.

"What are you doing? What were you running from?" Andonis asked, his heart still hammering in his chest as he scanned the area for danger.

"I was just out for a run. There's no danger."

"A run at this hour?"

"I always run with the coming sun. I didn't expect to see any two-legs out and about so early."

"Two-legs?"

"That's what my people call yours." She gestured to his two legs and then to her own four.

"I understand the concept." He lowered his sword and stretched his back. "I'd prefer you call me Andonis rather than 'two-leg.'"

"As you wish, Andonis. I am Lyric."

His mouth dropped open. This was Lyric, the one Pythia had told him about. She played a pivotal role in one of the four options before him. Was it fate that he had run into her today? Pythia had said that helping Lyric get home and saving her people, along with the path where he and Neiaphi stayed together and made it to Atlantis, were the two strongest paths.

"What are you staring at?" Lyric asked, stepping back slightly.

Andonis held out his hands. "I'm sorry. Forgive my rudeness. I spoke with Pythia last night and was just thinking about what she said."

Lyric snorted. "That's one strange two-leg—predicting the future and all. Well, I must be off."

"Will I see you again?"

"I'm sure of it. I'm not leaving anytime soon. I need to find a way to save my people." With that, she set off at a brisk trot.

Andonis stared after her, a swirl of thoughts in his mind. How could he possibly help her save her people? He had only just learned of her existence.

"Good morning, dear," Altesse said as Neiaphi ducked out of the tent, squinting against the bright morning sun.

"Good morning, Mother. Have you seen Andonis yet?"

"A few moments ago." She nodded in the direction he had gone.

"I'll be back."

Neiaphi hurried down the path her mother indicated. Up ahead, she spotted Andonis walking slowly.

She slowed to match his pace as she reached him. He flinched slightly but relaxed when he realized it was her.

"Good morning," she said softly. "I'm sorry."

He stopped and turned to face her. "For what?"

"For taking off yesterday and making you and my father worry." She kept her gaze on the ground, her voice barely above a whisper. "Hearing about Cret being here just before us, then finding my way up that mountain and talking with Pythia—it was all just too much." She crossed her arms, hugging herself for comfort.

Andonis stepped closer, wrapping his arms around her and pulling her into a warm embrace.

"I'm just glad you weren't hurt." He led her over to a log and sat down.

They settled into silence, his arm still draped around her shoulders.

"What did Pythia say to you last night?" he asked tentatively. She stiffened at the question. "You don't have to tell me if you don't want to," he added quickly.

She slowly relaxed her muscles and let out a sigh. "No, it's all right. I can tell you. But first…" She looked up at him, searching his eyes. "Have you spoken with her?"

He nodded. "When your father and I were searching for you, we ended up at her temple."

"She told me that I have several paths to choose from," Neiaphi said softly.

"She told me the same thing."

"She said that only one of my paths leads to you." She fell silent, her gaze dropping to her hands in her lap.

"How many are with Cret?"

Without lifting her gaze, she replied, "One."

"How many other paths do you have?" he asked gently.

"Two. How many do you have?"

"Four," he said.

"We travel to Atlantis; you secure a top position; we flee with my parents after Atlantis is attacked," she murmured.

"I have that path, too. Do you want to share any of the others?"

"I don't know any details, just that one is with Cret. Pythia said I would find out when the path selects me. Do you know yours?"

He opened and closed his mouth, realizing Pythia hadn't shared her other paths with her. That meant his choice would determine hers. He could simply decide the path that kept them together and ignore the others. But could he lie to her about Pythia withholding that information from him?

"What's the matter?" she asked, concern creeping into her voice. "She told me details about all of them," he admitted.

"Why would she tell you yours but not mine?" Neiaphi asked, her brow furrowed in confusion.

"I think my choice will ultimately determine yours."

She frowned, concern etching her features. "I don't like the sound of that. So, my only options are to stay with you or leave, without knowing what I'd be stepping into. Not that I would ever choose to leave," she added hastily.

"I know that," he reassured her, squeezing her shoulders gently. "But I guess that's how life works. Knowing I have these choices—and that I'll find happiness no matter which I choose—kept me up all night."

"I'm sorry. It's not fair," Neiaphi murmured, resting her head against him. "Do you want to share any details?"

"I'm not sure just yet," he replied, his voice hesitant. "One path is extremely upsetting, and I don't know how I'd find happiness afterward. It's not a path I would choose; it feels more like a possibility if I don't act. Another is to stay here by myself." He took a deep breath, steadying himself. "And one path involves traveling with Lyric to help her save her people."

"Who is Lyric?" Neiaphi asked, curiosity flickering in her eyes.

"One of the centaurs. I ran into her this morning—well, more like she almost ran into me." He hesitated, feeling the weight of the conversation. Neiaphi reached up, placing a gentle hand on his cheek.

"It's okay. You don't have to tell me."

He nodded, grateful for her understanding. "You deserve to know, but I need a bit more time to think about it."

"Take all the time you need," she reassured him.

After a moment, he stood and offered her his hand. "I've made my decision."

She took his hand, still seated. "Already?"

He gently pulled her up until she stood beside him. "It's the only choice I know will make me happy. My place is with you if you'll have me."

"Of course, silly. I love you."

He pulled her into a tight hug, feeling her warmth against him. She pressed her head against his chest, and he closed his eyes, lost in the moment. But then, unsettling images flashed through his mind: advancing on Cret with his sword drawn, the terrible moment of betrayal as he ran him through, Neiaphi's horrified scream echoing in the background. Chills raced through him, his heart pounding with the weight of that choice. How could he ever do such a thing to her, to them?

"Are you okay?" she asked, tilting her head up to meet his gaze, concern etched on her face.

"Everything is just fine." He leaned down and kissed her, sealing his resolve. That path would never happen; he would do everything in his power to protect their future together.

As they pulled apart, Neiaphi smiled, a light spark shining in her eyes. "So, what now?"

"Now," he said, taking her hands in his, "we face whatever comes our way—together."

"Together," she echoed, squeezing his hands tightly. The promise hung in the air, a beacon of hope against the uncertainty ahead.

## ∞ 31 ∞
## PATHS

**NEIAPHI** left Andonis, leaving him to rest in his tent before his watch shift.

"Lyric? Do you have a moment?" Neiaphi called out as she approached three centaurs gathered around a fire at the edge of their village.

"Of course! Who are you?" Lyric replied, her eyes widening with interest.

"I'm Neiaphi," she said, and Lyric nodded, rising to her feet.

"Let's go for a walk," Lyric suggested, leading Neiaphi away from the other centaurs. Cypress bounded after them, tail wagging.

"Is that wolf yours?" Lyric asked, eyeing the dog curiously.

Neiaphi laughed. "He's not a wolf; he's a dog. His name is Cypress."

Lyric nodded, though she seemed a bit unsettled by Cypress's presence. "How can I help you?" she asked, clearing her throat.

"How long did you know Cret?" Neiaphi inquired.

"We met a couple of moons before the snow season," Lyric replied.

"Was he well when you parted?"

Lyric nodded. "Yes. Have you read the letter he left for you?"

"Yes, but it left me with more questions than answers," Neiaphi said, frowning.

"How can I help?" Lyric asked.

"Why did he leave? He said he knew I was coming; why would he just leave? He even says he misses me, but he chose to go anyway."

"Pythia told him to," Lyric replied flatly.

"That's not a good enough reason. Couldn't he have waited just a little longer?"

Lyric frowned and crossed her arms. "I've had very little interaction with two-legs; Cret is the first I've ever seen. But from my limited experience, I find your mating rituals quite confusing."

"We don't have a mating ritual. We simply find someone we're interested in and pursue them, or our parents arrange the marriage. Nothing like that is going on between Cret and me; we are just friends."

"Okay, that first part makes sense, but the last part? That's not what I'm seeing."

"What do you mean?" Neiaphi asked, furrowing her brow.

"Well, I don't know if you want to hear this or if Cret wants me to tell you, but I'm going to say it anyway.

"I've noticed how Cret says your name—the tone of his voice and how his scent changes with attraction and longing." Neiaphi dropped her eyes to the ground, shuffling her feet. "And then there's you; I can see and smell the same changes in you. You feel the same, yet you're with that other man. I know it's possible to love more than one person, but that's uncommon among centaurs. The mating bond is very special; once you choose, that's your mate for life. Don't two-legs do the same?"

"Some do, but not all."

"You have chosen two," she stated matter-of-factly.

"No, I haven't," Neiaphi protested, stopping to place her hands on her hips as she looked at the centaur.

"Your scent and heartbeat tell a different story."

"Well, in my defense, I didn't know if I would ever see Cret again. I was told to pick from the options in front of me. Pythia was the one who told me that."

Lyric cocked her head to one side. "Pythia? But you only met her last night."

Neiaphi shook her head and resumed walking. "She came to me in my dreams. My heart told me to wait, but my mind said he was lost to me. What would you do in my position?"

Lyric paused to consider her words. "I understand your dilemma. What's your decision now?"

Neiaphi sighed. "I still have only one option in front of me. I love Andonis, but I love Cret as well. Cret isn't here, and I may never see him again. My choice has to remain the same, but it's breaking my heart." She sank to the ground, burying her head in her hands. "Especially when he sends me a letter saying he loves me, that he wishes he could be with me, but he's happy I've found someone who cares for me. It's so frustrating! How can he express his feelings and then say goodbye in the same breath?" She sobbed, the weight of her emotions overwhelming her.

"I imagine this is hard for him as well," Lyric said softly.

"Oh, I know it must be," Neiaphi agreed, wiping her eyes. "I just wish he would have stayed a little longer."

Lyric snorted. "And then what? How would you choose between your two loves? One will end up heartbroken, and you'll still Neiaphi's mouth dropped open. "I—I don't know," she stammered, struggling to process Lyric's words.

"No, this is the best way. Cret made the choice for you; he has set your path."

"Why do you say 'my path'?" Neiaphi asked.

Lyric shrugged. "I didn't mean anything by it. Why?"

"It's just something Pythia mentioned. I have several paths before me, but I don't get to choose."

"That doesn't seem fair. Everyone should have a say in how their future unfolds."

Neiaphi stood up and brushed off her skirt. "I agree. Thank you for talking with me. You've really helped."

Lyric paused and turned back to Neiaphi. "Prophecies can be vague. They often hint at future challenges that aren't visible yet."

Neiaphi frowned, trying to wrap her mind around it. "So, you're preparing for something that might never happen?"

"Exactly. It's about being ready for whatever comes. We centaurs are proud of our heritage and will do anything to protect it."

"Is there anything I can do to help?" Neiaphi offered, her concern genuine.

Lyric smiled, appreciating the sentiment. "A prophecy says I will save my people from certain doom."

"Are centaurs in danger?" Neiaphi frowned.

"Not that we know of."

"Then how are you supposed to save them from the unknown?"

"I don't know. But I've found new friends and helped them with their quests. So far, I feel I've made a difference."

"Sounds like it." An intense wind suddenly ripped through the village, tossing their hair around and threatening to knock Neiaphi over. Just as quickly as the wind started, it stopped. "That was strange."

"Very strange," Lyric agreed, glancing around as if expecting something to appear. "Winds like that often carry warnings or omens."

Neiaphi shivered slightly, the abrupt change in the air unsettling her. "Do you think it means something?"

"Possibly. It could be a sign that changes are coming, both for you and for my people." She looked thoughtfully into the distance. "We should stay vigilant."

"Right," Neiaphi said, trying to shake off the unease. "I'll be on the lookout. I don't want to let anyone down."

Lyric nodded, her expression serious. "Good. And remember, sometimes even the smallest actions can have a significant impact."

"Extremely," Neiaphi replied.

Lyric lifted her nose to sniff the air. Cypress mirrored her action. "Danger is coming; please, come with me." She motioned for Neiaphi to climb onto her back. Neiaphi complied, and Lyric broke into a canter. "We need to find your leader."

"I saw him heading into the village earlier today," Neiaphi said as they turned toward the village. They soon spotted Addident rushing back to the tents.

"Danger is coming, sir!" Lyric shouted. "Please have your people head to the Temple."

"Why the Temple?" he asked, a look of concern crossing his face.

"There's no time for questions! Grab your weapons and hurry. Many lives will be lost if you delay." He nodded and sprinted off.

Within moments, the entire group rushed through the village, heading for the Temple Mound. The wind picked up again, roaring toward them and urging them up the hill. A chorus of howls shattered the morning stillness, driving everyone to run faster. Fearful villagers ran for their homes and slammed their doors shut.

Pythia stood in front of her temple, frantically waving them inside. "Quickly, everyone, get in!"

As soon as the last person crossed the threshold, the heavy temple doors slammed shut behind them.

Once the initial shock settled, nervous murmurs, frightened cries, and angry questions erupted into the air, directed at no one in particular. The Temple, usually dimly lit, gradually brightened as more torches flared to life.

"Please, everyone, calm yourselves. You are safe," Pythia's voice rang out, carrying unnaturally loud from where she stood.

"Safe from what?" someone shouted.

"The Wolvers are surrounding the temple, but they will not be able to enter." A wave of cries and sobs followed her words.

Several local villagers who ran to the temple for shelter shouted at once, asking what a wolver was. Pythia raised her hands until the noise subsided.

"My people, please hold your questions for later. We are entering trying times, and new information will be shared with you all. What I'm about to tell you may shock and frighten you, but please rest assured that everything will be fine."

"Wolvers are creatures from our home world," Pythia explained. "For many generations, it was unknown that they had made their way to this realm. When centaurs walked among us and shared our villages, they posed no threat; we had strength in numbers. As we chased the centaurs into hiding, the wolvers focused their harassment on them, leaving the two-legs"—she smiled at the term—"alone for the most part. Until recently, that is." She nodded toward Neiluios and Altesse.

"But what are they?" someone asked, breaking the tension in the room.

"No one knows for sure," Addident replied. "They resemble the wolves you have on this world, but much larger." He turned to Pythia. "Are you certain they are wolvers?"

"Oh yes, they most certainly are. Most of them possess a high level of intelligence." Pythia turned her attention to Lyric. "Will you and your band please join me in my waiting room? Addident, Neiluios, Andonis, please join us as well." As she began to walk away, she glanced back and added, "Yes, child, you may join us," her eyes landing on Neiaphi.

Neiaphi's heart raced at the invitation. Was she truly speaking to her? Hopeful yet hesitant, she followed after them slowly.

"I find it hard to believe that wolvers made their way to this world unnoticed. Someone must have brought them here," Addident said, addressing Pythia.

"Believe it or not, those are wolvers. I have spoken to several of them," she replied calmly.

"Spoken to?" Neiluios exclaimed, his brows furrowing in disbelief.

"As I mentioned, most are quite intelligent," Pythia clarified.

"How can you communicate with them?" he pressed.

"Through dreams. Most wolvers are Dream Walkers, and some even claim they are shapeshifters."

"Now it makes sense," Neiaphi blurted out.

"What does, child?" Pythia asked, her gaze shifting to Neiaphi, drawing everyone's attention.

Her cheeks flushed with embarrassment. "When Mara visited me in my dream to say that my brothers would be returned to us, she mentioned that Kayson had been sent back to his kind for punishment. She called him a Dream Walker and said he had gone to Romota and returned, which wasn't allowed."

Addident frowned. "He must have stowed away on a transport ship."

"He was on ours," Neiaphi said sadly.

"How do you know?" Neiluios asked, placing a reassuring hand on her shoulder.

"He appeared in my first dream about Earth. He had to have been on board our ship," she replied, her voice heavy with regret.

Andonis wrapped an arm around her waist, offering comfort.

"At least one mystery is solved," Pythia said, her tone shifting as she cleared her throat. "Lyric, you and your band are the current targets of these creatures. In fact, all centaurs are. There are two factions of wolvers: those that despise your kind, known as the Wers Clan, and those that simply seek to live in peace, called the Lyca Clan."

"Is that my destiny? To stop them?" Lyric asked quietly.

"No, my child. Your true destiny is to help your people flee and return home," Pythia replied.

Lyric's mouth dropped in disbelief. "How do I do that?"

"With your necklace," Pythia said, her gaze steady. "I will reveal to you the location of the missing technology that your people once used to communicate with Romota. Your mother's clan was the guardian of this technology. The Wers sought to sever your connection to Romota, leaving you vulnerable."

She continued, "You will use that technology to call for help. Your Romotian brethren will send you a means of transport and welcome you all home."

"How will I convince them to leave the only home they've ever known and venture into the unknown? Centaurs aren't exactly known for their adventurous spirit," Lyric said, her brow furrowed.

"All except you, that is," Justic chimed in with a grin. Lyric blushed and shrugged, a shy smile tugging at her lips.

"That's something you'll have to figure out," Pythia said gently. "I'm afraid not everyone will wish to leave. But given enough time, they will all have to leave this planet, one way or another."

"I wish to help them in any way I can," Andonis declared. Neiaphi's eyes widened in surprise.

"Are you sure this is the path you wish to take?" Pythia asked, her tone stern. "I told you about the paths before you, and only one can be altered once it has been set in motion. I did not mention that one chosen path might lead to all others unfolding."

Andonis stared at her for a moment, then glanced down at Neiaphi. The silence stretched between them, heavy with meaning. After what felt like an eternity, Neiaphi placed her hand on his chest, grounding him.

"We will help Lyric and the rest of the centaurs," Neiaphi asserted.

Pythia nodded, "So be it."

"How do we address the issue at hand?" Addident inquired, his voice drawing everyone's attention. He gestured into the air, "The wolvers? How do we get them to leave us alone?"

"We know the basics of defense, but all-out war is something we are not prepared for," Neiluios added, his brow furrowed in concern.

"They will disperse shortly," Pythia replied calmly.

"How do you know that?" Justic pressed, skepticism lacing his tone.

"Please come with me," Pythia said, sidestepping the question. "We can make everyone comfortable for the evening.

The wolvers will be gone by morning, and then Lyric's group can get underway."

"Where will they be going?" Addident asked.

"Lyric's mother's clan lived on an island not too far from here."

"Wait, what? No, my mother's clan was killed not far from my father's clan, northwest of here. Not on an island!" Lyric exclaimed, her eyes wide with disbelief.

"That is true," Pythia acknowledged. "But they were not in their home territory when they were attacked last. They were fleeing the Wers Clan at the time. I'll explain more tonight. For now, let's get everyone settled."

Later that evening, the howling of the wolvers faded to an occasional distant call. People huddled in small groups, quietly conversing or attempting to sleep. Pythia's acolytes moved among them, ensuring everyone had food, water, and bedding.

Once everyone was settled, Pythia gathered the same small group in her private study. "Addident, Neiluios, you are not obliged to follow my advice, but I do recommend it," she said, her tone serious.

"What is your advice?" Addident asked.

"You two should remain here until Crelian's group arrives. Then, all of you can continue on to Atlantis. I can arrange a ship that will take you to The Pillars, and with my endorsement, you should be allowed to proceed from there with minimal delay."

"That sounds like a reasonable plan," Neiluios replied, and Addident nodded in agreement.

"Good. Now, for you, Lyric. My dear child, your journey will be more challenging. I will arrange a ship for you as well, one that will take you to The Star Clans' home territory."

"The Star Clan?" Lyric asked softly. "My mother could never remember the name of her clan."

"You will begin your journey there. Once you arrive, you'll understand what steps to take next."

"How?" Justic pressed.

"You'll simply know," Pythia replied.

"What about us? How can we help?" Neiaphi asked.

"Andonis, you and Pelagios should assist the centaurs. They will encounter other humans, and your guidance will be essential in helping them navigate those interactions."

Andonis nodded. "I will help them."

"What happens after they return home? Can I go back too?" Pelagios inquired.

"Yes, my son. If that is your wish, you may return home. But keep your heart open to any other possibilities that may come your way."

"What do you mean?" Pelagios asked, puzzled.

Pythia smiled but remained silent. "Andonis, your path will reveal itself before you, but remember, if you choose this path, all the options I've presented could unfold. Are you ready for that?"

Andonis hesitated, gazing at Neiaphi's warm smile.

"Andonis?" Pythia pressed.

"I'm ready," he replied. Neiaphi beamed at him, but he cast his gaze downward. Would she still love him when she understood what he was risking by selecting this path?

"What about me?" Neiaphi asked, her brow furrowing slightly.

"You, my blessed daughter, as I mentioned, will not choose your own direction. You will join Andonis, and your path will reveal itself as you journey together."

"Wait, what?" Neiluios interjected, rising from his seat. "Neiaphi can't leave. She's supposed to join her mother, me, and her brothers in Atlantis."

"I'm afraid her path does not lead directly to Atlantis," Pythia stated firmly.

"I will not allow this," Neiluios insisted, his voice rising with concern.

Andonis stood up, his expression resolute. "With all due respect, Neiluios, Neiaphi's going to be my wife. She's starting her life with me now." He turned to Neiaphi, his voice firm yet tender. "Marry me now before we leave." Neiaphi's eyes widened, and her mouth fell open in surprise.

Pythia rose, nodding to Neiaphi as she stepped forward to stand beside Andonis. She took his hand in both of hers and said, "It is not her time to marry just yet. She will join you on your adventure, but only as your bride-to-be."

"B-B-But why?" he stammered, confusion and disappointment etched on his face.

"Do not worry; everything will work out as it's meant to," Pythia assured him. "And Neiluios, this is the path she must take. In order for her to become the woman she is destined to be, you have to let her go."

Her mother and I can't lose her again," he said, his voice trembling.

Pythia stepped closer and placed her hands on his shoulders. "You both will see her again; that is my promise."

# ∞ 32 ∞
# FAREWELLS

**NEIAPHI** stood at the ship's stern, waving goodbye to her family as they sailed into the bay. Andonis stood beside her, one arm wrapped around her shoulders, while Cypress sat attentively on the other side. Was this the right decision? A new chapter of her life was beginning, but was she truly ready for it?

"Are you okay?" Andonis asked, giving her shoulder a reassuring squeeze.

"I will be," she replied, forcing a smile. "How about you?"

His body went rigid at her question, and for a moment, he seemed lost in thought.

"Yeah, why wouldn't I be? I'm going on an adventure with my girl, helping creatures I didn't even know existed until recently save their species from some strange, angry wolves that aren't really wolves. Who wouldn't be okay?" He cleared his throat and chuckled, trying to lighten the mood.

Neiaphi turned to face him, her expression serious. "You didn't have to choose this path. You had other options, right?"

"I had others," he nodded. "But this is the only one that felt right. I can't explain it. When I met Lyric, it just clicked. I knew I had to help her; it just feels… right somehow."

"Then this is what we need to do," she said with certainty, her voice steady.

On the second day, the ship finally approached the shore. "Is this it?" Lyric asked the captain, her heart racing.

He eyed her nervously. "That's the island Pythia told me to take you to." He nodded, adding, "No one lives there, you know?"

"Not anymore," she whispered, a chill running down her spine as she stepped away from him. Turning to her group, she said, "As soon as we land, we'll split into two groups. Justic, Andonis, and Neiaphi will be with me." Everyone nodded, gathering their belongings in preparation.

The captain's voice called out, "This is as close as I can get; I'll lower the cargo raft. Everyone aboard!"

Several crewmates rowed them to shore, the tension palpable as everyone braced for the unknown.

"Let's establish a base camp here," Ambrite suggested as the cargo raft drifted back out to sea. "We'll reconvene in three days or sooner. If you discover anything or run into trouble, return here immediately. Let's spend the night and set out fresh with the sunrise."

Nods of agreement rippled through the group, a shared determination evident in their expressions.

"He left the ship with the creatures, sir," the crew member reported.

Brutus snarled, "We are called centaurs, two-legs."

"Does it really matter what everyone is called?" Hepluosis replied, raising his hands in a placating gesture. "The important question is, what are they doing on this island?"

"We'll swing around to the other side of the island and then spread out," Hepluosis commanded. "If you see anything of interest, report back. If you encounter any of their group, stay hidden. Observe and follow, but do not engage unless that pilot is completely alone and won't be missed for several minutes."

"Yes, sir!" the soldiers snapped to attention in unison. Hepluosis, Six, and the centaurs acknowledged their agreement with a quick nod. Captain Rirmell noticed the subtle exchange but chose to remain silent.

"There it is, boys! Welcome to The Pillars. Now let's get you conscripted into the Royal Atlantean Navy," Captain Matteas announced.

"Will it be difficult for us to get enlisted?" Tivadarios inquired.

"Well, I don't doubt that two of you will be welcomed," he said, glancing pointedly at the two centaurs.

"What's that supposed to mean?" Myreia huffed, crossing her arms.

"No insult intended, ma'am. I just don't see how a naval ship would make use of you and your mate," he replied.

"We'll show them just how valuable we can be," Cret said flatly, gazing up at the massive stone statue of a man straddling the bay, sword held high and shield at the ready—an imposing marker for the entrance to the Great City of Atlantis.

"Do you think she's okay?" Altesse asked, glancing down at Annas, who slept peacefully in her arms.

"I'm sure she's fine, dear. She has Andonis by her side, and Pythia assured me we would see her again," Neiluios replied, trying to sound reassuring.

Altesse looked up at him, her brow furrowed. "Can she truly be trusted?"

He shrugged. "So far, I see no reason not to. Don't worry; we'll see her again." Altesse rested her head against his side, letting out a soft sigh.

"The horses have escaped again," Lars growled, pacing back and forth along the shoreline.

"Calm down, Lars. We'll catch them soon enough," Staps replied, snapping his massive jaws. "My sire was part of the raiding party that destroyed the settlement on that island. There's nothing there for them. They'll be back looking for the second machine before long."

"If everything was destroyed, how would they know where to look for the second machine?" Lars snapped, hunching his shoulders and keeping his head low.

"Don't worry about that. We left clues for any stragglers to find. It'll lead them right to us. Now, come on, pack. We have an ambush to prepare." With that, the pack erupted into howls and trailed after their leader, ready for action.

"They are coming!" Dyna said, looking out the window of her sitting room at The Center Palace.

"Who is my lady?" asked her attendant, glancing up from her tasks.

Dyna looked at the young woman kneeling before her, placing the final touches on the elegant gown she would wear to the banquet that evening. She wasn't aware she had spoken out loud.

"That's not important," she murmured, and then she smiled, *They're almost here. The final pieces are falling into place. Salvation is almost upon us,* she thought to herself.

*To Be Continued...*

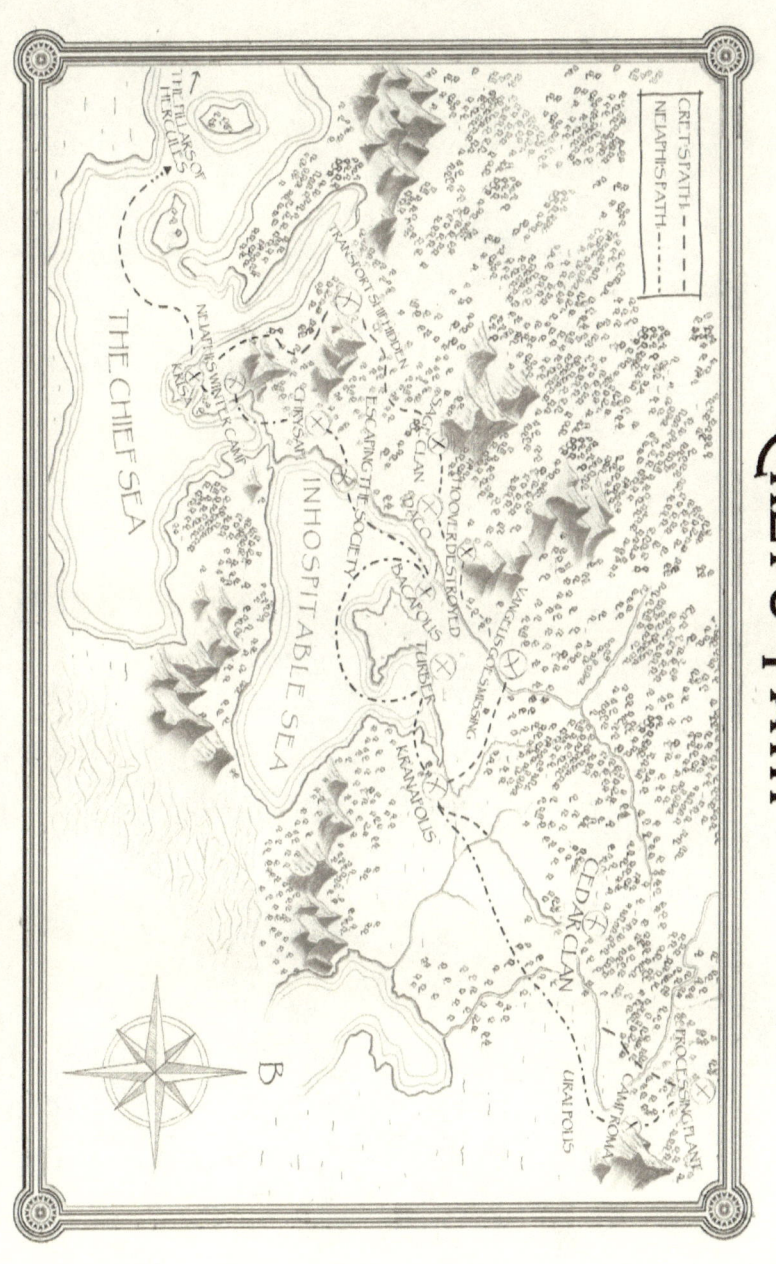

CRET'S PATH

Thank you for reading *THE JOURNEY CONTINUES* - Book 2 in the
**CHRONICLES OF ATLANTIS**

Book 3 - *THE END OF ATLANTIS* is currently in the works.

**⇗ MAY THE GODS SMILE ON YOU ALWAYS ⇗**

NeiaphisAtlantis@gmail.com

Sarah M. Wasson currently lives in Las Vegas, Nevada, with her husband and son. She is a business entrepreneur, pet groomer, amateur golfer, horse enthusiast, falconer, and lover of sci-fi/fantasy.

www.ingramcontent.com/pod-product-compliance
Lightning Source LLC
Chambersburg PA
CBHW020556120726
47903CB00001B/278